"**I** don't need a mission board," Roger repeated, his voice softer. "But I do need you, Anna. All through the years, I've yearned for you as no man ever yearned for a woman. Isn't it time that I had a little happiness in my life?" Then he grew angry. Pounding the steering wheel with his fist, he said, "Why should one mistake sentence a man for life? Why, Anna? Why?"

# ANNA

## MARGARET
## GRAHAM

LIVING BOOKS

Tyndale House Publishers, Inc.

Wheaton, Illinois

Second printing, June 1987

Library of Congress Catalog Card Number 85-51656
ISBN 0-8423-0020-1
© 1986 by Margaret Graham
Printed in the United States of America

*For*

## JEAN ABRAHAMSEN

*an exceptional teacher, the consummate professional,*

*committed to students, to American History,*

*and to excellence. Integrity and impeccable*

*ethical standards; an uncommon sensitivity for the*

*worth of every individual; and high expectations,*

*have made her a blessing in the high school classroom.*

# CHAPTER
# ONE

As soon as she walked into the classroom, Anna Petersen knew something serious was going on. There were only three girls and a boy in the room—in the back of the room—and they were whispering one at a time, their heads pressed close together. Unnatural.

With automatic proficiency, Anna sealed herself in, a device equivalent to climbing into a rubber suit and checking gear to do battle with sharks. Whatever the trouble, it would take everything she could muster to cope. Normal routine was challenge enough. Now this.

Anna opened the deep drawer of the desk, put away her thermos and pocketbook, then settled down to reading the morning bulletin, not with concentration but pretense. After eighteen years of reading morning bulletins, there was nothing new to anticipate. Taking a tissue she cleaned her glasses, then glanced at the absentee list and the lunch menus for the week. She would wait to post the three sheets on the bulletin board; to walk to the back of the room would invite trouble.

Standing up, Anna reached to pull down the Territorial Expansion Map, which she knew by heart: Thirteen Original Colonies, pink; Louisiana Purchase, green; Mexican Cession, orange; Oregon Territory, beige; Gadsden Purchase, white. Pinching the sides of her skirt at the thighs, she pulled it straight again.

The flyswatter still hung between the map and the movie screen even though bee season was past. It was time to change the cartoon poster but she would wait.

The poster came at the end of the pictures of the first sixteen presidents which hung on the right wall. To take it down would attract the students' attention. Anna sat down again and began arranging paper clips and thumbtacks in the wide, flat desk drawer. Not until she was wiping dust from the vase of plastic daisies was she ready to tune in again.

It was not fight talk—that would be loud and filled with contradictions and challenges. Nor was it the buzz of gossip. This was something deadly serious. Something scary.

"Shh," one of them said, and there was silence— silence as when the timer clicks and the washer pauses between cycles. *Here it comes*, Anna thought.

She raised her head. The four of them were looking at her. Louvenia, who wore her hair in cornrows and usually held her head with the elegance of an African queen, was staring at her with frightened eyes, her lips pale and parted as if to speak. The boy nodded, urging her to say something. She spoke rapidly. "Miz Petersen, did you know a girl's had a baby in the bathroom?"

Anna ran the words through her head a second time, unwilling to believe what she heard. "Oh, come, Louvenia, you know that's not true."

"Oh, yes, ma'am, it is true."

Anna's heartbeat quickened. Louvenia was not given to wild tales. It could be true. Anything can happen here.

They were coming toward her now, pushing aside desks, talking all at once. "It's in the toilet. She left it in the toilet."

"In the commode?"

Louvenia nodded. "Head first. A full-term baby!"

"Nonsense."

They did not argue, but their eyes, pinned on her, said, "Go and see for yourself." Anna was refusing, standing her ground behind the desk.

"Miss Petersen?" Paul Elroy, department chairman, was standing in the doorway. "The kids say something's going on in the girls' washroom. I think Mrs. Porter's in there, but would you check? I'm calling the office."

He didn't wait for an answer. Anna hesitated even after she reached for her purse.

In the hall she knew it was true. A knot of students was huddled together, talking nervously, glancing at the closed door of the girls' room. The bell for homeroom rang ten minutes early. Once, twice.

Anna stood waiting for the students to disperse. The intercom sputtered momentarily before the voice of Liza Minnelli belted out the words of "Come to the Cabaret" on the radio station that was typically played during homeroom. The principal had signaled business as usual.

Anna's heart palpitated wildly. Reluctantly, the students were gathering their books together, dillydallying, hoping to see something. One of them, a girl Anna did not know, spoke. "Miz Petersen, did you know—"

Anna stopped her. "Go to homeroom!"

The girl slammed her locker door, sauntered past Anna, and started toward the girls' room.

"Oh no!" Anna stepped between the girl and the door. "You can't go in there."

"Why not?"

"You know perfectly well why not. Now get to homeroom before the tardy bell rings."

In defiance, the girl banged on locker doors all the way down the hall. When she was out of sight and the hall was clear of students, Anna drew a deep breath and pushed open the restroom door.

In the far corner, the school nurse, Suzanna Porter, and the P. E. teacher, Nellie Malloy, stood close together, mute with shame. Their eyes held the misery of generations of humiliation.

Oh no! Not a black baby! That Uncle Tom look on

their faces—it must be a black baby.

A stall door was half open, and Anna sensed the baby was still there. She wanted them to say, "Don't look," but they didn't. Their dark faces turned away from her, waiting for her to look. What did they want from her? Why must she share this burden?

Lying on the floor on two brown paper towels lay the little, lifeless form. Anna's stomach lurched. The baby's lips were bloodless, its small body mauve in color—cold as stone in death, cold as the ceramic toilet bowl above its head.

Anna felt hot, then chilled; her stomach convulsed, roiling. She retreated into the next booth, too weak to stand.

Elbows on her knees, head reeling, eyes pressed closed, still she could see the baby—womb-shaped, helpless. Least of all could she erase the ashen look, the mauve tinge—like some fading haze caught midair and eternally preserved.

Trying to pull herself together, Anna opened her eyes. But there, beneath the wall dividing the stalls, were the infant's feet, its tiny toes curled back the way fingers close against the palm. Though she shut her eyes against the sight, the image of the baby lingered. Anna could remember the closed eyelids, the soft mouth ready to suckle a mother's breast.

The tardy bell was ringing. Anna stood, limbs weak and trembling. As she came out the women were waiting. Their eyes pleaded with her. "It's been reported?" Anna asked. Nellie nodded.

Nellie was stronger and more determined than the nurse. Even so, her shoulders were bowed, drawn in around her body as if she were being whipped. Everything they had worked for, suffered for, everything they had achieved, was being dealt another blow. They would recover, as they had before, but their anguish first had to be endured. Anna wanted to put her arms around the suffering women, but thought better of it. No white woman could possibly understand or relieve them now.

Out in the hall, a group of girls swarmed past the washroom, purposely ignoring the tardy bell. Instinctively, Anna barred the door, ordered them to move along. "The bell has rung!"

She needed to get back to homeroom—no telling what was going on there—but the girls were taking their time to clear the hall.

Finally, as she was walking back to the room, Anna felt the shock wave in full force. All voices were hushed except Louvenia's. "I was in deah when dis girl come in but we don' pay her no mind. She was in de johnny and de rest of us was rappin'. We din't hear nut'n. Not nut'n. Fust thing I knowed, some woman come to de doah and dat girl run out. We was rappin', didn't pay her no mind."

"Who was she?"

"None of that!" Anna commanded, walking into the room. The students were clustered around Louvenia and looked up.

"I don't want to know who it was, and that will be the end of this conversation. Do you understand?"

Slowly the students moved away from Louvenia and slunk back to their desks. It was understandable that they wanted to know all the lurid details, but this time they would have to get the details somewhere else—in another class, in the locker room, but not in here. Anna was determined.

Although her legs were wobbling, she stood behind the desk with a silent sternness she did not often like to use with students. As she eased into her chair, she kept her eyes on them, convincing them she meant business. But as soon as she began checking attendance cards, the whispering began again.

A girl leaned across the aisle to ask Louvenia, "How'd she cut the cord?"

Anna looked up. Louvenia motioned with her head and the girl looked Anna's way.

"Miss Petersen," she said, "Samantha Johnson was looking for you."

Anna nodded. "Thank you."

Samantha was a retarded girl who came from one of the black communities across the creek. Her handicap was an odd one. She took everything literally and could not understand figures of speech much less abstractions. Yet in her poor brain were islands of intelligence that sometimes gave her clearer insights than people with better, analytical minds.

Yes, Samantha would be terribly disturbed by this.

Anna monitored the whispering as she flipped through the attendance cards. A boy's high-pitched voice rose above the others'. "It happens all the time. My daddy works at the disposal plant and they're all the time gettin' babies in the sludge."

"Stop it!" Anna leapt to her feet, angry. "There will be no more talk like that in this classroom!" The bell was ringing. Students grabbed their books and rushed to leave the room.

But there would be more discussion. Every period, students no doubt would recount their share of the news. It would go on for three days. Experience had taught her that. No matter what happened—race riots, drug busts, killings—three days was the attention span. Neil Armstrong's walk on the moon scarcely caused a ripple in Scotsville. But a local happening titillated the fancies of bridge players and teenagers until the subject was milked dry. They were expert in embellishing anything they heard—exaggerating, dramatizing any incident into something sensational. After three days the gossip would be stored in memory, ready to be resurrected every time the name of the subject was mentioned. At fifteen, the McCrory girl had run off to spend the night with a boy. Now, even though she was thirty-three, happily married, and a good mother, the mention of her name invariably evoked the question, "Isn't she the girl who ran off with that Indian boy?"

Yet, to be sure, this case was unlike anything that had ever happened at McAdden High School. If it wasn't handled right, it could do irreparable harm. Anna pondered the matter. *I don't see any way in the world to make something constructive out of this*, she thought.

Samantha Johnson burst into the room, stopped dead still, and stood trembling. Her voice quivered. "Oh, Miz Petersen, do you know what happened?"

The brown skin of Samantha's face was streaked with tears. Anna got up and went to her. Other students were streaming in, brushing past them. Samantha stood immobile, devastated. There would be no joy from her today, no big, wet kisses.

"Oh, that baby, Miz Petersen, that poor, poor baby!" Anna put her arm around the girl and led her to her desk, but Samantha would not sit down. "Oh, Miz Petersen, how could she do it? Oh, if I ever have a baby I'm going to love it with all of my heart."

"I know you will, Samantha."

Ken Tompkins put down his books and came up to straddle the desk in front of them. There was a heartless grin on his face. "What's up, Samantha?"

"A girl lef' a baby in de john."

"So?"

"She killed it! She killed it! She drowned it in de john!" More tears washed down her cheeks. Anna went for tissues.

"Lotsa' babies die that way," Ken teased.

"Dat don't make it right."

"Who says?"

"God says!"

Ken was getting her really riled and his pleasure was obvious, yet this wasn't the time to stop him—not with Samantha losing.

"Did he say that to you?"

"To me, to you, Ken Tompkins, to Miz Petersen— to everybody in de worl'."

"When? Last night? This morning?"

"In de Bible. He say, 'Thou shalt not kill.'"

Ken leaned back on his elbows and laughed. Then, with some softening in his voice, he said, "Aw, Samantha, what's with the thees and the thous?"

"You be quiet, Ken Tompkins. Don't you know dat's de way God talks?"

Ken rolled off the desk laughing. Samantha would not be put off by him. "Don't nobody got good sense make fun o' God and dey don' laugh at de way he talks neither!"

The tardy bell was ringing and stragglers dived for the door.

"All right, Samantha," Anna said gently. "You go to your seat now and we'll talk about this later."

She cooperated, but as Anna was taking the roll she could see out of the corner of her eye Samantha's grief-stricken face and knew there was more to come.

The roll finished, Anna put the top back on her pen and turned to the lesson plan for the day. Samantha put her head down and began sobbing.

Anna went over to her, putting her arm around her shoulder. "Samantha, would you like to go to the nurse?"

"Oh, Miz Petersen," she sobbed. "It's just murder, just plain murder!"

"Aw, Samantha, don't cry." It was Alfred Stegall trying to comfort her. "She can have another baby."

Anna turned to him. "Alfred, it's not a matter of

another baby. It's that this one has been denied life."

Ken Tompkins wasn't listening. "Miz Petersen, wanna buy a 1972 yearbook?"

"Not now, Ken."

"Miss Petersen, tell Samantha that baby went straight to heaven," Judyth said, trying to be helpful.

Alfred whispered so Samantha wouldn't hear. "Not if it wasn't baptized."

"Now, Samantha," Anna began again, "we don't know all the circumstances about this. Don't you think we should wait until we know all the facts before we judge?"

"I s'pose so," she answered meekly. Anna patted her shoulder reassuringly. But as Anna turned away Samantha said again, "It was just plain murder, just plain murder."

Anna observed a respectful silence before beginning the lesson. None of the students could honestly concentrate on the Louisiana Purchase. She wouldn't try for discussion or questions; all she could hope to do was get through the period without further incident.

With every class that morning, it was the same scenario. The only subject the students wanted to talk about was the girl and the baby. Anna met them head-on. "This is not our business," she told them and went on with the day's work. A few students seemed relieved, but most of them sat in sullen silence, anxious for the bell to ring.

After every class, Samantha made a beeline to Anna's room to ask, "Did they call the police?"

Of course, Anna did not know because she hadn't ventured from her own classroom. The only way to avoid the talk was to stay out of the teachers' lounge, the cafeteria, and the restroom.

Even after school Anna graded papers in her classroom with the door shut, hoping no one would come in. When it was time to leave, she put her things together, pulled on her car coat, locked the door, and left.

The winter sun that hung in the sky offered some cheer. North Carolina had its pluses. Wind whipped her hair as she walked across the schoolyard but it held no chill. The January weather was mild. Placing her things on the backseat, Anna crawled under the steering wheel and backed out of the parking lot.

As she drove down Trade Street, the bare limbs of trees arching overhead made her think of Mrs. Carey, whose father had planted the trees a hundred years before. Two squirrels were chasing each other, leaping from branch to branch. She needed groceries, but they could wait. The scandal would be all over town and she didn't want to be put on the spot by women in the supermarket. Anna went straight home.

Home was a one-bedroom apartment in the new Raefield Arms, the first apartment complex built in Scotsville. The living-dining room area was divided by a studio couch. The hutch and the dinette suite were on one side; the bookcases, easy chair, and rocker were on the other. The marble-top tables and two of the lamps were inherited from the mother she never knew, and in the bedroom was a French provincial suite that had belonged to Aunt Helga. Beside the television set stood the cello, her father's legacy, and on the set, a pink conch.

Anna checked the refrigerator to make sure the chicken was defrosted and calculated the time it would take to cook the vegetables. The phone rang. *I'll bet that's Thelma*, Anna thought.

It was. "My husband came home from work with some story about a baby born at the high school today. Is that true?"

Anna spoke guardedly. "Yes, I'm afraid it is true."

"Really? George said the mother's a black girl named Briggs. Is that right?"

"I don't know, Thelma. All I know is she gave birth in the girls' room."

"I don't suppose you saw her?"

"No."

"Did you see the baby?"

Anna hesitated. "Well, yes, I did," she said, angry that Thelma pressed her.

"Oh, my! That must've been awful! What did it look like? Was it a boy or a girl?"

For the first time, Anna realized she didn't remember the sex of the child. "I don't know, Thelma. I don't remember."

"Oh you poor girl. You're still in shock. Listen, I'll come right over."

"No, Thelma. Thanks, but I'd rather you wouldn't come now. I have a few things to do."

"Well . . . are you sure now?"

"Yes, I'm sure."

Anna did have a few things to do. Slipping out of her blouse and skirt, she put on a housecoat. Going through the mail, she saw there was nothing worth opening—Helga's letter would only acknowledge receiving the check. Anna called the beauty shop and canceled her appointment. With school gossip making the rounds, the last place she wanted to be was a beauty shop.

No sooner had she put down the receiver than the phone was ringing again. Automatically, she reached for it, then, against her nature, decided not to answer it. If it were Thelma again, she simply couldn't talk to her. Walking into the living room, Anna counted the rings—four, five, six. *It's got to be Thelma*, she thought, turning on the television set. Eleven, twelve, thirteen . . .

Lying down on the couch, she watched Don Knotts, pop-eyed and gesticulating frantically, amusing Andy Griffith.

After the sixteenth ring, the phone fell silent. *Glory be! That was Thelma all right.* She closed her eyes, hoping to fall asleep. *That baby . . . that poor girl. And Samantha . . . will Samantha ever get over this?* As she waited to doze off, a tear slid from the corner of her eye onto the sofa pillow.

When Anna woke up it was because the phone was ringing again. The TV was sputtering news about Secretary of State Rogers and the Viet Cong. Anna turned it off and answered the phone.

"Where were you?" Thelma asked, not waiting for an answer. "I found out the baby was a girl, a black baby. I guess it's just as well she's dead—anybody who'd do a thing like that is no fit mother. I always tell my boys, 'If you ever get a girl in trouble, come straight to me. I promise you there won't be any fuss. Whatever you do, don't take matters into your own hands.' "

Anna stopped listening, her eyes on the kitchen clock. Thelma chatted non-stop for more than thirty minutes.

Anna hung up the phone and went into the kitchen to start supper. The chicken looked uninteresting, the pink liquid slippery beneath the plastic wrap. She closed the refrigerator. *I think I'll call Marge.*

Marge lived in Georgia, and talking to Marge sometimes helped. Anna glanced at the clock. The nighttime rate was on as she dialed the number.

As soon as Marge answered the phone, Anna knew she was drinking, but she told her about the baby anyway. Marge was furious.

"Anna, what're they going to do about it?"

"Well, I don't know. I guess the authorities will do something."

"Authorities, my eye! That bunch of rednecks won't

do anything. The whole time I lived in Scotsville there wasn't a decent man on the force. They're nothing but a bunch of sots chasing every woman in town. They'll never do anything about one more little black baby."

"Oh, Marge, you're wrong. I taught some of the men on the force, and they don't come any finer."

"Well, things must have changed an awful lot since I was there." She paused, probably to sip her drink. "Tell you one thing, if they don't do something it's up to you."

"What do you mean it's up to me?"

"To do something. You can't let this pass, you know."

"For crying out loud—it's not my responsibility!"

"What do you mean, it's not your responsibility? You're the very one who ought to follow through on this. Everybody in town knows you and they'd respect whatever you say. Promise me . . . " Her voice trailed off as if she were distracted. "Promise me you'll do something, Anna."

"No, Marge, I can't promise that. My job is to teach school and keep my nose out of other people's business."

"Other people's business? Is that poor little baby, dead in the ground, going to speak its own defense?" She stopped short. "Did they bury it?"

"Oh, Marge, I don't know. I can't get all involved in this. It's enough that I had to look at the little thing. If you could've seen . . . "

"I'm upsetting you, Anna. Tell you what—I've told you a hundred times before—get out of that town. I'm telling you for the last time. It's a no good town!"

"Marge, it's not like it used to be. This town's been good to me."

When she hung up, Anna was sorry she had called. Sober, Marge was sensible; drinking, she was impossible.

Anna went back to the refrigerator, looked inside, leaned on the door, decided not to cook supper. She ate a cookie, then another one. *Never too upset to eat cookies,* she mused ironically. She decided to grade papers and go to bed.

Anna lay the sheaf of papers on the desk, turned on the lamp, and sat down. The paper on top was grimy and dog-eared. Unconsciously, she opened the folded corners and smoothed them flat. The writing was in pencil and nearly illegible. Straining to make out the cramped script—so light it was almost invisible—she found many corrections to mark. She got up to get another cookie, then painstakingly wrote a note at the top of the paper with the grade.

The refrigerator came on humming an A-sharp. There were times when perfect pitch was a curse. It was hard enough to concentrate on the monotonous papers without identifying every tone she heard.

At 10:30, Anna stopped grading papers, slipped them back into the briefcase, and went to the closet to choose what she would wear the next day. It was an unnecessary exercise because her five outfits hung in a row, one for each day in the week. She remembered her thermos, washed it, then took a bath and got ready for bed.

Ordinarily, Anna fell asleep easily, but she knew she wouldn't that night. Propped up in bed, she tried to read. When, page after page, she couldn't remember a word she read, she turned out the lamp and lay there staring at the ceiling. An eerie feeling crept over her. The mercury light from the parking lot cast a mauve hue in the room—the same mauve color of the baby—and Anna was unsettled by it. The uneasiness grew. She turned on the lamp to dispel the haunting shade, but her mind's eye was full of the color. There was no escaping it.

All night Anna struggled against troubling thoughts

that would not lie down and sleep. Marge kept intruding, disturbing her. But Marge had been drinking, she told herself. *I can't get involved in this. It's not my business.*

Dozing fitfully, waking up hot, then cold, Anna finally got up, went into the living room, and turned on the television. The test pattern came into focus with its signal sounding middle-C. The hateful mercury light was inescapable; eyes open or shut she saw it, and in her mind the color fused with the signal to create an unrelenting beam that held her captive.

In the hours before dawn, Anna prayed for relief, for tears, for anything that would help. Opening the curtains, she saw signs of daybreak coming up over the dumpster. The mercury lights would soon dim.

Anna fingered her cello, its fern-shaped neck familiar to the touch, its lovely red wood gleaming in the light. Carrying it to the middle of the room, she sat in a chair, positioned the instrument, and tuned it. She began hearing Muhling's *Warum* or *Why?* Drawing the bow across the strings, she closed her eyes and swayed to the sobbing sounds of the music. Aunt Helga called the cello the grieving instrument. So it was, and Anna was grieving now.

# CHAPTER TWO

In 1954, when Anna Petersen came to Scotsville from Jersey City, she left nothing behind—nothing except Aunt Helga, who insisted on selling the house so she could move into a retirement home, eat chocolates, and play cards to her heart's content. There was the memory of Tory Petersen, Anna's father, but memories she took with her. Pleasant or unpleasant, they went along on the long trip south to North Carolina.

Anna boarded the night train in Newark, lugging a suitcase and carrying the cello carefully. The trunk, which held the rest of her possessions, would follow by Railway Express. It would have saved money if the trunk could have come with her in the baggage car, but the nearest terminal to Scotsville was a place called Weston—thirty miles west of the town—and Anna wasn't sure how she could transport a trunk from Weston to Scotsville.

The coach was not filled, which meant she could have a seat to herself. Anna started to lift the suitcase to the overhead rack when a sailor jumped to his feet and offered to do it for her.

"Thank you," she said as he swung it into place.

He tipped his cap. "My pleasure, ma'am."

*Ma'am?* At thirty did she look that old? Old enough to be called *ma'am?* Taking off her raincoat to lay it on the seat, she ran her palm over the upholstery and felt grit. "Uff-dah!" she said in Norwegian. Even her nose told her the car was filthy.

Anna checked her bag for the *jule-kae* and *gjestost* wrapped in wax paper. The bread and cheese would tide her over until she reached Scotsville.

She sat next to the window, positioning the cello against her leg and propping her feet on the rail on the back of the seat ahead. A film of dirt on the outside of the pane distorted her view as the train pulled out of the station, jerking and hissing. A porter slid open the door between the coaches and came down the aisle bearing pillows for rent. Anna debated about spending the quarter and decided it was worth it.

It was going to be a long night—this, her first trip below the Mason-Dixon Line.

Across the aisle, a Negro woman and her four children had folded back a seat so they could ride facing each other. The tallest girl held an obviously wet baby who was alternately sucking a pacifier and crying, his nose running. They were eating chicken—even sucking the marrow from the bones—and licking their fingers.

*Uff-dah!* Anna thought and turned her face away. She wouldn't think about what might lie ahead in Dixie Land. The important thing was she had a job waiting for her and that was a miracle. Anna Petersen, with no college degree, no teaching certificates and no experience. Yet Philip Gilchrist had hired her. No matter what difficulties Scotsville presented, she had to succeed there because she had no other option.

The clickety-clack of the train was rhythmic now, as predictable as the rhythm of the metronome that had stood like a household god on the piano at home. When Anna was only seven years old, Aunt Helga had drilled her in the absolute necessity of perfect timing, its function in music, and its control. "A mathematical mind serves a musician well," Aunt Helga said. "Four-four time means four hundred and forty vibrations per second. Do you understand? Of course not. You don't have a mathematical mind. Never will have. Just like your mother.

"Every note has its own vibration. That's why an A is an A and not a C." She would march around the room, thump a table, tap a vase, strike the radiator, saying, "Notes are sounds," and Anna, in her head, was answering, "That's a C-sharp, that's an A, that's a B-flat," but Aunt Helga didn't hear what went on in Anna's head.

Living with Aunt Helga had never been pleasant. She had never let Anna forget that she was sacrificing her life for a motherless child who was not her sister's child but her brother's—as if that made some great difference. She blamed Anna's mother for dying, as if the brain hemorrhage was her fault, her own doing. Nor did Helga let Anna forget that Tory Petersen could have been a professional musician if he had not been left with a child to care for. "But one-night stands and traveling about is no life for the father of a little girl," she said.

From her earliest recollection, Anna spent part of every day waiting for her father to come home from Klein's Clothing Store, where he worked in the men's department. In good weather she could walk up Neptune Avenue, but she was not allowed to cross Garfield. When the bus stopped, her father would jump off and run to meet her. Scooping her up in his arms, hugging and kissing her, he would put her down only long enough to reach in his pocket for licorice.

Of course, Aunt Helga disapproved of licorice. When Anna chewed it, Aunt Helga would see the blackened teeth and say, "Ish-a-miy!" the Norwegian equivalent of "Poor me!"

Aunt Helga disapproved of almost any pleasure the two of them enjoyed. They loved Ocean Grove, and every summer during the week of the Fourth, the three of them went there on vacation. Helga enjoyed the boardwalk, the paddleboats, and especially the tabernacle organ as much as her brother and his daughter, but she never would admit it. Once they found a lovely pink conch buried in the sand and brought it home. Tory worked hard to clean its surface, soaking and bleaching it, only to have Helga tell them it was not to be put on the mantel. Anna kept the conch in her room on a fern stand and from time to time held it to her ear to hear the surf sounds of Ocean Grove. At night, in her dreams, she heard the sound as undulating music, a whispering, velvety sound.

If the three of them went to Radio City or Carnegie Hall, Helga criticized the performers or felt a draft in the theater. On Sundays, when they sat in the cool quiet of the little Episcopal church, Helga invariably reminded them that it was not a Lutheran service.

Sometimes, in the late afternoon, Anna and her father went to Journal Square to feed pigeons, but Helga said pigeons were diseased so would not go with them. On the way home, the two of them would stop at Cushman's Bakery and bring Helga a seven-layer chocolate cake to pacify her.

Another pleasure Helga would not share was going outside to look for rainbows after every storm. Once when Tory was home from work, he and Anna hopped a bus and went all the way to the Palisades hoping to see one—and they did. It arched across the Hudson from Manhattan and disappeared over Ft. Lee. The thrill of it made Anna squeeze Tory's hand and shiver with excitement. In all her years she had not experienced such ecstasy as she did that day, watching the broad band of sapphire steal across the river half-circle, seeing the spectrum fused with violet and the faintest blush of pink. In her head the colors murmured harmonies as soft as the wisps of fog from the river.

They stood spellbound. Her father finally whispered,

"Dear God, it's beautiful!"

The spell continued even after haze had obliterated the rainbow.

Climbing back to the path, they sat down on a bench. Tory Petersen leaned forward, elbows on his knees. His thin face had grown serious. "Love, as beautiful as it is, you must always remember that a rainbow comes only after a storm." His voice trembled even as his hands did at times. "And, Love, not every storm has a rainbow."

The two of them sat there a long time, the wind tousling Tory's graying hair, raindrops from the trees spattering them. He looked old and drawn. The pair lingered as long as they could, but at last they had to go—Helga would be waiting for them.

There was one enjoyment Helga could not deny. Every evening after dinner they played their instruments; Helga, the piano, and Tory and Anna, the mandolin, marimba, recorder, cello, or violin. There was scarcely an instrument Tory Petersen could not play by ear, and Helga had studied many years at the Eastman School of Music. She taught Anna everything she knew about music—its history, theory—everything. But when Anna showed too much fondness for the cello, Helga was quick to discourage her.

"It's no life for a girl. Now your father, that's different. He could have made a fortune. He could have been famous. But music is no life for a girl. Straddling a cello is one of the best ways I know to become an old maid. I rue the hours I spent on that piano bench when I might have been finding myself a nice young man. Look at me! If it hadn't been for all those scholarships, I'd be a happily married woman today."

Well, one thing was sure. Anna didn't want to be like Aunt Helga—fat and dimpled and disagreeable.

Tory Petersen cautioned Anna as well. "You're a pretty girl, Anna. You'll fall in love, settle down with a good husband, and have a lovely family."

During her freshman year at Douglass, Anna decided to do just that. Roger Metcalf was a pre-med student at Rutgers, and they met in the hospital where she worked as a part-time ward secretary and he as an orderly. The first time she saw Roger she noticed his built-up shoe, not because he limped, but because his uniform pants were ankle-high. He was blond and shy and had an appealing, mellow sound in his voice.

Leaning on the counter of the nurses' station waiting for the morning shift to come on duty, Roger told her, "I'm a '4 F.' " He was rolling a pencil back and forth in his palms, deep-seated hurt showing in his clear blue eyes. "They wouldn't take me in any branch of service . . . not in any capacity . . . not even in the reserves." He snapped the pencil in two and turned away from her, a muscle twitching in his jaw.

Anna poured coffee and set his cup on the counter. Turning around again, he rubbed his thick forearm as if it ached. "I want to do my part, Anna. If I can get through med school in time, they'll have to take me as a doctor."

Anna didn't say it, but she thought, *He'll never get through med school before the war ends.* He was pacing in front of the counter, hiking up his pants by the belt. "Even if the war's over soon, there'll be plenty of work overseas for doctors. Europe'll be devastated, and there'll be all kinds of casualties and disease."

Elevators were beginning to whine up the shafts. Roger leaned over the counter and pinched her cheek. "Time I punched out." Absently leaving the coffee, he walked swiftly down the hall.

Desperation drove Roger Metcalf day and night. If he was not in class, he was studying or working, striving to put school behind him so he could get on with what he conceived to be his duty. That was a quality to admire, but Anna did not need to look for more qualities in Roger to admire—and love. Night and day she thought of him, yearned for him.

In his poverty, Roger worked extra shifts or sold his own blood to finance dates. He was determined to show Anna a good time. He insisted on New York restaurants, the opera, concerts, or the theater. "Can't we just walk through the park?" she once asked. Instead, Roger hired a hansom cab, and they rode in style.

Anna pondered the poverty that made him extravagant and wondered what he could possibly see in her, the plodder, the plain girl with no high-flung ambitions or expensive tastes. In his arms she didn't wonder about anything. Their bench on the hospital lawn was shielded by a copper beech—at least he said it was a copper beech—and from that bench they watched the leaves of autumn fall, the snow of winter fill up the bare branches, the green come again in the spring.

With all the years of schooling ahead of him, marriage was out of the question. In her sophomore year, Anna was prepared to wait a long time for Roger Metcalf. But Roger was impatient.

Late one night in the hospital cafeteria, her head aching and her body bone-tired, Anna was waiting for him to come off duty. At that hour, the cafeteria was deserted. The hall door swished open and there he was, smiling from ear to ear. He was wearing the only sweater he owned and his uniform was unironed, yet the sight of him striding across the room sent a sharp pain through her breast. She was hardly out of her chair before he was sweeping her up in his arms. Holding her close, he murmured, "I've thought about holding you this way all day."

"And what do you think I've been thinking about?"

He kissed her and released his hold. "I have something for you."

"What is it?"

He held out her chair for her and drew up another

for himself. "This isn't the place I would choose, but I can't wait." From the pocket of his old sweater he pulled a jewelry box.

"Roger! You sold your blood!"

"Shh. Open it."

Anna lifted the lid and there inside was a ring, a tiny diamond gleaming against the black velvet. She couldn't speak. Roger reached for her hand, took the ring, and slipped it on her finger. Tears welled up in her eyes as he kissed her fingers, then took her in his arms and kissed her again and again.

When Roger finally found his voice, he whispered coarsely, "I wish we didn't have to wait so long. Will you wait for me, Anna? Wait until I can make enough money to support us?"

Holding his dear face in both her hands, she looked deep in his eyes. "I'll wait for you if it takes forever."

Even now, in the swaying railcar, Anna felt a surge of passion for Roger Metcalf.

The Parkinson's changed everything. Tory Petersen suffered tremors for years before his illness was diagnosed correctly. At Klein's they were kind, took him out of the men's department, and gave him a desk job. But eventually they had to let him go.

Aunt Helga insisted that her health was too frail to care for Tory alone and told Anna to come home from school. In the middle of her senior year, interrupting practice teaching, a requirement of certification, Anna came home.

By then Tory Petersen's eyes were set back in his head, giving his face a skeletal appearance, and his voice was raspy. Roger explained the nature of the disease as a disorder of the brain and drew a sketch to describe the interrelationships of ganglia, ventricles, muscles, impulses. "The shuffling gait, the mask-like face are both symptoms of Parkinson's," he said. "But no one knows enough about the brain to tamper with it. As marvelous a mechanism as it is, the brain has yet to know itself."

Roger went to Columbia to study medicine. In the beginning, his love was as ardent as ever. Every brief break in his schedule, Roger came to Jersey City. Sometimes he studied all night in order to be with Anna for an hour or two. But even when in his arms, Anna sensed unnamed fears that worried her. "What's the matter?" he asked, and she evaded the question, unwilling to say what she felt.

"Roger, the drugs do so little. Is there nothing more?"

"Anna, it may take years for the Parkinson's to catch up with Tory. If he can hang on, maybe they'll find a cure."

Tory Petersen did more than hang on; he had a determination that caused Anna and Helga constant anxiety. Slipping away from them, he would try to do more than his stiff, rigid muscles allowed, and they would find him in a heap where he had fallen, unable to get up. When they couldn't get him on his feet, there was a neighbor, a policeman, who helped. If Mr. O'Flannery was not at home, Tory had to lie where he was until someone came from the precinct station. He wouldn't listen. No matter how much they explained the dangers, Tory persisted in taking great risks. Yet with all his perseverance, nothing slowed the relentless disease.

Tory Petersen's savings were soon depleted. Anna advertised for cello students and two beginners came, but they did not stick with the instrument. One student after the other tried and despaired of playing, which made giving music lessons a frustrating experience. In the fourth year of the illness, Helga began borrowing on the house to pay the bills.

As graduation from Columbia approached, Roger applied for internships in the area, but there were none available. In the end he went to Denver, Colorado. "It's too good an offer to turn down," he explained. Anna agreed, but the move worried her.

At first, Roger wrote every day and phoned regularly, but there was never enough time or money to come East for a visit. When the letters and phone calls became less frequent, less ardent, Anna could feel him slipping away and braced herself.

But bracing was not enough. The anguish of waiting for the final break was more than Anna could stand. She called Roger and asked him if he wanted the ring back. He protested heatedly. Half-teasingly, she chided him, " 'Methinks thou dost protest too much.' "

Instead of reassuring her, Roger began arguing, something he had never done before.

When she did not hear from him after the phone call, Anna knew she had lost him. She mailed him the ring. Within a week he acknowledged receiving it and, as with a great sigh of relief, wrote, "I'll always love you, Anna, but if this is what you want, I'll let you go."

Anna slipped the note in the bundle of Roger's letters she had kept, pressed her lips against the packet, and let the tears roll. It seemed as if there was nothing else to live for, nothing else to hope for—only long days of caring for her poor, sick father and enduring Helga's never-ending harangue.

Tory Petersen grieved that his illness was costing Anna so much. After dinner, the only instrument Anna wanted to play was the cello, and although she did not cry, she knew her father did—inside—for the sorrow he felt. In her dreams she heard music in the minor key, slow and dirge-like. The grief it sounded made her toss in her sleep, seeking release. *Someday, when the pain is gone*, she thought, *I'll write the music if I can remember it.*

Her father worried about her future and cautioned Anna, "There's no percentage in music. When I'm gone, Love, promise me you won't chase rainbows."

"I promise, Dad," she said and put away the cello. There would, indeed, be no more rainbows. After he died she would find steady employment, with a retirement plan and insurance.

Tory Petersen had an old Navy buddy, Philip Gilchrist, living in the South. Philip called him once in a while, and Tory had followed his friend's career as he moved up from science teacher to superintendent of schools in Scotsville, North Carolina. When Phil would call, Tory, straining to be heard, would anxiously ask, "Phil, you'll have a place for my daughter, won't you?" and Phil would promise him again and again that he would have a teaching job for Anna when the time came.

After the calls, Tory's tremors usually subsided. Anna, sitting by his bed, would read aloud from the Bible and the prayer book until he began sleeping. When she turned out the lamp, he always roused and the predictable whisper would come. "Best decision I ever made, hiring on at Klein's. Where would we be today if I didn't have my pension?"

Smoothing his covers, Anna would kiss his forehead. "Good night, Dad. I love you."

Love him she did. Despite the drudgery, the loneliness, the ache in her heart, caring for her father gave Anna some reason to live. He loved her, and it seemed there was nothing that mattered more than that.

The last thin thread to Roger was broken when the Rutgers Alumni Bulletin announced his marriage to a Jewish girl. Anna took the packet of his letters to the basement and burned them all.

In the eighth year of his illness, Tory's mind was rapidly failing. Anna, in an impulsive, desperate moment, spoke of taking him to the shore. Helga demurred, then agreed. "It might help him. At least it will give him something to look forward to."

Anna regretted the decision. There was no way she could get her father to Ocean Grove alone, but Helga had told him they were going, so every morning he woke up asking, "Are we going to the shore today?" He agitated until they packed his bag weeks in advance of the trip.

When the time drew near to go, Anna spoke to Mr. O'Flannery about the dilemma. Right away he offered to go with them. He drove them in his own car and twice a day he helped Anna get Tory in the water. It was a Herculean effort, but to see her father's joy as the water laved over him was worth all the trouble.

The day they came home, Helga settled Tory in his bed while Anna unpacked the dirty clothes. Later in the afternoon, Anna heard her father awake from his nap and ask in his coarse voice, "Are we going to the shore today?" He had not remembered any of it. Every morning afterward, until he slipped into a coma, he asked the same question.

When her father died, Anna wept, but she did not grieve. Mr. O'Flannery and the rector joined Helga and Anna at the graveside. Turbulent clouds hovered overhead and Anna caught herself glancing at them, looking for a rainbow. The rector's voice droned on as he read from a book, but Anna wasn't listening. She was hearing her father's voice saying, "Love, as beautiful as it is, you must always remember that a rainbow comes only after a storm."

Soon after the funeral, Helga put her plan into action. She sold the house, disposed of the furniture, stored a few things, and moved into a retirement home in the Poconos.

With the insurance money, Anna paid the funeral expenses and medical bills. Two hundred dollars were left. Anna was thirty years old and alone.

# CHAPTER
# THREE

The Greyhound bus, waiting to pull into the street, rumbled and wheezed impatiently. Anna had ridden most of the night on the train to get to Weston, missed the morning bus to Scotsville, and waited until four in the afternoon for the next one. Finally, on the last lap of her journey, feeling miserably tired and dirty, she fell asleep. When she woke up it was raining. The tires of the bus were singing on the wet pavement as they coasted down a street. *This must be Scotsville*, she thought, and a little knot of fear formed in her chest.

"Scotsville!" the driver yelled. "Home o' the Fightin' Scots! And, for that matter, Home o' the Fightin' Colored Folks. Home o' the Fightin' Croatans. You name 'em, they fight here!"

Passengers chuckled and Anna wondered, *What in the world is going on?*

"Home of the thuteen millionaires and six thousan' po' folks!" Negroes on the back of the bus chimed in. "Dat's right! Dat's right! Shore as shootin'!"

"Worl' cap'tal cantaloupes, cukes, and melons; tobacco, cotton, and cawn. Dry as a chip, folks, so if you wanna wet yer whistle, better stay on this here bus till we cross the line."

His words ran together lazily, melding like dominoes in a row. So many different sounds rose and fell. Anna, listening, caught the meaning of a sentence only after it had passed. *Glory be! Am I still in America?*

They were rounding a curve, the driver guiding the

big wheel with both hands and leaning with the curve. The rain slackened. "Only town in the Yewnited State's got a monument to a school teachah."

*Good,* Anna thought, *at least I'm still in the Yewnited States!*

"Stands proud as the Washington Monument on Cross Street, direckly in front o' the co'thouse." The bus was slowing. "Scotsville's full o' critters, cranks, and town characters. I'll show you one up ahead in a minute—ol' Roosevelt Carey. He'll be smack dab in the middle o' Trade and Cross directin' traffic—thinks he's a cop. Crazy as a bedbug and black as the Ace of Spades. Can't miss him." The brakes were squealing as they came to a stop. "Theah he is, what'd I tell ya?" The driver cranked open the window vent. "Hey, deah, Roosevelt!" And to the passengers craning their necks to see the little man, he added, "See 'im over yonder, wavin' his arms, blowin' 'at whistle?"

The little man darting about the intersection ignored the bus driver. Intent on his work, busy waving two cars past and excitedly holding the bus at bay with his billy club, Roosevelt Carey had no time for kibitzing.

"See 'at cap? That uniform? He got it off a railroad conductor. Thinks he's a trainman, too. Everybody in town knows if they want a letter to get on the last train outta here, all they gotta do is give Roosevelt a nickel and I guarantee you that letter'll git on 'at train. Can't nobody git that letter away from Roosevelt." The driver stomped the gas pedal to make the motor roar. "Rides McCurdy's coach to Raleigh or Florence with only McCurdy aboard. Two of a kind, I say. McCurdy as rich as cream and Roosevelt po' as dirt, but they both got all they want and that's what it's all about, ain't it?"

"Yassuh, yassuh!"

The driver leaned into the aisle. "Where's 'at little lady got on in Weston?" He was looking at Anna. "A new school teachah, ain't cha?" And without waiting for her to answer, he continued, "Gittin' off at the teacherage, right? I go right past there so I'll drop you off soon's Roosevelt lets me go."

"Thank you."

As he turned his attention to Roosevelt again, Anna said to herself, *Well, this is it.* "Lord, I have to make a go of it here," she prayed silently. "You know I've no other place to go. Please help me to trust you and not be so nervous."

The driver was leaning out the window again, letting the cool air escape. "Hey, Roosevelt, don't you know 'at rain water's wet?" Passengers whooped and hollered at that one. "Better run between 'em raindrops, Roosevelt!" The bus was pulling away now, crossing the intersection. Anna looked back at the small figure in the middle of the streets glancing furtively this way and that, waving his arms at imaginary traffic. She felt sorry for Roosevelt Carey.

Two blocks up the street the rain had stopped, the street was dry. The bus pulled to the curb in front of a two-story, brick veneer house with square columns that supported one porch on top of another. *Must be the teacherage*, Anna thought. The driver took down her bag from the overhead rack, and she followed him with the cello. Until the trunk arrived, she would have to make do with what was in the suitcase.

"What's that thing?" the driver asked, nodding toward the cello. "A coffin?"

"It's a cello."

"Too bad. There's a body right acrost the street's been needin' a coffin fifty-eight years." He was carrying her bag to the porch. "You from up No'th?"

"Yes, I am."

They reached the porch. Inside the house someone was banging on a piano. "I'll mash the button for you." He set down the bag, took off his cap, and wiped his brow with his forearm. "Comin' here to teach?"

She nodded.

"Lawd, he'p you!"

He waved aside the money she offered him and went back to the bus, shaking his head.

The inside door of the teacherage and all the windows were open. Dancing feet were thumping to the beat of boogie-woogie in the front room as Anna pressed the doorbell again and waited.

The glass in the doors was oval, the side panels leaded glass. Anna looked across the street at another brick house twice the size of this one and in better repair. A sign hung in front: McSwain Funeral Home.

Philip Gilchrist had sent Anna instructions and the names of everyone she needed to know. Mrs. Milligan, the house director, would probably come to the door. A woman was moving through the hall, her white hair piled high on her head, her pearl-rimmed glasses studded with rhinestones. "Miss Petersen! You must be Miss Petersen." She was opening the screen door with one hand and shooing flies with the other.

"Yes, I'm Anna Petersen."

"Well, come right in! I'm Mrs. Milligan, the den mother here." She laughed at her own little witticism. "Horace! Come here, Horace, if you will, please. Get this—thing."

"Cello," Anna supplied.

"Yes. Cello."

The young man bopping with a girl in the parlor on the right stopped and came into the wide hall. Tall and balding, he was wiping perspiration from his face with his shirttail. Anna tried to keep her eyes from gravitating to enormous white buck shoes protruding beneath the cuffs of his pants.

"Horace, this is Miss Petersen. Miss Petersen, Horace Wigglesworth. Mr. Wigglesworth teaches English. Horace, would you be a good boy and take Miss Petersen's bag upstairs? And the cello?" Then turning to Anna she said, "It's the first room on the left at the head of the stairs. You'll share a room with Marge Penry, Miss Petersen. A fine girl. Let me know if you need anything. Supper's at six."

Horace led the way, the bag bumping against the bannisters. "Did cha have a good trip?" he asked.

Another one who ran his words together. "Yes," she answered.

"Rode-all-night?"

That was worse. "Almost all night."

"Jeet jet?"

"Pardon?"

"Jeet jet?"

*What in the world is he saying?* she wondered.

"Supper. Jeet supper?"

"Oh, no."

"Good. We're havin' po'k chops." They reached the landing, then the top of the stairs. "This is the room," he said, rapping on the door. "Marge, it's me."

"Just a minute."

Suddenly, a sound like a foghorn blasted several times. Horace thrust the cello at Anna. "I gotta go— fire!" Leaving the bag at her feet, he bounded down the stairs.

The room door opened slightly and a girl peeped out, her hair in curlers. "Hey, there. Come on in. Here, let me help you with that bag." Anna came inside the room and glanced about for a place to put the cello.

"By the mantel, right over there," the girl said. "I'm Marge Penry. You must be Anna Petersen. We've been looking for you all day."

"You have? Well, here I am."

The horn kept sounding, drowning them out.

Marge was a good-looking girl, as tall as Anna but slender and tanned.

"Listen, I know you're exhausted. I'll see if the bathroom's free, and if it is, I'll start your bathwater."

After she left, Anna thought, *Well, so far so good. At least I can understand Marge Penry and Mrs. Milligan.* Looking around the room at the high ceilings, Anna was impressed with its size. There was a wardrobe, a chest of drawers, and a wall mirror. On the far side of the room was a bay window, its wavy old panes clean against the afternoon light. Some kind of gentle fragrance scented the air as the breeze came in the window. Shoes were strewn about the floor; a tennis racket lay on one of the beds. Looking down on the house next door, she saw huge trees, a wide lawn, some red flowers. Coming up the street was a horse-drawn wagon, an old Negro man hunched over the reins. The wheels were slanted at different angles, making the wagon—and the old man with it—lean like a listing ship. Anna felt strange. Everything was so different.

Marge breezed back into the room. "Good, I got the bathroom. Clara's been in there taking one of her long, hot baths so it's all steamed up. It's her arthritis. She's always soaking her bones, as she calls it. Now here's a towel and washcloth. Better shake a leg. Mrs. Milligan doesn't like us to be late to supper."

Anna unpacked the clothing she needed as Marge took the rollers out of her dark hair and talked about the P.T.A. picnic. Even Marge's toenails were manicured. No doubt about it, Marge knew all there was to know about grooming.

"I'm really sweaty," Anna said wearily.

Marge laughed. "Honey, ladies do not sweat. Animals sweat, men perspire, but ladies feel the heat!"

Anna laughed. "I guess that's my first lesson on being a Southerner."

"It may be your first, but it won't be your last. Don't worry. I like Yankees. I used to visit relatives in Michigan, and I really like the people up there."

Anna crossed the wide hall that served as a sitting

room. Someone's heavy oxfords were beside the couch. Following the sound of the running water, she found the bathroom. Inside, she slid the bolt, felt the water temperature, then began taking off her clothes.

The enormous tub had old-fashioned plumbing fixtures and a stopper for a drain. As she submerged herself in the cool, deep water, she breathed a sigh of relief. *Ahh. Does that feel good,* she thought. *Hope my grime doesn't clog the drain!*

Stretching her toes apart and wiggling them, Anna admired her slim feet. Above everything else, Aunt Helga had taught her to take care of her feet. "Never walk on floors barefoot," she had told Anna, and Anna never did. If Anna had one vanity above another, it was her soft, slender feet. And if she had a phobia about anything, it was athlete's foot—and, of course, animals. She prayed that no one in the teacherage would have an animal pet.

"Feet," she said, "I may become an old maid schoolteacher, but I promise you one thing: you'll always wear high heels. I give you my word, your perfect form will never be disgraced with ground-grippers as long as I live."

By the time Anna returned to the room, Marge had made space for Anna's clothes in the wardrobe and emptied half of the dresser drawers, dumping the contents on a bed. She was plucking her eyebrows as Anna unpacked. Anna put her underthings in the drawers and hung her Sunday dress, two skirts, and two blouses in the wardrobe. Then, with a brush, she tackled the tangles in her hair. "Does humid weather make your hair curl all over the place?" she asked Marge.

"Uh-uh. Wish it did. Bet you don't have to pluck your eyebrows."

"No, just darken them a bit." Anna was out of the habit of doing even that, but now she would. Fumbling in her toilet kit for the pencil, she worried that she wouldn't do it right. For a thirty-year-old woman, she looked too innocent—or was it immature? Perhaps a little more makeup would help.

Marge, with the tips of her fingers, dabbed rouge on her temple and brought the color down along the cheekbone. Anna followed her lead. *There*, she thought, *that's the best I can do.*

At supper, Anna was introduced to sixteen teachers sitting around two long tables. There was no way she could remember all their names as she was introduced. Mrs. Milligan seated Anna to her right and Marge on the other side of Anna.

Someone banged the back door and came running down the hall. It was Horace. "Where was the fire?" Mrs. Milligan asked.

"No fire. Fellow from Raleigh hit a fire plug. Ambulance took him to the hospital with a lump on his head."

Marge was admiring a plant in the center of the table. "Clara raises African violets," Mrs. Milligan explained to Anna and nodded toward a dumpy woman at the end of the table. "You have hundreds of them, don't you, Clara?"

"Fifty-nine," replied Clara, obviously impatient to get on with the meal.

At the tinkle of Mrs. Milligan's bell, a heavy-set Negro woman in white uniform brought in a platter of fried pork chops and set it on the table. Anna felt her stomach revolt at the sight. Pools of grease puddled the chops and drained onto the platter in rivulets.

The woman came in again with two bowls heaped high with fluffy rice. The poor woman's cheek was swollen and Anna thought she must have a toothache.

Then came the beans—string beans with chunks of fat meat, the skin of it limp and brown. Anna closed her eyes. When she opened them, a dish of cole slaw was set before her and it looked remarkably edible.

Then came the hot biscuits nesting in white linen. *Glory be! Everybody's dripping from the heat and they're serving hot bread!*

As Horace asked the blessing, Anna, in all earnestness, prayed, "Lord, help me get this down." She would worry about keeping it down later.

As the dishes were passed Anna watched to see how much Marge took to determine how small a portion she might dare take. In order to camouflage the sparsity on her plate, she took generously of the rice; it looked really good.

Miss Chicora Pendergraft, a thin lady sitting across from Anna, minced her food, cutting it into measured bites and lifting it to her mouth robot fashion. Chewing and chewing, her small mouth nibbling like a rabbit's, Chicora Pendergraft was undoubtedly the embodiment of Southern culture. Anna thought, *If that's the way they eat here, I'll never make it!*

Clara-who-raised-violets put Anna's mind at ease. Clara ate everything in sight, all in a rush, smacking her lips with relish. Aware that Anna noticed Clara, Mrs. Milligan, embarrassed, tried to divert her attention. "How was your trip, Miss Petersen?"

"Rather uneventful until we were coming into Scotsville. Then the bus driver started talking like a tour guide. Everybody was laughing at the things he said."

"What kind of things?" Miss Pendergraft asked.

"Oh, he told us about the crops raised here and the people—a lot about the people who live here."

Mrs. Milligan raised her eyebrows. "The people?"

"Yes. He said this is the home of the fighting Scots. At least, that's what I think he said. And the fighting colored folks and the fighting Croatans. I didn't understand Croatans. Are they Indians?"

"Yeah," Horace answered. "The woods are full of 'em 'roun' here."

"Now, Horace," Mrs. Milligan chided, "we don't

have nearly as many Indians in McAdden County as they have in Beaver County."

"True, but we have more 'n our share."

Miss Pendergraft put down her fork and raised one finger the way a person does if a fish bone is caught in his throat and imminent demise is threatening. She was calling for attention. Taking a sip of iced tea, she lightly dabbed her lips with the napkin, then commenced. "Miss Petersen, you may be interested to know that the Indians here may be descendants of the first colonists in this country. You have heard of the Lost Colony?"

"The Lost Colony?"

"I'm sure the present company will forgive me for repeating a story they have heard many times." She did not wait for their consent. "Sir Walter Raleigh sent men to the New World to find a suitable place for a colony. After ten weeks of sailing, they came to the North Carolina coast and found an inlet near an island which the Indians called Roanoke."

Every syllable was delivered intact, chiseled in stone. Anna listened to keep her mind off the food.

"When they landed, they took possession of the land in the name of the Queen, then returned to England with a glowing report of the bountiful country here. They even took two Indians back to England with them, Manteo and Wanchese."

Clara forked another pork chop. Mrs. Milligan gave her a look to wither a cabbage, but Clara was undaunted. Sticking her tongue between her teeth, she made a sucking sound, then washed down her mouthful with tea.

Miss Pendergraft talked the way she ate, deliberately, savoring every word. "The Queen knighted Raleigh and laid claim to all the land from Florida to Canada. They named the territory Virginia in honor of the . . . virgin queen."

At the word *virgin* she discreetly took a sip of tea as if to legitimatize an impropriety.

Anna put a forkful of greasy beans in her mouth, then chased them down with the bland rice. The rice was definitely a lifesaver.

"A second expedition came to Roanoke that summer and in September, returned to England."

The other people at the table were conversing with one another, leaving Anna as Miss Pendergraft's sole listener.

"In April 1585, one hundred men came to prepare homes for their families, who would come later."

"Why haven't I heard about this in history books?" Anna asked.

Miss Pendergraft's mouth twisted in bemused satisfaction. "Miss Petersen, textbooks are written by Nawthaners. There's no other explanation unless, of course, the colony's mysterious ending is the excuse." Enjoying the suspense she created, Miss Pendergraft took another sip of tea, her outstretched pinkie as straight as a clothespin.

Anna cut the last bite from the pork chop, leaving as much meat on the bone as she dared. "Won't you have another pork chop?" Mrs. Milligan asked.

"No, thank you," Anna replied. But remembering Helga's dictum, "Ask for seconds to compliment the hostess," she asked for more rice.

*Glory be!* she thought. *If I have to do this every meal, I'll be as big as the house!*

Miss Pendergraft continued. "The men had problems and abandoned the colony, but another expedition came in 1587—men, women, and children. They built a settlement and named it 'The City of Raleigh in Virginia.'

"They held the first Protestant service in the New World and baptized the first Indian, Manteo. Also, the first English child was born—Virginia Dare."

Everyone at the table had finished eating and, exasperated, waited for Miss Pendergraft to wind down. No sooner did Chicora place her knife and fork across her plate than Clara boomed, "Good. Bring on the dessert!"

Mrs. Milligan rang the bell and the cook appeared, her poor cheek puffed out like a balloon.

"Dora, will you remove the plates?" Mrs. Milligan asked.

When the woman left the room, Anna whispered to Marge, "That poor lady must be in agony."

"Agony?"

"Yes. Didn't you see her face? Her jaw is swollen. She must have a toothache."

Marge had a fit of laughing and couldn't stop. Tears rolled down her face. "That's snuff," she managed to say. "Dora dips snuff!"

*For crying out loud! How am I supposed to know that?* When Dora brought in the pie, Anna tried not to stare, but curiosity got the better of her. Never in her life had she seen anyone who used snuff.

Chicora Pendergraft declined dessert and was carrying on with her saga. "John White gave each settler five hundred acres of land and then went back to England for more supplies. Before he left, the colonists agreed that if they left the settlement, they would write on a tree where they were going. If they were in distress, they would carve a cross.

"It was four long years before John White could return. Catholic Spain had mounted an offensive against Protestant England, hoping to crush it with their fleet." She paused. "Miss Petersen, you're not Catholic, are you?"

"No, Miss Pendergraft, I'm Episcopalian."

Heads turned her way registering the surprise of people seated at the table. "We don't have an Episcopal church," Miss Pendergraft informed her. "You'll have to go to the Methodist."

"She doesn't *have* to go anywhere," Horace argued.

"Don't interrupt, Mr. Wigglesworth. I haven't finished answering Miss Petersen's question about Croatans.

"When the Spanish fleet was finally defeated, John White returned to Roanoke Island, but he could find no trace of the colonists. They had built a fort, and their homes were still standing with furniture and food inside, but none of the settlers was anywhere to be found."

"Were they massacred?"

Miss Pendergraft shook her head vigorously. "There was no sign of killings, no skeletal remains, no evidence of resistance. He did find the letters C-R-O cut in a tree, but he did not find the sign of the cross. On a doorpost was carved CROATOAN."

"You mean the colonists just disappeared off the face of the earth?"

"Apparently. When White returned to England, Raleigh sent him back to search again. He went up and down the coast, but found no trace of them.

"Some historians think the settlers went somewhere with the Indians. Even to the present, there are Croatans who have the same English names that the colonists had, and they have curly hair—sometimes blond. Their dialect is definitely old English. They could, indeed, be descendants of the colonists."

"That is very interesting, Miss Pendergraft. Will I teach any of these people?"

"Indians? Well . . . "

"Only those who pass for white," Marge said. "Indians have their own schools."

Horace laughed. "Those who pass for white? In Beaver County they have three doors in the theaters: One for white, one for colored, and one for Indians. Some families use all three doors!"

"Oh, I get it," Anna said. "You mean there's been intermarriage and some families . . ."

There was polite amusement at her naiveté. Mrs. Milligan, annoyed, tried to change the subject. "What else did the driver tell you, Miss Petersen?"

"Did he tell you this is one of the last empiah towns?" Horace asked.

"Empire towns?"

"Yeah. You know, owned by one family. In this case, the whole county's owned by McCurdys. They own all o' the fahmland, cotton mills, cotton gins, guano plant, oil mill, feed mill—you name it, McCurdys own it."

Color rose in Chicora Pendergraft's neck. "Scotsville is not an empire town, Mr. Wigglesworth! It is a community of wealth and philanthropy. We have a great heritage and it is all due to Cecil Blackmore McCurdy, Esquire. He rescued this county single-handedly from total destruction! When Sherman's renegades came through here carrying out his scorched earth policy, it was Cecil Blackmore McCurdy, Esquire, who came to the rescue!"

Miss Pendergraft turned to Anna to explain. "I use his full name, Miss Petersen, because there has always been a Cecil Blackmore McCurdy. The first, Esquire; the second, Junior; the third; and now Cecil Blackmore McCurdy IV—a fine man, chairman of the school board.

"But the gentleman I am telling you about is Mr. Cecil Blackmore McCurdy, Esquire, whose portrait hangs in McCurdy Department Store. A finer Christian man never lived!"

Horace grinned. "Miss Pendergraft, I guess you knew him well."

She ignored Horace. "When General Sherman's men

marched through McAdden County stealing stock, burning crops, houses, barns, desecrating churches—forgive me, Miss Petersen, I know you are a Yankee and are mortified that one of your own could be so heartless to our women and children—"

Anna nodded solemnly.

The woman's voice escalated to a higher pitch. "Cecil Blackmore McCurdy, Esquire, championed the cause of his neighbors. He loaned them money on their property so they could replant and rebuild. Unfortunately, without slaves they could not prosper. In time, Mr. McCurdy had to foreclose."

Miss Pendergraft drew in her breath for a fresh start, and when she spoke again her voice was stronger, her cheeks redder. "But Cecil Blackmore McCurdy, Esquire, was a man of foresight and will. He raised a standard against the carpetbaggers from the nawth—kept them *out!* Kept out the Klan and used the resources of this county to —" She came down on the last words with an oratorical roar that would do Joan of Arc credit. "To *build!*"

A volley of words bombarded them as Miss Pendergraft spoke rapidly. "Cecil Blackmore McCurdy, Esquire, built gins, a mercantile store, and a cotton mill. He organized farms. That put people back to work, and when there were profits, he built churches and schools. McAdden County owes everything, *everything*, to him!"

As if to douse the fire in her eyes, Miss Pendergraft clutched the glass of tea and gulped down its contents in one fast swallow after another.

Unconsciously, Anna expected applause. Instead, Marge smiled and asked, "What else did the bus driver say, Anna?"

"The bus driver?" She had to think a moment. "Oh yes, he said something very strange. He thought my cello might be a coffin and when I told him it wasn't, he said, 'Too bad. There's a body across the street that's needed burying for more than fifty years.' What did he mean by that?"

Miss Pendergraft jumped up, raised both hands, palms flat out, heading off any answer. "Miss Petersen, I'm afraid that is quite a long story. I don't think you're quite ready for that yet."

The teachers burst out laughing.

# CHAPTER
# FOUR

In the heat of the September morning, Anna walked three blocks up Trade Street from the teacherage to the high school where Mr. Philip Gilchrist's office was. The administration had yet to tell Anna what or who she would be teaching. That in itself was nerve-racking.

Gnats swarmed around her nose and mouth despite the alcohol Marge had splashed on her face. "Gnats give children pinkeye," Marge said. Miss Pendergraft corrected her. "Conjunctivitis," she said primly.

The old brick school had three stories. The ground floor, which was half underground, was marked by whitewash on the wall and long, flat windows. The first floor was reached by a wide flight of uneven, steep steps. Cracks and broken pieces of cement were evidences of the generations of feet that had walked up and down them, feet that went in and out of this old school.

Horace swore the building had been condemned twenty years ago. Perhaps it was condemned, but somewhere in the past there had been great pride in this place. Four cement columns, with cornices imitative of the Parthenon, crowned the steps, and above them was raised the American flag. It hardly stirred in the still air.

Walking inside from the bright sunshine, Anna found the interior dark and cool. A strong smell of lacquer and wax pervaded the air. Floorboards creaked beneath her feet. Like the steps, they were uneven, warped with age.

The clicking of a typewriter led Anna to the superintendent's office. A pleasant-faced woman looked up from her desk. "I'm Mrs. McMillan," she said. "I'm Mr. Gilchrist's secretary. We're so happy to have you in Scotsville, Miss Petersen."

Mr. Gilchrist came out of his office. The seersucker suit he wore was rumpled, the tie conservative. He was of medium height and a rather rotund build. He extended one hand to shake hers and held a pipe in the other hand.

"Welcome to Scotsville, Miss Petersen," he said warmly. "Come right in." He ushered her into his office and held her chair until she was seated.

Anna's stomach was churning. Gilchrist, smiling, did not take his eyes off her. Dumping tobacco from the pipe into an ash tray, he slapped the bowl against the heel of his hand before he spoke. "You look exactly like Tory," he said. "Same hair, straight nose, clear eyes." Brushing flecks of ash from his trousers, he walked around the desk and sat down.

Gilchrist had a white streak running from a widow's peak through the waves of his dark hair. He was not a handsome man, but there was a winsomeness in his eyes. They brimmed with merriment as if a chuckle were in the making.

"You know, your father and I were in the Navy together before the war broke out and we were discharged. After Pearl Harbor, we both tried to reenlist." The smile left his face. "They took me, but Tory was over the age limit. It broke his heart. I offered to pull some strings for him, but he wouldn't hear of it.

"I never knew a more principled man. When we were given shore leave, most of the men went on binges, but not Tory. He'd do a little sightseeing, send some postcards, buy gifts. But if there was an orphanage or a mission, he'd spend most of his time there, playing his mandolin and singing."

Mr. Gilchrist turned the chair around to look out the window. "Tory felt it was his privilege to serve his country—never even cashed in on his benefits. I tried to get him to go to a military facility when he was sick, but no, he said, he would manage.

"Tory had two pictures in his wallet—one of himself with your mother and one of you when you were a little girl."

He was leaning back in the swivel chair as he enjoyed his reminiscences. Anna felt comfortable with him, this stranger who knew and loved her father.

"Miss Petersen," he asked without warning, "why have you chosen to be a teacher?"

"Chosen?" She hesitated. "Well, Mr. Gilchrist, to be perfectly honest with you, it's all that's left to me. I like teaching. When I did my practice teaching, I more than enjoyed it—I loved it."

"Are you a good disciplinarian?"

"I can't answer that. My practice teaching was cut short by my father's illness. I really don't know."

Gilchrist brought the chair around to face her again. "Which brings me to another matter that must have caused you concern."

"My certificate?"

He nodded.

"Yes," Anna explained. "The State Department of Education told me I'm three hours short in practice teaching."

"That's true, but I called Raleigh, and they agreed to issue you a B certificate. If you complete one year of teaching satisfactorily, that'll meet the practice teaching requirement, and next year you'll have an A certificate. It does mean a cut in pay. Let's see, I have the pay scale right here." He shuffled through papers in a basket. "Here it is. Hmmm. Let's see. Here's what you'll make." He leaned across the desk, his finger pointing to the figure.

"Two hundred and fifty dollars a month?" she asked, surprised.

"That's correct." He leaned back in the chair. "It isn't nearly enough, Miss Petersen."

But Anna was pleased at the prospect of earning two hundred and fifty a month.

"We hope salaries will improve. We do have a teacherage for single teachers which cuts down on the cost of room and board. I believe the rate is twenty a month for the room and . . . I don't know how much for meals. Of course, you can get your noon meal at school for thirty-five cents.

"Now you must be eager to know what you'll be teaching." Adjusting his glasses, he went through the basket again. "Here's your teaching assignment. I'm sorry we couldn't get it to you sooner, but our principal Mr. Secrest had some rearranging to do. Hmmm. You'll be teaching eighth grade in the morning and high school in the afternoon. All the classes are in this building."

Anna's heart sank. "Eighth grade?"

"Yes. We have a departmental setup. You'll teach English grammar and North Carolina history in eighth grade. Someone else teaches science and math."

Anna felt panic. The last grammar course she had was in junior high, and she'd never studied North Carolina history!

"In the afternoon, you'll teach American history in the high school." He reached into the basket again, lifted a folder, and thumbed through the papers. "Here's your transcript. You've had American history, haven't you?"

He scanned the transcript. "Well, you've had good courses in history but only a survey of American history." He dropped the folder on his desk and looked up at her, smiling. "Don't worry, Miss Petersen, if you passed International Relations and Ancient Culture of Egypt at Douglass, you can master American History. All I ask is that you keep one chapter ahead of the students." Mr. Gilchrist was chuckling with a confidence Anna did not share. "You won't have any trouble," he reassured her. "You'll do just fine."

Gilchrist leaned back in the chair and looked out the window again. He grew pensive. "You can be a great help to us, Miss Petersen. Last May in the Brown vs. Board of Education case, the court decided in favor of the plaintiff—the law now bans racial discrimination in the public schools.

"The initial reaction here was short-lived because it happened just before school was out. We've been told to proceed with all deliberate speed. A lot of Southerners are prepared to fight this thing to the finish, but President Eisenhower will enforce the law. I'm afraid we're in for trouble.

"The law had to come. In a free and just society, Jim Crow laws have to go. But I can't express my views publicly in Scotsville. Parents here are far from ready to accept colored children in their schools. The trouble won't come for a while, but it will come, and what we do now will determine how much difficulty we'll have later."

He turned to look at her. "Miss Petersen, I'm counting on you to do whatever you can to change attitudes. I daresay the students we teach in the next few years will be the parents of that generation of children that will be totally integrated."

He stood up. "I'll take you in to meet Mark Secrest, the principal. He's a fine man—rank of colonel in the service. After the teachers' meeting this morning, he'll show you your classrooms and introduce you to your colleagues."

Mr. Secrest was a tall, good-looking man. He led Anna down an aisle in the auditorium through a hubbub of voices. Seated on the platform with other new teachers and several elementary principals, Anna was careful about her skirt and her posture, but there was nothing she could do to quiet her stomach. She felt like heading for the nearest door and running all the way home to Neptune Avenue.

When Mr. Secrest stepped to the lectern, people stopped talking and sat fanning themselves with the programs. The upturned faces scrutinized the newcomers on stage. As Anna returned their gazes, she noted a sameness about their faces—as if they had been born of the same mother, thought the same thoughts.

The meeting began with the singing of "America the Beautiful," but the piano was off-key by a whole note and the pianist did not compensate. Some of the voices strained to reach the high notes of the chorus, while others fell to another key to finish the song.

After Mr. Secrest led in prayer and welcomed the teachers, Mr. Gilchrist rose to introduce the newcomers. Anna was last in the alphabetical list. "Miss Anna Petersen, all the way from Jersey City, New Jersey."

Anna stood while the audience politely applauded.

Next, Miss Amy Esmeralda McLean stood to talk about membership in the professional organization. She was a modest woman with a soft voice. "As you all know," she said sweetly, "we of the Scotsville school district are always one hundred percent in NCEA membership and each of us serves on a committee."

Something told Anna that no one bucked Miss Amy.

Other principals made announcements, then Mr. Gilchrist began his opening day address. He told in-house jokes that Anna did not understand, then became serious. "There is a common agreement among many people that the Golden Age lies somewhere in the past. This is a natural attitude which rises out of a very urgent necessity. The most important function of any generation is to pass on the cultural heritage to the next. The generations are held together by the subtle magic of things in common known and felt.

"Underlying the fear of individual parents that they may fail their own children is the social fear that a whole generation may fail to grasp the magic link and humanity itself falter in its long climb towards the light.

"My own conviction is that the Golden Age lies somewhere in the future. Each of us has a God-given opportunity and obligation to make a little contribution towards the coming of that day. This generation of students and the schools which they attend are being subjected to some very harsh criticism. My prediction is that the loyalty, ambition, and seriousness of present-day students will confound the pessimists.

"In years ahead, look back to the students you teach this year and see how many of them will have made their mark and with it, their contribution to the dawning of that better day which is the hope of good people everywhere.

"As you teach them, you will need all the knowledge, wisdom, and patience you can call up. But above all, you will need love, for 'Though I speak with the tongues of men and of angels and have not charity, I am become as sounding brass, or a tinkling cymbal. . . .'" He quoted the entire thirteenth chapter of 1 Corinthians.

Anna was so moved by the speech she expected the audience to stand to its feet and give a rousing ovation. Instead, there was a slow patter of applause and the meeting was over. The hubbub resumed.

Walking to the teacherage with Marge and Horace, Anna asked, "Didn't you think Mr. Gilchrist's speech was wonderful?"

"I really wasn't listening," Marge confessed, slapping at the gnats. "Darn gnats!"

"You weren't listening?"

Marge laughed. "Anna, after you've heard as many opening-day speeches as I have, you stop listening. He always says the same thing."

"The same speech?"

"He always quotes that love chapter."

"Well, he sure inspired me."

Horace kicked a can down the sidewalk as they were walking, his white buck shoes taking a beating. "Inspi'ed?" he asked. "Wait'll this time tomorrow, after the first day with all o' those screamin' hellions. I thought landin' in Normandy on D Day was bad, but that first day o' school was a beachhead that beats all I evah saw in combat! Just wait'll tomorra, then tell us how inspi'ed you are!"

*What a jerk,* Anna thought.

But the first day was horrendous. Anna took pains to dress well, even pulling on a girdle, which was not an easy task after going all summer without one. The plaid dress was full-skirted—hot for the climate, but the best-looking outfit she owned. Marge was diplomatic. "You look nice, Anna, but I think you'd also look good in a straight skirt." Then she tempered it. "Looks nice with those heels. Blue is your color."

The day before, Marge had said yellow was her color. *Better wise up,* Anna decided as she walked out of the teacherage. *These Southerners are too quick with the compliments. Never have I been told by so many that I have pretty hair, pretty eyes, pretty skin. Today, above all days, I need a reliable judgment on how I look. But I'll have to be satisfied with knowing I've done my best.*

As early as she was, there were already students crowding the sidewalk going to school. As she drew near McAdden High, she dreaded walking across the schoolyard with students everywhere. Going up the steps where they flocked like birds would be the hardest. Anna walked straight ahead, the crowd parting for her like the Red Sea parted before Moses. So far, so good, but heading for the steps, Anna felt her legs start to shake. The students who sat on the steps or stood by the walls on either side were horsing around and yelling. But as soon as they saw her the horseplay stopped. There was dead silence. Every eye was on Anna.

A girl ventured to speak. "Hey."

Anna didn't like the "Hey." It sounded impertinent.

"Hullo," she responded. A ripple of giggles went through the crowd. Anna's cheeks flushed. Students moved aside to make way for her, and Anna picked her way up the steps.

For the second time she would have to be on the platform, this time to be introduced to the student body. Until Mr. Secrest came in, she sat in the back of the empty auditorium, fighting to bring her nervousness under control.

Mr. Secrest bounced through the door and motioned Anna to the front. She followed him to the platform, stepping carefully on the worn, wooden steps. *Klutz*, she told herself, *don't fall*.

While students and teachers streamed into the room, Anna sat alone on the stage. She tried not to think about the people. The old auditorium was built like a Bijou theater. The floor sloped to the front; the wooden seats squeaked; the rows curved in a semicircle and were sliced with two aisles. Embossed tin squares covered the ceiling, which was stained brown by leaks in the roof. The lighting was poor, and, despite the open windows, a warm, human smell permeated the room.

An open pulpit Bible rested on the podium, a baby grand piano with one leg askew was on the stage, and the American and Christian flags flanked the old velvet curtain.

Mr. Gilchrist joined her and when Mr. Secrest was finished running about, he too sat down and mopped his brow.

Anna was glad for the full skirt; she didn't have to worry about anything showing. They sang the national anthem, accompanied by the awful piano, pledged allegiance to the "Yewnited States of Amuracah," and prayed. After announcements, Mr. Secrest introduced Anna and she stood. "Miss Petersen will teach eighth-grade English, North Carolina history, and American history."

A boy groaned loudly and the crowd laughed.

The business lasted an hour, but before students were dismissed, teachers were asked to go their classrooms. Anna felt conspicuous crossing the stage with everyone looking at her, and her legs were not steady. On the last of the wooden steps, she tripped and fell sprawling. Mr. Secrest was quickly by her side, holding her arm as she scrambled to her feet. "Are you all right, Miss Petersen?"

Everybody was standing up, craning their necks to see what had happened. Anna's face burned with embarrassment. "I'm fine," she insisted, but Mr. Secrest continued holding her arm as they went up the aisle. The students found that to be funnier yet. Whistling and making a big hullabaloo, they applauded the pair out of the auditorium.

Anna's face was still warm when, standing by the classroom door, she greeted eighth graders as they came in. Too shy to speak, they giggled and rushed to grab desks in the back of the room.

Anna wrote her name on the board and then spoke the words she had memorized the night before. "I'm happy to be your teacher this year. You may notice that I talk a bit differently than you do, and I hope that won't be a problem. I'm going to work hard on getting a nice Southern accent. But in the meantime, if you don't understand something I say, please let me know."

She had stayed up until one o'clock writing lesson

plans and was up again at five to go over them. It was paying off. The students were so quiet you could hear a pin drop. *It's really going well*, she thought, and glanced at her notes.

The next item on the agenda was the roll. "I will now pass around this sheet of paper and ask you to sign your names. While you're doing that, I'll go on with the lesson."

There seemed to be some consternation among the students and some whispered discussion, but soon they began signing names and passing the paper.

"When I arrived at the teacherage, the first evening I was here Miss Pendergraft—" At the mention of the name, fleeting signs of recognition crossed their faces. Anna continued. "Miss Pendergraft asked me if I had heard of the Lost Colony. Since I'm not from North Carolina, I had not. So she told me the story. . . ."

Their faces were blank. Obviously, they had never heard of the Lost Colony either.

As Anna recounted the story, the students were spellbound, so much so that they forgot to swat gnats. Anna's confidence soared. The heat, the gnats—nothing seemed to distract them.

Stealing a glance at her watch, she was delighted that her timing was perfect. Reaching the climax of the story seconds before the bell rang, she could see by their expressions how mystified and curious they were about the disappearance of the colonists. "Think about it and come back tomorrow and tell us what you think happened to the colonists." The bell rang.

As students filed out of the room, Anna stood by the door smiling. Her performance could not have been more perfect.

The last boy to leave was a good-looking, crew cut blond with a smile to melt the heart. "Miss Petersen," he said with boyish charm, "I didn't understand a word you said, but you sure talk good."

Anna's mouth dropped open. "You mean . . ."

"It's your accent, ma'am. My name's Ted McGill, and that's my sister sits in the corner. Remember the girl with red hair? That's Anita."

Anna was stunned.

"She's smarter'n me. That's why we're in the same class. I got held back in second grade, but Anita makes all As." His books were sliding under his arm. "I gotta go, Miss Petersen," he said, straightening the books. "Bye, now."

Anna sat down. *How could I be so dumb?*

The English classes were as polite as the history class. The students had the same mystified look, but there were no lost colonists to mystify them. Anna was unnerved; they were not comprehending one word she was saying! If she looked at her watch once, she looked fifty times. *The bell is never going to ring*, she fretted. *Lunchtime will never come.*

Too nervous to eat, Anna went to the cafeteria hoping to find Marge. They were serving meat loaf and squash, nothing Anna could eat and keep down easily. A Negro cook behind the counter poked a platter of fried meat toward her. "Dis 's fo' you teachahs."

"What is it?"

"Fatback fried crisp."

*Uff-dah*, Anna thought and shook her head. "No, thanks."

When she couldn't find Marge, Anna headed for the classroom where she would teach high school history. When she reached it, another class was in session so she waited outside for the bell to ring.

A girl came tearing down the hall, distressed. "Ma'am, can you help me?" Her face showed panic. "My friend's in the girls' room. She's wearin' falsies and they come a'loose."

"Help you?"

"Yes, ma'am. We gotta have a pin."

"Sure. I think I have one." Anna searched her pocketbook and came up with one.

The girl grabbed it. "Oh, thank you! Thank you, ma'am! You don't know how much I 'preciate it!"

The bell rang, the door burst open, and students charged out, racing for the lunchroom. When the last student was gone, Anna went into the room, spoke to the teacher leaving, and put her things on the desk. Then she took up her position at the door to welcome incoming students.

The first newcomer sauntered down the hall, a boy dressed in draped, pegged pants and a polo shirt. The shirt tended to cling to the boy's body, so with his thumb and forefinger, he bounced the shirt back and forth against his chest to cool himself. He was chewing a wad of gum and blew a bubble that popped and plastered his lips, but his eyes never left her. Unceremoniously, he examined her from head to toe. Anna's stomach began churning.

The next boy was just as intimidating, coming close enough to her that the smell of brilliantine made her draw back. Each boy in turn appraised her as he walked past. Anna's knuckles were white against the doorknob.

A slip of a girl approached and with a barely audible "Hey," slipped past her. Following her was a plump brunette with an armload of books. She greeted Anna properly. "Good afternoon, Miss Petersen."

"Thank you," she answered absently. The bell rang. Anna glanced up and down the hall to see if anyone else was coming, then stepped inside and shut the door. Her mouth was dry. She reminded herself to show confidence. *Stride across the room,* she told herself. She drew in her breath and started forward, but was halted mid-stride. Her skirt was caught fast in the door! *Too late—it's ripping! Definitely ripping! Don't panic!*

Immediately the students saw her predicament and started laughing like they'd never seen anything so funny in their whole lives.

The rip was at the waist, separating the skirt from the top part of the dress. Anna slapped her hand over the tear and used the other hand to open the door and release the skirt. Her cheeks were blazing—the boys were howling!

The brunette who knew enough to say, "Good afternoon," and call her by name, admonished the boys. "Hush! You better lay off. You want Mr. Secrest comin' in here?" But the girl herself was giggling.

Anna sat behind her desk so the rip wouldn't show. A tall, T-shirted boy, who had a pack of cigarettes rolled in his sleeve, stretched his legs on either side of the desk ahead of him, jabbed a finger toward Anna, and asked, "Ain't choo the lady fell offa the stage this mo'nin'?"

Another burst of laughter, this one in no way subsiding.

The door opened and in came a skinny, disheveled-looking boy, his hair wild and unkempt.

"Hey, Pluto," Peg Pants called. "Where ya been?"

"Jus' gittin' to school," he mumbled and flopped in the front desk.

"Shall we come to order?" Anna pleaded, her voice strained.

"To order what? Hamburger and french fries?" a boy quipped. He had a ducktail haircut and was too busy squeezing a pimple to look up.

"Let's not have any wisecracks," Anna suggested, her voice high and squeaky.

"You talk funny," Pluto informed her.

The students howled. "Good, Pluto, you noticed." T-Shirt again.

"You a Yankee?" Pluto asked.

T-Shirt answered. "Yeah, she plays first base—gonna win the series for us."

"Miss Whatever-Yer-Name-Is, when the Worl' Series is on, we don't do nothin' but lissen to the game till the series is over," Ducktail informed her.

"What do you mean?"

Peg Pants explained. "We lissen to the ball games over the intercom every afternoon."

"Listen to ball games?" she exclaimed.

"Sure. It's the World Series," T-Shirt said, as if no further explanation were necessary.

"There will be no listening to ball games in this classroom," Anna said emphatically.

"All you have to do is tell Mr. Secrest to turn on the game over the intercom and he'll do it. Want me to ask him?" Pluto offered.

Anna was indignant. "I do not!"

"Why not?" Peg Pants argued. "Ain't cha patriotic? Ain't this Amuracun Hist'ry?"

T-Shirt stood up, stretched, laced his fingers behind his head, and walked around the room holding the back of his head, elbows akimbo. "Teacher, lemme tell you how 'tis. If you don't let us lissen on the intercom, we stay home an' lissen."

"But you'll be suspended."

"Naw, we won't. It don't work that away. Our mommas'll write us excuses. In this town, mommas is the law and the gospel. Mr. Secrest, Mr. Gilchrist, they all lissen to mommas."

"I don't want to hear any more of this!"

Ducktail stood up, imitating Napoleon's famous pose. "I second the motion."

T-Shirt sat down, drew his knees up under the desk, and folded his hands like a child. All the others followed suit and, with mock respect, fastened their attention on Anna.

Now it was up to her. *What am I going to do?* she

wondered. Rising slowly, her left arm wrapped around her waist to cover the rip, Anna wrote on the board: "Miss Anna Petersen."

Turning around, she smiled and lied, "I'm happy to be your teacher this year." A pause. "If you have trouble understanding me, please let me know."

In unison, with mock meekness, they answered, "Yes, Miss Petersen."

Holding up a sheet of paper in her right hand, her arm still wrapped around her waist, she instructed them. "I have here this paper that I'm holding in my hand." Nothing seemed to come out right.

"Yes, Miss Petersen," they responded with rapt attention.

"I'm going to pass the paper around the room." The paper was shaking. "Just write your name on it and pass it to the next person."

The awkwardness of trying to hide the rip and hand Pluto the paper at the same time was not lost on them. With feigned seriousness, one of them quipped, "A body could grow to an arm like that."

"Tomorrow I'll begin learning your names," she promised, "and we'll get better acquainted."

"Yes, Miss Petersen."

There was nothing to do but ignore them. She sat down again. As the paper went around the room there was a lot of snickering, but she was too unnerved to worry about it. What could be so funny about writing your name on a piece of paper?

By the end of the day, Anna was drained, depleted, exhausted. Lugging an armful of books to the teacherage, she collapsed on the steps and let the books slide onto the porch. Perspiration was trickling down her neck, gnats were swarming about her face, and her dress was sticking to her back below her shoulder blades.

Horace was coming down the street, loping along as

if he had all the time in the world. He was supposed to be at junior varsity football practice. It was too late to escape him; he was crossing the street from the funeral home.

"Hey," he called, coming up the walk. "Still in-spi'ed?" He flopped down beside her, and Anna got a whiff of body odor that would do honor to a dead fish.

Horace rubbed his face on his shoulder to wipe away sweat and lifted the sleeve of his shirt to wipe his forehead.

"You were right, Horace. Normandy couldn't have been any worse."

"Aw, come on. So you stumbled on the steps—that coulda' happened to anybody."

She had forgotten about that.

"Anything else happen?" he asked.

"Well, for starters, they couldn't understand me. I talked the whole period and the eighth graders sat there like angels, but they didn't understand a word I said."

"How'd ya know?"

"Some boy told me."

"Who was he?"

"A nice-looking, crew cut blond. Had on a white shirt and dungarees. He told me his name but I forgot it."

"A white dress shirt?"

She nodded.

"Only boy I know wears a white shirt is Ted McGill. He wears a white dress shirt and dungarees every day of his life."

"That's his name."

"Well, so they didn't understand you. They'll learn. Anything else?"

Anna groaned. "Oh, Horace, you wouldn't believe that sixth period history class."

"Who's in there?"

"I don't know their names. Some tall boy in a T-shirt

with a pack of cigarettes in his sleeve. A boy named Pluto. Ducktails, crew cuts—all shapes and sizes."

"Didn't you make a roll?"

"Oh, sure I did. Do you think you might know some of them? Here, I'll get it for you."

Horace held the paper in both hands as he read the names. "Hey, you couldn't 'a had Harold Appleton in your sixth period—that clown's in my English class sixth period."

A grin spread across his face as he read on. "Oh, I see what they've done." He was laughing.

"What're you laughing at?"

"Anna, you've fallen for the oldest gag in Scotsville history. They've given you all phony names!"

"What do you mean, phony names?"

"Just that. Here's the name of the janitor, Willie Pellem; Tom McAllister is the sheriff; Ray O'Reilly is the bootlegger. The rest o' these are different students who're always gettin' into trouble . . . Now here's a girl who might be in your class, Sue Marie Ellsworth. Her mother's a teacher. Did you have a girl in there who's chubby? Dark hair? I have her in English third period. Nice girl."

"Yes, I remember her."

"Well, that's the only valid name on that list unless this Ellen Wheatley is some girl I don't know. You'll have to start all over tomorrow."

Horace was chuckling as he stood up and brushed the seat of his pants.

Anna gathered up her books and tried to hide the rip in her dress by holding the books against her hip. When she struggled to her feet, Horace held the screen door for her and followed her inside. "How'd ya tear your dress?"

"Caught it in a door," she answered, annoyed.

"Wonder what's for supper? Got a date for the PTA

picnic?" Picking up the Raleigh paper, he thumbed to the sports page.

Anna left him in the downstairs sitting room and trudged upstairs to her room.

Marge was stretched out on the bed in her slip. "Hey, there's some mail for you on the mantel."

It was the Rutgers' alumni bulletin. Anna scanned it to see if Roger's name was in it. There it was—Dr. and Mrs. Roger Metcalf—announcing the birth of twin sons.

Anna looked at the announcement for a while, then crumpled the bulletin in her hand. *So,* she thought, *she's given him sons, two of them. How grateful and proud he must be.*

"Your trunk came today."

She had seen it beside the wardrobe. Anna unlocked the latch and lifted the lid. On top of everything else, wrapped in newspaper, was the conch. Unwrapping it, Anna could hardly see for the mist blurring her vision.

"What's that?" Marge asked.

"It's a shell I found at Ocean Grove." She held it for Marge to see. The inside curl was pink, the surface smooth as glass. The lip was fan-shaped, its pink edge tinged with lavender.

"How pretty," Marge said. "Why don't you put it on the mantel?"

Anna placed it carefully and, still holding it lovingly in her hands, fought back the tears.

# CHAPTER
# FIVE

Miss Amy, spinster principal of Montgomery Elementary, saw to it that all new, single teachers had dates for the PTA picnic. Anna was no exception. Her date was Woodall Jackson, a bachelor Presbyterian minister. Kind he was, but shy—the type Marge called "painfully shy"—and with good reason. The poor man had an eye badly disfigured by shrapnel during the war. It was not fair to him, insisting that he escort some woman he did not know to a picnic sponsored by an organization to which he had no reason to belong. But he was such a good man, Marge said, he'd do anything anybody asked him to do.

Even though Anna had been warned about the eye, still it was a shock to see it. They were driving to the country club in Woodall's station wagon, which was neither new nor clean but which, as Marge assured Anna, was at least paid for. Woodall was a man who made less money than a teacher, Marge said, yet he paid his bills and put down cash for things like a car.

Anna admired that. She had been having money troubles. The NCEA dues were an unexpected expenditure and Anna worried about spending part of her two hundred dollars from her father's insurance. That money should be kept intact, she felt. Well, she'd pay it back payday.

The car was really old and dirty. The night was too hot to ride with the windows rolled up and the wind tousled her hair and made talking difficult. Anna had mended the blue plaid dress, washed and ironed it. Now, sitting on a lumpy seat, the springs pressing her bottom, she could well imagine how wrinkled the dress would be by the time they arrived at the club.

"Country club" meant elegance to Anna and she felt anything but elegant.

Anna tried to talk to Woodall, but after he asked, "What church do you go to?" and she answered and then asked him where he preached, it was his turn to speak. At least he could have asked her what she taught, but he was too nervous to say anything. Besides, the roar of the motor drowned out comfortable conversation.

Woodall preached in two churches, each in an opposite end of the county, and while Anna waited for him to say something else, her mind played with the idea of Woodall tearing across the county every Sunday morning in his old Pontiac, making chickens and dogs scatter on the back roads.

"He's steady, reliable," Marge had told her as if Anna were considering marriage. "Much more so than the Methodist preachers. They're here today, gone tomorrow. Don't ever get involved with a Methodist minister, Anna. Marry one of them and you'll live in a different house every two or four years, never have furniture of your own, and have to entertain the flock regularly—and be criticized by the same. You'll never make a friend without making two enemies."

Anna didn't understand how Marge could know so much and be so dumb. David Garston was a handsome man, a CPA, and he called Marge several times but she wouldn't go out with him. Instead, she went with Peter Waldo McSwain who owned the funeral parlor. He was bald, fat, fortyish, and dull.

Horace claimed that Waldo was wanted by the FBI, but he wouldn't say why. Waldo could be anything—a Red or a Mafia man or a numbers dealer—except for one trait: Waldo was lazy, too lazy to be anything.

Hurricane Hazel had struck Scotsville the week before, and after enduring such a storm cloistered in the room with Marge and oatmeal cookies, Anna felt close enough to her to ask why she went with Waldo.

"He comes from such a good family, Anna. McSwains were among the first settlers in McAdden County."

The logic escaped Anna. "Why won't you go out with David Garston?"

"David's from North Scotsville." Marge said it as if that should answer the question. It didn't and she saw that it didn't. "You really don't understand?"

Anna shook her head.

"Sit down. North Scotsville is where the mill people live. You might think it's a part of Scotsville because one town runs into the other one, but it has its own mayor and city council." Marge began buffing her nails but she kept glancing at Anna, hoping to see some light of understanding.

"The reason it's set up that way is because mill people don't like to mix with town people. They have their own school. McCurdys built the school and it has better facilities than we have in town schools. Their school goes through eighth grade and when students finish eight grades, it's hard to get them to come uptown to the high school. Of course, an eighth grade education is all they need to work in the mill."

"Do they have to work in the mill?"

"No, but that's all most of them want to do. You have to understand, Anna, that working in a cotton mill is more than a job; it's a way of life. Their culture isn't at all like ours. They talk different, go to different churches, do everything different."

"But David Garston is an educated man. He's hard-working and well-mannered."

"Anna, believe me, you can take a man out of the mill, but you can't take the mill out of the man."

Anna was pondering Marge's words as Woodall turned the Pontiac off the paved road and onto a sandy lane. There sat the country club, nothing but a farmhouse in a field, cars parked randomly in the yard. Limbs ripped off by the storm were strewn about, making the place even more unsightly. Anna wondered why anyone would want to come so far to such a dump. She ventured another question to Woodall. "Tell me, why do single ministers come to PTA picnics?"

"Miss Petersen," he replied, "bachelors never miss a free meal." He smiled sheepishly and she laughed. Woodall hopped out of the car and raced around to open the door for her.

Inside, people were already lined up on both sides of long tables, heaping their plates with fried chicken and ham biscuits. The chicken was delicious—crisp and tender. Before the opportunity had passed, Woodall trotted back for seconds several times.

As sweltering as it was, the after-dinner program was not shortened. Every member of the school board was introduced—a woman doctor, a lawyer, a banker, a minister—and then Cecil Blackmore McCurdy IV, chairman, was asked to speak.

McCurdy was a mild-mannered man, thirtyish, with a town-and-country look about him; nothing distinguished him from the others except the keen intelligence in his eyes and a quiet reserve. He looked through rimless glasses from beneath heavy brows and made a few remarks. No frills, no humor, all business.

"He went to Harvard," Woodall told her. "His wife's an invalid. Been in an iron lung over a year now. Polio."

"Any children?"

"A son and a daughter. Aunt Charlotte looks after them."

It was good to know the children had an aunt to care for them.

"Aunt Charlotte's been with the McCurdy family three generations."

"Is the boy named for his father?"

"Of course. The girl's named Judyth."

The tragedy of Cecil McCurdy's wife affected Anna's attitude toward him—anyone with a situation like that deserved consideration, she reasoned. Yet even Woodall showed little compassion for the man.

"Don't worry about McCurdy," he said. "He has cooks, maids, all kinds of servants to take care of things at home. He gets in an aeroplane any time he pleases and goes to Miami, New York, Tokyo—anywhere he wants to go. Got his own private railway coach, too."

On the way home, Woodall couldn't get his mind off McCurdy. "A man like Cecil McCurdy doesn't have any problems." Suddenly, without warning, he turned to Anna and blurted out, "What do you think McCurdy would do if he had a problem like mine?"

Anna hesitated, then surprised herself by saying exactly what she thought. "He'd wear a patch over it."

Woodall's mouth dropped open. When he clamped it shut again he did not open it until he delivered Anna to the door. "Good night," he said and left.

As Anna was undressing for bed, she told Marge about the conversation. "I wonder why Woodall reacted that way?" she asked.

"Don't you know, Anna? Woodall isn't ashamed of that eye—it's his pride, his red badge of courage, his Congressional Medal of Honor."

"You've gotta be kidding!"

Marge smiled. "Anna, you've got a lot to learn about men," she said and left for the bathroom. Anna sat on the side of the bed, bewildered.

When Marge came back she had dismissed Woodall from her mind. "I heard something today that'll cheer you up. Be advised that the students now understand you. Ted McGill told my class, 'All you have to do is remember that Miss Petersen makes all her *ing*s and her *r*s stand up straight.'"

It did cheer her. Anna stayed up until the wee hours getting ready for the next day's classes.

Yet in the eighth-grade English class, there was a turn of events that threw all her plans out the window. Ted's sister, Anita, whispered to him, "Ask Miss Petersen."

The boy turned to Anna. "Miss Petersen, our cousin lives in New Jersey, and he says they have air-raid drills in his school. Do they?"

"Yes, Ted, it's true. America is very concerned now that Russia has the atomic bomb. Students in many schools have bomb drills regularly just as you have fire drills."

"You mean they get out of class?"

Anna did not smile. "It's very serious, Ted. One atomic bomb would destroy New York City, and everything within a hundred-mile radius would be affected. That would mean parts of New York State, Connecticut, New Jersey. New York City would be a prime target. Everybody who lives there is very alarmed."

"Boy, I'm glad I don't live up there," Ted said.

Andrew Lawton, the tallest and smartest boy in the class, began to unwind his lanky frame and, with nothing less than a sneer on his face, proceeded to take over. "That's nothing. Scotsville's only forty miles from Ft. Bragg, and Ft. Bragg just happens to be the most strategic military base on the Eastern seaboard. If the Russians picked a target, it'd be Ft. Bragg, not Broadway." The sarcasm was aimed directly at Anna and he didn't intend to let up. "When scientists tested the bomb in New Mexico, they told GIs not to even look at the explosion or they'd be blinded. Well, we're close enough to Ft. Bragg that if they dropped a bomb there we'd see the flash. What's more, we'd be hit by shock waves and a lotta fallout. I don't see why you people up north think you got any more danger than we have right here where I'm sittin'."

"True," Anna began, baffled by his animosity.

A fat boy named Charles interrupted. "Them Russians ain't about to drop a bomb on us, Andy. We'd wipe 'em plumb offa the map."

Andrew snapped back, "Not with that bunch of Republican fatheads sitting in Washington."

"Well, we won World War II, didn't we? Wasn't Ike the one who dropped the bomb on Japan?" Charles argued.

Andrew looked disgusted. "No, Ike didn't drop the bomb on Japan. It was Truman and the Japs surrendered, but that's a different story. Back then we were the only country that had the bomb. Situation's different now that Russia's got the bomb."

"Shoot, Charles, there's no way we wouldn't get a bunch o' people kilt," Eddie McLaughlin said. Eddie was the oldest of three boys; their mother was dead and their father was a traveling salesman. At fourteen Eddie was a surrogate father in the family.

"That's right," Anna agreed. "Charles, one atomic bomb would take many lives and we don't want that. No nation can say it will win in an atomic war. The cost in human lives and health would be astronomical. Civilization would be seriously threatened. The whole human race would suffer radiation fallout. How could any nation feel like a winner?"

"Oh, Miss Petersen, you're making me scared," Anita said, her face pale. "Do you mean that if they dropped a bomb on New York City or some place big, they wouldn't stop there?"

"Not unless we surrendered, Anita."

"Amuruca would never surrender to the Reds," Charles said confidently.

"Shut up, Charles," Andrew said. "There wouldn't

be anything left. Communications would be disrupted, water and food contaminated, hospitals and medical personnel destroyed. Plagues would spread and people would die because there wouldn't be facilities or medicines."

"Please, Andrew, we do not say, 'shut up.'"

"We do down here," he informed her and the class laughed.

"Miss Petersen, my uncle was in Japanese waters when Hiroshima was bombed," Eddie said. "He was one of the first GIs to go in after the bombing. It was so bad he won't talk about it even now."

With great bravado Charles tried to be blasé. "Well, if you gotta go you gotta go. If you get blown up, you won't know what hit cha. That's a good way to go if you ask me."

"Charles, if you're lucky, you get killed," Andrew told him. "What if you're burned all over or you go crazy or you lose your arms and legs?"

"Yeah, Charles," Ted said, "there's lotsa things worse than death."

A girl named Jennifer spoke up, "What're we gonna do about it?"

"I'm not gonna worry about it," Charles said. "Whatever will be will be. You ain't goin' no place till it's your time."

Clearly the others did not agree with him. They were white-faced and shaken. When the bell rang, they didn't want to leave.

Disturbed as she was by Andrew's behavior, Anna felt it was a good discussion. She felt so good about it, the situation in the afternoon class did not dampen her spirits. None of the boys showed up for high school history. Sue Marie Ellsworth and Ellen Wheatley were the only students who came. At first Anna didn't recognize Sue Marie because she was no longer a brunette but a blonde.

"I peroxided it last night," she said, giggling. "I'm glad the boys aren't here to tease me. Too bad we can't have class—nobody's here."

"You're here," Anna said.

"I know, but the boys aren't and you'll only have to repeat all the stuff when they come back."

"No. That's their problem. We won't go over this material again."

Surprised, the girls looked at each other. "You mean—"

"That's correct. If the boys choose to listen to the World Series instead of coming to school, then it's up to them to make up the work. You came to school and you deserve to be taught. When the boys come back I'm not going to bore you by repeating the lesson we'll have today."

Anna brought out the roll sheet. "Now, before we begin the lesson, there is a little matter you can help me with. Ellen, Sue Marie, here's the roll the boys signed. Do you know what they've done?"

The girls looked at each other sheepishly. "Yes'm," Sue Marie answered. "Do you?"

"Yes. Mr. Wigglesworth told me. Will you help me? Will you write the correct names on this sheet for me?"

The girls agreed and Sue Marie began writing the names. "Don't feel bad," she said. "Students played this trick on Mama once. Most of the boys in this class are football players and Mama said it wasn't fair giving you all the football players your first year. They cause a lotta trouble. When the boys from across the state line come over here, Scotsville boys fight them with broken bottles, baseball bats—anything they can get their hands on."

"Why?"

"No reason, Miss Petersen. It's rumbling."

"Could you girls help me put names with faces?"

"Sure. Pluto Martin is the boy who sits here on the

front row. You know him. He's the one with the big ears and freckles—a really sweet boy but the other fellas torment the soul outta him. His mother's crazy and he's had a hard life. He's got all these brothers and sisters who drink all the time. Pluto's the youngest."

"Well, I don't need to hear all the personal information, Sue Marie, but if—"

"All right. Do you remember the boy with the ducktail? He's Earl McClendon. He's crazy about cars. He's got this Chevy that's all souped up and he drives like crazy. Goes out to Eddie McLaughlin's place and those two boys do nothing but work on motors.

"The boy who wears T-shirts is Oren Wallace. He's quiet and stays out of school a lot. Lester McKenzie's the boy who draws pictures in class—zoot suiters. His daddy's the fire chief. The fella sits next to me is Marvin Locklear. He's Indian, only he passes for white."

"He doesn't look like an Indian."

"He is. Locklear's an Indian name. His mother's white and that's why his granddaddy shot Marvin's father. You know, he didn't like Indians. He killed Marvin's daddy."

"Was he prosecuted?"

"He went to jail for a while but before he got out, Marvin's mama married another Indian." Sue Marie was coming to the end of the list. "You know Ellen and me."

Anna smiled at the thin, little girl beside Sue Marie. "You're a sophomore, aren't you?"

Ellen gave a slight nod of her head.

"What are your plans for the future?" The girl shrugged her shoulders.

"Tell Miss Petersen how you want to be a beauty parlor operator," Sue Marie prompted. Still the girl didn't talk.

"Where do you live?" Anna asked.

"North Scotsville."

"What street?"

"Second Street."

"Would you like to go up to Charlotte or Raleigh and study cosmetology?"

"I heered them's bad places," she ventured.

"Not *heered*, Ellen, *heard*."

"How do you say h-e-a-r?"

"Well, you say, *hear*."

"Well, ain't it *heered* when you put an e-d on it?"

Anna gave up. "Well, girls, let's get down to the lesson."

Because there were no interruptions, they covered most of the material. When the bell rang, Sue Marie stood up, wrapped her arms around her books, and held them against her flat chest. "I hate to admit it, Miss Petersen, but you did the right thing. It's what my mama would've done. She woulda taught the lesson even though there were only two in the class."

Anna felt it had been a very good day at school. She came home eager to tell Marge about the good discussion on war and about how she had handled the boys being absent and the fake roll. Later, she might talk to her about Andrew, but not now. At the teacherage there was a phone call for her to return. Anna dialed the number and in the middle of the first ring, a woman answered abruptly. "Hello?"

"I'm Anna Petersen and I'm returning—"

The woman cut her off. "Are you the Miss Petersen who teaches English in the eighth grade?" Her voice was strident.

"Yes, I am."

"Well, Miss Petersen, my daughter Jennifer came home from school today scared to death and I want to know what went on in that class that upset her so."

"Well, it was a discussion about atomic war."

"Atomic war! What does that have to do with English?"

"Well, nothing but—"

"Lemme tell you one thing, Miss Petersen. My child is thirteen years old and to you that might mean she's grown, but to me she's just a little girl and if I, a grown woman, don't know anything about atom bombs, I don't see any reason for scarin' the daylights out of Jennifer with a whole lot of scary stuff. I'd thank you to stick to teaching English because in my book you're no expert on all that military mess. In Scotsville we're peace-loving people and there's no sense in talking about things that're goin' to upset children. Why, Jennifer won't sleep a wink! She's cryin' right now."

Anna's head reeled. "I'm sorry, Mrs. Bradbury."

"Sorry isn't enough, Miss Petersen. I'm calling Mr. Secrest about this!"

The receiver clicked.

Anna was stunned. *Glory be! I can't believe this!*

The phone rang. She picked up the receiver. "Teacherage. Miss Petersen speaking—"

"Miss Petersen, you don't know me but I'm Charles Simpson's mother." Her voice was as sweet as honeysuckle. "He's in your eighth-grade class and he came home today all upset about the atomic bomb. Now, I don't mean to be critical, you being a beginning teacher and from another part of the country, but I thought you might like a little advice from a mother. I understand you're from New York?"

"New Jersey. Jersey City."

"Well, whatever—it's all the same. You're from up No'th. Down here things are a lot different. I guess you've found that out already?" There was a little nervous laugh. "We raise our children a lot different, if you know what I mean.

"Now my little Charles is a smart boy. I guess you've

found that out? He had the highest IQ in Montgomery School and I reckon it's the same story there at McAdden High. I don't say that to brag, but you might as well know what you're up against. Charles takes things like war serious. I'm sure that up No'th you think nothin' about exposin' children to the horrors o' wa', but down here we don't talk about people gettin' burned alive and gruesome things like that.

"You people up theah have juvenile delinquents in your schools. We don't have them around here. Now, I don't mean to hurt your feelin's, but you can't expose children to horror stories and not expect them to lose their—you know what I mean—their tenderhearted-ness. That's the word I'm lookin' for.

"Oh, once in a while Charles goes to see a Fran-kenstein movie but that's just fun, it's not the real thing. Know what I mean? I can't stand to think about blowin' up places and all that. It upsets me—think what it does to a child."

Anna wanted to spit in the woman's eye.

"I do hope you understand, Miss Petersen. I'm not tryin' to be critical. I know you teachers have your hands full with my Charles. My, he's a handful for his daddy and me, but we bought him the encyclopedia and when he asks us all those questions, we just send him to the encyclopedia.

"It'll take you a while to catch onto our way of thinkin' down heah so if I can be of any help, I'll be more than happy to oblige. I do want to meet you, Miss Petersen.

"Oh, one thing more—if you don't mind—would you let Charles sit by the window? In this heat, with his weight problem, he needs all the air he can get."

"Mrs. Simpson, I seat the children alphabetically. There isn't anything preferential in the seating."

When she hung up, Anna was really mad. "Marge!"

"Up here."

Anna bounded up the stairs two at a time. Shutting

the door behind her, she said, "Oh, Marge, I've had two parents call me!"

"What about?"

"We had a discussion today in English about atomic warfare—"

"In English!"

It did sound far removed from the subject. "Oh, Marge, what have I done? Jennifer Bradbury's mother was ready to take off my head. She's going to call Mr. Secrest!"

"Uh-oh." Marge stopped combing her hair.

"It's that bad, huh?"

"It could be worse. She could call Gilchrist."

"Oh, Marge. What did I do wrong? All I told them is how horrible it would be if we had war with Russia."

"Anna, the first thing you learn is never upset parents. Whatever you do, you can't do that. Oh, they'll get upset no matter how hard you try, but let it be over grades or discipline—something like that—not war or sex or politics or religion. Those things are definitely no-nos."

Anna felt sick.

"Who was the other person who called?"

"Her name was Simpson, said she just wanted to give me advice."

"Charles Simpson's mother?"

Anna nodded.

"Humph. That hypocrite. She's real mealy-mouthed, isn't she? That woman's a pain in the neck and they tell me her know-it-all son is worse. Don't worry too much about Mrs. Simpson, but Mrs. Bradbury—well, she carries a lot of weight. She's big on the bridge circuit and she's in the DAR. She has clout."

Anna was nervous. "What can I say to Mr. Secrest in my defense?"

Marge thought hard, tapping her mouth with the

comb. "Well, how'd it come up? Did you bring it up or did the children?"

Anna had to think about it. "Let's see, how did it come up? Oh, I think Ted McGill asked me if it was true that schoolchildren in the North have air-raid drills. That's how it came up."

"Good. Tell him that. Secrest is a reasonable man. He won't be too hard on you the first time."

Anna did not sleep very much that night. When she did, she dreamed of loud cacophonous sounds, dissonant and running together rapidly as if percussion instruments warred.

Too nervous to eat breakfast, Anna left the teacherage before anyone else. Sure enough, there was a note in her box to see the principal. She went in right away.

Mr. Secrest closed the door behind her and nodded toward a chair. Anna could not hold the note in her hands steady. He looked grave. "Miss Petersen, it's about a phone call from Mrs. Bradbury—Mrs. Bradbury and a few other parents, for that matter. I'd like you to tell me what went on in your eighth-grade English class yesterday."

Anna cleared her throat. "Well, one of the students asked me if it's true that in the North schools have air-raid drills and I said, yes, it is true. They wanted to know why and I told them."

"All right," he said and sat down. "You know, Miss Petersen, I was in intelligence in the army and, frankly, I know the danger we're in. If I had my way, we'd have bomb drills in McAdden High. I hate to think of what would happen to America if we were attacked now. We're far from being prepared in civil defense. I appreciate what you were trying to do and I wish I could tell you to go ahead, but I can't. We're in a small community and we're dependent on its support for our very existence. Whatever you can do within the confines of that classroom to inform students is all well and good, but when it gets beyond those walls it can cause us irreparable harm. You'll have to feel your way, Miss Petersen. Soon you'll learn how much you can teach and how much you'll have to leave unsaid."

Mr. Secrest still looked grave and his eyes never left hers. He was a fair man, the kind who would never leave you in the dark as to where you stood with him, but he was not a man to take chances. "We're glad to have you," he was saying. "I'm sorry you had to experience this so early in your teaching career. I hope it won't happen again."

"Thank you, Mr. Secrest. Is that all?"

"That's all, Miss Petersen." He rose to open the door for her. "Oh, I almost forgot. Mr. Gilchrist wants to see you but he's at Montgomery School this morning. Would you drop by his office this afternoon?"

"Thank you. I will."

The butterflies returned. So Mrs. Bradbury had called Mr. Gilchrist as well.

When the English class came in, Anna was determined not to talk about atomic war. The fright was still in some of their eyes. Andrew was in a baiting mood and he was not going to let her avoid the subject. "In those great drills in the schools up North, do they tell anybody how to survive an atomic attack?" he asked.

Charles Simpson was eyeing Anna, daring her to answer. She had to make a split-second decision. "Yes, Andrew, they do give instructions about survival. Each student is given a particular space in the hall—so much room." Using her hands, she showed them.

"In the hall?" Anita asked.

"That's right. You see, the outside walls of a building can be permeated by radioactivity. It can seep through the walls. An inside hallway would therefore be safer than a classroom."

"Safe? Ha!" Andrew was challenging her. She ignored him.

"Each student is assigned his own space in the hall and there are a certain number of teachers with each group. They're told that if they survive an attack, they must stay in the hallway for two weeks. That's how long it would be before it might be safe to go outside."

The students were full of questions but Anna had satisfied what was necessary without backing down to Charles or his sweet-as-honeysuckle mother. She smiled. "We'll talk about this some other time but, remember, we missed English yesterday and we have to catch up."

The class cooperated and Andrew let her alone until the bell rang. As he passed through the door he spoke deliberately for her benefit. "I've never met a Yankee yet who didn't think he knew it all."

The morning dragged by. Facing Mr. Gilchrist was made doubly hard by Marge's warning at lunchtime. "He's temperamental. If he's in a bad mood, he'll take your head off."

The afternoon crept along and Anna's imagination began running wild. She prayed and she talked to herself. "If he reprimands me it'll go in my permanent record. How many reprimands can a conditional contract survive?" She couldn't keep her mind on what she was doing.

When the last bell finally rang, before the students cleared the room, Anna was on her way to the superintendent's office. Mrs. McMillan looked up from her desk smiling. "Oh, Miss Petersen, you've come to see Mr. Gilchrist, haven't you? He isn't in."

Anna collapsed inside. She couldn't stand the tension much longer. "When will he be in?"

"He won't be back today but I know what he wanted to see you about. Mrs. Gilchrist heard that you play the cello. Is that right?"

"Yes, I play cello."

"Well, she wants to know if you'll play for the Thursday Afternoon Book Club?"

"I'd be delighted!"

Anna walked out of the office, butterflies quiet, knees steady. She was hungry for the first time all day.

# CHAPTER
# SIX

For Anna, the school year became increasingly difficult. Keeping one chapter ahead of students was not nearly enough with Andrew Lawton in the room. Every day he challenged her, corrected what she said, argued, disputed. More often than not, he was right and Anna was left defeated and humiliated.

They were discussing China's taking of Formosa's offshore islands. President Eisenhower sent the U.S. Air Force to Formosa to support the Seventh Fleet and a student asked Anna, "Why?" She fumbled. Immediately, Andrew answered. "It's because last year Ike signed a treaty for the defense of Formosa and the Pescadores Islands."

The defeats were not because Anna did not try. Every night she was up past midnight and every morning up before six, studying and making lesson plans.

"Bluff," Marge advised. "Every teacher bluffs."

"I'm not good at bluffing, Marge. Besides, I want to learn all I can; I'll be teaching the rest of my life."

"But you don't have to have a detailed plan every day."

"Marge, when I did my junior practicum, I observed a crackerjack of a teacher, and one thing I learned from her is never to teach a class without a plan. She told me that if you don't know where you're going, you'll never get anywhere. I believe that. It works for me."

"To each his own. For myself, I just wing it some days."

English was the real headache. Anna didn't remember her junior high school grammar, and the textbook used here was confusing.

"Darnest book I ever saw," Horace said. "You know what I do, Anna? If I don't know the answer, I put the question to two of the brightest students in the class, and whatever they think the answer is, I go with that. If it's a split decision, I pick one and skip the reasons. Now, who're the brightest students in there?"

"Andrew and Anita."

"Okay. Just ask them."

Anna did and it worked, but she didn't feel good about it.

The problems made Anna wish for her own church—the cool quiet of St. Andrew's Episcopal. Every Sunday she went to a different church, trying to find her own kind of worship service. Although she didn't find it, Scotsville religion was interesting. There were three main churches: Presbyterian, Methodist, and Baptist, with a small Catholic congregation tucked away close by the mill village. In North Scotsville the Church of God and Pentecostal Holiness churches led the field, with smaller Baptist, Presbyterian, and Methodist groups. Marge said Anna positively could not visit Negro churches.

"Wouldn't I be welcome?"

"Yes, you'd be welcome, but if it got out in town that you went to anything more than a funeral or wedding in a colored church, you'd be branded a radical, a Northern liberal, at best. That would put you in a category somewhere between a Republican and a Communist."

The restriction was unconscionable to Anna, but she had her own misgivings about going into the Negro community uninvited.

Of all the preachers, Woodall Jackson was the best.

He believed the Bible and lived it better than most. He was well prepared, reverent, forceful and, after a while, she forgot about his bad eye. Woodall invited her to play the cello for a service, but that was a mistake. The only people in Scotsville who appreciated classical music were the ladies in the Thursday Afternoon Book Club. Horace Wigglesworth poked all manner of fun at the cello, called it a sawhorse.

Going to a Pentecostal church came about as the result of Anna's seeing several girls and women with beehive hairdos. "They're holiness," Marge explained. "They have lots of 'don'ts' for women, few for men. They're against jewelry, makeup, slacks, pedal pushers, shorts. They don't go to movies or dances but they're full of inconsistencies. The same girls who won't cut their hair wear see-through blouses."

"We all have our inconsistencies, Marge."

"True, but they're so 'holier than thou.'"

Marge, aren't we all 'holier than thou'? People in mainline churches here are opposed to liquor, they say. They vote like teetotalers, but you told me yourself there are places you can buy liquor in town. You know as well as I that Horace has his beer and Miss Pendergraft keeps wine in her wardrobe."

To get to the Pentecostal church, Anna walked past McAdden High. Just beyond the school, on the north end of town, was the mill village. There the scene changed noticeably from modest bungalows to rows of small frame houses painted white. "Shotgun houses," they were called—three rooms in a row with a privy outside; one street after another of them, and each street numbered, "First, Second, Third." No other distinctions were made.

The mill itself was as bleak as a prison, with flocculent gray cotton clinging to the chain link fence around it. The heavy machinery inside ran twenty-four hours a day, with mill workers filing in and out at the shrill sound of the whistle—three shifts a day.

In all these houses Anna passed, there were people trying to sleep while other members of the family worked or went to church. The beds served every shift and lay warm in between. How people could sleep with freight trains rumbling past was a mystery to Anna.

Deeper in the mill village, beyond the company houses, were the shanties of even poorer folk. The McCurdy shortline railroad running beside the mill separated the shanties from the village and, by comparison, the whitewashed shotgun houses seemed quite tolerable.

Behavior in the Pentecostal church was different from anything Anna had ever experienced. The first time she went she was disturbed when everyone began praying at once. In the midst of the praying there was shouting and two women danced in the aisles. That frightened her and she wanted to leave but the church was so packed there was no way she could leave gracefully.

The longer she observed, the more she came to realize the earnestness with which many of the people prayed. While some people did not participate, there were others for whom the fervor had great meaning.

Anna liked the music. It was pure Americana with a twang of the Grand Ol' Opry style, the kind of country tenor and alto she and her father used to imitate. There was a swinging rhythm that made her want to tap her foot, and although it was not the kind of church music she was accustomed to, some of the words were good.

McAdden students were shocked when Anna visited their mill village churches. "What are you doing here?" one of them asked her.

As soon as revival season rolled around, the young people were quick to invite her to services and she felt obligated to go.

"Anna, you can't make a habit of this," Marge cautioned. "You can't go to holy roller meetings. Once or twice is fine—good community relations—but if you make it a habit, people are going to think you're a linthead fundamentalist."

"Marge, at the risk of being called a damnyankee, or something else, I must tell you I resent hearing people being called holy rollers, lintheads, all those names. I don't even know what they mean, but they sound awful."

"I don't like names either, Anna, but you get used to them around here. Lintheads are people who work in cotton mills: they get lint in their hair. I know it's derogatory, but that's just the way it is here. You should hear what they call Negroes—jigaboos, jungle bunnies, spades, niggahs."

"Please! I don't want to hear all that!"

"Anna, you must be careful. The worst name in Scotsville is 'niggah-lover,' and if you ever get hung with that, you might as well kiss this place good-bye."

"You don't have to tell me, Marge. That Andrew Lawton lets me know in no uncertain terms that Yankees aren't welcome here. He's so prejudiced against me I can hardly teach the Civil War in North Carolina. Talk about Sherman's march, and he blames me personally—wants me to go with him to a church where Sherman's men camped. They wrote their names in the belfry and he swears there's a Petersen name there."

Anna fought back tears. She could not bring herself to tell Marge all Andrew's impudence. Only that day when she had begun to explain something by saying, "This is my first year of teaching . . . ," Andrew had remarked, "That's not hard to see."

He was smart and he knew it, and he never let Anna forget that she wasn't.

The high school classes were a headache as well. By some secret signal the boys would burst into song. "Hernando's Hideaway" was a favorite because of its sinister beat. They overrode her efforts to teach and talked about their rumbles or mooning down at the Hub, the teenage hangout.

"What's that? What's mooning?" Anna asked.

The students howled.

"Tell her, Sue Marie," Lester prompted.

Sue Marie came to the front of the room and, giggling, whispered in Anna's ear. "They bare their bottoms out car windows."

Anna could feel her cheeks grow warm as the class laughed at her embarrassment. "Don't you know you can be arrested for that?" she scolded, her voice getting shrill.

"For what?" Marvin asked.

"Indecent exposure."

"Miss Petersen, don't worry your curly head about that. Worse thing can happen to us is sunburn or frost-bite."

The class was out of control. Every day there was something going on to distract them from history. The boys tormented Pluto about his ears. "Here comes that taxi with the doors flappin'! Wind hold you back, Pluto?"

They ridiculed Sue Marie's shapeless figure with words that made her furious.

"Hubba, hubba,

Cement mixer

Putty, putty!"

Mr. Secrest forbade parties in classrooms, so the boys defied him. They had the coffee percolating and donuts served by the time Anna arrived. They munched donuts and talked about Noodles, the name of the corpse that lay unburied in the funeral home.

"He's some fella got his head busted open with a axe," Lester McKenzie told her. "A carnival worker. You can see where it split his skull."

It was disgusting. They wanted her to react. Sounding

calm, Anna asked, "Why don't they bury him?"

Lester did not raise his eyes from the drawing he was shading, but he was grinning. "Why, Miss Petersen, Noodles is Scotsville's leading tourist attraction. We've kept him nigh on to fifty-sixty years. People come from all over to see Noodles."

Anna pretended interest in his drawing. The drawings never varied—zoot suiters with broad-brimmed hats, exaggerated shoulders, draped pants. Lester sketched in the watch chain that hung to the knees. "Naw, Miss Petersen, they can't bury him. It's against the law. They can't bury an unclaimed body."

"You wanna go see 'im?" Oren asked her. "Looks like a mummy, his skin's so brown and dried. Kinda' like Miss Pendergraft's."

They thought that was very funny.

Oren Wallace jumped up, his cigarettes falling to the floor. "Hey, lissen! We could have a field trip— go see Noodles!"

"Yeah!" they hollered.

Anna tried to keep calm. "Why do they call him Noodles?"

"He's Eyetalian."

As much as they disturbed her, Anna never let on and eventually they seemed less interested in trying to unnerve her. By no stretch of the imagination could the situation be described as education unless it was that they were educating her. Only when report cards were due did the boys show any interest in grades. Then the question was, "How many points do I have to make to pass?"

"Is that all you're interested in—passing? Don't you want to learn all you can, make the best grade possible?"

They looked at each other as if that were an entirely new concept in education.

No measure of decorum lasted long. The day they

were to have the six weeks' test, in came Sue Marie five minutes late, making a grand entrance. Anna's mouth dropped open. Sue Marie was no longer flat chested—beneath her blouse two inverted ice cream cones poked straight ahead giving her a remarkable anatomical appearance!

The boys were hysterical! The girl looked so ridiculous even Anna could not control herself. She turned her back to the class trying vainly to stifle the giggles. Leaning against the blackboard, struggling for composure, her shoulders shook uncontrollably. Never had she seen anything so hilarious! The boys were whooping so loudly they wouldn't hear her if she shouted.

The door opened and Mr. Secrest stood in the doorway with a "What's going on?" expression on his face. His presence did nothing to diminish the uproar. Anna could only look at him, wipe tears and fight for control.

"All right! All right!" she yelled. "I'm ready to pass out the test!" Some of them seemed to hear. In desperation, she shouted, "Are there any questions?"

Mr. Secrest stepped inside, waiting for order.

Lester, red in the face, tears streaming down his cheeks, raised his hand. "Yes, ma'am . . . I have a question. Are there any true-falsies on this test?"

At that there was no stopping them! Helplessly, Anna turned to Mr. Secrest. The man was easing out the room, closing the door behind him.

After school, Mr. Secrest asked Anna to come to his office. He began in his grave manner. "Miss Petersen, I appreciate the problems you have with that particular history class. Boys in this school call beginning teachers 'fresh meat.'" He paused to see if the term meant anything to her. "It means something like 'fair game' or someone to initiate. They test your patience and your ability. But, Miss Petersen, you'll have to get control of that class if you are to succeed as a teacher."

The threat was obvious.

"Last week I took my daughter to see 'Blackboard Jungle' and I must say, Miss Petersen, the boys in your room are not above behaving like those hoodlums in the movie. First thing you know, they'll be calling you 'Teach,' and we can't have that."

He shuffled papers on his desk. "The guidance counselor came to me about Sue Marie today. Quite frankly, she's concerned about this young woman's behavior. Have you observed anything out of the way?"

The implication angered Anna. "Mr. Secrest, Sue Marie Ellsworth is a nice girl. Adolescents are trying to find their way—improve themselves in one direction or another. Now that we're grown, some of the silly things we did in youth are an embarrassment to us. It is a comfort to us if those things are forgotten."

"Then you don't suspect—?"

"I suspect, Mr. Secrest, that Sue Marie Ellsworth will become one graduate of McAdden High School who will go places and make all of us quite proud."

There was a lapse in the conversation as Secrest leaned back in his chair, pressed the tips of his fingers together, and studied her. Finally, he cleared his throat. "That will be all, Miss Petersen."

By spring, Anna marked off the high school class as a fiasco she could not redeem. The boys had no ambition to do anything and the clowning never ceased. Anna had worked, prayed, wept—but nothing improved. Ellen Wheatley eloped with a Marine. Sue Marie gave up falsies and pursued one diet after another. Anna despaired of accomplishing anything with any of them.

One evening Marge came in from a date with Waldo and found Anna in tears. "Anna, what you need is a treat. All you ever do is work, worry, and pray. Listen, since neither of us smokes, why don't we consider the money we would spend on cigarettes as ours to do with as we please? Tell you what. Every Saturday from now on, we're going downtown and spend our 'cigarette money.'"

It was fun. Every Saturday they woke up singing Petula Clark's "Downtown," and away they went to spend their money. They bought records for the record player they planned to buy as soon as they had saved enough money. They bought cookies and licorice, went to the movie, or spent the two dollars on costume jewelry.

One movie they did not see was "East of Eden," but every student at McAdden High saw it and James Dean became an instant idol. Poor Sue Marie was smitten most of all and hid movie magazines inside her notebook and mooned over them in class.

It was spring and Sue Marie wasn't the only one in love. Eddie McLaughlin, as shy as ever, was in love with Anita McGill and they were an inseparable couple.

In the teacherage several single teachers became engaged and wedding plans dominated the conversation at dinnertime. When parties began to fete the brides-to-be, the discussion at mealtime revolved around what each would wear. "Scotsville believes in conformity," Marge said. "If one girl wears cocktail length, they all wear cocktail length."

Going to all the parties was a problem for Anna. She had one Sunday dress and couldn't afford anything new. Somehow she had to get out of accepting all the invitations.

Even Clara grew tired of the parties. "If I eat one more pressed meat sandwich, there won't be enough bicarbonate in town to help me!"

"It's tough enough going to school, studying to go back the next day, without anything extra," Anna complained.

Bone tired, Anna was not her best at school. Neither were the students. With warmer weather they were all irritable, more difficult. Tempers blazed as if by spontaneous combustion.

Anna stepped to the water fountain just up the hall and a fight broke out in her room. Sensing the commotion, she ran back and found Andrew Lawton and Eddie McLaughlin going at each other tooth and nail! They were knocking over desks right and left. Eddie's glasses went sailing across the room. Ted tried to separate them and was knocked sprawling.

"Boys! Boys!" Anna yelled, but it did no good. They were slugging each other, red in the face, vicious. No one could get near them. Blood spurted from Andrew's nose. Mr. Secrest rushed into the room and saw that the boys were locked in a to-death struggle, rolling over and over on the floor. "Get the coach!"

Ted ran to obey.

It took both men to subdue the boys, and only then by wrestling them apart, straddling them, and holding them down on the floor.

Not until it was safe did the men release their holds, and even then Eddie was white with rage.

After they were led away, Anna asked, "What happened?"

Ted McGill was beside himself. "It's all my fault. I can explain everything."

"Your lip's bleeding." The front of his shirt was spotted with blood. "Wet this tissue, Anita, and help your brother."

Students were setting up the toppled desks. "Look, Miss Petersen, they broke this chair in half."

"Ted, what do you mean, this was your fault?"

"Oh, Miss Petersen, lemme go to the office. Eddie'll be in a lotta trouble all on account o' me."

"Ted, you stay right here."

"Miss Petersen," Anita explained. "It was all over a penny. Ted saves Indian head pennies, and the boys thought Andy swiped one of them."

"It doesn't matter," Ted insisted. "I don't care about the penny. Please, Miss Petersen, let me go tell Mr. Secrest what happened."

"Ted, if it was your penny, why was Eddie fighting?"

"Well, you know my brother," Anita said. "He's good-natured and lets people get by, but Eddie's not like that. He's always sticking up for those two little brothers of his, and when he thought Andy stole the penny from Ted he just lit into him, that's all. He's like that."

"Please, Miss Petersen, let me go tell Mr. Secrest," Ted begged.

"Ted, you go to the boys' room and wash your shirt, and don't you go near that office. Mr. Secrest can handle this."

Mr. Secrest did handle the matter. After suspending the boys, he called Anna to the office. "Miss Petersen," he began, tight-lipped. "It's against the law for a teacher to leave a classroom unattended. Perhaps now you understand the wisdom of that law. Those boys could've killed each other!

"I hate to think what this may lead to. Andrew's father is a lawyer and, as you know, he's on the school board. Andrew's black-and-blue. Eddie has loose teeth and his glasses are broken."

Mark Secrest's eyes snapped with anger. "I'll support you any way I can, Miss Petersen, but there is a limit to what I can do in a situation like this. It's only fair to warn you."

"Mr. Secrest, I'm sorry this happened. I stepped out of the room only long enough to go to the water fountain. I wasn't gone two minutes."

"Miss Petersen, earthquakes destroy cities in less time than that."

Everybody was talking about the fight. Marge slipped into Anna's classroom to comfort her. "Don't worry about it. You couldn't have stopped it even if you had been in the room."

Later, at the teacherage, after Anna told Marge about Mr. Secrest's warning, Marge looked worried. "Yeah. I guess you are in hot water. Tell you what, I'll speak to Waldo. He plays poker with Andrew's daddy. He'll put in a good word for you."

"What good will that do?"

"Well, Anna, in this lousy town it's who you know that counts. There's the big league and the little league. Waldo's in the big league with men like Benjamin Lawton."

The school board met, and the next day there was a reprimand in Anna's box. Anna had never been so humiliated in her whole life. Marge read the letter. "This is bad, Anna, but school will soon be out. You ought to know in a couple of weeks if you're coming back."

Anna felt sick. Every day she looked for a notice that would tell whether or not her contract was renewed. When none came, Anna decided it was a sin to worry about it and committed it to the Lord.

Even so, she was anxious and when she could stand the suspense no longer, she asked for an appointment with Mr. Gilchrist.

Philip Gilchrist closed the door and took a seat in the swivel chair. He looked tired and none of the jovialness she had seen before was apparent.

"Miss Petersen, I've talked to the board and, granted, they gave me a hard time, but so long as I'm superintendent I have the final word. McCurdy backs me up. I say you stay. Next year you can recoup your losses, and if things go well you'll be with us for a long time."

Whatever encouragement his words gave, the weariness in his voice betrayed doubt.

As Anna walked outside and looked up at the clear sky, she wondered if the storm was over. If it was, it was one without a rainbow.

# CHAPTER
# SEVEN

Marge lined up a job for Anna at a summer camp in the Blue Ridge Mountains. Anna was grateful if not enthusiastic, dubious about living in the woods and the responsibility of caring for young girls.

As it turned out, camp was a disaster. There were nasty little girls who draped snakes around their necks and fondled them as pets. Everybody knew everything there was to know about nature and thought Anna should know it, too. To Anna, all flowers were lilies; if it moved, it was an animal, whether an ant or a giraffe; if it flew, it was a bird. Who cares if it's a petunia, a fox, or a pigeon? She had absolutely no interest in becoming any more intimately acquainted with any beast or flower of the field.

Marge was trying to convince her otherwise as they walked through the pasture toward the barn. A sudden fluttering in the hedgerow startled Anna and she gasped when a flock of birds rushed up and away.

Marge laughed at her—laughed so hard she had to sit down and hold her sides. "Anna, they're only sparrows! Harmless little birds! Be brave—this wilderness holds none of the dangers of Jersey City!"

"It's not funny, Marge. I'm not used to all these wild creatures."

Marge tried not to laugh. "Anna, if only you could see the look on your face when those sparrows flew up."

Approaching the barn, Anna was wary and refused to follow Marge inside to the stalls. The horses were stamping and blowing, swishing their tails, and Marge walked right up to them, sweet-talking in their ears as if they were human. *Uff-dah!*

From the dark recess of the barn, a cat ambled out, stretched itself in the sun, and then twined around Marge's leg. "Uff-dah!" Anna exclaimed. "I bet this barn is full of cats."

"Five in all." Marge grinned.

"Then this is where we part company!" All the way to the playhouse she kept looking over her shoulder, fearful of what animal might be following her.

In the playhouse Anna rehearsed the choir and played the piano. It was an indoor job where she felt safe from animals, both wild and tame.

Cabin life was a trial to endure. Even twelve-year-olds sometimes wet the bed and it was Anna's job to air their linen, their underwear, and whatever else might need it. But she did feel for the poor little rich girls that came to camp. Their stories were pitiful and between their activities she spent the better part of every day listening to their problems and counseled them. At night, she read the Bible to them and talked with them about Christ.

But the starchy meals and community showers were another matter. As careful as she was about her feet, Anna was the one counselor who contracted athlete's foot. She was so ashamed she wouldn't tell anyone. The children saw her scratching her toes and told Marge.

"It's no disgrace," Marge told her as she applied the ointment.

"Give me your solemn word, Marge Penry, that you will never breathe a word of this to anyone!"

"My solemn word," she pledged.

By heaven's grace, Anna survived the summer and

returned to Scotsville "with only my sanity impaired," she wrote Aunt Helga. "Please, keep your eyes open for a job for me next summer. I'll wait tables, change beds—anything indoors. Repeat! INDOORS!"

# CHAPTER EIGHT

Anna settled into the school year, determined to succeed. On the first day of the term she learned she would no longer teach eighth grade, and that was a definite answer to prayer. No more English grammar—no more North Carolina history. She could concentrate on her first love, U.S. History, and with the Lord's help she would cause high school students to love it as she did.

Anna also wanted to save money to buy a car and that would take discipline. No more spending of cigarette money. That became easier as the school year wore on because Marge began going home weekends. Every Friday afternoon she caught the bus for Sumter and came back late Sunday night.

Marge never invited Anna to go home with her and that seemed more strange than rude. Only during the holidays did Marge invite her for Christmas Day. That day, Marge's mother drank too much, and Anna wondered if she were an alcoholic and if that was the reason Marge was reluctant to take anyone home with her.

Without Marge the weekends were long and boring. Sometimes Woodall took Anna to the Dairy Queen, but students were always there. Scotsville didn't offer much in the way of recreation.

Anna tried to make friends outside the teacherage but it wasn't easy. She didn't play bridge and didn't have time to learn. She taught the Ladies' Bible Class in Woodall's Springhope church but the members were too feeble to socialize. In desperation, Anna told Marge,

"The next time somebody says, 'Come see me,' I'm going to take them up on it."

"All right, but I warn you. Sometimes 'Come see me' doesn't mean a thing. It's just a friendly saying—a kind of 'How are you?' meaningless expression."

"I know. You told me before, but they shouldn't say it if they don't mean it."

"Spoken like a true squarehead; but don't say I didn't warn you."

After the Thursday Afternoon Book Club meeting, where Anna had played the cello, Miss Amy was driving her back to the teacherage. As they slowed to stop at the back door, Miss Amy said, "Won't you come go home with me?"

"Yes, thank you, I will," Anna answered.

Miss Amy's face flushed a bit. "Oh, my! Well, yes, please do." Then she paused. "On second thought, perhaps we'd better make it another time. I just remembered that my sister is away and she'd be terribly disappointed if you came and she didn't get to visit with you."

"Very well," Anna answered and opened the car door.

"You will come some other time, won't you?" Miss Amy said convincingly.

"Yes. Some other time," she answered and got out of the car.

She found Marge in their room standing before the mirror, dressed in a gorgeous lime green taffeta, her hair falling about her shoulders.

"Wow!" Anna exclaimed. "You look beautiful!"

Marge turned slowly to show off the dress. "Does it fit right?"

"Looks like it to me."

"How'd the club meeting go?"

"So-so."

"Anybody invite you to go home with them?"

"Miss Amy."

"Why didn't you go?"

"You were right, Marge, they don't mean it."

"Don't say, 'they.' Some of 'em mean it. Miss Amy would love to have you visit but her sister's a war horse—rules the roost." Marge was holding the hand mirror to examine the back of her hair. "How does it look in back?"

"Great. You going out with Waldo?"

"No." She laid down the mirror. "I'm going to Sumter."

"Tonight?"

"It's something special." Marge changed the subject. "If you think 'Come see me' is something Southerners run in the ground, what about the weather? Do they talk about the weather up North?"

"No. Not like here."

"Even I get sick of it. They'll never quit talking about Hurricane Hazel. Ever notice how Clara dates everything before or after Hazel?"

A horn beeped. "There's my taxi. Gotta go." She grabbed her bag and dashed out of the room only to dash back. "Forgot my pocketbook." Marge was plainly excited. "See you Sunday!"

Anna stood at the window to watch Marge get into the cab. Strange that Marge would take a day off from school to go home. Whatever it was, it must be something very special.

After the cab pulled away, Anna went downstairs.

Clara was in the parlor waiting for supper, looking as hungry as a horse. Anna sat down at the piano to play.

"Where's Marge goin'?"

"Sumter."

"On Thursday?"

"It's something special."

"Well, I'm afraid she's in for bad weather. I can tell

it's going to be rough out. Whenever it's going to rain, I can feel it in my bones."

"Well, so far the weather's been nice today."

"Yes, but mark my words, it'll be rough."

Anna teased her. "But your lilies don't seem to mind the weather. They thrive regardless."

Clara smiled. "African violets, Anna. The name is African."

"I know, I know."

Clara was one person who was comfortable with herself. Anna envied her for that. Clara was just what she was, a plodding school teacher who had only three subjects to talk about—weather, school, and family—but she had the good sense to stick to the weather in a house full of talkers.

Talking, the occupational hazard of teachers, was not shared by librarians who could be mummies but there was only one librarian in the teacherage. The others were classroom teachers who never left the classroom; they talked loud and clear, non-stop and with authority. Not so, Clara. Although she talked, she never said much. If she didn't know something she said so. Clara was genuine.

Fortunately, there were few subjects the teachers seriously disagreed on. They were all Protestants and all Democrats. In the history of McAdden County there had been very few Catholics, and they came in during the war when local girls married servicemen. As for Republicans, Mrs. Milligan said there were seven registered the last time she served at the polls, but she felt honor bound not to reveal their names.

Even in the Eisenhower landslide, McAdden County voted solidly for Stevenson. When the news broke that the President had suffered a heart attack, little concern was shown for him. Mrs. Milligan said, "If he dies there's Mr. Nixon to take over. One Republican is no better or worse than another."

"Still," Miss Pendergraft said, "I wish we could follow the news more closely."

"Why don't we all chip in and buy a TV?" Horace suggested. "Then I can watch the Ed Sullivan Show."

Horace was appointed to shop around. When he reported his findings, they agreed on an Admiral and it cost each of them ten dollars. Anna had to dip into her savings.

Like a leak in a dike, the break of resolve grew bigger. Anna bought a record player. After all, what good did it do to have a stack of forty-fives if there was nothing to play them on?

Had Anna known the great financial reverse she was about to suffer, she would not have bought anything. The loss came with the theft of her three sweaters hanging on the clothesline.

Anna was not the only victim. Clara's corset and one of the teacherage tablecloths were stolen.

"It's Miss Letitia," Mrs. Milligan explained. "Poor Letitia, she could buy and sell us all but she's a kleptomaniac."

She was dialing a number. "Maybe if Jack can get 'round there before she hides them, we can get them back."

Mrs. Milligan stood with her hand on her hip, waiting for someone to answer. "Jack, this is the teacherage," she said. "Would you come over here, please?"

The police car drove in the rear of the teacherage and Jack came to the back door. "It's Letitia, Jack. She's taken the girls' clothes off the line."

"What'd she take?" He took out a pencil and pad.

"Miss Petersen's three sweaters."

He looked up at Anna. "I never knowed a teacher who had three sweaters," he said, winking.

"A tablecloth. And, well, a girdle, if you must know."

"That all?"

"Yes, I believe so."

"Well, don't feel bad. The other night we had a whammy across the street clockin' traffic, and Miss Letitia stole that."

"She stole the whammy?" Mrs. Milligan laughed. "Now, Jack, you'll be nice?"

"Sure. If I don't find these things all I have to do is bill her son and he'll pay for 'em."

Jack's efforts were futile. He came back to the teacherage to have them sign an affadavit so he could bill Jim Oakes, Miss Letitia's son.

Mrs. Milligan had second thoughts. "I better call Mr. Gilchrist about the tablecloth. You know how he feels about the Oakes. They're such nice people."

While she went inside to call, the three of them stood talking. "Why does Miss Letitia steal?" Anna asked.

"A long time ago she got bad off sick, hadda high fever," Jack explained. "When she got better she was left with this klepto thing. She'll steal anything that's not nailed down and some things that's nailed down! When I make my rounds at night, I see Miss Letitia in the wee hours of the morning prowlin' 'round alleys lookin' for stuff she can haul home. That house is so full o' plunder I don't see how she gets in it."

Mrs. Milligan came outside again. "Mr. Gilchrist said, no, we mustn't charge Jim for the tablecloth."

"What about you, Miss Clara?"

"Jack McClendon, you know there's no way under the sun I'm going to ask Jim Oakes to pay for my corset! Besides, it was about worn out."

Jack grinned and looked at Anna questioningly. As costly as it was for her, Anna could not bring herself to charge the sick woman's son. "No. I'd rather not do that," she said.

Although Anna bought only one sweater, she had to take the money out of savings. That worried her, but she wouldn't have panicked if her dental work had not started costing her a fortune. There was one dentist bill after another for teeth that never stopped aching.

Seeing her savings dwindling, Anna was determined that the two hundred dollars left from her father's insurance money would not disappear, as well. She had to do something to make sure that didn't happen.

"Marge, if I leave that two hundred in savings, the first thing you know there'll be an emergency and I'll use it. I want to put it somewhere I can't get hold of it easily."

"Want me to ask someone who knows about safe investments?"

"Would you?"

The next weekend, Marge came back to the teacherage with a prospectus on robot stocks. Anna frowned. "Robots?"

But Marge was confident. "Anna, my friend says you're liable to make a fortune. Robots are the wave of the future. True, it's speculative but you have to take risks if you want to make money."

"I don't want to lose this money, Marge."

"I know you don't, Anna, but you can trust what I'm telling you. Harry has made money hand-over-fist and he says that if you just leave that two hundred in robots and wait long enough, you'll double your investment."

"Don't I have to have a broker?"

"Harry'll take care of it. I'll take him the money, and they'll send you the stock."

After she had made the transaction, Anna worried about it. *What's got into me? It's so unlike me to do a thing like that—take a chance with money Dad left me.*

But it was done.

The cello would ease her mind if anything would. With Marge away on weekends and everyone else deserting the teacherage, Anna felt free to play to her heart's content. Unzipping the case, she told herself, "Well, I've done it. I've put the money where I won't touch it. I'll just pray it's the right thing. I know I should've asked the Lord first."

As she played, she could visualize her father's hand on the bow, his fingers pressing the strings, walking them up and down. It no longer made her sad to think of him. For such a long time she could think of her father only as he had been during his last months—ill and crippled; now she was remembering him as he had been before, in health, when they chased rainbows and ate licorice.

In her room she could see the conch now placed where it deserved to be, on the mantel, reflecting in the mirror behind it. There should be music that expressed the feelings the conch aroused. Thumbing through the sheet music, she looked for a piece that would remind her of the shell or rainbows. She tried a Bach sonata with its slow second movement and the dancelike *scherzo* before the last movement. It wasn't what she was looking for. If she had the time she might try to compose something herself, but there was never time.

Anna kept looking. In all her books there was nothing that expressed what she felt, nothing that translated the convolutions of the shell, its rhythms and wet-pink lip; nor music that translated the colors of rainbows, the misty graphics after a storm.

She closed the books. Maybe she was off her rocker. Being alone gave her too much time to think.

Leaning on the cello, she closed her eyes. Risking the two hundred was, indeed, chasing rainbows. *If only Dad was here to play the violin and Helga the piano, I'd feel better. It's no fun playing solo when you're by yourself.*

Music written for the cello alone was more difficult because the instrument had to become several instruments in one. *Well*, she thought, *I'll have to get used to that—I'll be playing solo the rest of my life.*

People were coming in downstairs. She put away the music. "Well, Dad," she whispered, "at least I've chased only one rainbow."

She knew Tory Petersen wouldn't hold it against her. Her eyes misted. "Dad, if some day you can look down and see that I made it here in Scotsville, I'll be satisfied."

The easiest way to succeed in Scotsville was on the town's terms, but Anna couldn't do that. In December, Negroes began boycotting buses in Montgomery, and Scotsville people were of one opinion about that. Anna kept quiet. Demonstrations threatened violence and she was afraid of that, but she couldn't blame the Negroes. Martin Luther King, who organized the boycotts, was fast becoming the most hated man in the South. Only in church was there any voice of reason raised. The Methodist minister went away to conference and came back talking integration; and in Sunday school, the literature denounced racial bias. The congregation grumbled but they asked for the same minister to stay another two years. Anna realized that, despite the verbiage, there were good people in Scotsville who were beginning to think, to question what they had accepted all their lives to be true and right. It was a beginning.

At school there was some racist talk but the young people were too caught up in the Elvis Presley craze to think about much else. "Rock Around the Clock," they sang and shimmied disgracefully.

Woodall deserted the Dairy Queen and took Anna to the Hub where the students congregated to drink milk shakes and dance in an open pavilion. The spectacle of so many bodies shaking so many parts at one time struck Anna as more comical than decadent. She came home singing "You Ain't Nothin' But a Houn' Dog" to Marge's delight.

Elvis created a battle royal between Horace and Miss Pendergraft one Sunday night when the star appeared on the Ed Sullivan Show. Horace shouted, "It's un-constitutional!"

"What?" Miss Pendergraft asked.

"Can't you see what they're doin'?" he yelled. "They're shootin' Elvis from the waist up. That's censorship!"

Miss Pendergraft pursed her lips. "Mr. Wigglesworth, the television networks have a moral responsibility to protect the public from Mr. Presley's vulgarity."

"Hogwash! A man's got a right to see what he wants to see."

"A man, perhaps, but innocent women and children must be protected."

"Ha!" Horace whooped. "I've known a few women in my day that were far from innocent, and if you wanna know the truth, Miss Pendergraft, we got high school students who can tell you more about sex than any biology book you ever saw!"

Miss Pendergraft was indignant. "Mr. Wigglesworth! I would ask you to watch your tongue! There are—"

"Some of those little darlin's you think are saints because they sing in the church choir are down at the beach shackin' up every chance they get!"

"Mr. Wigglesworth, I won't sit here and listen to such trashy talk." She got up and went to her room.

A few days later Anna discussed Elvis with Sue Marie who enjoyed popular music and did some singing herself. In the Four-H Talent Show, Sue Marie had won first place, and to Anna her voice sounded professional. Whether or not the girl ever made singing a career, it was important to encourage her.

"He sings some things really well," Sue Marie said. "You know that song 'Love Me Tender'? I think that one'll be around a long time.

"Did ya see Andy's blue suede shoes?"

"Andrew Lawton's?"

"Hmmm. I just love those shoes. Andy's no Elvis

fan, he just likes the blue suede." She was biting a fingernail. "I guess you'd say I have a big crush on Andy. A lotta good it'll do. Every other girl in school has a crush on him."

Anna smiled. "So I noticed. Well, Sue Marie, don't give up hope. You stay on that diet and first thing you know all the boys will be noticing you."

Sue Marie didn't think so. Anna could tell by the way she changed the subject. "Eddie and Anita make a cute couple."

"They are a nice pair."

"Do you think they'll get married, Miss Petersen?"

Anna laughed. "Oh, Sue Marie, how could I answer a question like that? They're only ninth graders."

"Ellen Wheatley was only fifteen when she married that Marine. Of course, her mother had to sign for her, but Ellen didn't love that boy. She just married him to get away from home. And, boy, did she get away! They're at some base in Cuba!

"Anita and Eddie do everything together and they're nice, Miss Petersen, if you know what I mean. Eddie's shy and everything and if he wasn't nice, Anita wouldn't have anything to do with him."

Anna watched Sue Marie reflecting on the case, her eyes dreamy, her thoughts far away. "I hope they get married some day. You know Eddie's never had a— what you might call a real home. His daddy travels all the time and Aunt Chloe's raised him and his brothers."

"Aunt Chloe?"

"The colored woman. She's a skinny little woman who wears a starched cap and white apron. She loves those boys but she's so old and everything. She raised their daddy. But she makes those boys mind. I don't know how she does it—they just love her to pieces. I guess that's it."

Sue Marie was in a talking mood and Anna had papers to grade.

"Like I say, Miss Petersen, I hope Eddie and Anita get married some day. You know my granddaddy is kinda crazy but he makes good sense, too. He lives upstairs and Grandmama lives downstairs. She's a little bit off her rocker, too, but if you ask Granddaddy why he lives upstairs and she lives downstairs, he always says, 'There's no love like the first love,' and then he clams up very mysterious like. I take it he loved somebody before he loved Grandmama and made a mistake when he didn't marry her.

"I hope Eddie marries Anita. He's such a nice boy— he deserves a girl like her. Don't you just love her red hair?"

"I think you call that color chestnut."

"Whatever. I'd hate for Eddie to wind up like Granddaddy, living upstairs and his wife living downstairs because he didn't marry his first love.

"Besides, can't you just see their children? They'll be beautiful with blond hair mixed with red. Maybe one will look like her brother, Ted."

"Do you think Ted's going to make the team?"

"I dunno. Coach Wigglesworth keeps telling him to hit harder. Do you see Ted very much?"

"He comes by every day. He brought me these flowers he picked on the way to school. He knows my weakness for Hershey bars so he sometimes brings me candy."

Anita came in the door. "You busy, Miss Petersen?"

"Not really."

"I told Eddie I'd wait for him here."

"Good. Sue Marie and I were just visiting."

Someone was whistling in the hall. "That's Ted," Anita said. "Whistles all the time."

Ted poked his blond head in the door. "What cha doin'?"

"Come in, Ted." Anna gave up on the idea of grading papers. "On your way to practice?"

"Yep. Wanna hear a moron joke, Miss Petersen?"

"Sure," she said and listened to the one about the little moron who jumped off the Empire State Building so he could make a hit on Broadway. They all laughed.

"I thought you'd like that one since you're from New York." He straddled a desk. "Here, have some gum."

"Ted, you better go," his sister warned.

"I know. Coach doesn't like us to be late." He gathered up his books. "Sorry, I gotta go." At the door he paused, looked back wistfully. "Miss Petersen, I know you're busy but I sure wish you'd come see us play."

"I'll try, Ted."

After Ted left, Eddie came. He stuck his head in the door. "You comin', Anita?"

"Just a minute."

Eddie came in to wait. "Hey, Miss Petersen."

Anna returned his smile.

Eddie tried not to smile because smiling made his dimples show. He pressed his forefinger to his glasses on the bridge of his nose and spoke softly to Anita. "Andy's waitin'."

"Okay."

"Miss Petersen, you gotta come see us play. We're bound to have a winnin' season. Andy's gonna quarterback and that boy can really run. He's a natural born athlete."

Sue Marie interrupted. "How're you and Andy gettin' along now?"

"Well, if you're talking about that fight we had last year, I don't know. I say I won and he says he won, but he kept Ted's Indian head. I know he's got it and that's not right." He looked at Anita. "Come on, I'll buy you a Pepsi."

Ted did make the team but his junior-varsity games were played after school and Anna never found the time to go. There was always more work to do than she could get done—papers to check and lessons to study. Scotsville was sports crazy and no team ever lacked spectators. She was sure she'd never be missed.

Football season passed, then basketball, and still Anna had her nose to the grindstone. Even during Christmas vacation and Easter, she worked.

The pressure made her sleep fitfully and in her dreams she heard beautiful music, so enjoyable she didn't want to wake up. Once it was organ music—so original she imagined her father playing an organ in heaven.

By spring, when Woodall Jackson asked Anna to chaperone a retreat group, she agreed. The church would pay her ten dollars and she needed the money, but more than anything else, she needed a break from routine.

The retreat was at a mill pond near Scotsville where there were summer cabins and a place for vespers. Two college students, Tom and Bruce, were counselors, and when Woodall was called out of town for a funeral, the young men took charge. They did the speaking and led the singing.

Anna liked them. They believed the Bible and spoke of faith and commitment the way Woodall did. A few of the young people were students Anna had taught— Ted and Anita McGill, Lester McKenzie, and Eddie McLaughlin. They came in Earl McClendon's hot rod. Sue Marie and Pluto Martin came on the bus with the rest of the group.

The group seemed well behaved but Anna felt nervous at the responsibility she had.

The campground was beautiful, with tall trees standing in the tea-colored water of the pond. After the cookout Friday evening, they built a bonfire and watched the moon rise over the water. Tom and Bruce played guitars and sang fun songs, then Christian choruses.

Anna sat across from Ted, Eddie, and Anita. In the

firelight, their young faces were cherubic. Anna smiled and said to herself, *Yes, Eddie, I forgive you for the mayhem—for nearly getting me fired. And, you, Anita, some day I'll tell you how you helped me teach English grammar.* . . . But, Ted—There was no way she could tell Ted what he meant to her. With his simple kindnesses he had made life bearable when it was the hardest.

Trees in the lake had trunks that were strangely swollen at the bottom. The moon tipped the trees on the other side of the lake and a path of moonlight rippled across the water. The young voices carried easily over the water and Anna was pleasantly surprised that Lester and Earl joined in the singing and that they could harmonize.

When the time came to put out the fire and go to bed, Anna was as reluctant as the young people to leave. She could not remember ever feeling so close to God.

Walking the sandy path made white by moonlight, their voices singing softly, Anna heard the pines swaying and wondered if perhaps there were angels nearby.

After lights were out, Anna took a flashlight and patroled the grounds to make sure everyone was inside a cabin. From a sandhill she saw some shadowy figures. "Hello, there," she called.

One of the college boys answered. "It's okay, Miss Petersen. Ted's with me. We won't be long."

In the moonlight she could see Ted's blond head.

From down on the main road, Anna heard the roar of a car racing, "va-room! va-room!" *Glory be! I wonder if that's Lester and Earl taking off? I don't see the Chevy. Oh, I hope not.*

The sound of the motor was fading fast. Well, if it is, there isn't anything I can do about it. I can't chase them in the church bus.

Saturday was a scorching hot day but because there

was no lifeguard, Anna forbad swimming. Naturally, some of the retreaters purposely fell in the water and to discipline them, Anna sat in the cafeteria with the culprits Saturday afternoon while the rest of the group played softball.

At four o'clock, Tom rang the bell for boarding the bus. Like a swarm of bees they came in from the field, wet with perspiration. They gulped water and doused their faces and heads—splashed water on each other. Bruce called them, "Come on, gang, let's make a friendship circle under this tree."

They were happy and tired, sorry the retreat was ending. Arguing over a stolen base, they formed a ragged line, holding hands, getting ready to sing. When the circle was formed, Anna asked, "Before we leave, would anyone like to express appreciation to Tom and Bruce for this time together?"

There was silence for a few minutes. Lester McKenzie was looking at the ground, moving a pebble about with the toe of his shoe. Slowly he raised his head and in a voice so soft it was hard to hear, he said, "I would just like to say that I accepted Christ as my Savior on this retreat."

His words first stunned them, then someone began sniffling and across the circle Sue Marie's eyes brimmed with tears. Another voice spoke, "I want to be saved, too."

They began to let go each other's hands and turn to Tom and Bruce. The men took them aside in two groups and Anna watched, speechless, as they huddled together to talk. The young people were oblivious of her, the bus, of everything but their spiritual concerns. The quietness was so unlike them. Pairs of them stood with heads bowed in prayer; some of them wept softly, holding on to each other. Tom and Bruce were speaking quietly, first with one, then another. Whatever was happening, Anna felt she could not interrupt.

As they lingered, she became nervous. Parents would be waiting at the school to meet the bus—the bus shouldn't be late.

Eventually, the young people began getting on the bus, too full of their own thoughts and feelings to speak. After they were all aboard, Anna counted them. Lester and Earl were standing beside the bus waiting for them to leave before they got in the Chevy to drive home.

On the way back to McAdden High, students stared out the windows, absorbed in their own thoughts. It would have been a sacrilege to dispel the mood.

As the bus pulled into the schoolyard, the young people got off one by one, but instead of going to the waiting cars, they gathered beside the bus. Then they moved under a shade tree and began praying together, one after another.

Anna felt uncomfortable with the parents watching, wondering what was going on, yet she could not intrude. She was as much a spectator as the parents.

It was not until Monday that Anna realized to what extent the retreat had taken effect. The small group of those affected had become larger. All day long students at McAdden High talked about nothing else but their personal relationships with God. At every opportunity they huddled in a hall or in the back of a classroom and talked in serious, thoughtful tones. There were bowed heads and wet cheeks, yet the young people were in control. There was nothing out of hand.

Eddie McLaughlin was the first student to seek out Anna privately. They were standing beside the water fountain and Anna looked up to the broad-chested young man and waited for him to speak.

"Miss Petersen, I've been thinking all weekend about something Bruce said. He said, 'It doesn't take much of a man to be a Christian, but it does take all of a man.' I guess I didn't have the guts to accept Christ at retreat but I want to. Can I accept him right now?"

"Why, of course. But wouldn't you rather—"

"No, I want to do it right now," and with that he bowed his head and prayed, "Lord, I believe Jesus died for my sins and I wanna be a Christian from this day on."

When they opened their eyes, he shook Anna's hand and left for class.

At lunch time there were so many students around Anna's desk she had to give up the idea of going to the lunchroom. "Miss Petersen," Sue Marie said, "Earl says he's been stealing from the drugstore, slipping boxes of candy from the showcase under his shirt. His dad's on the police force, and Earl went home Saturday night and told his parents, 'If ever you're going to help me, help me now.'"

Anna felt encouraged. Even teachers were talking about the phenomenon. "What's come over them?" Marge asked. "I heard them singing on the way from school and they sounded really good."

"I don't know, Marge. I can't say for sure what happened. Maybe this is what they mean by a revival."

"Oh, no! Not a holy roller revival!"

"No, not that."

On Tuesday afternoon, Mr. Cecil Blackmore Mc-Curdy called Anna. "Miss Petersen, this is Cecil McCurdy," he said. "Mr. Gilchrist is out of town or he would be calling you. There seems to be a matter of serious concern to parents regarding a retreat you chaperoned last weekend. I've talked with members of the school board and they feel you should meet with us this evening to explain your role in this matter."

He was not unpleasant but he meant business. Anna felt the room begin to spin.

"We'll meet at the courthouse at seven sharp."

When she hung up, Anna held onto the chair so she wouldn't fall. My role in this? "Lord, it wasn't me!"

# CHAPTER
# NINE

Anna appeared before the school board—a lady doctor, a minister, a red-faced banker, an old merchant, and Andrew Lawton's father, a lawyer.

Mr. McCurdy tapped the gavel and the meeting came to order. For some reason Anna felt calm. McCurdy rose to his feet and stood looking down at his notes. He hitched up his pants and Anna thought of Roger, the way he hitched up his pants.

McCurdy seemed taller than Anna remembered him to be at the PTA picnic. His Brooks suit and narrow tie set him apart from the other men, and there was a poise about him that contrasted to the champing at the bit so obvious in the other men. Only Dr. Jennie seemed relaxed. She smiled at Anna as if to put her at ease.

Anna had the feeling that McCurdy knew what the outcome of this meeting would be before it began; her fate lay with him.

"This is a called meeting of the school board," he began, fingering a paper before him. "We are here to review the recent retreat which Miss Petersen chaperoned. Reports from parents indicate that there has been some religious enthusiasm generated by that retreat.

"Unfortunately, Reverend Mr. Jackson is out of town due to a death in his family, but I understand that when he was called away, he left Miss Petersen in charge. Is that correct, Miss Petersen?"

He turned toward Anna, looking at her through the

rimless glasses, his eyes a cold blue. She nodded. "That's correct."

"Well, then do you, Dr. Jennie, gentlemen, have any questions you would like to ask Miss Petersen?"

The minister was first. He was perspiring profusely and mopped his brow with a handkerchief. "Miss Petersen, I speak for the Ministerial Association and let me express, on their behalf, our appreciation for your interest in our young people.

"My daughter tells me that all over McAdden High School, students are getting saved." He grinned at the idea. "Is that right?"

"I really can't say. Only time will tell who is saved and who isn't."

"That's not what I mean. You've seen students crying and carrying on, haven't you? I understand they've been very emotionally upset."

"I've seen some tears."

"Well, doesn't that disturb you? As a history teacher surely you ought to know the evils of religious fervor. Why, back in the old days in the tent meetings, there were all kinds of goin's on. In Scotsville we've put that kind of sawdust religion behind us. It isn't healthy for young people to get all wrought up over religion."

"Young people get emotionally disturbed about a lot of things. If they read a novel that's touching, they cry. They cry at movies."

"That's different, Miss Petersen." The grin left his face and his jaw hardened. "Here in the halls of our high school crying and carrying on over Jesus—that's fanaticism."

"If I may say so, it is strange to me that adults find it acceptable for young people to get emotionally involved over James Dean or Elvis Presley but unacceptable for them to become emotionally involved with the Lord Jesus Christ."

The words came out easily as if she had practiced saying them.

Dr. Jennie liked her answer and was about to say something when Mr. Lawton spoke. "Miss Petersen, I worked late Friday night and as I was driving down the road near that camp, two boys in a souped-up Chevy almost sideswiped me. They were headed for that drag strip in the sandhills. Could they have been from your group?" Benjamin Lawton was a sharp-faced man with piercing dark eyes.

"They might have been."

"You mean you let them run around the county in the middle of the night?"

"It was not a matter of letting them, Mr. Lawton. Young people with automobiles are not easily controlled."

"But it was your responsibility to chaperone this group, was it not? It was your responsibility?"

The minister interrupted. "Getting back to this business of religion in the school. You do understand the principle of separation of church and state, do you not, Miss Petersen? We have respect for the law in Scotsville, and it seems to me that you have—" The fire horn was blasting. He waited until it stopped to continue. "It seems to me that you have started something."

Mr. McCurdy stopped him. "Let's not blame Miss Petersen unduly. After all, she was asked to chaperone the group before Woodall Jackson was called away. The full responsibility fell on her shoulders as an exigency she did not anticipate."

The banker spoke. "Miss Petersen, you're new in our community, and we're glad to have you here. May I ask what faith you are?"

"I'm an Episcopalian."

He nodded his head, thought a moment, then continued. "Some of the parents complained to me that you have no right to impose your religious beliefs on their children. Did you indeed approve of the evangelistic emphasis of this retreat?"

"Yes, I did."

He grunted his disapproval, looked at the other members for agreement.

Running through Anna's mind was the voice of the Sanhedrin, "What further need have we for witnesses?"

The banker shook his head. "Well, you're entitled to your own beliefs, but all I'm interested in is getting people to quit calling my house. Phone nearly rang off the hook last night. People call me in the middle of the night and tell me to do something about this. It's my duty, Miss Petersen, to call you to account."

He was a bull of a man, thick necked and barrel-chested. Eyes pinned on her, he expected Anna to equivocate, offer some excuse, anything that he might tell the people to satisfy them. "I suppose there were soft lights and soft music that got them all worked up?"

"No. It happened at four o'clock in the afternoon when the students came in from playing ball. They were hot and dirty."

Dr. Jennie seemed to regard Anna approvingly and was about to say something when the minister began. "Would you say that my daughter needs to be saved? On the day my little girl joined the church she said, 'Daddy, this is the happiest day of my life.' Now, what if she came to me and said, 'Daddy, I want to be saved'?"

Anna did not answer and his question hung suspended in air.

The minister turned to McCurdy. "Mr. McCurdy, you haven't had your say about all this. What's your opinion?"

"My opinion is unimportant," McCurdy snapped. "My judgment is that if this is not of God, nothing will come of it; if it is some kind of spiritual work, we should not fight against it."

The men were non-plussed. Dr. Jennie laid her slender hands flat on the table and said, "Cecil, if this is, indeed, a work of God, is it enough that we do not oppose it?" She was a woman in her sixties, small and well-groomed. Her independence was obvious. "As Christians shouldn't we give our full-fledged support and encouragement to the young people?"

Before McCurdy could answer, the phone began ringing. Dr. Jennie was wanted at the hospital. She picked up her bag and left.

The manager of McCurdy's Department Store cleared his throat. "We seem to be going in circles. Our concern is for the parents. We must make them feel that their children are in good hands when they're in a teacher's charge, whether it's at school or on a trip somewhere. Miss Petersen, what do you propose to—well, let's say, 'to mend fences,' that sort of thing?"

McCurdy cut in. "I think that question may best be answered by us, not by Miss Petersen. I propose that we make it a school board ruling that members of the faculty may not chaperone religious retreats."

"Good idea," the merchant agreed. "I make the motion."

Someone quickly seconded it and the motion carried unanimously.

Cecil McCurdy had indeed known the end from the beginning. The man was a marvel to watch. He had let them vent their spleens, then moved swiftly at the right moment to bring the matter to a close.

As Anna walked down the courthouse steps, she wanted to quit. Scotsville and its provincial narrowness, its demagoguery, were too much for her.

When she told Marge about the meeting, Marge was furious. "You spend your whole weekend with other people's children and this is what you get? That's appreciation for you!"

"Do you think they'll rehire me for next year?"

Marge hesitated. "It all depends. Every one of those men on the school board work for Cecil McCurdy except the preacher and Dr. Jennie. The only one who's not intimidated by his power is Dr. Jennie.

"It's hard to explain, Anna, but there's always been a wall around this town to keep out people like yourself. Scotsville considers itself liberal and tolerant, but they're only tolerant until their way of thinking is threatened.

"In all fairness, I must tell you that it all boils down to what McCurdy decides."

Marge was polishing her nails and thinking through the case. "If I were you, I'd wait until school's out, then I'd write a letter of resignation. I'd get out of Scotsville."

Anna's eyes filled with tears. "I can't do that, Marge. I have to succeed here. I don't have any other place to go."

They sat in silence a long time. Marge sighed, "Well, I know you're right. I wish I could tell you that things will get better, but it's been this way as long as I've lived here." She patted Anna's head. "You're too nice a person to be treated this way." And then, as an afterthought, "Oh, by the way——"

"What is it, Marge?"

"You don't need to know just now."

"Know what?"

Marge shook her head. Anna insisted. "You started it, you might as well finish."

"Lester McKenzie's mother is coming to see you tomorrow. She called tonight—said she'll see you here at the teacherage when she gets off work."

The message was another body blow. "What next?" she groaned.

Anna did not sleep well. The next day she couldn't keep her mind on anything she was doing.

Rushing home from school, she tidied up the parlor and asked Mrs. Milligan to keep everyone out so she could talk privately with Mrs. McKenzie. The palms of her hands were moist when the doorbell rang.

Mrs. McKenzie was a large woman. Unceremoniously, she flopped in one of the upholstered chairs. "Miss Petersen, I just want to know what happened to Lester on that retreat."

Anna hesitated, framing the words in her mind. "Mrs. McKenzie, Lester professed faith in Christ as his Savior."

The woman looked back at her long and hard. "Is that what it is? That's what he said it was."

Anna nodded.

"Well, Miss Petersen, I can't believe the change that's come over my boy. He came home from that retreat a different boy. I've had a hard time raising my boys. Lester and his brother have always fought like cats and dogs. Now, since he came home from that retreat, I haven't heard a cross word from him! He's been talking to his brother, and you know what Harold said? He said, 'Lester, I gotta have what you got!' I can't get over it, Miss Petersen. It's like a miracle."

# CHAPTER TEN

Woodall Jackson came back from the funeral wearing an eye patch over the bad eye. When he heard about the school board meeting, he came straight to the teacherage. He was so upset he forgot any self-consciousness he felt about the eye patch.

"Woodall," Anna told him, "you have nothing to apologize for, nor do I. Whatever happened was the work of God. If insurance companies accept 'acts of God,' I believe it's reasonable for us to accept them no matter what the consequence."

When Woodall left, Anna knew she had relieved his mind. Not until she could talk with Philip Gilchrist, though, would her mind be at ease. In the meantime, she took comfort in the fact that at least Lester McKenzie was a different person. His behavior in school was so much better, teachers commented about it. Horace was skeptical. "Anna, Lester's putting on a good show hoping it'll help him graduate."

When Philip Gilchrist asked to speak with Anna, it was to apologize. "If I had been here you would never have been brought before the school board."

His serious expression changed. Amused, a mischievous smile played about his lips. "I hear you won your case hands down." He was chuckling.

Try as she would, Anna could not laugh.

Lester McKenzie did graduate but only by the skin of his teeth. As he loped across the stage, gown flowing and cap at a rakish angle, he blew a kiss to Anna. Then, he was off to the National Guard for the summer.

"He'll go back to boozin'," Horace predicted, but he didn't. In July, Lester's mother called Anna to tell her he was thinking about studying for the chaplaincy. Anna didn't say anything; Lester was no student.

In late August, Lester came home and Anna was forced to face the problem. "I wanna go to college," he told her and sat waiting, as if she could wave a magic wand and get him accepted in the college of his choice. As she looked at him she wondered if he had forgotten that he was fifty-fifth in a class of fifty-six, yet she couldn't bring herself to remind him, to tell him that there was no way. "Well, Lester, it's too late to be applying for this term so why don't you wait until next year. You could get a job, save some money."

"Can't wait, Miss Petersen. I know now what I want to be and I'm ready to go." He leaned forward in the chair. "Miss Petersen, I don't think we have much time left before the Lord comes back."

"Do you have any money?"

"Nope, but God's got the cattle on a thousan' hills. You told me that, remember? If he has to, he'll just kill some of those cows and send me the money."

Anna winced at his brashness. He sat there looking back at her with all the confidence in the world.

"Where do you want to go to school?"

"Anywhere. Just so long as they teach Bible."

"Not many schools offer a Bible major on the undergraduate level. Why don't you go to a junior college first, then finish college and go to seminary?" Even as she suggested it, she felt ridiculous.

"Tom and Bruce go to a college in Nashville that teaches Bible."

"Okay, I'll call Mr. Jackson," Anna offered. "He'll know how to get in touch with them." Anna felt less than sincere. Lester's ambition was an impossible dream.

Woodall Jackson knew the president of the college Tom and Bruce attended and agreed to call him. Later, he reported to Anna. "When I called Dr. Robinson, he told me they didn't have room for another student, but as a favor to me he'd knock a hole in the wall and give Lester a chance. He'll have to prove himself. Dr. Robinson said they can't accept him on his record. His admission is only provisional. Make that very clear to Lester, Anna."

Anna did her best to explain the tenuousness of his admission, but Lester was so excited he wasn't listening. "Thanks, thanks a lot! Mama said all I had to do was ask Miss Petersen and you'd fix things up for me. She was right!" He hugged Anna, then dashed out the door to pack his clothes for Nashville.

When Anna told Marge about it, Marge shook her head. "He'll never make it. You know as well as I, he'll never make it. Get ready to pick up the pieces, Anna. Lester'll be back in Scotsville after the first grading period."

Marge was wrong. Every week or so Anna received a postcard from Lester with glowing reports of his progress. With the first marking period he sent her a copy of his grades—he was on the Dean's list!

Anna couldn't wait to tell Marge, but, as usual, Marge was away for the weekend.

That Saturday morning when the letter from Lester came, Anna and Miss Pendergraft were having a second cup of coffee alone. "I wish Marge were here," Anna said. "She'll be so happy for Lester." To herself, Anna wondered if Marge would be interested. Lately she had seemed too preoccupied to listen to anything or to care about anything except Fridays and the weekends away. Perhaps Marge's mother was giving trouble—yet Marge didn't seem worried. In fact, she seemed happier than usual.

Miss Pendergraft nibbled a piece of toast, finished it, and brushed crumbs from the table with her hand. "Marge Penry is quite a mystery person these days, isn't she?" A silly, self-conscious smile played at the corners of her mouth, as if her mind were enjoying a secret pleasure. "Have you noticed how she's away every weekend, never says where she's going, never talks about it later?"

Anna refused to pick up on the insinuation. Miss Pendergraft persisted. "There's good reason why she doesn't talk about her weekends."

*Uh-oh,* Anna thought, raising the cup to her lips. *Something's coming.*

"She's going with a married man, you know."

Anna set the cup down with a rattle. "A married man?! How do you know? I mean, who?"

"He's from Sumter but he travels so she hops a plane from Raleigh or Charlotte and meets him in Cincinatti or Jacksonville, wherever he happens to be." Miss Pendergraft's eyes glinted maliciously as she watched Anna's shocked reaction. "The man has a wife and three children. He'll never leave those children for Marge Penry, no matter how pretty she is." Her mouth twitched. "No man ever does, Anna. The wife holds all the cards."

The way Miss Pendergraft rolled the words around on her tongue and popped them out for effect was serpentine. "No man will marry a woman he can . . . have."

The way she said "have" was disgusting. Anna got up from the table. "Excuse me, Miss Pendergraft. I shouldn't have asked you about this. I have laundry to do."

Sunday evening when Marge came in, Anna found it hard to talk to her. Never had she felt so betrayed, and yet it was indeed none of her business. Instead of staying in the room, Anna sat in the sitting room watching television. In the middle of an aria Robert Merrill was singing, the fire alarm blasted. Downstairs, Horace ran through the house and out the back door. Horace Wigglesworth gloried in the excitement of disaster. By the time the blasts stopped, Robert Merrill's singing had ended. Anna picked up the Sunday paper. There was an article about the Salk vaccine. Too bad it didn't come in time for McCurdy's wife, she thought.

It was eleven o'clock and Anna was tired, but she was giving Marge plenty of time to get done with her makeup ritual before she went in to get ready for bed.

The Salk article described the effects of polio, showed a picture of an iron lung patient. *Poor Mrs. McCurdy*, she thought. *Think of being in that contraption year in and year out.*

Marge came through the sitting room on her way to the bathroom. Anna tried to sound natural. "Wonder where the fire is?"

"I think that was the rescue squad—two blasts and a long one." Marge brushed her teeth, then came and sat on the couch beside Anna. "What're you reading?"

"An article about the Salk vaccine."

"Too bad they didn't discover it in time for McCurdy's wife."

"I was thinking the same thing. Which hospital is she in?"

"Johns Hopkins." Slowly brushing her hair, Marge was pensive. "Anna, they say all kinds of things about McCurdy."

"What kind of things?"

"That he's unfaithful to his wife."

"Why do they think that?" She lowered the paper to look at Marge.

"Because he's out of town all the time. You hear it all over town. 'McCurdy's got a girl in every port.'"

Anna felt angry, the heat of her anger rising up her neck. If Marge Penry was going to sit there and pass judgment on a man she knew nothing about when she herself was guilty of the same sin, Anna was going to let her have it.

Marge was looking off in space, the brush held limply in her lap. "There isn't a word of truth in it, Anna. McCurdy's a decent man. He wouldn't do a rotten thing like that." Marge's chin began to tremble as if she were going to cry. She got up and went into the bathroom.

Anna was stunned. She felt awful—trapped by her own quick judgment. Poor Marge, in the bathroom crying, feeling rotten. It must be true—she must be involved with a married man.

When Marge came out of the bathroom, she avoided Anna and went straight to the bedroom. After a while, Anna followed. Marge was in bed, her face to the wall.

Anna had not fallen asleep when someone came upstairs and rapped on the door. "Marge?" It was Horace. "Anna?"

Anna threw on her robe and stuck her head out the door. Horace's face was white as a sheet. He was too shaken to speak.

"What's happened?" Marge was by her side.

"There's been an accident."

"Accident? Where? Who?"

"Ted and Eddie. . . . They were killed."

"Killed? No!"

Horace sat down heavily on the couch, head in his hands. The girls followed—sat on either side of him.

"A car wreck?" Marge asked.

He nodded, too full to speak. Marge put her arm around his shoulders. Horace broke down sobbing.

Someone opened a door. Clara peeked in; Anna looked her way. Clara joined them. Anna spoke softly, "There's been an accident. Two boys were killed."

Clara went white.

"Ted and Eddie, Clara." She took the older woman in her arms and realized then that her own body was shaking. "Better tell the others."

The news spread quickly, and hurriedly the other women got up and came into the sitting room. They stood like marble figures in moonlight, pale with shock.

"It was on the Old Mill Road," Horace was saying, his voice thick and halting. "They didn't make that curve."

"Was anyone with them?"

"Andy Lawton, but he's okay. Didn't get a scratch."

"Who was driving?"

"Eddie. Andy said he went onto the shoulder of the road and that's when he lost control."

"Were they killed instantly?"

"I think so. Eddie was pinned in the car but he was already dead. Ted—" His voice broke.

"What about Andrew?"

"He was thrown clear." Horace blew his nose, tried to get control of himself. Hands shaking, he folded the handkerchief and put it back in his hip pocket. "I have to go to their homes. Will you go with me, Anna?"

She nodded. While she dressed, the women kept asking questions. "Whose car were they in?"

"Earl's hot rod. They were goin' too fast, just goin' too fast."

"You don't suppose they were drinking?"

"No. Those boys don't drink. They were just goin' too fast."

Anna was ready and pulled on a sweater as they walked downstairs.

Horace fumbled with the keys, couldn't get the car started—let out the clutch too fast, choked it. He swore. Finally they were underway.

The McGills lived only a block away from the teacherage. Every light in the house was blazing; already cars were along the curb. Horace parked, cut off the engine, and crossed his arms on the wheel. They watched people arriving, helping each other in the darkness. "I can't go in, Anna. I can't go in there."

"Maybe we ought to go over to Eddie's house. Those little brothers may be alone with Aunt Chloe."

"You're right. Jack McClendon was trying to get Eddie's daddy. He's on the road some place and the colored woman didn't know exactly where."

They drove down Trade and turned east on Cross. The wrecker was coming toward them, lights flashing. It was towing the Chevy into the Ford place. Horace turned in behind the wrecker and got out to look at the demolished car.

From where Anna sat she could see the crumpled car—shattered glass, twisted metal. She felt sick.

When Horace got back in the car, he leaned over the steering wheel a long time, saying nothing. Anna waited. Without raising his head, he spoke. "Anna," he croaked, "Eddie wasn't driving that car. Andy Lawton was driving."

"Are you sure?"

"Positive."

"How do you know?"

"Andy's blue suede shoes are on the floorboard of the driver's seat."

"But couldn't they have been thrown there?"

He shook his head. "We found Eddie pinned in the back seat—Ted almost in the trunk."

"And Andrew was thrown clear?"

"That's right. The force of the impact jerked him right outta his shoes. I remember now when we got to the scene of the accident, Andy was barefooted."

"Maybe you're mistaken."

He shook his head. "Andy lied. He was driving that car."

"Well, are you going to tell the police?"

"I dunno." He was quiet for a while. "What good

would that do? It won't bring Eddie and Ted back." He laid his head against the wheel and wept.

After a while, Anna spoke. "Horace, let's go back to the teacherage. I don't think we'd be any help to anyone just now."

They were up all night at the teacherage—Mrs. Milligan, Miss Pendergraft—all of them. One after another they spoke of the boys. "I had Eddie in fifth grade, the year he broke his arm in September and his collar bone in the spring."

"That was soon after his mother died, wasn't it?"

"Let's see, she got sick the first year I came to Scotsville . . . it must have been in '49 . . . no, '50."

"Automobiles, that's all he cared about," the librarian remembered. "So long as he had one of those magazines about automotive mechanics he would be quiet in the library. I used to save the old copies and let him take them home. I know it was against the rules to let them go out of the library but I couldn't deny that sweet boy."

"Remember, Clara, when Ted was in Cub Scouts, how proud he was of that uniform? Every Tuesday he'd meet you at the car dressed in his uniform, knowing you'd make a fuss over him."

Clara nodded, sniffling, "I had him in second grade. He used to bring me flowers. He'd stop on the way to school and pick violets along the ditch bank." She covered her mouth to stifle her sobs.

"He didn't make his grade that year and I had to hold him back but he didn't hold it against me like so many of them do. The next year he still brought me flowers."

The music teacher cleared her throat. "When Ted was in Montgomery School, when I'd walk in the room he'd throw up his hand and I knew what he wanted to ask. He always asked if we could sing 'Fairest Lord Jesus.' Every time I hear that song I think of Ted."

Anna poured coffee and listened.

Unconsciously Horace twisted a pillow in his hands. "When I had to cut the team, Ted got a place on the first string, but right away he went to the boys who were cut—couldn't get excited about his own good luck, so concerned about them."

A pang of remorse gripped Anna. *Football—Ted asked me please to come watch the team play and I never went. It was the least I could've done.*

Miss Pendergraft had been standing by the window watching the McGill house, cars coming and going all night. The first streaks of daylight were beginning to show behind the funeral home. Slowly, she turned around and, as she did, everyone looked at her expectantly, knowing she had something important to say.

Her face was transfixed as she spoke. "Only I, of all in this room, know the tragedy of this night. I alone know what they have lost, their lives snuffed out before they know the full freedom of adolescence, the ecstasy of love, the joy of being twenty years old and embarking on a life full of promise—of being thirty and settled into that life, of being forty and reflecting upon it, casting an eye to what is over the hill. I alone know what it is to be fifty and satisfied with maturity—to be sixty and looking forward to retirement."

Her voice rose to a higher pitch. "Three-score years and ten are promised to us but whether by fate or childish error, there has been a default here."

Everyone in the room felt the anguish that made Miss Pendergraft tremble from head to toe.

Mrs. Milligan rose and, without a word, stood by the light switch waiting. One by one they got up and filed past her to climb the stairs. They would lie on their beds until it was time to go to school. Somehow they must absorb the impact, brace themselves for the onslaught of grief-stricken youth come morning.

# CHAPTER
# ELEVEN

Andrew Lawton came home from the hospital in a daze. His father held onto him as they came in the house and saw that Andrew was safely seated at the table before he went for the wine. Andrew's teeth were chattering, not from cold but from the terror he felt.

"Here, drink this," his father was saying. "Your mother went to McLaughlins'. She'll go to the McGills' before she comes home, but she won't be gone long." He was putting an afghan around Andrew's shoulders. "Now drink this, son. Dr. Jennie knows how you hate shots so she told me to give you some wine. Here, I'll hold it for you."

Andrew could not feel the glass against his lips.

"I know it doesn't taste good," he coaxed. "It's a port somebody gave me at the office, but it'll help calm your nerves. Take a sip, son."

He felt the liquid in his mouth and swallowed.

"Good. Think you can drink the rest while I get your bath ready? Dr. Jennie said to put you in a warm tub."

Andrew had not drunk the wine when his father returned. Benjamin Lawton sat down beside him, put his arm around his shoulders and held the wine to Andrew's mouth. Patiently he waited as, sip by sip, Andrew drained the glass.

"Good boy! Now let's get you in that tub."

After the bath, Andrew lay under the covers, stiff and staring. He did not hear his mother come into the room nor feel her kissing him. Vaguely, he knew she was there.

Some time before dawn, Andrew came to with a start. His shoes! He remembered his shoes. They were still in the car! What if they—? He looked about the room. His mother was sitting in a chair beside the bed. "Get Daddy," he said coarsely.

"What is it, son? What is it? Mother's here. Mother's here."

"Get Daddy," he repeated with force.

She hurried out of the room. Andrew raised himself up on the side of the bed. Without turning on the light, he reached for his pants and was pulling them on over his pajamas when his parents returned. "What is it, son?" his father asked.

"I need you to take me someplace." His voice did not betray the fear that made his body clammy with sweat.

His mother protested. "Andrew, you can't go out—not at this hour!"

"Be quiet, Mary. Let the boy alone." Benjamin Lawton put on his jacket. "I'll get the car."

Leaving his mother pleading but silent, Andrew went out the back door and crawled in beside his father. "We gotta go to the Ford place," he said, and Benjamin Lawton turned the car in that direction.

Neither of them spoke as they drove straight down Cross. The street was deserted. It wouldn't do for anyone to see them, yet that was the chance they had to take.

As they neared the garage, Andrew said quietly, "Go 'round the back." His father turned the car into the alley. "Turn off the lights." In the darkness the car crept along the rutted gravel. At the back of the garage they stopped and Andrew told his father, "Turn it off." His voice was quivering.

"Do you need me?"

Andrew shook his head and opened the door. He could hardly stand, he was trembling so badly.

Of course the doors were bolted shut. Andrew tried the service entrance. No use. His father was getting out of the car, coming toward him. Andrew cursed. Why couldn't he stay in the car!

"Andrew, you know the police have the Chevy impounded. It wouldn't do for us to be seen here." Andrew didn't answer. "I'll move the car out of the alley and park it on a side street. There's less chance—"

Andrew was trying the windows. If he had to he could break the glass and crawl inside, but in an old building like this there was no way all the windows would be locked. Too many times he had gone back to school at night to get something from a locker and, with all the doors locked, he had always found a way to get inside. The garage proved to be no more of a challenge. There was a window propped open part way—it had only to be opened wider for him to slip through. All he needed was a leg up. He glanced at his father. Without a word, Benjamin Lawton leaned over and hoisted Andrew to the window ledge. The boy pulled the sash out and up, setting the prop in its last notch. Pulling himself up over the edge, he dropped down inside the garage. No sooner did he hit the floor than things began falling, clattering in back of the big room. Andrew froze! Something was moving among the clutter that lay piled in the darkness. His heart pounded in his chest. He waited, hearing only the car easing out of the alley, then silence. But he knew there was something alive in the garage.

Suddenly automobile headlights flashed along the walls—a car turning into the alley! Moving slowly along the gravel, the searchlight of a patrol car swept the windows back and forth. Andrew flattened his body against the wall, waiting. *Probably Jack McClendon*. The car stopped; the motor still running, the door opened but did not close. Footsteps sounded, coming toward the window above his head. A flashlight beam bouncing off the ceiling, the footsteps crunching beneath the window. The patrolman was trying to reach the window prop with the flashlight. Reaching it, he gave the prop a jolt that slammed the sash shut. Andrew did not breathe, listening. More footsteps, the car door slammed, the tires began rolling in the gravel, the car moving out of the alley.

Andrew slumped to the floor. Beads of perspiration rolled down his face; he was breathing hard. The street lamp cast squares of light on the cement floor, making patterns that would not lie flat. Outlined in the light was the demolished car, the hood ripped away from the motor. Twisted pieces of chrome reflected the light.

Another noise sounded in the blackness of the far side—something sliding, a tool, hubcaps, something. Andrew's lips were dry despite the sweat. There was something alive in the place, something moving. He could feel it coming toward him, and in his panic he felt that he was smothering. Then he saw the eyes reflecting green and a striped cat stepped into the square of light, arching its back, stretching sleepily. Andrew stared at it. The cat mewed, came toward him, wound around his leg, rubbing itself up and down. Andrew flung the cat aside.

There was a smell about the place—oil, grease, gas—familiar fumes, but there was something else— something foul. The cat was coming toward him again. He kicked at it weakly. Outside, he could hear his father working to get the window open.

Andrew crawled across the floor. Get the shoes, he told himself. Get the shoes! Peering inside the car, the stench of blood overpowered him. That was the smell— it was the smell of blood! He began to retch. Nothing would come up. Holding his nose, still he gagged. He lay back on the floor and the cat again purred about his legs. He felt too sick to throw it off him. The animal stealthily crept up his body and sat on his chest looking down in his face, its tail moving back and forth.

Andrew's father was tapping on the window. Andrew rolled the cat off his chest and tried again. He would not breathe the foul odor, he would hold his breath. He would not see the blood or hair or flesh, he would see only the blue suede shoes.

Again pulling himself up beside the car, he searched inside. He felt for the inside handle and opened the door. There on the floor beneath the clutch and brake pedals lay the shoes, the laces still tied as if he had slipped out of them to go barefoot. One whiff of the blood smell and his head went reeling. Snatching the shoes, Andrew clutched them to his chest, slammed the door, and stumbled back to the wall.

Slumped against the wall, waves of nausea swept over him. Water filled his mouth and spilled down his neck. He could not wait for the nausea to subside— he had to get out of there.

To reach the window he needed something to stand on. Casting about, he saw the cat sitting on a barrel. With his foot he turned over the barrel, dumping the cat. Then he rolled the barrel beneath the window and climbed up on it. Lifting the window handle, he pushed out the sash, fixed the prop in its notch, and threw the shoes out ahead of him.

Crawling out the window, Andrew dropped to the ground, falling in a heap. Benjamin Lawton helped him to his feet, steadied him, picked up the shoes, and handed them to him. Then Mr. Lawton wondered how he could shut the window. With a stick he was able to lift the prop so the sash swung shut again. Without a word the two of them slipped to the waiting car.

The smell of blood came and went, making Andrew nauseous. He would drink some more of the wine; maybe that would help.

They were pulling into the driveway when Andrew spoke. "Daddy, it wouldn't do for anyone to know about this."

"I understand, son."

# CHAPTER
# TWELVE

Anna sat in the teacherage waiting to go to the funeral. Lester McKenzie had hitchhiked all the way from Nashville to be there. Sitting on the couch across from her, he was hollow-eyed and thin. He was working as an engraver to pay his way through school and, though the work paid well, it was tedious.

"Miss Petersen, you probably don't remember it, but on that retreat Ted was the first person to accept Christ."

"No, I didn't know that."

"Bruce told me about it. On that Friday night, after lights were out, Ted and Bruce were down by the lake talking. Ted wanted to be sure he was a Christian and after they talked, Ted prayed. Later, he told Bruce he was sure everything was all right between him and the Lord."

"Oh, that's wonderful. Now that you mention it, I do remember something about that. I was checking cabins when I saw this blond head duck down in a ditch. When I called, Bruce answered. He said it was all right, that Ted was with him. I wonder if that's when it happened?"

"It probably was. Bruce said they were in a ditch."

His face clouded. "What about Eddie, do you know if Eddie was—"

"Oh, yes. Eddie prayed right in the hall. We were standing by the water fountain and I heard him ask the Lord to save him." The thought of it made Anna's eyes fill with tears. "One of the counselors had said, 'It doesn't take much of a man to be a Christian, but it does take all of a man,' and that's what impressed Eddie.

"Later the same day, Eddie led Earl McClendon to the Lord. Earl said they were in the lunchroom."

The room was filling with teachers ready to go to the church. Fingering their gloves and adjusting hats, they drew deep breaths and hardly spoke. Miss Pendergraft led the way out the door and they walked in a group down Trade Street to the church.

There was not room in the church nor in the church-yard for all the people who came to the double funeral. Jammed in close together, sitting, standing, they stared straight ahead at the bank of flowers above the caskets as the McAdden Glee Club sang, "Fairest Lord Jesus."

The boys' two ministers spoke, their voices warm and professional, yet they did not break through the mute grief of those to whom they spoke. The sanctuary held heart sickness of a kind and degree no words could assuage.

Aunt Chloe sat with great dignity, her head held high, but when the little boys began sobbing, she gathered them in her arms and held them close. Eddie's father reached for his handkerchief and held it to his mouth. Aunt Chloe reached for him and he leaned toward her, his tears falling in her lap.

Andrew Lawton, sitting between his parents in the row behind Aunt Chloe, never raised his head.

When the last prayer was spoken, the audience stood for the caskets to be removed. In the silence, the only sound to be heard was the rubber wheels of the biers rolling down the aisle.

Anna glimpsed Anita, white-faced, walking unsteadily behind her brother's coffin, Eddie's coffin following.

People streamed to the cemetery, in cars, on foot, like forlorn survivors of disaster. At the graveside services, Woodall Jackson's voice was strained but it never quavered as he lifted the words above the crowd and prayed.

When he was done and had offered comfort to each family member, he stood ramrod straight, the eye patch giving him the appearance of a swashbuckling soldier of fortune. But as soon as the families were ensconced in limousines and driven away, Woodall Jackson turned away and, shielded by the great live oak, wept like a stricken child.

People began milling about, scarcely acknowledging each other, yet lingering, not wanting to be alone. Workmen, waiting to finish the burying, leaned on their shovels, their heads hung like mourning doves.

Horace and Anna stood on either side of Clara, waiting for the others to leave. From time to time, they touched her, comforting her. Clara clutched a brown paper sack in her hands and shifted her weight from one bunioned foot to the other.

As if by some signal, the three of them stepped over the coping and moved toward Ted's grave. The gray metal casket had been lowered part way into the ground and dozens of flowers blanketed the earth on all sides.

Clara opened her bag, reached in, and drew out a handful of violets. Stooping down, she laid them in the open grave and, weeping, backed away.

# CHAPTER
# THIRTEEN

The flag atop McAdden High flew at half-mast until the end of the funeral day. Scotsville did not easily recover from the grief they felt.

The student body voted to have portraits of Ted and Eddie hung in the school library. The yearbook would be dedicated to their memory. But nothing they did dispelled the pall that hung over the town. It lingered long.

Andrew Lawton could not get hold of himself. Irrational fears stalked him. The Russian Sputnik had frightened everyone but in Andrew's emotional state, the Russian threat became a personal terror. Desperately trying to hold onto his sanity, he knew he mustn't tell anyone. *They'll think I'm crazy. It's only the violence of the wreck, linking up in my mind with atrocity*, he reasoned. But he could not shake the fears.

Classmates hovered around Andrew, seldom allowing him to be alone, but they were no help. They hovered around Anita as well, loving her, trying to help her, but Anita reached out only to Andrew.

Intelligent as she was, Anita spared him words, and Andrew went through the motions he hoped would help them both. Together they visited Aunt Chloe, did Eddie's chores, took his brothers to games, bought them things.

In a rare private exchange, Anita asked him, "Do you still have nightmares?"

Andrew nodded. "Dr. Jennie says they'll go away in time."

The nightmares were no worse than the horrors he feared in the daytime. The mere mention of the word "communism" struck panic in his mind. All the agitation about Sputnik heightened his fears. *We're so far behind the Russians,* he thought, *we'll never catch up. They'll invade us, take over.*

He heard commentators and educators saying the same things, yet their sanity was not threatened. Andrew felt the threat personally, knowing he would suffer most, and he was hysterically afraid.

Even his mother did not know of his fears. She complained that Andrew was quiet and tried to cheer him up. She bought him a tonic and fretted that Dr. Jennie should be able to give him something to improve his condition.

If Anita suspected anything more than the grief they shared, she didn't let on.

"You'll never get over it, Andy, until you face it," she said.

Andrew had forgotten what they were talking about. "What did you say?"

"I said, you'll never get over the nightmares until you face it."

"That's what I thought you said," he lied.

Anita drew in a deep breath, struggling to say what she must. "Like I couldn't bear the sight of his clothes, his football and stuff." Her chin trembled. "My parents didn't make me—it was hard for them, too. Ted did so many sweet things. At night, when he went upstairs, he'd leave a note on the steps for Mama. Sometimes he'd say he was sorry for something he'd done or he'd just say he loved her and Daddy. Mama keeps grieving because she didn't save the notes.

"Well, I knew I had to face it—had to deal with it in my own way—by myself. Then one day I made up my mind. While Mama and Daddy were away, I walked into Ted's room all by myself. I sat on the side of his bed and remembered him sprawled there sound asleep. On Saturdays he'd sleep till noon.

"Mama had packed Ted's shirts and dungarees in a box to give to the welfare, but I opened the box and forced myself to look at them. It was, oh, so hard, Andy, but I did it—like I was saying a proper good-bye—not ignoring his leaving.

"His football was on the closet shelf. Of course, Ted never had a place for that football. Usually it was in the middle of the living room floor or under the table someplace. I held it in my hands and remembered how his hands looked wrapped around it.

"I even looked in the drawer of his bedside table. There were marbles, comic books, all kinds of junk, but on the top of it all was his New Testament. Ted didn't like to read but there in the Testament was a bookmark to mark his place. Ever since that retreat he had read it every night."

Andrew studied the girl's small, delicate face, knowing full well what she was asking of him.

"Andrew, somehow, some way, you must face head-on the thing you dread most—the fears you feel, or they'll never stop haunting you."

He agreed with her. For days he thought upon it. He could go to the police, tell Jack McClendon that he, not Eddie, was driving the car. Perhaps Jack would tell him to forget it.

Andrew rolled over in bed, lay on his stomach, the pillow wadded in his arms. No, Jack would not do that. He was stupid. He'd enjoy the theatrics of a trial, enjoy seeing Benjamin Lawton, corporate lawyer, humiliated.

Confessing would turn the whole town against him and without friends to see him through, as strong as he was, Andrew knew he couldn't survive.

He rolled over on his back and thought about Anita

looking at her brother's clothes, sitting on his bed.

Andrew got up and in the dark began rummaging through stuff in the bottom drawer of the dresser. Somewhere he had that penny he took from Ted. It was in an old shotgun shell box where he kept the rattlers from a snake he once shot. Sitting on the floor, he opened the box and felt for the penny. Rubbing the Indian head between his fingers, he wondered if he should give it to Anita.

After a while, Andrew got back in bed. *The penny has nothing to do with the fears or the nightmares,* he told himself. *I hadn't thought of it until just now. The fight was nothing; it only meant I outwitted them. Just three boys having a squabble and in the end we were friends again.* What did it matter?

*Anita might not think of it that way. If I give her the penny it will only bring the fight to mind, and she might hate me for taking advantage of Ted.* It would accomplish nothing, he decided. Zero!

Andrew lay on his back and watched the curtain billow in the night air. He tried to think of something else—what he would wear the next day, what he would say to Anita, where he would take Eddie's brothers. He had not worn the blue suede shoes since the accident. Since the night he retrieved them from the garage, they had been stashed in the back of his closet. Sooner or later, somebody would ask him why he wasn't wearing them and he'd have to say he didn't wear them any more because they reminded him of the wreck. Or, he could say he had outgrown them. Neither answer would work. People expected Andrew Lawton to be in control. Any excuse he could give about the shoes would make them wonder.

Not once since he brought them home had he looked at the shoes. Getting out of bed, he went over to the closet, reached for them, felt the texture of the suede. Just the feel of them made him giddy.

Taking the shoes to the light he examined them to make sure there were no stains. Looking at them made him smell the blood, but there were no spots, no tell-tale marks.

The next morning, Andrew wore the shoes.

Anna was working in her classroom after school trying to get the last things done for the NCEA banquet so she could go home. The North Carolina State seal had been drawn and had only to be hung behind the speaker's table. Marge was sending a boy to help Anna move it to the cafeteria. It never occurred to her that Marge would send Andrew. As he came in the door, Anna was startled by the sight of the blue suede shoes!

"What's the matter, Miss Petersen?" Andrew asked coldly, his eyes as dark and piercing as his father's.

"Nothing, Andrew. Here's the seal; do you think you can lift it by yourself?"

Andrew ignored her question and hoisted the seal, held it sideways to get through the door, then balanced it on his head and carried it down the hall and out the building to the cafeteria.

Anna felt weak. Her shock at seeing the shoes had not gone unnoticed by Andrew. Something had passed between them—yet how could he know she knew? There is no way, she told herself, but even as she said it she knew he could. Andrew, with his shrewd, calculating sense could have perceived the truth. His rapier mind had a way of penetrating to the heart of a matter.

*Well, I mustn't worry about that now,* she said. *There's hardly time to go home and get ready for the banquet at seven o'clock.*

The phone was ringing when Anna came into the teacherage and she answered it. The woman's voice on the other end had an unmistakable Jersey accent.

"Josephine Marotti here. Who's talkin'?"

"Anna Petersen. Did you say, 'Josephine'?"

"The same. Josephine Marotti. I'm yer aunt Helga's girlfriend." The voice was loud and coarse. "We been girlfriends evah since P.S. 30 and we ain't seen one anothah in forty years! Can you imagine that? Forty years?" Her voice was booming. "Soon's Helga went away to music school, I got married and me and my Mickey moved around a lot, an' we got lost track of, know what I mean? 'Cept one day in Bloomingdale's I'm waitin' at the glove countah an' I look up and see this beyootiful skin and I remember that face, only she had got a lot fattah than I remembered her! Still, right away I sez to myself, 'Josephine, that is Helga Petersen, the piano player.' And, sure enough," she squealed, "it was Helga!

"We forgot all about Bloomingdale's and headed straight for Schraft's where we ate hot fudge sundaes and drank coffee 'til they nearly run us outta the place. We talked and we talked and we talked an' when it come time to say g'bye we promised to keep in touch, call one anothah, visit back and forth, yeah, do all o' that but we dun't. You know how it goes." The voice grew melancholy, philosophical. "She had her troubles, I had mine." Just as quickly the voice bounced back cheerful. "But last summer me and my Mickey was up in the Poconos and who do we bump into but Helga Petersen!!"

The woman was so loud Anna held the receiver away from her ear. "Hold on, there's some man here tellin' me to git offa the phone." Josephine must have clamped her hand over the mouthpiece. In a minute she was back. "I gotta make this short. I'm here at yer local bus station on my way to Flowrida. My husban' he dun't wanna come on 'count his sisters. They live upstairs and me down but that can wait. I'm on my way to Flowrida to visit my son who's in used cahs, and when

I saw Scotsville so close U.S. 301—practically on the way—I sez to my Mickey, 'I'm gonna detour ovah and see Anna—that niece of Helga Petersen—the school-teachah.' So, could youse pick me up or should I call a cab?"

Anna was flabbergasted. "Well, Josephine, I live in a teacherage—"

"Teacherage? What's that?"

"I mean, I really don't have a place of my own."

"Dun't worry! I can make myself at home anywhere. Besides, I'm only here on layovah. Soon's my bus comes, I'll be on my way to Flowrida. I jus' hadda see ya, I heard so much about cha and I got a lotta stuff ye'r dyin' to hear. So whadda ya say? I dun't mean to rush ya but I gotta hang. This here man—this low-life—got no manners."

"Josephine, just stay right where you are. I'll have to find somebody with a car, but I'll come and get you."

Anna hung up and yelled for Marge. "Help!"

Marge met her at the head of the stairs.

"Some old girlfriend of my aunt is waiting at the bus station for me to pick her up. What in the world will I do? I have this banquet—"

"Call Woodall, he'll go get her."

"I can't ask him to do that. She sounds like a real character—as tough as you've ever heard."

"Relax. Sounds like fun. I'll help you. Oh, I've got a good idea. I'll call Waldo and he'll go for her in a limousine!" They ran downstairs. "We'll ride with him!"

There was no mistaking Josephine Marotti. She was standing by the phone booth—very short and very wide all the way around, smiling from ear to ear, a floppy hat on her head, and two shopping bags at her feet. Like Helga she was in her late sixties but, being fat, she had few wrinkles. Apparently, pasta gave Josephine a high energy level—she hefted the parcels with ease.

But when she realized the limousine was for her, she dropped the shopping bags and changed from tourist to royalty.

Waldo got out of the car and Josephine waited demurely for him to put the bags in the trunk, then open the door for her.

Anna made the introductions. "Pleased to meet cha, I'm sure," Josephine said, pursing her lips, smitten with her own importance. Sitting between the girls on the back seat, she clasped their hands and explained. "You might say I was momentarily rendered speechless riding in a limo." Her nose crinkled at the bridge displaying effusive pleasure. "I rode oncet in a limo to a wedding in Manhattan when I stood up for my girfriend who was marryin' a Puerto Rican. You know how they are, them Puerto Ricans make a big show. Don't get me wrong. It was nice. Very nice. I enjoyed it. First the civil, then the church. My church. Catholic."

They arrived at the teacherage and Waldo drove around the corner to let them in the side door. That made it easier for him to wheel into the funeral home, and Waldo always did what was easiest for him. "Just call me when Mrs. Marotti's ready to leave," he told Anna.

Miss Pendergraft was sitting in the parlor when Anna and Marge brought Josephine inside. The introduction was as awkward as pretense and utter self-confidence could be at first meeting. Miss Pendergraft lowered her glasses and peered over them, examining Josephine from head to toe. Josephine did not so much as cast an eye toward Cichora Pendergraft. She was busy pawing through the shopping bags for the "little something I brought cha," and having trouble finding it. Out came the contents of the first bag—rubbers, sweet roll, paperback novel, two newspapers, sun glasses—all dumped on the floor. "Must be in the othah one," she said, turning it upside down. A loaf of Italian sausage rolled across the floor. "There! There it is," she exclaimed happily. It was a cardboard picture and she rubbed it across her backside to dust it. "Sorry, I dun't have wrappin', but isn't that beyootiful?" Proudly she showed them the picture, the sacred heart of Jesus. "I betcha got one a'ready?"

"Oh, no. No, I haven't," Anna assured her. "Thank you."

Not satisfied, Josephine, pointing out its features, held the picture before each of them to admire. "See deah—you can see the blessed prints of the nails. An' his h'art—his deah blessed h'art open like that for all to see."

Miss Pendergraft shuddered visibly.

Anna interrupted. "Josephine, could I get you a cup of coffee, something to drink?"

"That would be nice and a cookie, too, maybe? Piece of cake?"

By the time Anna returned with the coffee and cake, Josephine was well into a story. "I was seventeen and there was this hold-up man. I was all alone in the deli when he come in and I knew he was up to no good! I knew that! Soon's I saw him, I sez to myself, 'He's gonna kill me,' an' that's exactly what he was goin' to do. He was goin' to kill me and take all o' the money. That gun was this big!" Josephine balanced the tray on her lap precariously and, using both hands, showed how long the gun was. Pausing long enough for a sip of coffee and plopping a piece of cake in her mouth, she continued. "That man told me he was goin' to kill me! The gun clicked. Right away I think maybe he's not goin' to kill me but worse!" She rolled her eyes. "I call out, 'Jesus, save me! Jesus, save me! Save my virginity!' I musta cried out seven, eight, ten times, and him standin' there, six feet eight and me five feet, eighty-nine pounds, same as now, and he pushes me to the back room. I keep callin' out, then I grab a bottle o' cream soda in my hands like this—" Leaning down, she placed the tray on the floor then demonstrated the way she brought the bottle across the man's head. "He falls right ovah! Then he lays there, out cold. I step ovah him and run outta the store. That day I became a born again!"

Josephine took another mouthful of cake. "Of course, I done things I shouldn' oughtta done but I paid fer 'em. Like my Mickey's sisters. Every night of our married life one of 'em comes downstairs with a full course dinner for Mickey. Not me, just Mickey. God gives me patience. I say, 'Good. Now my Mickey has got a choice!'

"Living with these characters is what's give me all o' my virtues. Them sisters think I dun't know how to make gravy. God gives me patience.

"Take my neighbor, Tony. He lay dyin' o' TB so I told him I am a born again. At first he dun't wanna hear nuttin' like that, but after a while he ast me, 'Tell me 'bout how you bein' a born again.' So I tell 'im. Then I sez to 'im, 'You wanna pray wid me?' and he sez, 'Yeah.' So we pray. We holdin' han's like so." Down on the floor went the tray again and Josephine put out her hands, raised her face, closed her eyes and continued. "Tony he sez the 'Our Father' while I'm saying the real words. An' he's saved!" Josephine slapped her thigh and laughed heartily. "I know he's a born again so I tell 'im it's good he's dyin', and he ast me why it's good he's dyin' so I tell 'im the Scripture—you know, the one about Jesus comin' back again. I sez, 'Tony, when Jesus comes the dead will come up first! Youse'll get up and go! Youse'll get there first!' Tony ast me if that's in the Book and when I tell him it is, he laughs. He likes that. And you know something? I know he's saved 'cause he died without no fear. His mudder will tell youse that. No fear. I tell you he died without no fear!"

For the first time the woman stopped talking, marveling at the mystery and the miracle of it.

Anna hated to break the mood but—"Josephine, please, forgive me but we have a banquet at seven o'clock and we have to get ready. If it was any other time—"

"Anna, I only came by to say hullo. In a minute I'll freshen up a bit and be on my way. Bus comes eight o'clock. I'll talk fast. I know youse wanna hear about yer dear mother, God rest her soul. I lived four doors down on Neptune Av'noo when youse were born and your father was out at sea, but because he loved the Bible so much, your mudder named youse Anna. Now don't ask me why. She told me already, but—seems somebody in the Bible had a daughter named Anna?"

"No, an old lady who saw the baby Jesus was named Anna."

"And Helga—I know ye're dyin' to hear about Helga." She lowered her voice. "I take it we're among yer intimates?"

Anna didn't know what to say. Miss Pendergraft leaned closer to hear.

"Confidentially, I think youse Aunt Helga has just about run through her money. She don't want youse to know it but sooner or later, youse'll hear. And, if youse'll pardon my sayin' so, can that woman talk!" She slapped her thigh, laughing good-naturedly. "She never knows when to shuddup!"

Anna took Josephine's tray. "Can I get you something else, Josephine?"

"Drink of water maybe? A little sandwich? A little seltzer?"

Marge followed Anna to the kitchen. Anna threw up her hands. "Gid-av-mig! Marge, what'll I do? I can't get rid of her!"

"Stop worrying. I just thought of something. I'll call Waldo—tell him to drive her around town. She'll have the time of her life in that 'limo,' as she calls it."

While Marge called Waldo, Anna made a chicken sandwich and served it. Miss Pendergraft was holding forth with a long spiel about the UDC or the DAR and Josephine kept opening her mouth to interrupt.

As soon as Miss Pendergraft caught her breath, Josephine started in on the "IUPIMC."

Miss Pendergraft was puzzled. "I beg your pardon?"

"The IUPIMC," Josephine repeated, "means Italians United for the Preservation of Italian Manners and Customs. My Mickey and me are very active members. I'm the secretary of our local chapter."

Marge came into the parlor. "Mrs. Marotti, I have a wonderful treat for you. That nice Mr. McSwain who drove us from the bus station would like to take you on a motor tour of Scotsville."

"Ain't that grand! Tell the gentleman I'll be ready in half a' hour." Josephine wolfed down the sandwich and chased it with seltzer. "Now, show me where I can freshen up," she asked, and Anna led her upstairs.

As luck would have it, Marge had chased Clara out of the bathroom, cutting short her long soak, and had barricaded the door, holding up a line of teachers anxious to get ready for the banquet.

Josephine took her time in the bathroom, but when she came out she looked no different. Only the smell of sweet powder pervaded the air, following Josephine about like a cloud.

Anna saw Josephine to the car, endured profuse hugs and kisses, and waved her good-bye as the disgruntled Waldo swung the limousine away from the curb.

By some doubling up in the bathroom, all the teachers were able to complete their toiletries and arrive at the banquet, harried, but on time. They ate the crusty chicken and peas that rattled on the plates, endured the gubernatorial candidate's speech, then stayed on to clean up the cafeteria. It was midnight when they came home.

When the lights went on in the teacherage, the telephone rang. It was Waldo. "What, in heaven's name, have you done to me?" he screamed at Marge. "What kind of a fool woman was that?"

Marge handed the phone to Anna. "Did she get on the bus?" Anna asked.

"Get on the bus? I should say she did but not nearly soon enough. She nearly drove me nuts! That woman threatened me with everything in the book!"

"Threatened you?"

"For having Noodles here."

"Noodles?"

"That's what I said. Marge told me to take her on a tour so we toured the funeral home. After all, what's there to see in Scotsville but Noodles? That woman's Eyetalian and she belongs to some kind of Eyetalian organization. She told me to bury Noodles or else!"

Anna groaned. "G'night, Waldo."

"Don't 'good night' me, Anna. That woman means business. She's one of those 'What Lola wants, Lola gets' types!"

"Not Josephine. She's my aunt's old grade school friend. If she's upset I'm sure she'll forget about it. I'm tired, Waldo. Go to bed. That's what I'm going to do."

# CHAPTER
# FOURTEEN

Andrew woke up screaming and neither his mother nor his father could quiet him. He was incoherent, trying to tell them about the shoes, how Miss Petersen held up the shoes in his face. How they were coming after him—men in uniform marching toward him and that woman holding the shoes—saying nothing—holding the shoes.

He fought his parents viciously as they struggled to restrain him. Finally, his father wrestled him flat on the bed, gripping both his wrists and pressing his knee against his chest.

Andrew lay panting, tossing his head from side to side. He heard his father tell his mother, "Call Dr. Jennie."

When Dr. Jennie arrived, she did not talk. She took one look, filled a syringe, swabbed Andrew's skin, and pressed the needle into his flesh.

"The boy needs help, Ben. Let me make an appointment with a psychiatrist."

"No, Dr. Jennie. We can handle this."

Andrew could not resist the effect of the drug. He was floating dreamily into sleep.

The next day, he slept late and didn't go to school. Refusing breakfast, Andrew got in his mother's car and drove to his grandfather's farm. The old man was dead now, dead over a year. If only he were alive there would be someone to listen, someone to tell him what to do.

At the farm, Andrew walked through the woods to

the pond carrying a package under his arm. The old boat was bobbing beside the dock and the dark water lapped against the pilings the way he remembered it from childhood.

Andrew untied the boat and, stepping into it, shoved away from the dock with the paddle. Dragging the paddle in the water, he let the boat glide. The spot he had in mind was in the middle of the pond where the water was deepest, but he was tired and there was plenty of time.

Doves were cooing and the familiar sound soothed his weary mind. A crow flew over the water cawing, telling him that this place was the same.

Andrew scanned the entire lakeside twice, making sure no one was in sight. Then he saw the cat, a lazy alley cat ambling onto the pier. Sitting on its haunches, the cat's eyes followed his every move. The sight of the animal unnerved him; it reminded him of the cat in the garage. He scooped up water and tried to splash the cat but he was too far away. Andrew began paddling away from the dock.

In the middle of the pond he guided the boat so that a cluster of cypress trees stood between him and the pier. Of course, the stupid cat could not see him, nevertheless—

Andrew reached for the package. Water in the bottom of the boat had wet the paper; the blue suede was damp. He held one of the shoes over the side of the boat, paused, then let it drop. The shoe plopped, turned over once and sank from sight. He waited a few minutes and dropped the other one.

For a long time he sat watching the ripples, thinking about the look on Miss Petersen's face when she saw him wearing the shoes. Miss Petersen was like the cat—always watching, always seeing whatever he did. She puzzled him. More than puzzled him, she scared him.

He heard the doves and the crazy crows as a kind

of reassurance, a kind of "all's well." He would not think about Miss Petersen or the cat but he would give the cat plenty of time to be gone before he turned back to the dock.

*If only Granddaddy were here,* he thought, *I could tell him. I know what the old man would say; he would tell me about Stonewall Jackson and how he was his own man, kept his own counsel, the bravest man who ever lived. He would approve the way I'm handling this. In fact, if for no other reason then to keep faith with the old man, I have to be strong. Still . . . it would help if I could talk it over with him—relieve the pressure.*

Andrew could not tell his father anything. Benjamin Lawton prided himself in being a man of steel but when it came to his only son, he didn't want to hear anything adverse—not the slightest imperfection. Andrew's father expected great things of him and Andrew had never disappointed him, not in grades nor athletics, and he wouldn't disappoint him in this. He would keep his troubles to himself.

Andrew scarcely thought of his mother. She was a good but simple woman, catering to his father and to him. She hardly mattered at all.

The ripples were gone; the water lay smooth as silk. Then Andrew saw a bubble rising lazily to the surface. He would ignore it. *Maybe a mud turtle,* he told himself and fought the uneasiness that rose in him. He breathed deeply and looked toward the dock. The cat was gone. Good! He stroked the paddle in the water, turning the boat toward shore.

Andrew drove to the high school and waited there for Anita. When school was out, she came to the car and without asking why, she said, "I'm sorry you had to miss today."

She knew. She was having her own bad dreams. Anita knew about the night before. They went to Anita's house and, as he always did, he shunned the living room where Ted's picture hung. They ate a sandwich, then got in the car again.

"Andrew, let's drive out on the Old Mill Road."

"You mean—?"

"Yes. We have to face it all. I'm ready, are you?"

He could not let on that the scene of the accident was something he dreaded most. "Sure," he said and headed out of town.

The nearer they came to the curve in the road, the tighter he felt. As they came down between the mimosa trees where the road was straight and Andrew had floored the accelerator, flashing in his mind were the lights as they had bounced off the trees, the radio blasting, the motor wide open—Ted, or was it Eddie, shouting in his ear, "Slow down! Slow down! You wanna get us killed?"

Now, as he drove the stretch, he crept along, repeatedly braking the car. Anita glanced at him oddly. "It's soon now," he whispered.

The car was barely moving as they came around the bend. Gripping the wheel, Andrew's knuckles were white. He let the car roll onto the shoulder and stop. Neither of them moved to get out.

Anita's voice was soft. "If only Eddie hadn't been going so fast. . . . Andy, how fast can you go and still make the curve?"

"Fifty, fifty-five."

"How fast was Eddie going?"

Andrew felt he couldn't breathe. "Let's get out."

They walked across the road. She was saying something about what the cops said. "Mr. McClendon said you must've been going eighty miles an hour or more."

He examined the pavement for skid marks. There were none, only one deep tire rut and the tall grass stripped where the car had slid on its side. "He ran off the edge of the road on this side," he explained, "cut back too sharp, and landed over here." His voice was remarkably controlled.

"What's that over there in the cattails?"

Andrew walked over to the edge of the water where something glinted in the sun. It was the side view mirror, torn from the body of the car and smashed. Andrew turned it over, looked at the other side, flipped it in the pond.

Anita stood on the edge of the road, her arms folded about her waist. She was shaking. Andrew put his arm around her, drew her close.

"Oh, Andy, I'm sorry but I can't forgive him. I can't forgive Eddie. He must've floorboarded it to have come around that curve so fast."

"Don't blame Eddie, Anita. It could've been any one of us. It could've been Ted or me. Boys do crazy things." He stroked her hair, tried to concentrate on the gold strands that glistened in the sun. *Like copper*, he thought to himself.

"Not that crazy. Not on a road everybody knows is dangerous. Eddie was just showing off, wasn't he? Trying to be a daredevil. What was it, Andy, what was he trying to do?"

Andrew couldn't answer. But taking the girl in both his arms he held her, trying to stop her trembling, trying to think about something else—anything.

"Andy," she whispered, "help me. I'm so angry!"

That night Andrew tried not to sleep knowing the terror that awaited him if he turned off the light. Even awake he could not deal with the irrational fears that gnawed at his insides, worming their way through every defense raised against them. He sat in the chair and stared at the ceiling trying to think logically, trying to face up to the reasons why he did what he did. What made them, laughing and yelling, go faster and faster?

Andrew could hear the floorboards in the hall creak.

His mother was standing there, listening. "Son, are you all right?" she asked timidly.

"Of course!" he stormed back at her.

He would have to turn off the light if he wanted her to go to bed. He switched it off and, still sitting in the darkness, struggled.

He tried to make nonsense of the fear the cat gave him, the threat Miss Petersen was to him. The mention of her name, even the thought of her, made him quake inside. *Guilt, of course, but I didn't do it maliciously. Why do I feel so guilty?*

He told himself he admired Eddie, admired his spunk. Ted? *Ted was a simple, good boy—I liked him. I didn't mean to hurt either of them. It was an accident. It was just the kind of thing Eddie would have done, or Ted. Not what Andrew Lawton would do—not sensible, suave Andrew Lawton!* He slammed his fist into his palm and swore.

Is that why he let the cat and Miss Petersen frighten him so? They were both harmless, senseless. Fear of them was as irrational as the fears of communism. Easy to explain, he argued. The result of the violence of the wreck, the terror of losing control. *She can't prove anything,* he told himself.

Andrew got up and walked around the room. He took the penny out of the shell box, decided to put it in his wallet.

He was doing what he could to make up for everything. He was helping Anita. *I'll always be a brother to her and I'm doing everything I can think of for Eddie's brothers. What more can I do?*

Andrew thought again about turning himself in but dismissed the idea. *I've been through all of that,* he said. *I'm satisfied that what I've done is best. Not one good thing could come from telling the truth. It would only ruin everything. As it is, I can at least do something to make up for whatever I've done.*

He wished again for his grandfather. In the darkness of the room he tried to visualize the old man there, sipping his homemade blackberry wine. The last time they had talked Andrew told him about the bomb scare Miss Petersen gave them in eighth grade. The old man had exploded, called her a damnyankee, and told Benjamin Lawton the school board should fire her.

Yes, the old man would be on his side if only because Miss Petersen was from the North. Andrew smiled. He felt eased now. Maybe if he drank some of his father's port he could sleep an hour or two. Going to the kitchen, he poured the wine into a jelly glass and gulped it down to avoid the taste. He went back to bed but sleep never came.

# CHAPTER FIFTEEN

The ingathering at Barnwell Memorial Church was always well attended. An old country church, it was famous for pit-cooked barbecue, homemade cakes and pies, jams and jellies, quilts and handwork. Townspeople turned out in droves and everybody at the teacherage went. Anna wished she had ridden with one of the teachers instead of Waldo.

"Lan' sakes, here comes Miss Letitia!" one of the ladies exclaimed and the women flew into action. "Count the silver! Count the silver!"

Anna spotted Miss Letitia on the far side of the churchyard approaching the picnic tables. There was nothing out of the ordinary about her appearance. In fact, she looked better than some of the other women huddled around a table counting knives and forks and giggling like schoolgirls.

Waldo was standing with Anna carrying on about Josephine's letters. "Five this month! One of 'em was seven pages long! When she was here she insisted that I look up Noodles' name—it's Costa-Vincent Luigi Costa. Now she's callin' every Costa in the state of New Jersey tellin' 'em there's a relative of theirs down here that needs buryin'. The woman's crazy, Anna. You gotta get her to stop botherin' me or I'm goin' to a lawyer."

"Maybe that's what you should do, Waldo."

"Whadda you mean?"

She didn't answer.

"Say, are you tryin' to tell me something?"

"I'm not trying to tell you anything. You know Italians, though—"

"You mean wops, don't you? That's what we used to call 'em in the Army. Gangsters, that's what they are."

"You mean the Mafia?"

"Right. That's it."

"No, they're law-abiding, family people."

"Anna, whose side are you on?"

"I guess you'd say I'm on the side of Vincent Luigi Costa," she said and walked away from him.

As soon as the words were out of her mouth Anna knew it was the wrong thing to say to Waldo, but it was the truth. It was unconscionable to leave a human corpse lying unburied to be made fun on. Yet it made Anna nervous that she had said anything. *Waldo can jeopardize my job!*

Waldo followed her across the yard. "You know, I don't understand you people. I got no authority to bury Noodles. It all happened when my granddaddy was the mortician here. The wop gets killed at the carnival. Takes Granddaddy a week to locate his old man. The old man comes, identifies the body, says he'll be back with the two hundred to bury him, and that's the last we see of him. Now what do you expect my granddaddy to do? Bury him and risk a whole pack of Eyetalians descending on him with papers?"

"I can't discuss it, Waldo. It just seems there should be some way. How would you like it if you were a corpse and people gawked at you?"

Waldo laughed. "Anna, I wouldn't know anything about it. When you're dead, you're dead."

"He's a man, Waldo. A man made in the image of God."

"That old carney? Anna, if you'll pardon my saying so, it's people like you that give Yankees a bad name. You sound like a know-it-all." Waldo was being his nastiest. "It's your fault that eager beaver came here in the first place. When this thing blows sky high it's not going to look good for you, Anna. I'm going to talk to Ben Lawton. If you won't get that woman to stop pestering me, maybe the law can. Don't be surprised if Ben calls you about Josephine."

Anna left Waldo. She skipped the barbecue, sweet potatoes, and hush puppies and settled for pie and coffee. Only Marge could put Waldo in his place, but Marge was never in town on weekends.

Anna found a bench with gray-haired ladies and took a seat beside Mrs. Carey and her maiden sister, Pearl. Miss Pearl was an avid news carrier, but Mrs. Carey was a gentle soul. Pearl leaned over her sister to talk with Anna. "Guess you've heard the stories they tell about Letitia?"

"Now, Pearl," Mrs. Carey cautioned. "I don't believe Miss Petersen's interested in hearing all those tales."

"Tales? Sally Mae, it's public knowledge how Letitia is. Look at her there—she's just as likely to steal one of those bedspreads as she is to eat barbecue without paying."

Mrs. Carey was embarrassed. "You don't know that, Pearl."

Mrs. Carey was no match for her sister. The older woman relished telling Anna every tidbit she could think of. "Miss Petersen, do you know there's not a gas station in town can keep soap or toilet paper in the public restrooms? Letitia makes the rounds night and day, steals everything in the ladies' rooms and maybe the men's rooms, for all I know."

"Pearl, really now!" Mrs. Carey protested.

"She got so bad—she's worse when there's a full moon—Jack McClendon, you know, the policeman—Jack's told her any number of times to stay off the streets after eleven o'clock at night, but Letitia doesn't pay him one piece of mind!"

"Pearl!" her sister scolded.

"Sally Mae, there's no harm done. Letitia's a sick woman, we all know that." Pearl was momentarily distracted. "Oh, there's Cecil McCurdy! I think I'll go over there and see how Esther's doing, poor girl."

Mrs. Carey was ashamed of her sister. "Miss Petersen—"

"Please, Mrs. Carey, call me Anna, if you will."

"Very well."

"You don't have to explain anything, Mrs. Carey. I understand Miss Letitia had an illness of some sort that left her, well, affected."

"Well, I guess you might call it an illness." Mrs. Carey was hesitant. "They tell awful stories about Letitia. Most people don't remember her the way I do. We went to school together. When we finished Mr. Logan's school—you know, he's the schoolmaster they built the monument to—well after we finished Mr. Logan's school, we all went over to Martin's Creek to the female seminary there. That's where all the young ladies went to study Latin and Bible and, oh, yes, art." She smiled. "I guess you've seen those oil paintings in the homes of people my age? Deer or flowers—all done in dark colors and looking very European. Well, the teacher did most of those paintings. What the seminary was truly famous for was its music. Our teacher, Mr. Hugo, was a German and he had studied in conservatories all over the world. He was very strict, but Letitia just drank in everything he taught. I tried to but I didn't have the gift Letitia had. She became an accomplished musician. Of course, in those days girls didn't think of going on concert tours—that kind of thing—but if it were today, Letitia would be a concert pianist.

"Letitia was the prettiest girl I ever saw. Not just pretty, she was a beautiful girl. Even now she's very nice looking when she's fixed up, don't you think? She was the belle of the ball, as they used to say in those days." Mrs. Carey pressed her fingertips against her mouth, worried by the faulty fit of her dentures.

"And then she married Mr. Oakes—Victor Oakes. He was a successful farmer and bought cotton futures. They moved up in the social set of Southern Pines, Pinehurst. That's where all the Northern people come to spend the winter, you know. Letitia had beautiful gowns and jewelry. She fit right in with all those wealthy people.

"Then Mr. Oakes lost all their money and most of their land. When he died, he was penniless. It was very sad. We were all upset about it, but Letitia pitched in and started growing vegetables to sell—worked like a Trojan, she and her little boy."

Miss Pearl rejoined them and was quick to take over the conversation. "Oh, Miss Petersen, you should have seen Letitia when we came to town to sell produce. She had this old, beat-up tin lizzie, and don't you know there was no floorboard in it! The boys used to stand along the sidewalk and look under the car to see if her feet were showing." She was laughing. "They declared Letitia stopped that car with her own two feet!"

"Pearl! You shouldn't talk like that!"

" 'Pon my soul, that's what was told me. And, that's not all—they said she'd drive up to Pinehurst and go to the back doors of all those beautiful homes and sell vegetables to the cooks. Then, at night, she'd get all dressed up and appear at the front door as a party guest!" Miss Pearl cackled with glee.

Mrs. Carey was annoyed. "Pearl, well now, maybe we ought to talk about something else awhile, seeing all that happened so long ago."

Miss Pearl brushed aside the suggestion. "Let me finish, Sally Mae. Miss Petersen, when those socialites found out about Letitia, they dropped her like a hot potato! That's when she started acting queer. She stopped raising vegetables and went to taking things."

"You mean her mind snapped?"

"Something like that." Pearl leaned across her sister to speak confidentially. "Why, you know, Letitia has this little wooden wagon she pulls and she goes out about the cemetery at night and digs up all the flowers and shrubs, brings them home, plants them in her own yard."

"Now, Pearl, let's change the subject," Mrs. Carey insisted.

Pearl ignored her. "Remember, Sally Mae, how Letitia stole all that porch furniture? Went down to the beach in a truck and brought back a whole load of lawn chairs!"

"Now, Pearl, Letitia isn't to blame for all that. She's done very well. Her son turned out really well, and Letitia's well fixed. She deserves a lot of credit."

"I'm not denying all that, Sally Mae, I'm just telling Miss Petersen what I think she ought to know. There's no harm done. Letitia might frighten Anna some time. I've known Letitia all my life but if I looked out my window and saw her peeping in the way some people have, I'd die of fright! I've known her all my life, but when a person's sick the way she is you never know what they'll do."

Anna didn't want to hear anything more about Miss Letitia. "Isn't that Mr. McCurdy over there?" she asked. She had never seen anyone hitch up his pants like that except Roger.

"Yes. That's Cecil McCurdy. Fine looking man, isn't he?"

"Are his children here?"

"I doubt it. They're probably at home with Aunt Charlotte."

"Their aunt?"

"Aunt Charlotte's the colored woman. She looks after the children just like she raised Cecil and his sisters."

The supper was ending, and the women were collecting the silver, counting each piece.

Waldo was driving Anna back to the teacherage and to keep him off the subject of Josephine Marotti and the corpse, Anna mentioned Marge. It was a mistake.

"I'm through with that hussy," he said.

"Waldo, how dare you call her that!"

"That's all she is, Anna. Everybody knows she's playing around with a married man."

"Waldo, Marge is my friend and I don't—"

That made him really mad. "Not only are you a know-it-all, Anna, now you're a holier-than-thou. Well, lemme tell you one thing, you're walking on thin ice as it is. When I tell Ben about this Marotti woman he's going to ask me why she came to town, and when I tell him it's not going to set well with him. He carries a lot of weight with McCurdy and the school board."

They took a wrong turn. "Aren't you going the wrong way?" Anna asked. He didn't answer. They drove onto a dirt road. "Waldo, where are you going?"

He pulled over to the side and stopped the car. His arm went around her. "Anna." His voice was oily. "How 'bout going to the beach with me next weekend?"

"What?" She was furious.

"I won't tell," he whispered.

"Waldo, if you don't take me home this instant I'll get out of this car and walk!"

He yanked his arm from around her and turned on the ignition with force. Angry, he drove fast and recklessly. Neither of them spoke. At the teacherage Anna got out of the car and slammed the door behind her.

The nerve of him! Upstairs in her room she paced the floor, her temper blazing. *To think I could be so naive!*

After a while, when all the other teachers were in their rooms, Anna went down to the parlor to wait up for Marge. Hussy or not, Marge Penry was the one person in Scotsville she could talk to. Pawing through a magazine, she felt restless. What in the world's keeping Marge? She went over to the piano, sat down on the bench, and began playing softly.

When the clock struck midnight, Anna stopped playing. *Well, I might as well go up to bed. Marge might not come home until morning.* She twisted around on the bench and was about to close the piano lid when she was startled by a face at the window, a straggle-haired woman! Anna stared at her and the woman stared back. It looked like Miss Letitia!

Anna hurried to the door and opened it. "Miss Letitia?" No answer. "Miss Letitia, is there anything I can do for you?" Anna walked to the edge of the porch, close enough to touch the woman. "You were listening to the music, weren't you?" she asked.

The old woman's head bobbed once.

"Please, Miss Letitia, won't you come inside. I'd love to play for you. They're all upstairs. All the teachers are in bed."

Glancing about as if afraid, Miss Letitia hesitated. Then, without a word, she dropped the handle of a child's wagon and pushing aside the shrubbery, came up on the porch.

In the light, Miss Letitia did not look like the woman Anna saw at the church supper. The gray hair hung loose, the dark circles around her eyes gave her a haunted, wild look. In the parlor she looked frightened. Anna motioned for her to sit on the settee.

Anna returned to the piano and played "Claire de Lune." Miss Letitia's eyes were fixed on Anna, intent on the music. When Anna finished playing, she turned to look at her and Miss Letitia mouthed one word, "Brahms." It was a request.

Anna thought a moment and played Brahms' *Concerto Number One in D Minor*. She could feel the woman's rapture as some kind of magnetic charge in the room. When she finished, Miss Letitia spoke, "Bela Bartok," and Anna responded with another concerto. *Is this a test of some kind?* Anna wondered.

When the music ended, Anna turned and the two women smiled self-consciously at each other. "Miss Letitia, I have no one to accompany me on the cello. Would you?" It was a bold risk.

The woman shook her head. "Liszt," she said as if she were ordering from a menu. Anna complied.

At the end, Miss Letitia's cheeks were wet. She got up from the chair, motioned Anna to move from the bench. "Get your cello," she ordered.

Anna dashed upstairs to obey. Marge was coming in the back door. In the room, she asked, "What's going on?"

"Later," Anna answered and hauled the instrument down the steps, careful to be quiet.

Closing the french doors of the parlor, Anna tuned the cello and waited for Miss Letitia to state the piece they would play. "Mendelssohn's Sonata, Opus 45."

They played well together. The woman was all Mrs. Carey said she was, a gifted musician and more. They went from one selection to another without music, seldom faltering, and the woman's touch was as fluid as Vladimir Horowitz's.

Marge tiptoed down the steps and stood at the doors peeking in, not wanting to disturb. Anna saw her, too late to warn her. Miss Letitia jumped up from the bench mumbling angrily. Rushing past Marge, giving no heed to her profuse apologies, Miss Letitia hurried outside.

Anna followed her but the old woman was retrieving her wagon and not listening. Quickly, she disappeared in the darkness.

"Well, I never—!" Marge whispered.

# CHAPTER
# SIXTEEN

Clara asked Anna to ride out to the cemetery with her
to put a flower on Ted McGill's grave. "I don't see how
you raise all those lilies in your room, Clara."

"Not lilies, Anna, African violets. This is a Hawaiian
variety—see the blue stars and white edge?" The short
woman could hardly see over the dashboard and to
divert her attention to the plant was a decided danger.

"They're pretty."

"They're not hard to raise—just break off a leaf, root
it, and you have another plant." The car swerved as
they zoomed around a curve. Clara didn't notice. "Of
course, you mustn't water them too much or put 'em in
direct sun. I don't put chlorinated water on my plants—
turns the leaves yellow."

Clara roared up to a stop sign and put on the brakes
hard. When Anna recovered she asked, "Isn't all water
chlorinated?"

"City water, yes, but I keep a pot of water in my
room. Sometimes a bucket. After it sets overnight the
chlorine is evaporated."

Clara was driving down Bridge Road and when they
came to the railroad she looked both ways, then gunned
the car over the tracks with one jolt after another.

"Ted loved my violets. I used to have them in the
classroom on the windowsill. Matter of fact, he liked
the wild ones, and in the spring he'd pick wild ones
and bring them to me."

"African violets are indoor plants but they'll last a

while outside. Under the live oak they'll get filtered sunlight. Beetles and bugs'll eat 'em if Miss Letitia doesn't steal them first."

They had turned onto the dirt lane that led to Ted's grave. "Heard you playing last night," Clara said, craning her neck to see the road.

"Did I keep you awake?"

"No, but you know my room's right above the parlor. Who was that playing the piano?"

"Miss Letitia."

"That's who Mrs. Milligan said it was."

Another car was in the cemetery, parked under the live oak near the McGill plot.

Clara glanced out the side window and back again, nervous. "I hate to tell you this, Anna, but Mrs. Milligan didn't like it. She said to tell you there's been a lot of criticism about the teacherage lately and the town wouldn't like it if they knew Miss Letitia came there. People in town would say she was stealing all the furnishings they contributed to the teacherage."

"You can't be serious."

"Yes, I am. Scotsville people emptied their attics to furnish the teacherage, so they lay claim to the place."

Clara screeched to a halt behind the other car, turned off the motor. "That's not all they're complaining about. The married teachers say the single teachers are getting a supplement by living in the teacherage." She opened the door and was struggling to get out of the car. "Looks like Anita and Andrew standing over there."

It was. Anna didn't mind seeing Anita but Andrew made her uncomfortable. He was in Anna's history class now, and the hostility he had shown in eighth grade was intensified by what had happened since.

"I'm worried about Andrew," Clara said.

"Why?"

Clara was looking down, stepping carefully. Anna

watched Anita standing in the sun, her hair coppery, blowing in the breeze. Her heart ached for Anita. As she stood there in her wide flared skirt, the sweet blouse, bobbie socks, and saddle shoes, she couldn't help but think of the fantasies Sue Marie had described for Anita and Eddie. How little did they know that day—

As Clara and Anna drew near, Anita greeted them. "We're on our way to the lake."

Andrew nodded to Clara, then stooped down to pull weeds at the base of Ted's tombstone. Anita admired the violet Clara held.

Andrew made no effort to be civil to Anna. In the classroom, whatever confidence Anna had gained through teaching, Andrew destroyed with one thrust of his rapier intellect. He relished contradicting her. When she taught about Abraham Lincoln, Andrew called Lincoln a traitor to his own beliefs and quoted from the Lincoln-Douglas debate in which Lincoln said he was not in favor of bringing about social and political equality of the white and black races. "Lincoln said he did not favor making voters or jurors of Negroes, nor did he approve of their holding office or intermarrying with whites. He said coloreds are physically different— the white race superior to the black."

Anna had not rebounded from the blow before he thrust another. "Lincoln wanted Frederick Douglas to take all the slaves to an island off Haiti. When that didn't work, he wanted to give them a state."

Andrew spoke rapidly, his lips white and drawn tight against his teeth. He frightened Anna.

"Lincoln was not an abolitionist. When the Emancipation Proclamation came, Lincoln freed slaves in the Confederacy, not in the North. Abraham Lincoln is a Yankee hero, Miss Petersen. To us he's a traitor to what he knew was right."

Anna did not quickly recover but she fought back, trying to regain her role as teacher of the class. She did not succeed and the boy looked at her, smarting as she was, and the curl of his lip was cruel.

As Anna watched Andrew pulling the weeds, she tried not to show the resentment that she felt for him.

He stood up, tossed a handful of grass in the road and announced to Clara, "Miss Campbell, we're going to Granddaddy's pond." The breeze caught his hair and for a moment his striking features caught the sun in a way that heightened his forehead and cast deep shadows about the eyes. He was indeed a handsome young man.

Clara and Anna stood watching the couple as they walked toward the car. "It's his nerves," Clara confided. "Mrs. Lawton's sick about it. He's still having nightmares. They have to call Dr. Jennie real often."

"You'd never know it. He's a three-letter man in sports, quarterback in football, captain of the basketball team, and in the Honor Society. In addition he's very popular."

"Too popular," Clara added.

"What do you mean?"

"Oh, Anna. I shouldn't say anything but I worry so about Andrew. There's a sophomore girl chasing him and she's nothing but bad news."

Andrew rowed the boat to the middle of the pond. Anita trailed her hand in the water as the boat idled along. "Andy, why don't you like Miss Petersen?"

He made another stroke with the paddle then laid it in the bottom of the boat. "So you want to know why I don't like Miss Petersen?" He leaned back on his elbows and let the boat drift.

"I love this place. My granddaddy used to take me fishing here. We'd sit in this old boat and he'd tell me stories about the past.

"He told me about his father and his grandfather who

lived on this farm—the struggles they had with drought and floods, the boll weevil and all.

"He told me about the Yankees coming through here during the Civil War. My great-granddaddy heard the Yankees were coming and he had all this cotton he wanted to hide. He had five hundred bales and that's a lotta cotton to hide. Well, he got this bright idea of dumping it in the pond.

"See that place right over there beside the dock? My granddaddy told me that on that spot his daddy stood as a young boy and watched the slaves bringing the bales down to the water's edge. Floating them on a raft, they took the bales to the middle of the pond and dumped them.

"Then, after Sherman's men were gone and the war was over, cotton was very scarce. They drained the pond, dried the cotton and sold it for a big price."

Andrew let his eyes feast on the sweet shape of the girl's face. There was no way not to love Anita. Love was one thing, what he got from the fast girl in tenth grade was something else.

"You want to know why I don't like Miss Petersen? It's because I don't like Yankees. My great-granddaddy outfoxed them, but think of the poor suckers who didn't have a pond or the good sense to protect themselves.

"When I look at McCurdy and his family and think how they took advantage of poor suckers, it makes me hate them like I hate Yankees."

"But your father works for McCurdy."

"Sure. Who else could a corporation lawyer work for in Scotsville?" Andrew flung a stick in the water angrily. He didn't like it that his father worked for McCurdy. All his father had ever done was go up to Chapel Hill for a few years and as soon as his schooling was over, came right back to McAdden County. He could have gone anywhere in the world—he had the ticket out—but, no, he came right back to the snug security of all that was familiar to him. He loved being a big fish in a little pond. Andrew hated his father. More than Yankees or McCurdys, he hated Benjamin Lawton.

# CHAPTER
# SEVENTEEN

Anna awoke with a sense of impending doom. It was the day for singing "Goober Peas" in history class and she did not relish making a fool of herself in front of Andrew Lawton. As musical as she was, Anna could not carry a tune, but singing "Goober Peas" had become a tradition in U.S. History and every class looked forward to Anna's terrible rendition. If students remembered nothing else about the Civil War, they remembered the Rebel soldiers who survived on peanuts and sang "Goober Peas."

Perhaps the feeling of doom was begun the day before when the letter came from Helga asking for money. She needed twenty dollars a month if she stayed on in the retirement home.

Twenty dollars a month was more than Anna could spare if she was to buy a car, but she would send the money. It seemed ironic that Helga who had never worked a day in her life, who had made life miserable for Anna and her father, should expect a return on such a small investment of herself.

Helga was even indirectly responsible for the threat Josephine Marotti had brought into Anna's life. The IUPIMC was becoming a household word in Scotsville because of the publicity given the organization in the local newspaper. For months every issue of the *Scotsville Herald* carried an irate letter, editorial, or news item about the Noodles case. On the front page or wedged between the Baby Beauty Contest winners, the

Happy Birthday ads, the court docket, or recipes, were items from or about the Italians United for the Preservation of Italian Manners and Customs. The most recent threat from Josephine's Army, as it was dubbed, was a notice in the *Herald* that a delegation would be arriving in town Saturday to serve notice on one Peter Waldo McSwain, that he must turn over the body of one Vincent Luigi Costa to the IUPIMC or else face prosecution. In answer, there appeared a big picture of Waldo on the front page of the paper. In a statement made from the steps of the funeral home, Waldo was holding firm. "Over my dead body," he declared and then left for Florida on vacation.

Waldo had made it his business to inform every member of the school administration that it was Anna Petersen's connection with this "subversive group," as he called the IUPIMC, that brought all this trouble to Scotsville. Anna decided it was time to defend herself.

Before school she went into Mr. Secrest's office. He listened to her side of the story, then said, "Miss Petersen, I suggest that you talk with Mr. Gilchrist." Then, leaning back in his chair, pressing his fingertips together, he dropped a bombshell. "It may be that Mr. Gilchrist will ask you to meet the delegation Saturday since Waldo's not in town."

"Meet with the group? Oh, no, not that!"

"Why not?"

"Well, to tell you the truth, I could only stand with them in their cause."

Mark Secrest became serious. "That's where I would stand, too, if I could."

Anna dreaded the interview with Mr. Gilchrist. When she walked in his office, Horace was sitting in the waiting room. "What's the matter, Horace? You look like you've seen a ghost."

Horace shook his head.

"Mr. Wigglesworth," the secretary called, and Horace went into the superintendent's office.

Anna waited ten minutes, and when Horace came out he was still upset. Mr. Gilchrist patted him on the shoulder. "I'm sorry, Coach. Try not to take it so hard. These things happen."

Philip Gilchrist turned to Anna. "Miss Petersen, it's good to see you. What can I do for you?"

In his private office, Gilchrist removed his glasses, wiped them clean. He looked disturbed.

Anna mentioned the delegation and explained her relationship with Josephine Marotti.

"Miss Petersen, I don't know how you feel about this matter, but if anyone can get that man buried my hat's off to them. Despite all the vitriolic rhetoric in the newspaper, there are many people in Scotsville who feel as I do about Mr. Costa. His case is more than an embarrassment, it's a sacrilege." Then Mr. Gilchrist smiled. "The problem is, how do we handle Mrs. Marotti and her Army?" There was a twinkle in his eye. "You'll have to help us, Miss Petersen. The mayor's in Raleigh and the commissioners voted to abstain from this matter. Will you meet the delegation? Be their hostess, so to speak?"

"The delegation?" The bell was ringing. She had to get to class.

Mr. Gilchrist waved her out the door, chuckling. "You'll think of something!"

Going down the hall, Anna's head was spinning. She'd just as soon handle a live hand grenade as to handle Josephine Marotti.

But, for the moment, she couldn't worry about Josephine. Somehow she had to get through the singing of "Goober Peas." "Lord, help me," she prayed.

Anna cut short the preliminaries in order to get through with the singing as quickly as possible. Andrew's cold dark eyes never strayed from Anna's face as she sang lustily:

"Peas, peas, peas, peas,
Eating goober peas,
Goodness, how delicious,
Eating goober peas!"

As she sang, she walked up and down the aisles passing out peanuts. The students were laughing so hard they scarcely heard the seven verses that followed. "Sitting by the roadside, on a summer's eve. . . . "

Even Andrew smiled. Anita nudged him. "What do you say, Andy?"

The laughing subsided a bit. "I say any Yankee who has the nerve to sing 'Goober Peas' has got to be either brave or crazy. With a voice like hers she's both brave and crazy!"

The class howled and Anna with them.

Anna recounted the event to Clara, hoping to relieve the older woman's worry about Andrew. But Clara only shook her head and went about pinching wilted leaves from her plants. Anna was sitting in Clara's rocker and when Clara didn't respond, Anna remained quiet. Did the boy's nerves concern Clara or was it the sophomore girl?

"Excuse me, Anna," she said at length. "I have to go soak my bones."

"Oh, sure," Anna said, but when she got up from the rocker the chair tipped over a jar of water. "Good night! Look what I've done." Clara handed her a towel and the two of them mopped up the water.

"Is this the water you let stand overnight?"

"Yes. But I won't water the violets today. I'll just fill this jar again and water them tomorrow."

Anna got up from her knees. "Well, I'll see you later."

She had wanted to discuss the problem of Josephine with Clara. There wasn't much time to plan and Anna needed all the help she could get. She went downstairs and found Horace in the sitting room looking glum. "Horace, are you okay?"

"No, I'm not okay," he grumbled. "But I can't talk about it."

"Horace, could you help me with something?"

"Maybe."

"It's this Josephine Marotti thing. Mr. Gilchrist asked me to meet the delegation, serve as hostess."

"Meet the delegation? I'd meet 'em with tar and feathers. Who do they think they are, comin' down here tellin' us what we can do and what we can't do? All my life I've heard about Noodles and there's not a person in this county that don't know Noodles. What's so wrong with making a man a celebrity? Who'd know anything at all about him if he was buried under the ground? What's the sense in buryin' him now after all these years?" Marge was coming in the back door. "Ain't that right, Marge?" he yelled.

She came in the sitting room. "What?"

"Noodles. Anna's got to meet that bunch o' Eyetalians Saturday and she wants to know what she should do."

Anna followed Marge upstairs to their room and closed the door. Marge dumped her books on the bed. "Why you, Anna? Is it because you're the one she visited?"

"That and the fact that Waldo is out of town, the mayor is in Raleigh, and all the city commissioners voted to keep out of this."

"Whew! This is a biggie. We might as well stretch out—Clara's gonna be in that bathroom till suppertime." Marge flopped on her bed.

"The paper said the bus gets in about nine, right?" Marge asked. "And they'll stay overnight. Why don't you make arrangements for them to stay at the Gibson Girls'?"

"The tourist home?"

"Hm-mm."

"Those little old ladies wouldn't want a swarm of irate Italians in their place. After all, it's their home and it has all those elegant antiques and everything. We don't know who might be in this delegation."

"Don't worry. The Gibson Girls might look fragile but they're quite capable of taking care of themselves. In fact, they have a kind of added dimension."

"What do you mean?"

"It's hard to explain. They're aristocrats and all that, related to all the other old families, but they can accept people who're, well, different. It's funny. They're very Southern and the way they dress you'd think they were Queen Victoria's ladies-in-waiting, but they're, well, they're Christians. One of them was a missionary in Cuba most of her life and, well, they have something some churchgoers don't have. They'll treat the Italians well."

"Well, if you say so. Finding them a place to stay is a good start, but there's a lot more to this. I'll probably have to talk to this delegation—try to solve the stalemate."

Marge shook her head in dismay. "I'd hate to be in your shoes. If you satisfy the Italians you'll make Waldo mad. Waldo is a good friend, but he's a terrible enemy. When he gets back and learns you've taken sides with the Italians, he'll do everything in his power to pay you back."

"Marge, I know you're right but I'm in this now and I'll have to see it through. Let's get on with it."

They lay quietly, thinking. Then Anna had an idea. "What would you think of my calling the priest who serves this parish? Most Italians are Catholic and maybe he could help us."

"Maybe he'd say a mass for Noodles, burn candles or something."

"I don't know what he might do. Woodall should

know how to reach him." Anna got up and walked to the window, restless to get moving. "I don't know what we'll do with all those people for twenty-four hours."

"I know! Take them to the cemetery. Let them pick out a plot for the burial."

"That is, if there's going to be a burial." Anna wrote down the ideas they had come up with. "Marge, maybe we could have the delegation make speeches on the courthouse steps."

"Not on a Saturday. Too many people come to town on Saturday. There might be trouble." Marge stretched her arms overhead and yawned. "Why not have them make speeches in the Catholic church? It's very small and I've never known a Protestant to darken the doors. If they all talk as much as Josephine, the speeches'll take more than twenty-four hours!"

"Oh, Marge, I'm so nervous about this whole affair. What if—"

"You better go call the Gibson Girls and Woodall right away. Sometimes they book regulars—salesmen and all—with standing reservations. They might be full."

"Oh, Marge, I pray this all works out."

It did work out. Because it was a Saturday the Gibson Girls had not booked regulars. After a family "palavar," as they called it, they were agreed and excited about lodging the Italians.

The priest could not come to Scotsville but he gave the IUPIMC permission to use the church with certain restrictions.

On Saturday, Anna was up before dawn. With her Bible on her knees she prayed earnestly, then dressed and, without eating breakfast, went down to the bus station to wait.

After a while Woodall came roaring up in his beat-up Pontiac to help transport the delegation. Then Mr.

Gilchrist came and the cemetery salesman arrived in a brand new Lincoln. A young reporter from the Raleigh paper was on hand with a camera and the disconcerting news that the case had made the Associated Press.

Blacks, Indians, and poor whites crowded the little waiting room. They were quiet and curious, but harmless. Anna breathed a sigh of relief that no troublemakers were there. She preceded Mr. Gilchrist and Woodall outside to wait for the arrival of the bus. It was late.

Finally, it came roaring up to the station, charging like some enraged animal. Swinging open the door, the driver yelled, "All out for Scotsville," then, ducking his head, jumped down from the bus and bounced into the station as if he were running from something. Anna strained to see inside the bus, trying to find Josephine. Acting as tour guide, Josephine stood midway in the bus between the seats, shouting instructions. "Dun't forget yer parcels! Take it easy! Dun't push!"

Slowly the weary travelers were disgorged. As Josephine clambered down the steps, loaded down with shopping bag, sweaters, and newspapers, she was waving an umbrella. "Youse forgot the umbrella! Somebody listen! There's a umbrella heah!"

Seeing Anna, Josephine dropped everything, flung open her arms, and clasped her to her bosom.

"God bless you! God bless you!" And to the delegation, "Looka heah. This here is Anna, the one I told cha 'bout! She's a angel! Come 'ere, I want cha to meet her."

Anna survived the embrace, recovered from all the other hugs from the group, and turned to introduce Mr. Gilchrist and Woodall.

Most of the delegates were women very much like Josephine—talkative, using their hands, loud. The men were of the working class, awkward in suits and ties, broad-brimmed hats.

Mr. Gilchrist was ready to make his welcome speech.

Josephine, obviously thrilled to be in charge, pressed her finger to her lips and said, "Shush," to her Army.

"Welcome to Scotsville," he began. "We've arranged rooms for you in our most prestigious tourist facility. If you'll come right this way, we'll put you all in cars and be on our way."

Josephine took one look at the automobiles and asked, "Where's the limo?"

Anna didn't have to answer because there was a push to load everyone in the cars and Josephine had to secure her place on the front seat of the Lincoln.

The convoy motored down Cross to the Gibson Girls' Inn. It was an impressive old home with wide porches and steep gables. Roosevelt Carey, in his locomotive livery, stood on the porch ready to carry baggage. Together with the men, he carried all the bags and packages to the porch, then held out his cap for tips. Mumbling to himself, he counted the coins carefully and pocketed them.

The five Gibson "girls" appeared in the parlor to receive the guests. They stood all in a row according to age—Sister Maggie, Sister Lula, Sister Hortense, Sister Elease, and Sister Susan. They stood stiffly in a proper manner, hands clasped at their waists, heads tilted to one side. Their immaculate dress was matched by perfectly coiffured hair, tinted blue.

There were lengthy introductions before the receiving line dissembled. Miss Maggie proceeded to the desk to register the guests while Miss Lula explained the schedule. "As soon as you have freshened up, we will serve breakfast in the dining room. I suppose the proper word would be brunch but we're unaccustomed to anything but breakfast here. No lunch will be served but we will have an early supper at five-thirty."

Miss Lula tilted her head toward Miss Elease. "Sister Elease will explain the entertainment."

"Our guests are invited to hymn singing after supper and evening prayers. Perhaps, while we're waiting for everyone to register, Sister Hortense will favor us with a selection."

Miss Hortense nodded her acceptance and seated herself on the piano bench. With some aplomb she gave attention to spreading her skirt properly, adjusting her position so as to reach the foot pedals efficiently. Then she selected from the yellowed music book the song she would play. Strains of the *Blue Danube Waltz* filled the house. Josephine rolled her eyes at Anna then beckoned her to one side. "Come 'ere. Le's talk."

They squeezed into a corner and Anna began explaining the day's schedule. "After breakfast, we'll—"

Josephine interrupted. "We'll go to the funeral parlor and serve our petition to that low-life bum of a mortician!"

"No, Josephine, I'm afraid we can't do that. Mr. McSwain is out of town."

"Whadda ya mean he's outta town?" she yelled.

The newspaper reporter was at the door ringing the bell. Coming in with his camera, he looked toward Josephine. "Are you the leader of this group?"

"The same. Josephine Marotti, Joisey City, New Joisey." She was smiling broadly, her nose crinkled at the bridge. He raised the camera and she posed.

"I can't see nuttin' after that flash. What cha wanna know?" she asked him. "Ast me anything, anything you wanna."

The interview went on and on. The reporter could not get away from Josephine. She was pouring out details of the case with interminable tangents. The delegates had washed themselves, unpacked, and eaten a bounteous breakfast before Josephine let the man go. Only as the others were leaving to go to the cemetery with the salesman did Josephine tell the reporter, "I gotta go now."

Mr. Gilchrist caught Anna's eye and winked.

So, she thought, he approves. Big deal!

Roosevelt Carey was shepherding the delegates down the steps toward the automobiles. Opening each door, Roosevelt packed them into the cars and then poked his cap inside the windows for tips. The Italians were too busy talking to notice him—nothing he did caught their attention. As the cars pulled away from the curb, he saluted each one, standing at attention and thumbing his nose.

Anna, in Woodall's car, was third in the entourage. Woodall turned the key, the motor growled, and went dead. He tried again. Josephine, sitting in the front seat, was so busy talking she didn't realize what was happening. *It's just as well*, Anna thought.

One of the men got out of the car with Woodall, lifted the hood, and examined the engine. After trying one thing then another, Woodall getting in and out of the car, the engine fired. With a little puff of smoke, it got going loud and fast. "We're okay! We're okay!" Woodall shouted as the Italian ran to jump back in the car. Woodall gunned it and the Pontiac leaped forward. They were launched!

At the cemetery they had no trouble finding the group—before they saw them, they heard them. The Italians were red in the face, screaming at each other, arguing, waving their hands, crying. Josephine saw the situation immediately. No grave plot satisfied all participants in the decision. "Lemme out, lemme out!" Josephine bustled her way to the middle of the group, held up her hand, palm flat out requesting silence. Keeping her hand in an upright position, she held it there until absolute silence reigned.

Savoring their curiosity a moment, Josephine pursed her lips, closed her eyes, and announced, "Vincent Luigi Costa deserves the best!"

There was instant agreement.

Josephine allowed another moment to register their approval, then turned to the cemetery salesman. "Which one o' these graves costs the most?"

The weary man studied his clipboard, page after page, then went back again comparing. He looked across the graveyard, made his decision, and pointed. "That one right over there."

The Army followed Josephine who followed the man. At the plot, she asked, "You ain' got nuttin' costs more?" He shook his head. "We'll take it."

The salesman rifled through his papers, found a contract, and sat down on a headstone to fill it in.

As secretary-treasurer of the Jersey City chapter, Josephine signed the contract and wrote the check with the unanimous approval of the delegation.

That business finished, she asked, "And, where, may I ask, is the comfort station?"

"The what?" Woodall asked.

Anna ignored him. "We'll drive back to the Inn."

Roosevelt Carey was sitting on the curb when they returned, but he did not get up to open car doors. The Italians piled out and straggled up the steps. The Gibson Girls were lined up on the porch, each in a green rocker, each with a straw fan.

"I'm starved," Josephine announced.

"Perhaps you'd like a cup of tea?" Miss Maggie suggested.

"Tea, nuttin'. I need my coffee and anisette toast. You go make the coffee—I got the anisette upstairs in the shopping bag." She was going up the steps yelling back down, "Make it strong and make it black!"

The Army took turns in the bathrooms, milled around the downstairs looking at bric-a-brac collected by generations of Gibsons. But as soon as two of them were together, there was heated discussion. They were frustrated that Waldo was not there, that the funeral home was closed, that no city official had come to meet them.

Anna could feel tempers rising. "Could you play something?" she asked Miss Hortense.

Little Miss Hortense was happy to oblige and, with eyes closed, let her fingers caress the keyboard to the romantic strains of *Indian Love Call*. She was so enraptured, she sang the words with a voice that cracked, warbled, and gave out on the high notes. It did nothing to ameliorate the emotions of the Italians.

When Josephine's hunger was finally satiated, she bounced out of the kitchen with a full head of steam propelling her. "I'll make the gravy," she was telling Miss Lula. "Gotta go to the store but I'll be back shortly." She grabbed Anna's arm and pulled her close to whisper, "Nice ladies but they got no appetite." She rolled her eyes. "Finger sandwiches and chicken salad for dinner!" She glanced about the room. "Where's that Rev'rend? I need him to take me to the grocery."

With Woodall in tow, Josephine disappeared, leaving Anna to keep the lid on the situation. "Where's she going?" Mr. Gilchrist asked.

"To the store. She's going to make an Italian dinner."

"Do the Gibson Girls know about this?"

Anna nodded.

Mr. Gilchrist chuckled. "I doubt if they ever saw a garlic clove much less smelled garlic." He looked around. "I think we'd better circulate among the troops. Josephine's Army sounds explosive." Anna agreed.

By two o'clock, Josephine was in the kitchen preparing the ingredients for the gravy, as she called it. "I couldn't get none o' the right stuff. No bread. Youse got no bread in youse A & P here. Only white, soft, no crust. Why they got no bread in this town? And no wine, only soda. I look all ovah. What kinda crummy town you got heah, Anna?"

It was nearly four o'clock before Josephine finished in the kitchen. The Army dressed in their best to go to the church. When they arrived, they found the reporter sitting on the steps, his arms folded on his knees and his head on his arms. The Pontiac backfired and his head jerked up.

Woodall unlocked the church and Josephine herded the people toward the door. On such holy ground, Josephine held her tongue and used hand signals and facial expressions to give instructions. Understanding these communications, the women fished in their purses for handkerchiefs which they spread on their heads and, crossing themselves, entered the narrow door.

Woodall explained that each of them was invited to speak. "But first, Mrs. Marotti will read the petition and Mr. Gilchrist will receive and respond to it."

Josephine showed that she felt the gravity of the situation by the manner in which she cleared her throat and held a handkerchief to her brow. This was obviously the most important duty of her career and emotion choked her voice. "We, the members of the Italians United for the Preservation of Italian Manners and Customs, Local Chapter 63 of Joisey City, New Joisey, do hereby declare that one Peter Waldo McSwain is in violation of all that is legal, right, and holy in keeping the body of one Vincent Luigi Costa uninterred for a sum total of fifty-nine years and that his father and his grandfather before him were guilty of the same charge.

"We, the undersigned, do hereby declare that if the said person does not release the body of one Vincent Luigi Costa for burial by the Local Chapter 63 of the Italians United for the Preservation of Italian Manners and Customs, he will be sued in court and prosecuted to the limit of the law."

She read hundreds of signatures or more while the Italians sat ramrod straight, as united a people as Anna had ever seen.

Rising to accept the petition, Mr. Gilchrist bowed toward Josephine, thanked her, and pledged himself to carry out their wishes by presenting the petition to Mr. McSwain and to post a copy by special messenger to every city official.

Josephine interrupted. "May I ask if this here petition will be handled by Western Union or Postal Telegraph?"

Mr. Gilchrist was taken off guard. Then, with a twinkle in his eye, he replied. "Neither. The petition will be handled by special messenger only. Mr. Roosevelt Carey has been my personal courier for years. I wouldn't trust this document to anyone else."

Josephine beamed her satisfaction.

*Whew!* Anna thought. *Good thing she doesn't know who Roosevelt is!*

One after another of the delegation rose to read eulogies to the dead man whom none of them had ever known, but it was understandable that in their deep outrage they would do anything to restore the man's dignity.

When the speeches were finished, Josephine stood to announce the tolling of the bell, one toll for each year of Vincent Luigi Costa's life. Josephine explained, "Dun't nobody know Vincent Luigi's age but they think this deah mudder's son was twenty-five or so."

They stood with heads bowed as one of the men pulled the bell cord and counted twenty-five doleful dongs.

The mourners then walked out of the church in silence, wiping their tears.

The sun was setting as they drove back to the Inn and the faces of the Italians were dark with brooding rage. They could not be put off indefinitely. Anna did not know what more she could do.

When Woodall and Mr. Gilchrist deposited their passengers, they told Anna they must leave. "Think you can handle it?" Woodall asked.

. "She can handle it," Philip Gilchrist said and walked confidently down the steps to his car.

"Wait," she called after him. "Mr. Gilchrist, perhaps you should call Waldo, encourage him to talk to these people."

"I'll try."

The Inn smelled of tomatoes, herbs and spices—a delicious aroma! Josephine ordered Anna into the kitchen. "Come 'ere," she said, motioning with her head. Three of the Gibson Girls were standing at a respectful distance watching the sauce bubbling in a pot, their eyes wide with wonder. "No peppers, no nuttin'. None o' the right stuff," Josephine fussed. "I make do. Good cook can do that. It won't be my best but what can I do? It'll fill the stomach. Here, taste the gravy." She gave the sauce a stir, lifted a spoonful, blew on it, tasted it, smacked her lips. "Mama mia! That'sa good!"

Anna helped Miss Maggie set the table and arrange the chairs, and by seven o'clock the meal was served. Enormous helpings of spaghetti and sauce filled plates, and the Italians drank the Pepsi in good humor.

In the midst of the meal, the phone rang. Miss Lula answered. "It's a Western Union," she whispered. "It's from Waldo to the IUPIMC."

"I'll take that!" Josephine announced and took the phone. Holding up one hand for silence, she told the listener, "Josephine Marotti here, secretary-treasurer Italians United for the Preservation of Italian Manners and Customs, Local Chapter 63, Joisey City, New Joisey."

All eyes were on her as they sat waiting for the news. Josephine was nodding her head to the receiver as the telegram was being read to her.

Finally, she spoke. "Operator, I'd like youse to send me a copy of this very important message . . . . Yeah, I'm registered heah at the Gibson Inn." She clamped her hand over the receiver. "What's the name o' this street?" But before anyone answered, she was talking to the operator. "Youse'll send it right ovah? Know the place? Thank youse, operator."

Roosevelt Carey, sitting in the kitchen, grabbed his hat and went out the door.

Josephine put down the receiver and calmly faced the table. "Friends of the IUPIMC and members, our long struggle has not been in vain. Youse have labored long and spent much but—"

Even Anna could not stand the suspense.

"When youse is in the right, youse will win if only youse persevere. Am I not right?"

Quickly they agreed, hoping to hurry her up.

"Friends, it is my proud pleasure to announce to you that Mr. Peter Waldo McSwain has decided to release the body of our beloved Vincent Luigi Costa." The Italians went wild. Josephine held up her hand for silence but it was not easy to quiet them. "Mr. McSwain will set a suitable date for interment upon his return from Flowrida."

Whoops of joy rocked the room! They were hugging each other, kissing Gibson girls, laughing and crying at the same time! Someone collided with a Tiffany lamp, knocking it cockeyed. But Miss Lula waved it aside as nothing. They were intoxicated with joy.

Toasts were raised—first to the deceased, then to Josephine, to themselves, to Anna, to the Gibson girls—with one glass of Pepsi after another.

Not until the women cleared the table and sat down again for dessert did the revelry subside. Red in the face, they had just begun eating the fruit salad when the doorbell rang. There stood Roosevelt holding the telegram behind his back and his cap outstretched. The Italians rushed to the door, dug in their pockets for bills, not silver, and filled the cap with money. Roosevelt surrendered the telegram and busied himself counting his pay while the Italians toasted him.

Josephine opened the envelope, held up her hand to silence the hilarity, then read the telegram aloud. "It's true," she told them. "Now finish yer fruit."

They wolfed down the dessert, their excitement never waning. A florid-faced man, white linen napkin tucked in his collar, got up half way in his chair to announce, "Ladies, when the dishes are done, come in the parlor and we'll have some *real* music."

"Real" it was—arias from the operas. First a barrel-chested tenor singing *Figaro*, followed by *Pagliacci* and then, in chorus, they all sang the wedding march from *Aida*. They sang very well and kept singing on into the night.

The Gibson Girls were delighted—their house smelling of Italian food, their leaded windows vibrating with operatic music. Miss Maggie spoke for them all when she said, "Ladies and gentlemen, my sisters and I shall never forget this evening as long as we live. Thank you. Thank you very much!"

Miss Maggie's eyes were sparkling.

Josephine pushed back her chair and burped. "Youse ain't heard nuttin' till youse hear my Mickey sing that aria from Verdi's *La Traviata*."

It was one o'clock in the morning before the party ended. Anna walked home to the teacherage and fell into bed.

Sunday morning, after a breakfast of old ham, grits, and biscuits, the Italians piled their baggage on the porch and waited for the bus to pick them up. Anna was saying her last good-byes when the Gibson ladies, dressed for church, lined up on the porch to bid farewell.

When the last of the delegation climbed aboard the bus and the door was closed, Anna and the Gibsons were waving good-bye; the bus door swung open, and Josephine leaned her head out to shout, "Dun't forget to send the pitchu'es from the newspaper! And dun't forget when youse come to Joisey, gimme a call! We always got room for youse, Mickey and me!"

She blew them kisses, the door closed again and the Italians United were whisked away.

# CHAPTER
# EIGHTEEN

In the spring of 1959, Anna was seeing the end of the tunnel. At last she had mastered American history well enough to teach with some confidence. Her neatly-typed lesson plan book was in good order. On index cards she made notes on the books she read and added human interest anecdotes to the plans as she discovered them. There were students who, indeed, did love history.

The budget was under control. Although Helga required more money, Anna received an increment every year that kept her ahead of the wolf. The car fund contained two hundred dollars, much of it in pennies.

As for Scotsville, she knew she would never understand all the ins and outs of the way things were done, but she had grown to love the town and its people. With some exceptions, that is.

In a few weeks Andrew Lawton would graduate and as much as she hated admitting it, his leaving would be a relief. Try as she might, she had not won the boy over. It was a grief of mind to her. Worse, she could not make herself like Andrew. She was concerned about him, prayed for him, but she did not like him. It was not a good feeling.

Sitting in the dining room, waiting for the mail, she thought about the boy. No doubt he carried a lot of guilt about the accident. If only he understood the forgiveness that Christ would give him. Time and again when she prayed for Andrew she wished for the opportunity to talk to him. Of course, she was the last person he'd listen to.

Miss Pendergraft came in with the mail. There was only the Rutgers' alumni bulletin for Anna. She scanned it, looking for Roger's name. It was there—only a change of address. He was still in Denver but moved to a new residence. *Moving up in the world*, Anna mused. The twins were five years old.

Miss Pendergraft poured coffee and brought it to the table. "Anything interesting?"

"Not really. Alumni bulletin."

"It's hard to keep track of school friends. I sometimes wonder how close these McAdden seniors will be five years from now. Every class is the same, they promise lifelong devotion and cry buckets of tears at graduation, but no sooner are they in college than they forget. At their class reunions they're different people—most of them trying to impress each other with their money or position or degrees.

"They tell me all the old funny stories they remember about pranks and teachers and the ball games they won. Sometimes I think they laugh a lot to hide skeletons in their closets. Ten years after graduation they look back on all their wild escapades and they're ashamed."

"This class doesn't seem to have many skeletons in their closets. I think the accident sobered them. Losing two favorite classmates was a bad trauma for all of them."

"True." Miss Pendergraft rolled her tongue across her lips, her eyebrows raised. Anna knew the sign; there was something she wanted to tell. *Well*, Anna thought, *I won't encourage her. It can't be good.*

"True," Miss Pendergraft repeated, "but they have their skeletons."

Anna would not take the bait.

"I guess you haven't heard. It happened during basketball season. Remember how depressed Horace was?

He moped around for days about it and for good reason. The center on his team was in serious trouble."

Even though she was not a sports enthusiast, Anna knew the basketball center was Andrew.

Miss Pendergraft leaned closer and whispered. "Andrew Lawton got a girl in trouble." She paused. "They say she got rid of it—that Andrew paid fifty dollars and the girl went out of town to get the job done."

The woman was waiting for Anna to ask who the girl was. Instead, Anna stood up. "I'm sorry about that. Here, Miss Pendergraft, I'll take your cup to the kitchen."

"I'm not through with it. Neither are you. Sit down, what's the hurry? There's something else you ought to know."

"Well, I don't have time to listen, Miss Pendergraft."

"This is something you'd better make time for. It involves you and me and everyone in this house."

Anna would not sit down but waited to hear what she would say.

"The teacherage is going to close."

"How do you know?"

"Never mind how I know. The announcement will be made soon."

"Why are they closing it?"

"Criticism. Married teachers have always complained that the teacherage gives single teachers an advantage. When Clara bought a house and rented it out, they said that proved single teachers don't need to be given a place to stay. If Clara could afford to buy a house, she could afford to live in it."

"But that's not true. Clara's paying for the house with the rent; then, when she retires she'll have a place to live."

"I know, I know, but you can't make some people understand that." She drummed her fingers on the table. "And, people resent the pretty clothes some of these young teachers have. Not you, Anna. Tsk! I didn't mean that the way it sounded. But you know what I mean. Girls come here out of college and they still have their daddy's checkbook. They buy a lot of clothes to marry well."

"If this isn't the silliest conversation I've ever heard."

"Don't be so quick. It isn't all nit-picking. There are other things they're upset about."

"What kind of 'other things'?"

"The moral behavior of a certain you-know-who has tongues wagging all over town and if there's anything that gets people riled up, it's teachers who don't set a good example."

Anna took her cup to the kitchen and went up the backstairs to her room. Falling across the bed, she tried to think through the situation. *What'll I do? I'll have to find a room—have to eat out—maybe buy a car now. How am I going to do all that?*

Marge came in from the Laundromat. "Hey."

Anna rolled over and propped her head on one elbow. "Is it true, Marge? Is the teacherage going to close?"

"It seems that way."

Anna got up to help Marge fold her clothes.

"Boy! I wonder what we'll do?"

Marge stopped folding clothes and sat down on the bed. "Well, I have plans, Anna."

"Oh?"

Marge went back to folding clothes.

*Well*, Anna thought, *I guess that means I can't count on Marge taking a room with me or sharing an apartment.*

By the last week of school the news broke officially and residents of the teacherage were notified. It came as no surprise to any of them. The other teachers seemed better prepared for the change than Anna. Horace, sprawled on the upstairs couch, told them his plan. "Glad I got my Master's behind me. I been goin' to summer school all my life. Finished last summer. With a Master's in administration, don't you think Gilchrist'll gimme a principal's job? That way I can afford to get an apartment."

"You won't get a principal's job until Amy decides to retire," Miss Pendergraft told him. "If I know her and I know Gilchrist, she'll never retire. So, what if you don't get a principal's position?"

"I got a raise with the M.A. and coaches get a supplement. I'll teach Driver's Ed in the summer. I got it made."

"Where will you take your meals?"

"Down at Eleanor's cafe." Then Horace fired a surprise question at Miss Pendergraft. "What're you gonna do?"

"That's for me to know and for you to find out!"

Before the end of school, the whole town found out: Miss Pendergraft was retiring. Of course, it wasn't the first time she had retired and Horace said it wouldn't be the last time. Nevertheless, the town turned out for a testimonial dinner for her. Some of the former students who had made it big in the world came home to pay tribute. Sue Marie Ellsworth, who sang with a group aboard cruise ships, flew up from Miami to sing, "Till There Was You." She had grown into a stunningly beautiful young woman with a shapely figure. More than anything else, Sue Marie was poised and charming. It seemed miraculous.

Andrew Lawton, president of the McAdden student body, presented Miss Pendergraft with an orchid, whereupon she kissed him. Andrew, as suave as his father, was unperturbed by the silly woman. In fact, Andrew looked as if nothing could disturb him. Something of the luster had gone from his eyes, Anna thought; they seemed dull and gray. *Something must be going on inside him. Whatever it is, it's sucking the life from him.*

Mr. Gilchrist presented Miss Pendergraft with the customary Bulova watch and she kissed him. When Miss Amy, president of the NCEA gave her a life membership in the organization, Miss Pendergraft responded with a speech that lasted thirty minutes.

When she was finished, Marge muttered, "Boring!" Anna smiled.

The next day was Awards Day and, despite rain, the old auditorium was packed with relatives and friends come to see their young rewarded. As expected, Andrew carried away the highest athletic honors, two scholarships, and the yearbook hailed him as the Most Likely to Succeed, Best Athlete, Best Looking, and Most Popular.

At the end of the program, Mr. Gilchrist rose to speak. A rumbling of thunder made it impossible to hear him. Apparently he was introducing Mr. McCurdy, who walked from back stage to the podium. Standing there, he waited for the thunder to run its course.

"He's probably going to present the mill's scholarship," Marge said. She was straining to read the program in the dim light.

McCurdy was speaking familiar words. "Each year it is my privilege to make an award in which all citizens of Scotsville have a vote. Through the *Scotsville Herald* we conduct a poll to determine who shall receive the 'Young Teacher of the Year' award.

"To be eligible for this award, the individual must be thirty-five years of age or less. . . ."

Anna's fingers touched gum beneath the arm rest. "Uff-dah!" It was sticking to her fingers. Fumbling in her bag for a tissue, she wasn't listening, yet after McCurdy said the words, it dawned on her what he had said. "This year's award goes to Miss Anna Petersen."

The audience was on its feet clapping and Marge was trying to get Anna to stand up. Marge finally took her by the arm and pulled her to her feet. Pushing her into the aisle, Marge laughed. "Watch out, Anna! Don't fall flat on the steps!"

Anna was in a state of shock. All she could think about was how awful she looked. On the steps she was very careful. McCurdy was watching her coming across the stage. In her mind she was trying to remember to reach for the plaque with her left hand and at the same time shake his hand with the right.

Her "Thank you" was lost in the din of applause. McCurdy nodded, stepped back from the podium, yielding it to her. The people continued applauding and Anna was shaking from head to toe.

When the applause died down and people sat down, she spoke. "What can I say?"

Someone was walking out on stage. It was Sue Marie with red roses. She put her arm around Anna's waist. "I'm going to sing for you." Stepping to the edge of the stage, she spoke to the audience. "Join me on the chorus," and immediately she started singing:

"Sitting by the roadside, on a summer's eve. . . ." The audience roared! By the time the chorus came around, they gave a thunderous rendition:

"Peas, peas, peas, peas,
Eating goober peas,
Goodness, how delicious,
Eating goober peas!"

Anna was laughing so hard tears rolled down her cheeks.

When all the stanzas were finished pandemonium broke loose—clapping, whistling. Anna didn't have to speak: the people poured onto the stage, crowding around to congratulate her. In the midst of it all, by chance she glimpsed Cecil McCurdy standing in the wings, a certain smile on his face. When he caught her eye, he did not turn away.

For some time people milled about the auditorium

waiting for the storm to slacken. It was twenty minutes before Anna was able to slip out a side door and retreat to her classroom. There she could pull herself together, calm down, and gather up her things.

As she straightened up her desk her hands were still shaking. *I can't get over it,* she thought. Me, *teacher of the year!* She looked at the plaque again, rubbed it against her sleeve. *I can't* believe *it!*

The thunder had rolled farther away, the rain had slowed. Anna went to the window to look out. The traffic jam was over. A few stragglers were leaving the building, jumping puddles, covering their heads with their programs. Anna watched the retreating clouds. At first she didn't see it and when she did, she caught her breath—a rainbow, a *double* rainbow was spread across the sky, from one side of town to the other!

Her eyes blurred. "Oh, Dad," she whispered, "I made it! I made it! . . . I hope you know."

# CHAPTER NINETEEN

By the time school was out, the teacherage was vacated. Horace had a room in North Scotsville, Clara moved into her house, Mrs. Milligan (who inherited the television) went to live with her daughter, and Marge was packed up to leave for Georgia.

Only when they were standing by Marge's car, ready to say good-bye, did she confide in Anna. "Harry is developing offshore island property in Georgia and he's giving me a job. Harry says he'll teach me the business and by getting in on the ground floor I'll make some money."

"Oh, Marge. Sure you're not chasing rainbows?"

Marge smiled. "I'm sure. And just you wait. Your ship's going to come in, too, Anna."

"Sure."

"Checked your robot stock lately?"

"No. Last time I looked it had fallen another two points."

"Don't worry. I've never known Harry to lose a bet." Marge spoke without enthusiasm and there was a sadness about her that made Anna ask, "Are you okay?"

Marge didn't answer right away. She threw her raincoat over the back of the seat, straightened up, and faced Anna. Her violet eyes were misty. "No, Anna, I'm not all right."

Anna touched her arm. "Marge, is there anything I can—"

She shook her head. "Just say a little prayer for me

now and then." They embraced and Marge climbed under the wheel. "Don't worry about me, Anna. It's what I want to do. Thanks for all the good times." Marge started the car, looked up at Anna, and tried to smile. As she drove out of the parking lot, Marge did not look back.

Anna stood in the yard reluctant to go back inside the empty house. She had never felt so alone.

Philip Gilchrist asked Miss Pearl McCabe if she would rent Anna a room and she said she would. The only trouble was, Miss Pearl lived a mile from McAdden High.

Horace came to move Anna from the teacherage and as he was carrying her stuff to his car, he argued. "You gotta buy a car, Anna. You're gonna have to eat every meal out—you got a lotta stuff to carry back and forth to school, in all kinds of weather. How much you got in that penny bank?"

What Horace didn't realize was the biggest problem of all. Anna had to go to summer school to renew her certificate. The nearest school was Beaver Indian College, thirty miles away. She had asked around to see if she could ride with someone, but no one from Scotsville was going on the same days her classes were scheduled.

"Horace, I can't afford to buy a car."

"You have to."

Reluctantly, Anna agreed.

Horace checked the car lots and when he found a '57 Chevrolet that he thought was a good buy, he took Anna to see it. She carried the down payment, much of it in pennies, in a cloth bag. Horace haggled with the salesman and got the price down as far as he could, then told Anna, "Buy it."

The salesman took them into his office to draw up a contract. "Who's gonna co-sign your contract?"

"You mean I can't just sign for myself?"

"Not without collateral."

"Aw, come on," Horace argued. "You got the car as collateral."

"I gotta have a co-signer. Don't you know somebody owns property?"

"I'd co-sign for you, Anna, but I got no credit. How 'bout Clara? Clara Campbell's got a house."

"I couldn't ask Clara."

"Well, I can!" Horace said and picked up the phone.

In a few minutes, Clara's old Buick came bouncing into the car lot, headed for the plate glass. Just before crashing through the showroom, it halted.

Anna tried to thank Clara for signing the note. "I'm happy, happy to do it," Clara said over and over again and Anna believed she meant it.

As Horace gave Clara an enthusiastic run-down of the Chevrolet, Anna was thinking. *Where will I get fifty-seven eighty a month for the next two years, especially during the summer when I'm not working? Not working and going to school besides!*

When the two of them came back, congratulating her on her prize, Anna smiled. "There's one other minor detail I haven't worked out. Friends, I can't drive!"

"You mean you bought a car and you can't drive?" Clara asked.

"That's right," she said cheerily.

"Aw, anybody can learn to drive in a couple days," Horace said. "Come on. Clara, I'll drive Anna's car over to Miss Pearl's and you follow us. Then you can bring me back to get my car."

When they arrived at Miss Pearl's the Gibson Girls were sitting on the porch in rocking chairs, enjoying the breeze and chit-chat. As Horace opened the door for Anna, the gabbling stopped and the ladies craned their necks to see Anna getting out of the car. Horace yelled, "Come see Anna's new Chevy!"

The ladies had nothing but good to say about the car. Miss Pearl said it was a pretty green; Mrs. Carey said her husband always drove a Chevrolet; Miss Lula liked the interior, and Miss Hortense said the car looked roomy. The others nodded their enthusiastic approval.

Clara's Buick came charging up the street. As she tried to park she ran over the curb and down again. Getting out to join the admiring group, she announced, "I'm going to teach Anna to drive."

Miss Pearl was astonished. "You mean to say you bought a car and you don't know how to drive?!"

"That's right."

The ladies twittered. Miss Pearl turned to her sister and repeated, "Sally Mae, she bought a car and she doesn't know how to drive!"

Mrs. Carey smiled. "Anna, don't you think we should give the car a name?"

"Good idea," Horace said. "Let's have a christening. We oughta have champagne to launch this ship right. Miss Pearl, you got some Pepsi or somethin' in the house?"

"Yes, Pearl," Mrs. Carey said. "Don't you have some ginger ale in the ice box?"

The ladies chatted good-humoredly while Anna was trying to think of a name. Finally, she came up with an idea. "Since I saved so many pennies to buy this car, how about calling it 'Penny Slowpoke'?"

"Perfect!" They all agreed. Miss Pearl was coming, bearing the bottle of ginger ale.

Horace solemnly declared, "Penny Slowpoke be thy name," and Anna poured the ginger ale over the radiator.

The ladies applauded.

During the next week, Anna learned what it was going to be like living in Miss Pearl's house. There were advantages—a private bath and linen service. There was more privacy than at the teacherage. Still, she missed Marge and the others.

Marge was due a letter and Anna decided she'd better write before she started summer school and became too busy to write.

*Dear Marge,*

*I've bought a car! It's a green '57 Chevy and I've named her Penny Slowpoke. Surely, you know why.*

*I'm living in a room at Miss Pearl's. I wonder if Philip Gilchrist placed me here where so many maiden ladies congregate because maiden ladies have STANDARDS I'll need to have if I'm to be a proper spinster. Standards such as the proper length of skirts and when to come in at night. These ladies sit on the porch and 'rock around the clock'!*

*Rooms in these old houses are all alike, aren't they? Remember the Gibson Girls' Inn? Well, this one is like that place. The bed has a headboard six feet high which leans toward the footboard. If ever the bed collapses there'll be no escape.*

*The vanity has drawers that defy human strength. When you finally wrestle one open, you're in a heap in the middle of the floor. Then you discover that the drawer has fallen apart and you're frantic to get the thing back together again before SHE walks in.*

*Because SHE does walk in at the oddest times— like when I'm trimming my toenails.*

*In rooms like this one, if they don't have purple tulips on the walls with Persian rugs on the floor, they have green walls, red drapes, blue rugs, and yellow bedspreads.*

This house was built before they discovered closets but instead of a wardrobe such as we had at the teacherage, I have a chifforobe. One side is for hanging and the other side has drawers which smell like a rat palace. The chifforobe has all sorts of secret panels and clever racks for men's hats. It's plain to see it was designed for thieves or for the very rich. A person like me would be a fool to hide my Norwegian bracelet and high school ring in it because I'd forget which panel to slide and lose all my valuables.

Of course, the room has a fireplace. On the mantel is an orange vase and a built-in candle holder with a hurricane shade. Remember Hazel? They do.

Above the candlestick is a gold-framed picture of sheep grazing, and on the far wall a five-and-dime picture of a yellow rose. There's also a brown-toned picture of a moon-eyed maiden leaning against a shield—or is that Sir Lancelot? Beside that masterpiece is a poem expressing the sentiments of, you guessed it, friendship.

A marble top washstand is in the corner and I'm lucky, there's no cracked pitcher and basin on top! (Why do people want old stuff when they can buy new for even less?)

The bathroom plumbing is also antique. I haven't yet discovered what to pull up for what and how long to wait until. . . .

I eat out. Eleanor's Cafe is the best place in town and it's cheap—fifty cents for dinner. But Eleanor caters to menfolk. She either doesn't like women or she doesn't like Yankees and since I'm both, I stay clear.

Let me know how you're doing.

Love,<br>
Anna

Clara taught Anna to drive on the way to and from Beaver Indian College. The lessons were not without risks. There was something about letting out the clutch that Clara had not mastered and this resulted in jerking that threatened to snap their necks. Anna's first driving lesson was: "Now, when I start the car, slump down in the seat so your head's against the back of the seat. If the car jerks, you won't be yanked, only bounced."

Anna learned that lesson fast and survived without whiplash.

Clara, so short she could not see over the hood, drove either in the middle of the road or on and off the shoulder. Fortunately, the road was not well traveled but, even so, Clara ran a tractor in the ditch, grazed a mowing machine, and sideswiped a row of mailboxes all in one day.

In two weeks, Anna had her license. Clara refused pay for the driving lessons and seemed to sense Anna's financial stress. With a car payment, rent, Aunt Helga's allowance, gas, and food expenses, Anna needed more money.

Clara had a suggestion. "Anna, you know that area behind the courthouse where a lot of colored people live? They call it the Bloody Bucket. Well, every Saturday, people rummage clothes and stuff down there. Why don't you go through your things and see if there're things you want to throw away and we'll take them down there Saturday and sell them."

Anna was dubious but she was also desperate. Going through her wardrobe, she picked out everything she could spare and Clara pinned prices on them. Anna was disappointed at the low values Clara placed on her possessions, but she didn't say anything.

When they arrived at the Bloody Bucket, tables and clothes racks were already set up and the colorful array looked like an Arab bazaar. Women and children, dressed in faded, worn clothing, idled among the tables and racks. A thin, sunburned woman caught Anna's attention. The woman's sandy hair was pulled straight back and knotted in a bun on the back of her neck, giving her a severe look. The woman had to be younger than she looked because her children were small. On one hip she balanced a baby sucking a pacifier, and a toddler clung to her dress. An older boy trailed behind her. Anna smiled at the woman, but her workworn face was expressionless. With her free hand the woman brushed back a strand of hair from her forehead and blew at a hair about her face. Timidly, she looked at Clara. "Ain't choo Miz Campbell?"

"I am, and I taught you in second grade, didn't I? Now, what's your name?"

"I'm Brenda Homer now. Used to be Brenda McIntyre."

"Well, I remember you. You sat in the third seat from the back on the second row."

The woman was pleased. "I just come down here to see what they got. Gotta get thinkin' 'bout Billy here goin' to school come fall." She jiggled the baby, wiped the drool from his chin. "I can't believe dat dar young'un is old enough to go to school." The boy was picking at the baby, teasing. "I got two more girls at home nearly big as me. I was lookin' to find them a little somethin' to wear to church. They're good for goin' to church." A bit of pride sounded in her voice. "If I can't find nothin' down here I reckon I'll have to go up to McCurdy's Store. They give mill hands a fifteen-percent discount, but prices in dat store bees too high even wid de discount."

"Could your girls wear anything Miss Petersen has here?"

Clara held up a skirt. The woman eyed it up and down. "Hit might fit Daisy. She's got right smart hips. I heered her say she wanted a skirt."

"Well, you can have it for fifty cents."

The woman thought about it some more. Then she set the baby on the ground while she fished in her pocket for the money. The baby began crying as the woman was counting nickels and dimes in Clara's hand. Anna couldn't look. *This is awful*, she thought. *Taking that poor woman's money for a skirt I can't possibly wear.*

After the purchase was made, Clara introduced Anna. The woman nodded. "Well, I guess we better be gittin' on. Daisy'll be tickled to death to git this here skirt."

Anna couldn't stand it. "Brenda, I'd like to—"

Clara interrupted her. "Brenda, if the skirt doesn't fit, you call me."

Anna was aggravated with herself. When the woman was out of hearing distance, she said to Clara, "I can't do this. I can't take money from these poor people!"

"You'd take more than money from Brenda if you didn't let her pay. She's had a rough life, but Brenda would be hurt if you offered her charity. She has her pride. Do you want to take that away from her, too?"

Customers were arriving in droves, some on foot, in wagons, in old broken-down trucks and cars. People were swarming all over Bloody Bucket.

Across the way from their table, sitting beneath a patio umbrella, was one of the ladies from the Thursday Afternoon Book Club. Dressed in a wide-brimmed Panama hat, sunglasses, yellow sun dress, and sandals, she looked like a fashion model. "That's one of the McCurdy sisters," Clara told her. "She's here from the thrift shop the Junior Service League runs. What they don't sell in the thrift store, they bring here."

"Which sister is she?"

"Henrietta Standridge. She's Malcolm Standridge's wife. He travels a lot. Their children are in private schools and he has business interests in Spain, so Henrietta's involved in all kinds of charitable work. She's built a home for alcoholics—oh, there's Elijah."

An old Negro man with a woman and a wagon load of children was inching his mule through the crowd to a spot under a tree. When the wagon came to a stop, the woman and children piled out while the man took his time. He was crippled and moving seemed painful for him. Slowly he looped the reins around the limb of the tree and stood unsteadily.

Regaining his balance, he leaned on his cane and shuffled toward them. The overalls he wore were clean but much too large for his spare frame.

"That's one good colored man," Clara remarked. "He's worked for my family all my life. Papa gave him a little house and several acres of land. It's just a field house but he and Aunt Fanny made it home for a passel of children."

"G'mawnin', Miz Clara," Elijah said, lifting his hat, his eyes averted.

"Good morning, Elijah. How are you?"

"Tol'able, tol'able. Hot weather good for rheumatiz."

"I know. My arthritis isn't nearly so bad now as it was last winter. What brings you to town?"

Elijah chuckled. "I just brung all dese chuldrun to town for de day. Fanny, she need to come to town."

"Elijah, this is Miss Anna Petersen. She teaches at the high school."

He tipped his hat, nodded his head.

"Tell Miss Petersen who these children are, Elijah."

He chuckled. "I don' rightly know wheah dey all comes from. They's grans and great-grans. Fanny could tell you. Some of 'em is strays. Dey folks all up de road." He looked around trying to find them. "Dat talles' one, he bees my boy's baby. Dat's my boy wuz killed in service, Korean War.

"Dat gull ovah deah, she belong to my sustah's daughter and dat little light-skinned un, he jes' come home wid my grans and he ain' nevah lef'." The soft creases in his face showed no stress or strain but rather, contentment. "Me an' Fanny al'ays has a house full. Don' know how we'd make do widout dem chuldrun. Fanny, she jes' lay down and die." He leaned heavily on the cane and moved his lips, thinking upon it. He slapped at a fly pestering his face. There was a lull in the conversation as if each waited for the other to speak.

"Miz Clara, would you min' steppin' down to de chinaberry tree?" he asked.

Clara followed the old man to where the mule stood dozing in the shade. Elijah was rubbing the mule's nose and talking to Clara. In a few minutes, Clara came back to the table, got her pocketbook, and went back to Elijah. Elijah was patting the mule's neck and talking to him as Clara fished in her pocketbook. Anna watched her hand Elijah some money. He nodded his thanks, then slowly began counting the bills. Wetting his thumb he rubbed the bills between his fingers making sure they didn't stick. The fingers of his knobby old hands were stiff. Satisfied, he folded the bills and stuffed them in the pocket of the overall bib.

Clara came back to Anna. "Elijah's light bill is due," she explained. "He'll work it out. Of course, he's getting too old and crippled to do much but he does yard work and in the spring he plows gardens. Papa taught us to take care of our Nigras. Elijah's very deserving."

"What about the children's parents, I mean their mothers and fathers who live 'up the road,' do they send money to support the children?"

"Oh, Elijah's children are very good about sending money. But the others, well, most of the other children don't have parents—they have mamas who have boyfriends and some of those women dump their children on Elijah. Then it's 'out o' sight, out o' mind.' They stay in New York 'up the road,' they call it—and never lay eyes on their children."

"Why don't the women marry the men? Why don't

they make them support the children?"

"I don't know. The men act like they have free license. That's why there's so much disease and affliction among Nigras. A man has first one woman, then another; when the babies come, those children don't know they're related. One lives in Bloody Bucket, the other one across the creek; they grow up and can just as easily marry each other or have children by one another as not. Anna, it's a mess."

"You know what I think? I think this business of not getting married is related to slavery. Isn't it true that when the black people were brought over here the slave masters expected Negroes to produce children like farmers breed cattle? In other words, they weren't expected to marry, just produce children."

"I never thought about it that way. Maybe you're right."

An Indian family was strolling toward them. The woman was fat, the man brawny, the children were strong and half-naked. Their faces were expressionless but their eyes were big and brown as if full of wonderment. They did not speak or touch anything but their eyes examined everything on the table. They moved on without buying.

"Croatans," Clara remarked. "Only now they want to be known as Lumbees or Tuscaroras."

A Negro woman with a string of ragged children trooped through the rummage area picking over the racks of clothes. As the children passed a group of men eating watermelon, they stood and watched them. The men were squatting, holding long slices of melon in their hands. They took big bites of the luscious red fruit, the juice running down their chins, and spat the seeds on the ground, ignoring the hungry children. The children's eyes never left the men until the melons were devoured and the rinds tossed in a can.

The mother was separated from the children when Roosevelt Carey came along, attracting their attention. Roosevelt danced for the men which made the children giggle, covering their mouths with hands to hide their teeth. When he was done, Roosevelt held out his cap for donations and frightened the children when they did not pay.

The mother came back, rounded up the children, scolded them, and resumed her search through the racks. As the brood filed past Anna's table, she couldn't stand it any longer. "If it fits, take it," she told the mother. The woman looked back at her, questioningly. "That's right," Anna insisted. "If you can use anything on this table, you're welcome to it, free of charge. I'm ready to leave and I don't want to take anything home."

Without a word, the woman gathered up everything on the table, heaped a pile of clothes in each child's arms, too excited to speak.

As the woman hurried away, she looked back over her shoulder and she was grinning broadly.

Clara was understanding. "Well, we might as well go home."

"Clara, if I disappointed you, I'm sorry. I seem not to have the stomach for this. I never saw such poverty before."

"You haven't been at the right places. It's all over, Anna."

They were folding up their chairs. A thin little girl in a dress that hung like a sack was looking up at Anna with sad eyes. "Wait a minute," Anna told Clara. Looking at the little girl, she reached in her purse and found a dime to lay in her palm. The child's face brightened and without a word she ran to her mother, held up the dime, and explained her good fortune.

"Well, Clara, it looks like I'm a fizzle at this." They were trying to back Clara's car out of Bloody Bucket.

"I don't know what else I can do to make money unless I advertise for music students. Do you know anybody who might like to take cello lessons?"

"No, but it's worth a try."

The *Scotsville Herald* ran the ad two weeks before there was any response, then David McBryde appeared at Miss Pearl's door asking for Miss Petersen.

David was fifteen, musically inclined like his mother. "I'll take you as a student on a trial basis," she told him. "Please don't invest in an instrument until you're sure you enjoy the cello enough to pursue it."

"Oh, Miss Petersen, I'm dying to learn how to play. When the ad first came out in the paper, I started begging my dad to let me take lessons, but he thinks I've got too many irons in the fire as it is. It took a lot of persuading. Finally, he said, 'All right. If you don't neglect your chores.' So, here I am. Dad said he'll rent an instrument for a while."

David took to the cello so rapidly, Anna found teaching him a pleasure. When he asked for two lessons a week, she granted them. Payment for the lessons paid half Anna's rent; still she was having a hard time making ends meet. She reminded the Lord of all his promises to provide. She scrutinized the *Herald's* ads but to no avail; she applied for part-time work at McCurdy's Department Store without success. As she lay awake worrying, she kept thinking about the undernourished, sad people she had seen in Bloody Bucket. *If I can't get a job it's no wonder those poor, uneducated people are out of work. How in the world do they live?*

Miss Pearl put her mind at ease. "Oh, they're making plenty of money right now. They're working in tobacco or loading melons and cucumbers. Even Mr. Wigglesworth is working in crops now. He's crew chief for McCurdy's Seed Corn Company. They're detasseling corn. It's hot, dirty work but it pays well."

The answer for Anna's financial problem came the

next Sunday when Miss Pearl laid the Raleigh paper before her door. Listed in the classified ads was an opening for a book salesman. As much as she hated anything in the world, Anna hated selling encyclopedias, but for the rest of the summer she did and earned enough to keep body and soul together. But that was all.

# CHAPTER
# TWENTY

Andrew Lawton, in his second year at Duke, celebrated the presidential election by getting roaring drunk. In fact, since he was away from home, he was never far from a bottle. Wine steadied his nerves, kept the fears at bay, and he was making his mark at Duke despite the jitters. The young President Kennedy gave Andrew confidence that a new day had dawned on the world. The torch was passed. Republicans were out of the White House.

But in April that confidence was shattered. Hearing the news on campus, Andrew ran back to his room and switched on the television. Standing before it cursing, impatient for the picture to take form, he could hardly hear the voices of the nervous reporters for the crackling noises of a poor reception. They were prattling the news of the Bay of Pigs assault. Kennedy had called off the air support and confusion reigned.

Andrew felt the alarm like a blow to the solar plexis; he couldn't breathe. Easing himself into a chair, he didn't take his eyes off the screen as one report after another was made—conflicting reports—all tentative, nothing confirmed.

Muttering to himself, Andrew cursed the President. *The fool! He's playing into their hands. The commies'll make propaganda out of this that'll ruin us.*

As the day wore on, his anxiety accelerated. There was speculation that Russia would retaliate. A wild frenzy was churning inside him. He could not hold on—

the fear drove him, careening out of control! He jumped up, blackness threatening to engulf him. Blindly he stumbled to the phone in the hall. Dialing the number, he panted for air. *Why don't they answer!*

While the phone was ringing, Andrew forgot where he was. "Where am I?" he screamed.

His father answered. Andrew was sobbing. "Come get me," he whimpered.

His father asked him something but Andrew dropped the receiver and ran screaming down the hall. Hurling an ash tray through a window, he smashed everything he could get his hands on.

At least that's what the nurse in the infirmary told him he had done. Dozing, he was only vaguely aware of the restraints that bound him.

The next time he roused, his parents, standing by his bed, were blurred in his vision. His mother was whispering. "Benjamin, do as Dr. Jennie advised. Let Andrew go to a sanitarium. He needs professional help."

Lawton ignored her. Seeing Andrew awake, he spoke softly. "It's going to be all right, son. Dad's going to take care of you."

Andrew closed his eyes.

"You've been driving yourself too hard. It happens to a lot of boys. Duke's a tough school."

The soldiers were swarming around him and the woman was holding up the blue suede shoes, smiling at him. Not smiling, grinning. A whiff of blood caught in Andrew's nostrils. The fool woman was *grinning*. They were coming toward him! Andrew managed to grab his father's arm and, clutching it, dug his nails in the flesh. Through clenched teeth he demanded, "Get me loose! Get me loose!" He could taste the blood.

But his father wrestled his arm free. Terrified, Andrew thrashed from side to side until he was exhausted. He lay moaning while his father spoke. "Son, you need a rest. What would you think of taking a cruise—travel some place?"

The uniformed men were marching toward him, surrounding him. He couldn't breath! Anna Petersen stood smiling at him. Screaming, he strained against the straps that held him. A woman in white was leaning over him, pressing a needle into his arm. He fought until he had no more strength to fight.

When the crisis was over and the doctor said he was well enough, Andrew traveled to Spain. "Be sure you look up Malcolm Standridge in Madrid," his father had told him. Andrew ignored his father, scorning the mentality that believed if you knew the right people you'd be taken care of.

The streets of Madrid were jammed with revelers celebrating St. Isidro, their patron saint. Billboards were splashed with advertisements of contests, concerts, bullfights. Andrew pushed his way through a street festival to the *Cuevas de Luis Candelas.*

Sitting in the smoke-filled tavern, Andrew hardly noticed the swirl of dancing gypsies' skirts as he drank his wine. Sticky from the heat, sweat rolling down his chest, he watched a woman working the crowd, sidling up to men, picking their pockets, offering her favors. She was a hard-faced woman with slits for eyes. Dark and thin, she flashed yellow teeth between the red gash of her lips and laughed low in her throat. When she came to Andrew's table, she leaned against him, rubbing her cheek against his chest and murmuring in Spanish words he did not need to hear to understand. He had learned them all from the sophomore girl. The woman smelled of strong perfume and oil; her eyes were animal-like, like the cat's eyes, green with yellow slits—all seeing. The memory of the cat in the garage loomed in his mind ominously—the cat twining around his leg, sitting on his chest, staring down at him, its tail moving back and forth. He flung the woman off him, got up and stepped over her. The woman was screaming epithets after him as he stumbled into the street.

That night, lying in his bed, Andrew forced the woman and the cat out of his mind. He would think of Anita. In the whirlpool of anguish in which he lived, Anita was the vortex, the stabilizing center. Remembering the soft sound of her voice helped him. Remembering the silken feel of her hair, he yearned for her.

A shot—or something like it—sounded in the street, then another! Andrew jumped to the window. Fireworks were crackling in rapid succession like machine gun fire; explosions of red and orange sparks burst in the sky, popping, whistling!

Looking down on the street, he saw Franco's soldiers in the dim light of a street lamp. He wet his lips. *I've got to get out of here!*

The next week Andrew was aboard ship cruising the Mediterranean. There was little that interested him on the ship but he swam every day and lay in the sun. The jitters kept threatening him but, for a price, the ship's doctor gave him shots that more than eased his nerves.

Climbing out of the pool, Andrew towelled his face and hair and headed for the shower. He was anxious about his wallet. *I must be paranoid,* he told himself, *but you can't trust these people.*

The wallet was where he had left it. He felt in it for the penny. *There, there it is,* he said, relieved. Then he checked his money, his papers, and pictures.

Later, lying in the deck chair, he felt for the wallet in his hip pocket. Not satisfied that it was there, he slipped it out, removed the penny, and studied it. Rubbing its surface did nothing to polish the dullness, yet he rubbed it as he always did, making it warm in his palm. He examined the date and the face of the Indian. The strong profile and feathered headdress made him smile. The Croatans back home were far removed from that Indian image. He fished for another penny to compare the two. The face of Lincoln, as much as he despised him, drew another smile from Andrew. How easily he had bested Anna Petersen with the facts about Lincoln. How remarkably vulnerable she was. She was, by all accounts, a good-looking woman and she was smart, but she was unaware of either factor. That was why she was no match for him.

Andrew squinted against the sun glittering on the sea. In the warmth of the sun, floating as he was, it was hard to think of Anna Petersen as any kind of threat. He would forget about Miss Petersen and think again of Anita.

Remembering the day on the pond, the shimmering reflections of the trees so like the trembling fears he had felt, he could hear the bumping of the paddle against the sides of the boat. Andrew closed his eyes and tried to hear the cawing of the crows and the cooing of the doves, but he was seeing one bubble rising to the surface and all he could hear was Anita asking, "Andy, why don't you like Miss Petersen?"

Suppressing the turmoil, he gave himself pleasure by thinking only of Anita—her hand in his, the smell of her cologne, her thick chestnut hair, her eyes the color of a green sea. In her arms he felt loved. *If Anita were here*, he thought, *I wouldn't need the shots. Anita could lead me out of this hell.*

All evening Andrew thought of her. Sitting in the bar, he made up his mind. The next day, on the back of a postcard, he wrote: "Anita, I love you. Will you marry me?"

# CHAPTER
# TWENTY-ONE

David McBryde chuckled to himself as he walked down
the street lugging his cello. He enjoyed thinking about
the humorous situation at Miss Petersen's each time he
took a cello lesson. It took his mind off the fact that
his father would not let him drive the car, much less
own a car of his own. His father's penchant for making
David understand that privilege was not given to indulge
oneself nor one's children but a responsibility for which
meticulous accountability would be required was a burden David sometimes chafed under. But going to Miss
Petersen's for cello lessons eased the burden.

What amused him was Miss Pearl. Miss Pearl did
not like their music and made no bones about it. In
their long sessions after supper, Mrs. Carey came over
from next door to hear them play, but Miss Pearl sat
in the kitchen nursing the anxiety the music caused
her. To Miss Pearl it was dreary and depressing.

Not until they saw Miss Letitia at the window did
Miss Pearl come out of the kitchen. Then, determined
not to let Crazy Letitia threaten her further, Miss Pearl
took up a vigil at the window and every night stared
into the blackness, daring Miss Letitia to show her face.
To David it was comical and every time he thought
about it he laughed. What Miss Pearl did not realize
was that Miss Letitia was looking in another window
on the other side of the room. When Miss Pearl made
the discovery she went all to pieces and told Miss
Petersen she would have to move.

The Widow Carey took Miss Petersen in and the arrangement was much better because Mrs. Carey had a baby grand piano which she let them use to accompany each other. It also meant that Miss Letitia could come inside and listen as long as she liked or join them, playing the piano while they played their cellos.

None of David's friends could believe the stories he told them about Miss Letitia, and it excited him to be privy to the strange woman's company.

But playing the cello did not make David popular with his peers. Indeed, it made him the object of their jokes. Well, he was used to that. All through school he had excelled in everything he did and it was no wonder that many of them disliked him. He couldn't help it yet he regretted that he had to cope with all their spite. In second grade he had made up his mind not to let anyone dampen his enthusiasm and no one had. He was enthusiastic about almost everything. Everything, except sports. Not being sports-minded in a town of fanatical McAdden fans was another cross he had to bear.

In Floyd Berry, David met an antagonist more formidable than ever before. Floyd was a big strong Indian, notorious for fighting and wild escapades. Large for his age, he had the added handicap of being two grades behind his class in school. Not that he was dumb—not for one minute did David think him dumb—but because Floyd lived on a farm he didn't start school in the fall until the crops were laid by, and in the spring he stayed out of school for plowing and planting.

David could understand why Floyd loathed him. David was born with a silver spoon in his mouth—with a keenly musical mother and a successful father. When David wanted to please his father, he helped him build a harpsichord; when Floyd wanted to please his father, he jumped in an ice-covered pond in February or drove a truck thirty-six hours straight hauling watermelons.

In 1962, they were the last of the war babies and though they had a common spawning, their destinies did not appear to have common ends. David had read every volume in the town library on military history and he owned dozens of books on the subject. Floyd had never read a book. David aspired to be a cellist even though Miss Petersen told him, "David, there's no percentage in playing cello. You have the gift but a musical career is, at best, speculative." David thought about many possibilities. John F. Kennedy, in David's opinion, was the greatest man who had ever lived, and David often fantasized about himself becoming President and speaking immortal words such as Kennedy did.

Floyd had no ambition. If he was qualified for anything it was prize fighting because he practiced on everyone who offended him in the least degree. Or, so the scuttlebutt had it. David knew that sooner or later he and Floyd Berry would have a show-down. "He doesn't like me, Miss Petersen. Someday he'll corner me and I'll have to fight."

"He'll win, won't he?"

"Win? He'll *kill* me!"

"I doubt that. Can't you prove you're his match some other way?"

David pondered the possibility. As he sat in study hall beside the windows, he observed Floyd sitting on the front row to the right of him. The rest of the students had gone to the library. As he looked at Floyd he was thinking about himself in the role of a general in the army, the Army Chief of Staff, with men like Floyd Berry in his command. *How would I win the respect of troops like Floyd?*

Floyd was talking with Miss Petersen and David began listening, hoping for a clue, some indication of a way in which he might prove himself worthy of Floyd's respect without fighting.

"Ain't choo nevah et cooter?" Floyd was asking Miss Petersen.

"I don't think so. What's cooter?"

Her ignorance made David want to laugh.

"It's a turtle. Got the taste o' seven meats."

"Seven?"

Floyd nodded.

"Well, how do you cook them?"

David smiled. Miss Petersen was coaxing Floyd to talk. Floyd, like many Indians, never talked in any other class, too ashamed of his dialect. Chances were Floyd had a crush on Miss Petersen. Sometimes David thought he was in love with her, too. He had never met a woman like Miss Petersen. Unlike his mother who knew all the ins and outs of social maneuver, Miss Petersen was well-mannered but as transparent as glass. She could not be manipulative if she wanted to be. With her, something was right or it was wrong; no equivocation, no vacillation. He liked that but he wondered if her practicality had not limited her. There was no doubt in David's mind that Miss Petersen could have been a professional musician—even a composer—and his mother agreed. Yet Miss Petersen was content, even caught up, in being a high school teacher.

David couldn't understand it. He was champing at the bit to get on with his life—leave Scotsville, make his mark in the world. In fact, he was headed in more directions in one day than most of his classmates considered in a lifetime. Let his mother suggest medicine and his mind would go racing in that direction, or let his father show him a book on archaeology and immediately he wanted to go on a dig someplace.

"Fust, you gotta cotch de cooter," Floyd was saying. "In de spring o' de year, de females come outta de watah to lay eggs. Dat's a good time to cotch 'em. Some of 'em weigh thuty, fo'ty pounds. Or you cotches dem on trot lines wid a big chunk o' bait hooked on. De bes' kine bees a big snappin' turtle like so." He measured with his big, worn work hands. "Now to kill dat tu'tle you gotta coax 'im outta dat shell."

He got up and went to the blackboard. With a piece of chalk he lightly sketched the outline of the underside of a turtle shell. "Dis here bees de cooter. You takes a stick and poke hit at 'im like so. Fust thing you know, dat cooter bite de stick and when he do, you takes a'hold and snatch his haid outta dat shell an' cut it off like so." He sliced the air with his hand.

"To clean 'im, you throw him in watah hot 'nough to peel back de skin. De legs and neck bees white meat. Dey be bes' cooked parboil fust if they bees big or tough. Den you stew or fry 'im. Some people steak fry 'im or you kin stew 'im wid vegetables. Best eatin' you evah et. Taste o' fish, beef, pork, lamb, chicken—anything you want."

Amazed, Miss Petersen's mouth was half open.

David ventured a question. "Floyd, did you ever eat possum?"

"Many a day. You kin buy all de possums you want in Beaver County, ten cent apiece. I seen a man singe the hair offa a mama possum and all de little possums run around like they 'uz on fiah. He took a broom and kilt 'em."

Floyd nonchalantly picked his teeth and thought on the matter. "Bes' eatin' I know is frog legs. All you hafta do is skin 'em and pan fry 'em. Or crayfish. Wade 'round de river wid a seine and cotch 'em, throw 'em in a pot, boil 'em and you got yo'se'f a feast. Jes' break off de tails and dip 'em in butter what's melted. I kin eat a peck o' dem any day."

He kept picking his teeth and, without looking at David, remarked, "But I reckon as how a boy plays cello wouldn't cotton to nuttin' like dat."

"No, I wouldn't," David said honestly.

It wasn't what Floyd expected from him. "An' why

not?" Anger showed in his dusky face.

"In the first place, I never lived in the country so I don't know anything about stuff like that. In the second place, I have a weak stomach."

Floyd came up out of his desk ready to fight. Miss Petersen pushed back her chair. "Floyd, no! David meant no offense. He only spoke the truth. Can't you bear the truth, Floyd?"

The boy towered above Miss Petersen and stood looking down at her, torn between his admiration for her and his urge to hit David.

"Sit down, Miz Petersen, and I'll tell you what de truth be," he said.

After she sat down, Floyd folded his arms across his chest and began. "When de likes of dat lily white Scot come here, my people was waiting to welcome 'em to dis country. We wuz livin' in houses good as dere's, speakin' English an' fahmin' wid ways Englishman fahmed."

Miss Petersen interrupted. "What do you mean, speaking English?"

"I mean English, like I be speakin' right now. Me an' my people don't hab no other language but dis here one. We be Indians but we don't recolleck no other language, no other way o' talkin' but English."

"Then you must be descendants of those first settlers—the lost colony."

"Might be. We tuck dere names and dere ways but de strong blood ob de Indian race won out. We bees dark complected wid dark hair and we bees strong o' build and limb. I kin whup any white man alive and my sustah can whup mos' any white man." Floyd thumbed across the room to David. "My *baby* sustah can whup 'im."

"I don't doubt it," David said and laughed.

Floyd couldn't cope with David's defense. "Boy, you

got too many smarts. When I gits my fill of 'em I'll bust you one."

"Now, Floyd," Miss Petersen scolded. "You aren't going to *bust* anyone."

"See if'n I don't. That sissy-britches is scairt of his own shadder. When I gits through wid him he'll know what a man's about."

The threat worried David. Indians did not make idle threats.

Miss Petersen stacked papers on her desk. "Floyd, I wonder if you'd be interested in a yard job? Miss Campbell's yard man died and she needs help."

"You mean Miss Clara Campbell what failed me in second grade?"

Miss Petersen nodded. "Miss Campbell teaches second grade."

"I got me a job but I reckon one more won't hurt none."

"What kind of a job do you have?"

"Chasin' chickens."

"Chasing chickens?"

He nodded. "Chasin' half-grown game chickens in de attic of de old McCurdy building."

"Chasing chickens?" she repeated.

"Guess you wouldn't know 'bout dat. Dem chickens is against the law."

"How can a chicken be against the law?"

"Ma'am, dey fights 'em. Man gibs me a dime apiece for cotchin' 'em to sell. He don't have no part in fightin' 'em, jes' raises 'em."

"In an attic? In town?"

Floyd nodded. "Ol' McCurdy Building."

"Above the judge's office?"

"The same."

"What a place to raise chickens!" The bell was ringing.

David had an idea. Following Floyd out the door he asked him, "Floyd, I've never been to a cockfight. Would you take me?"

Floyd glared at him. "What makes you think I'd take you anywhere? You don't want to go to no cockfight. Yer yallar liver won't take hit."

"Aw, come on, Floyd. I'll show you I can take it."

"It's the likes o' you to run to the cops."

"I swear I won't tell anybody."

Floyd stopped in the hall, looked down at David with contempt. "You swear?"

"I swear."

"Not yer daddy? Nobody?"

"Nobody. I swear."

"I'll let cha know."

There was very little in the library about cockfighting and David was curious, as curious as he had ever been about anything. He hounded Floyd for information. At first Floyd was reluctant to talk but David followed him to Miss Campbell's where he was clipping a hedge.

"All I could get out of the library was stuff like cockfighting was the sport of kings and how it came from Asia thousands of years ago, stuff like that. What I want to know is how you train a rooster and what's to see when you go to a fight."

He reached for the clippers and took over cutting the hedge. Floyd stretched out on the grass. "So all your fancy books don't tell you what I been knowin' all my life. Ain't dat a switch! I'm gonna tell you what you need to know, but fust, get one thing straight. You don't talk rooster fightin' no place. You dumb cluck, you ast me all them questions in the lunchroom with people walkin' all aroun'. You ain't got biddy brains. This is man's talk and it ain't fer outsiders, you understand?"

The clippers were already making a blister on David's hand. He stopped working and sat down beside Floyd.

"So you wants to know how they's trained. You don't

train 'em. You worm 'em, delouse 'em, then you check dere backs, dere legs for three weeks." Floyd pulled a toothpick from his shirt pocket. "You give him so many flights on a runnin' board. Dat board's two feet wide and six foot long. Thataway you build up his muscles. He's trained like a boxer. You throw 'im up in de air tills he learns to lan' on his feet. When you get through wid him you kin throw 'im up on that car ovah yonder and he'll stay right there. He won't fly off—jes' walk roun' and roun'.

"Chickens got sense. People think chicken ain't got sense but all God's creatures got sense." Floyd worked over his teeth with the toothpick. "They's plenty stuck on theyse'f, too. When dey's moultin' dey don't wan' nobody see 'em. You pick up one o' dem roosters when he be moultin' and he squawk like a hen! But long 'bout de middle o' de wintah, dey strut dey so purtty. Some o' dem birds bring ten thousan' dollars at auction. My granddaddy sent all de way to Washington to git 'im a Black Indigo Stag. My uncle he got greys and he got reds, but de purtiest chicken I evah seen were a Lacy Roundhead. My granddaddy bred dem and Butchers, too.

"I useta go down his place long 'bout sunset to look at dem chickens. In de long slant o' de sun dey feathers glisten like dey was silk. Dat beady eye look out at choo like some kind o' king, wid dem long collar feathers splashin' down 'roun' his neck like cream. De breas' be orangey to wine color, claret dey calls 'em—de tail feathers curved way up an' fallin' roun' red an' gold, ripplin' in de sun. Dey is a sight to behold and dey knows hit."

"What about the fights? What're they like?"

Floyd's face took on an impressive seriousness. "When you go to a rooster fight you ain't goin' to, what I mean, eat hamburgers—you goin' to win the money." He flipped the toothpick over the hedge. "You got dat rooster in yo' arms like so. De referee feels de gaff, see if hit's okay."

"What's the gaff?"

"Hit's a steel blade put on where de spur ort to be. You cuts off de spur and de gaff go ovah de nub. Dere's all kinds o' gaffs—bayonet, slasher, jagger—razor-sharp."

"Where do they fight?"

"Mos' any place. In a barn, some place like dat. There's three pits 'bout sixteen foot wide—three, four foot deep." Floyd picked at the yellow calluses on his palms. "Evah chicken go by number. Let's say your number bees eight. They call out, 'Eight.' You go to the rooster house and get 'im weighed. Weighed up to de ounce. Dem chickens is matched to de ounce. Then you takes dat rooster to de main pit. You have him in your hand like so. Then you hold your rooster's head close t'other rooster's head; put 'em close together, head to head. Dere feathers rise up roun' dere neck. Dey get flustrated then, high tension. You hold 'im in your hands right under dere wings—let 'em fly at each other, maybe peck at one another. Referee say, 'Set 'em down!' You never turn dat rooster aloose till referee tell you to. He say, 'Pit!' and you turn 'im aloose. Time dey buckle it might be over. Dat's when dey go together. Mos' of the roosters is body type now, body slammer but I seen many a rooster go fo' de haid—peck out de eyes, de brains.

"But dem body slammers, after 'bout ten or twelve minutes, if your rooster gets cut up or tired, then you takes 'im over to de drag pit. He fights right on, only he ain't got as big a area, what I mean, to have to run an' fly. They jes' more or less fight till dey die. Sometimes dey give up and quit."

"If they give up, what happens?"

"That depends. Sometimes dey ring dere necks. Good bred rooster, though, sometimes quits if it's too hot. Most owners takes a wounded rooster home and feeds it bread an' buttermilk. Dat gets all de poison out uv 'em. In two, three days, he be okay."

"Well, Floyd, what's the fun of all that?"

Floyd spit between his feet. "Hit's a sport like any other sport. Dere's bleachers dere just like at a ball game. Watching dem high breakers go at each othah—dat brings de crowd to dere feet such as you ain' nevah saw at no ball game—that is, if you evah been to a ball game."

"High breakers?"

"Some o' dem chickens break five, six feet offa de groun'. When them body slammers light into each other it can all be ovah in seconds. Used to be they peck about the head 'stead o' goin' for body parts but them chickens is smart. A good rooster'll win you a pile o' money."

"Aren't you afraid of getting arrested?"

"Man, there's highway patrolmen, U.S. marshalls, all kinds o' law enforcement officers at rooster fights. They enjoy 'em same as me. It's all on de up and up. You ain' supposed to be drinkin', nuttin' like dat. You take a little sip and keep yer mouth shut inside dem buildings."

Miss Campbell was knocking on the window pane to get Floyd's attention. "Dat woman's the kind o' woman makes a man feel like he ain' a man. I don' need her tellin' me I ain' workin'. She so stingy she don' half pay me no how. I got a good mind to quit." Getting up from the grass he went back to clipping the hedge. "Sure you wanna go through with this?" he asked David.

"Of course, I'm sure."

"I'll let cha know."

# CHAPTER
# TWENTY-TWO

Anna sat in her room with her foot propped up, waiting for Anita McGill. Some student had stepped on her toe and bruised it. While she waited she went through the mail, opening Marge's letter first.

> Dear Anna,
>    Intelligence in a cat is to be admired especially so when it is used in self-interest. The little one from next door whom I've half adopted has worked out a plan: she scrambles to the transom over the back door. There's a ledge there where she sits and peers at me through the window. At these times she wants in to eat and enjoy companionship.

*This doesn't make sense,* Anna thought. *Why would she write to me, of all people, about a cat? This doesn't sound like Marge.*

The letter continued:

> Right now the cat is in. Oh, by the way, her name is Jewell. I don't particularly want her visiting. I don't want the responsibility. But, it's happening. Something's developing.
>    Besides, Anna, she's Mary Belle's cat. To take her as my own would be stealing.
>    Now she's sitting in front of the air condition vent cleaning herself. What can I say? Maybe

*the friendship is predetermined. You would
know about that. A great love we can't deny.*

*I'm trying to convince us both she's just a
visitor! She's just a visitor!*

*Love,
Marge*

Anna folded the letter. *Never a word about herself.
Nothing about the real estate business. Nothing about
Harry. And writing about a cat?* Anna shook her head,
bewildered. Chicora Pendergraft was right. Marge Penry was a mystery. But more than a mystery, the letter
was disturbing; Anna felt concerned.

*Maybe she's just being silly,* Anna decided, and in
the few minutes she had before Anita came, she dashed
off a silly response on a postal card.

Going back to the mail, she read a postcard from
Lester McKenzie. "One more year in seminary," he
wrote, "then the chaplaincy. Betty says she'll marry me
when I'm through school. You'll love her, Miss Pete."

So, she was "Miss Pete" now. Anna smiled and
looked down from the window to see if Anita was coming.

A car was parking behind Penny Slowpoke. A slow
drizzle filtered through the magnolia as Anna watched
the girl put a paper over her head and dash up on the
porch.

Mrs. Carey showed Anita upstairs to Anna's room.
Anna greeted her with a hug. "Home for the weekend?"

"Only for the day. I came especially to talk with you,
Miss Petersen." She smiled. "Took a chance, didn't I?
Oh, what's wrong with your foot?"

"Someone stepped on it at school. Happens every
once in a while."

Anita smiled. "We always admired you for wearing
high heels. I see you still do."

Anna laughed. "Well, yes. I have this perverse vanity about my feet. But you didn't come here to talk about that."

Anita grew quiet. "I need advice." She slipped off her shoes and curled her feet under her on the chair.

How uncomplicated she was—so like Ted.

"It's about Andy Lawton."

The name struck dread to her heart.

"I guess you heard—last spring Andy had something like a nervous breakdown. Ever since, he's been traveling. He's in Europe someplace, and he's due home soon." Anita's clear green eyes held a sadness too grave for one so young. "He wants me to marry him."

Anna waited.

"Well, you know Andy helped me when Ted and Eddie were killed. I'll always be indebted to him for that." Her voice faltered. "I guess Andy and I understand each other better than most people. . . . He's not an easy person to understand, Miss Petersen. He suffered more than anyone and if there's anything I can do to help him, I'm willing."

"You mean marry him?"

She didn't answer. "Oh, Miss Petersen, every time I hear anything about him, he's troubled. Everybody thinks Andy Lawton can handle anything, but I know better. The trouble with Andy is he keeps everything inside. He keeps things even from me. . . . I think he's drinking too much."

Neither of them spoke for a while.

"Do you love him?"

"Miss Petersen, how do you know if you love somebody? I care about him. I care a whole lot."

Anna waited, putting the words together in her mind before she spoke. Absently watching the rain falling softly on the magnolia leaves, she thought of Roger and what it meant to love him.

"Anita, the only reason for marrying anyone is

because neither of you can live without the other." Her voice threatened to quaver. "You might love Andy or he might love you but if either of you is not sure, don't risk marriage."

"But how do you know it's love?"

Anna studied the falling rain before she answered. "Love is putting the other's welfare above your own."

"Then I love him, Miss Petersen!"

"Then the question is, does he love you?"

"He must. He asked me to marry him." No sooner did she speak the words than she realized their fallacy. She dropped her head.

In the silence that followed, Anna could hear the vacuum cleaner running downstairs.

Anita looked up. "Andy's mother keeps calling me, crying, begging me to help him. Miss Petersen, Andy's coming home next week and I have to give him an answer. I'm afraid if I say no, he'll go off the deep end."

"Do you think Andrew loves you the way you love him, Anita?"

"Andy's too sick to put anybody ahead of himself right now. He wants me; isn't that enough?"

"Anita, I can't tell you what to do. I only know that it takes two people loving each other to make a marriage and a home."

The girl stood up, walked to the window. "Oh, Miss Petersen, I want to do the right thing. My parents expect me to finish school and I want to, but if anything happened to Andy I couldn't live with myself. Do you understand?"

"Well, Anita, if you marry Andy and it's not the right thing for him, won't that be more damaging?" The girl listened but didn't reply. "Two wrongs do not make a right."

Anita turned from the window. "You never liked Andy, did you, Miss Petersen?"

Anna paused. "No, Anita, to be perfectly honest with you, I never liked Andrew."

"But you care for him." She moved toward Anna, sat down on the edge of the bed. "I know you care about him. I can see grief in your eyes right now as we're talking about him."

"Yes, Anita, I care. It's very frustrating. He never gave me a chance, you know."

"I know that. I'm sorry. If you knew Andy as I do you'd understand. Oh, Miss Petersen, I want to see Andy made whole again! I want to see him the way he was before the accident. I want to help put him back together again. I don't know anybody else who can do it!"

"You're wrong, Anita."

She looked at Anna questioningly.

"Only Christ can put Andrew back together again."

Anita turned away. After a while she spoke, her voice so low Anna could hardly hear her. "How can you say that? I saw Ted give his heart to Christ. I saw the wonderful changes it made in his life but then God took him. When Ted was killed my faith was shaken and I'm not sure what I believe." She sat down on the bed again. "I might have gotten over feeling this way but in college I took a course in New Testament that made me think differently about the Bible and everything. The professor is a wonderful man, very intelligent, and he showed me how naive I was. He debunked everything I had ever believed, and I think I go along with his philosophy. Love is the key in Christianity. If someone needs love, what's so wrong about giving it? I'd live with Andy but it would hurt my parents. If I marry him, they won't like it but at least I won't disgrace them."

"But marriage—"

"Miss Petersen, you know I love and admire you, but it seems selfish to insist on love from both marriage partners. Perhaps we'll grow to love each other the way we should, but for the time being we may just have to make do."

"Anita, I hate to see you start out that way."

"You're still thinking the Ten Commandments and all that, aren't you?"

"Yes. The Ten Commandments and all that."

Anita began to cry. "Oh, Miss Petersen, I'm so mixed up. I know you're right. In my heart, I know you are." She blew her nose. "I have to go."

Anna followed her to the door. The girl turned and hugged her. "Say a little prayer for me?"

Anna nodded.

# CHAPTER
# TWENTY-THREE

David McBryde was late for his cello lesson. Standing on the curb, he threw out a thumb to a passing motorist. The car pulled to a stop and David hurried as fast as he could with his instrument in tow.

After he was in the car he wondered if he had made a mistake. The man looked like a beatnik. Then he recognized the tall rangy frame of McAdden's famous quarterback, Andy Lawton.

"I'm David McBryde," he said and stuck out his hand. It was ignored. "My daddy's the commissioner. You're Andy Lawton, aren't you?"

Andy was listening intently to the radio commentator.

"I'm a junior," David continued. Still no response. The radio was sputtering the news about the Cuban missile crisis. "Didn't you win the district from Beaver County for us? Didn't you run a long touchdown or something in the last few seconds of play? I remember hearing people talk about it."

Andy wasn't listening. When the news was over, Andy, speaking in a low, guttural voice, growled, "You know they're going to get us, don't you?"

"Who? Beaver County High?"

Andy looked angry, his face white and taut. "The Russians, you fool! The Russians are going to bomb us. They're going to take over."

"Well, it's scary all right," David admitted. "But I don't believe President Kennedy would risk our security. I'll bet he's one hundred percent sure the Russians won't strike."

"They're playing chicken—he and that stupid brother of his—like little kids showing how brave they can be. First letting the niggahs take over, now letting his pinko advisers lead us into the communist trap."

David thought about what Andy was saying and although he didn't agree with him, he didn't say anything. Andy was in a strange mood. What did sit-ins by Negroes matter if the President was at last getting the space program going? When John Glenn circled the earth three times, David knew his President was strong. *As for Cuba,* he thought, *it's high time somebody stood up to the Russians' influence in our part of the world.*

Andy stopped at the drugstore and without a word, got out of the car. David watched as he seemed to fumble for balance. Making it to the door, Andy stiffened, pulled his shoulders together in back, and walked through the door as straight as an arrow.

In a few minutes he came out and got behind the wheel. "Where you goin'?" he asked David.

"Mrs. Carey's house. That's where I take lessons."

Andy was checking the label on a bottle of pills. He slipped some of the pills in his mouth and gunned the motor.

"Miss Petersen teach you?"

David nodded. They came to a red light—Andy did not stop. Roosevelt Carey, standing in the intersection, blew his whistle and waved his arms as they sped past. If Andy noticed, he didn't let on. He was driving with the motor wide open. David was scared.

"Fools!" Andy screamed. "Lead us to the brink of war, will they? I'll show 'em!" They sped past Mrs. Carey's house and roared down the street. At the end of the street, the car careened around a curve leading out of town. David braced himself against the dash as the tires squealed and the car swerved to right itself.

"Andy, lemme out! Lemme out, Andy!" he yelled. He could smell rubber burning.

They were roaring down the highway heading south. Far behind them a red light was blinking. David saw it and told Andy, "Here comes a cop, Andy! Slow down! Slow down!"

Andy did not hear. The siren was sounding and in a few minutes, the patrol car was alongside Andy's car. "Pull over, Andy! Pull over!" David pleaded.

Without slowing, Andy ran off the road and bumped along in the dirt until they came to a stop beyond the South Carolina state line. As soon as the car stopped, David got out, taking his cello with him.

The patrolman approached the driver's side. Andy smirked. "You can't arrest me, mister. I'm in South Carolina."

The officer put the tablet back in his pocket. "You Andrew Lawton?"

"You better believe it!"

David walked back to the patrol car with the officer and asked for a ride back to town.

After they were in the car, the patrolman asked, "What's that?"

"Cello."

They were turning around in the road. "What're you doin' out here with Andy Lawton?"

"I bummed a ride with him. I didn't know he drove crazy."

"Wonder what's got into him? That boy was some football player."

"I think he's upset about the crisis."

"Well, who isn't?" The man kept glancing in his rearview mirror. "I'd of run him in but I've never won a case against his old man. There's no way I'd win if it was Lawton's own son in court." They were coasting down the street. "Where you goin'?"

"Mrs. Carey's."

Only slowly did David's heart resume a normal beat. It was good to know he was safe again. Good to know he'd soon see Miss Petersen. No, he decided, he wouldn't tell her about the wild ride.

The patrol car pulled up in front of the Mt. Vernon-style house. David got out, thanked the officer, and hurried up the walk.

Miss Petersen was waiting for him in the parlor and the sight of her made his heart skip. She was reading the *Scotsville Herald*. Folding it, she laid it aside.

"What's new?" he asked.

She smiled "You're late, that's what's new."

He tuned his instrument by the piano. "No, I mean in the paper."

"I see where Anita McGill and Andrew Lawton are engaged."

"Engaged? Anita McGill and Andy Lawton?"

"Why are you surprised?"

He shrugged his shoulders. "I dunno. I just saw Andy. In fact, that's why I'm late. He seems terribly upset by the crisis."

"Well, it's something to be upset about. Miss Pearl's so terrified she won't turn on the radio."

"Are you worried?"

"Yes, I am."

"You don't show it."

Miss Petersen smiled. "Neither do you when you're worried about Floyd Berry."

"I learned a long time ago, you don't let on you're scared of a bully."

"Is Floyd a bully?"

"I'm not sure. Say, what are we going to play?"

David wanted desperately to tell Miss Petersen about the upcoming cockfight as he wanted to tell her everything, but Floyd had made him swear. Besides, Miss Petersen would tell him rooster fighting was illegal and he didn't want to hear that. He had to convince Floyd that he was every bit the man Floyd was and, in addition, he wanted to convince himself.

After his lesson, David went home to sit up most of the night with his father, listening to the news reports.

By the end of the eight days when the Russians finally agreed to move their missiles, David understood the terror Andy Lawton felt. The more he thought about it, the more he admired Kennedy. If his own palms stayed wet through the ordeal, what must Kennedy have felt?

In late November, Floyd told David to meet him in back of McCurdy's store after dark. The anticipation excited David and when he climbed in the old truck beside Floyd, he sensed that Floyd was excited too. The big Indian drove recklessly, talking all the way. "They's big money goin' to be thar tonight. Mens comin' from South Ca'lina, Virginia, all roun'."

In a few miles they turned off the paved highway and headed down a dirt road that skirted a field and plunged across a bridge into the swamp. The sandy road was hard to maneuver but Floyd was skilled and the road was familiar to him.

They came to a chain strung between two trees across the road and Floyd wheeled the truck around one of the trees, dodging the chain. Further on there were "No Trespassing" and "Posted" signs, then a wire gate blocking their way. Floyd stopped, fished in his pocket for a key, got out, and unlocked the gate. "Dis here's my uncle's property," he explained when he was back inside the truck. "We got one more barricade to go, den we bees home free."

The road was deeply rutted with fresh tire tracks. "Lotsa trucks done come in here tonight. See dem ruts?"

A wall of vine-covered woods shut them in on both sides so that when they broke into the clearing, David was surprised to see a cotton field, the dead stalks not yet plowed under. They drove over the field road to the woods on the other side and again approached a barricade. A pole gate, the width of the narrow road, was fastened shut with wire. "I'll get it," David offered and hopped out. He swung open the gate and waited for Floyd to drive through. Fastening it again, he climbed back inside and they were off again.

The headlights followed the trees casting eerie shadows, grotesque shapes of nameless forms. David was exhilarated by the danger he felt.

Suddenly, without warning, the truck broke into another clearing and on the far side was a cluster of trucks and automobiles parked at random.

Floyd pulled up behind a tree and stopped. "This 's hit, McBryde." In the darkness, David could see the outline of an old barn and a doorway framing yellow light. Shadowy figures were moving about inside and the smell of tobacco hung in the air.

At the gate Floyd peeled two ten-dollar bills from a roll of bills and paid their admission. "My uncle's enterin' Red Fox, one o' his champs. You ain' seen nuttin' till you see Red Fox slam up aside one o' dem he'pless contenders!"

The big barn was ringed with makeshift bleachers already filled with spectators. A blue layer of smoke hovered overhead and dust, filtering the light, gave the place a clandestine aura.

Men stood around the wire cages where the birds were kept, bragging, betting, poking fun. In the center of the barn floor were the three rings. Three dead chickens lay outside the pits, their breasts slashed, their feathers wet with blood, their long proud necks limp. David stared at them, unable to pull his eyes away.

"What's the matter?" Floyd asked. "Sight o' blood make yer stummick act up?" He picked up one of the chickens and flung it aside.

David tried to enter into the spirit of the thing but it was all too new. The two boys moved to the center ring where a fight was about to get underway. "Dat's what cha call a handler," Floyd explained as they watched a man holding a rooster, blowing on its back feathers. "Dat makes dem roosters mad. See dem feathers standin' out like dat?"

The opposing cock was being fitted with a gaff. Its handler put the rooster on the ground to see if he could open his toes freely and David saw the curved steel blade. It was razor-sharp.

The plumage of the bird was magnificent even in the dusty, shadowy pit. The small quick head atop the full-throated neck graced the body with a splendid elegance. The way the tail feathers spilled down in back balanced the rooster on its tall strong legs in a way that reminded David of a stylized, primitive painting, perfect of form and grace.

The two men took their chickens into the pit, one on either side of the line. "Dat dere un's a quarter grey but he look so much like a full grey you can get good odds on 'im," Floyd said. "I put my money on dat white cock. Dere ain' no way dat phoney grey can beat dat white un."

David wondered how Floyd could be so sure. He watched the roosters flirting, their neck feathers full-blown, their glassy eyes excited. Agitated, they stretched their necks to peck one another, billing back and forth. "Lotsa tension," Floyd noted. The referee shouted, "Pit!" and the birds were dropped. The white dashed toward the grey, then stopped abruptly, luring the opponent into the air. The grey flew up and as he came down the white feathered warrior slashed him a multiple stroke! Then, clamping his claws around the grey's neck, he began choking him.

Floyd was on his feet. "Lookit! Lookit! He goin' to shuffle him to death!"

Barbaric glee rose from the ringside. David felt sick watching the helpless grey struggle. As the grey cock lay quivering in death, the crowd cheered the winner, then moved to another ringside.

David tore himself away from the spectacle and ran outside, gagging. He leaned against a tree, taking deep breaths.

Floyd came after him, grinned down at him. "You had enough?" he asked mercilessly.

"No!" David shouted, more angry with himself than Floyd. "I'll see every cockfight you can show me!" He was fighting back tears which made him angrier still.

Back in the barn, sitting on the bleachers, David and Floyd watched the drag pit where a rooster kept flying out of the ring, running for its life. The owner, furious, ran after it, brought it back only to have it fly out again. Finally, the owner grabbed the rooster and wrung its neck. David held his arm across his stomach, womanlike, hating himself for feeling sick.

"Here comes de Red Fox," Floyd announced.

Red Fox was rightly named. Standing tall and proud, its purplish-red plumage fell down about the neck and breast as resplendent as satin ribbon. Bronze-colored accents gleamed, rippling in the light.

Nearby a handler weighed a cream- and honey-colored cock almost as handsome as Red Fox. *What kind of human*, David thought, *would risk such beautiful creatures in a blood contest? How could Floyd sit there and relish all this?* If that was manhood, David decided he could do without it.

"Dat dar opponent's a Black Mug named Man-o'-War," Floyd said, nodding toward a black cock being pitted against Red Fox. "Mean lookin', ain' he?"

The warm-up was fast and furious. As soon as the roosters hit the clay, they flung themselves high in the air, buckling midair, gouging, fluttering, landing on their feet. The wild crowd loved it, cheered them on. The Black Mug sparred, eyeing Red Fox an instant before charging with lightning-swift speed, slashing

Red Fox's chest beneath the wing, blood spurting.

Red Fox flopped in the dirt, spasms jerking his body erratically. David could not look.

Floyd was jerking his arm. "McBryde! Raid!"

David jumped up, suddenly aware of commotion all around him—police at the doors using bull horns! People scrambling to escape!

Floyd pulled David past the pits, forced their way through the crowd to the other side of the barn. Floyd kicked a row of boards in the wall which fell away and the two of them, crawling on their bellies, wriggled to the outside. They jumped to their feet and, crouching, ran for the swamp.

A policeman rounding the corner of the barn saw them, and gave chase.

"Hit de watah!" Floyd yelled and David did! Splashing in the waist-deep water, they looked back at the policeman poised on the brink of the marsh. "He won't come no further," Floyd said, panting. "He ain' gonna mess up his uniform."

The policeman must have heard him because he got mad and started throwing everything he could get his hands on after them.

Floyd splashed ahead of David, leading the way deeper into the swamp. In the darkness they ran into trees, fell over snags, and were entangled in vines hanging low in the water, yet Floyd knew where he was going. David was numb with cold by the time they crawled out on a grassy bank.

They lay on the ground until they were breathing easier, then Floyd explained. "We made a half circle. Dem cops knows a road on de other side o' de swamp. They 'speck us to come out on dat side but we give 'em de slip comin' dis away. My people live roun' here. If we kin make hit to a house roun' here we be okay. While de moon's behind dat cloud le's try to make hit acrost de field. There's a house over yonder."

They made their way through the brush but no sooner had they reached the edge of the field than the moon came out from behind the cloud and they became as visible as in daylight. "Keep low," Floyd ordered, his breath white on the cold air. "Head for dem trees in the middle o' the field."

On the far side of the field they could see the head-lights of a car turning into a lane. "Hit de ground!" Floyd whispered. David obeyed, his body shaking from head to toe. "Could be cops," Floyd said.

In a few minutes he began crawling toward the trees. David followed.

Reaching the trees, David saw tombstones and graves. Dogs were barking, probably near the house they could see in the distance. They watched for the headlights to turn and go out the lane.

"We bees safe here. Come daylight dem cops'll be in town drinkin' coffee and we can get somebody roun' here take us home." Floyd seemed confident.

"You mean we have to stay here all night?"

"Yeah, lest you wanna go to jail."

"I'm freezin'." Wet to the skin, his teeth were chattering.

"Lie down on the groun' an' I'll cover you wid leaves. Soon's dat car leaves dat house, I'll sneak down dere and get us dry clothes."

David wanted to ask how but decided he better not.

As Floyd was piling the leaves on top of David he saw the car going back down the lane. "Dey's leavin' but dat cop he bees mad as a hornet—he ain' gonna give up easy. He be back to dat house all night long. I best go now if I'm gonna get us some dry clothes."

David hated being left alone. Beneath the leaves he shook as much from nerves as from the cold. He could see his mother right now, waking up his father, telling him to call the police—go look for him. His parents would be up all night, frantic.

Well, he couldn't worry about them. The main thing was to not get arrested. The thought of it made him shake all the more.

The dogs were barking frenziedly—Floyd must be nearing the house. What if the people weren't friends after all and turned him in? Floyd would never squeal on him, just leave him in that graveyard to get away the best he could.

It was not a happy prospect.

The moon was under another cloud which was good. However Floyd hoped to get the clothes, he'd need the cover of darkness to make it back across the field.

Before David saw him, he heard him. Floyd dropped down beside him, his arms full of clothes.

"Where'd you get 'em?" David asked, stripping off his wet shirt to change.

"Offa clothesline."

The pants were too big but they were dry and warm. David stuffed the shirttail in and pulled on another shirt. They were hardly dressed before they saw the patrol car, the lights bouncing ahead on the road. They lay flat on the ground. Again the car turned into the lane toward the house.

"Dat cop don' give up, do he?" Floyd chuckled, "Wal, he won't never find us here. Come daylight we hit one o' dese houses roun' here for some breakfust. While we eats somebody'll go git de truck. If'n dey can't get de truck bein's as how dem cops is dere, den dey'll take us back to town."

The plan seemed reasonable. If it wasn't, David had no choice. He lay looking up at the stars worrying about his mother, wishing the car would go away.

"Hit's movin' out," Floyd said. He leaned on one elbow watching. "Quit shakin', David! Here, pile up dese leaves, dat'll hold yer body heat."

"My mama's really gonna be worried. What about your mama, Floyd?"

"Women always worry. You got to think on other things."

That was good advice. "Floyd, how'd you know that white rooster was goin' to win?"

"I look at the leg scale. Dat rooster was a seven-crown special scale type. Now dat's a sign. The rest, you might say, be superstition, but my granddaddy taught it me and it works for me same as him. The moon has a effect on dem roosters. Specially if you got a white cock. If you fights a white un jes before de full or right on de full moon but not a'ter, you'll have a win. See dat full moon? Dat white-feathered warrior were a sure bet tonight. Dere wasn't a ace in dat place coulda beat 'im."

Floyd rolled over on his side. "Made you sick, didn't hit?"

"In a way."

"Well, dere ain' nuttin' wrong wid fightin' roosters. Hit's de nature o' game chickens to fight. In de jungles wheah dey comes from, dey fought off dogs, wolves, whatever and dey come up fightin'. You got to keep dem chickens penned up or dey kill one anothah. Dat's dere nature. Blind each othah, kill one another. De daddy rooster'll kill off de young roosters if'n you don't separate dem. De only way a young rooster keep alive is to go off by hisse'f, take some hens an' stake out his own territory. Den dat ol' cock won't come 'bout him less he wanna be kilt."

"What about the hens?"

"Hmph. Dem hens mean as a rattlesnake. Dey won't take no other hen's biddies—dey'll kill 'em fust. If some other hen's chick goes in her pen, it's dead on arrival! Dat's how high strung dem chickens is bred. Biddie run in rooster's pen, he kill it dead, peck its brain out. Dat's dere nature. When you puts two chickens in a ring to fight, you're lettin' nature take hits course. Ain' nuttin' wrong wid dat."

"Well, if that's the case, why don't you leave their spurs on—why use gaffs?"

"Them spurs ain't sharp enough to kill. Dey can't penetrate. Dem gaffs make quick, clean strike to vital organs. Spur jes' make a chicken suffer. Gaff bees humane.

"Now roun' here dey fights dogs. Dey uses pit bulls. But dey bred to dat, dat's not de dog's nature. Dem dogs makes gentlé pets if dey's allowed. I don't have nuttin' to do wid dog fights. Dey's pushin' dat dog fight business roun' here. Dey'll come in yer yard and steal yer dog to fight him wid pit bulls."

"If you can tame a dog, looks like you could tame a chicken."

" 'Course, you can tame 'em to men. Dey'll eat outta yer han'. You can pick 'im up and rub him an' he's easy to tame but you let another rooster come 'bout and you see dat ol' nature flare up."

"Okay. I'm not saying it's not right to fight roosters, but what about the gambling? You know that's wrong. It's against the law."

"Dere's a legitimate reason for dat. McBryde, do you know how much a settin' o' eggs costs? Three hunert dollars, give or take a few. Maybe some o' dem eggs bees et or trampled, so, say, you get two good roosters outta' de settin'. Den you got feed, doctorin', trainin', alla dat expense besides. Onliest way to git yer money outta dem chickens is to wager 'em. No harm in dat. It's business, dat's what it is."

David pondered the things Floyd told him. He was getting warmer and the dogs had stopped barking. *So what if it was the nature of roosters to fight, did that give people the right to exploit them?* he asked himself. *No.*

"So rooster fightin' makes you puke," Floyd concluded. "Know what makes me puke? Jes' the thought of hit makes me sick to my stomach."

"What's that, Floyd?"

"Men fightin' each othah in war."

David laughed. "Come off it, Floyd. You like to fight."

"I got me a reputation for fightin' but when did you evah see or hear o' me actually hittin' somebody?"

David had to admit he never had.

"I got me a reputation in fust grade. I knocked out a boy's tooth. Dat tooth was done shakey and ready to fall out, but all de way through school dey talked about me bein' de one dat knocked out Bo Williams' tooth. Nobody took de time to tell 'em we was in fust grade.

" 'Course, I keeps my reputation strong wid a few fights here and dere but mostly all I hafta do is ball up my fis' an' make like I be ready to bust somebody's mouf. Don't nobody in his right mind want to fight."

Floyd's confession was a revelation to David.

"As for war," Floyd continued, "I don't see no reason for hit. You got your nose stuck in dem war books alla de time—jes' gloryin' in all dat stuff. How come dat don't make you sick to yer stomach?"

"Well, war's a necessary evil, Floyd."

"Who says so?"

"The Bible says there'll be wars and rumors of wars."

"Don't say it gotta be." Floyd sat up. "David, you ain't nevah seen combat. When you read about some-body gittin' killed in battle, you think he's got a neat little hole in his head and how he's a big hero. Well, the truth is, he's mos' likely got his blood and guts splattered all over hisse'f. Dere ain' nuttin' you kin say dat will convince me it's de nature o' men to fight one anothah. We been bred to fight like dem pit bulls."

"The Bible says its our nature to fight and war."

"I ain't never read dat in de Bible."

"Another thing, Floyd, God uses war to judge na-tions."

"You blamin' God now."

"Not blaming him. Just stating facts. Also, we have to defend ourselves. God sent David and a lotta people out to fight Israel's enemies."

"I wouldn't know nuttin' 'bout dat."

"You mean to say that if the Russians invaded America, you wouldn't fight?"

"I ain' nevah started no fight but I have finished a few." Floyd rolled over on his back. "I even been known to run, though. Oncet I danced with this feller's girl and he come after me wid a gun. I run then. I knowed it was me or him and I couldn't nevah kill nobody, no way, so I run and I hid out ovah in McAdden County one whole summer." He yawned sleepily. "McBryde, hit's all right you got sick ovah cocks killin' one another, but if you evah tell anybody dat killin' people makes Floyd Berry sick, I'll whale de tar outta ya!"

"Gotcha," David said and laughed. He wasn't afraid of Floyd Berry any more. In fact, Floyd gave him something to think about. He snuggled down in the leaves and tried to sleep.

# CHAPTER
# TWENTY-FOUR

Anna and Mrs. Carey were sitting on the porch in April of '63. They were talking about the tree-lined streets and, as she always did, Mrs. Carey told Anna how her father had planted the trees—how once all the neighborhood had been her father's farm and how he planted the trees knowing that one day the dirt road would be the main street of Scotsville. Telephone wires mutilated some of the limbs, but on the whole the trees had survived and their branches arched like a cathedral above the street.

And then they talked about Ocean Grove, a mutual love. Again she heard dear Mrs. Carey tell her, "If Papa made a good cantaloupe crop he sent my sisters and me to Ocean Grove. We went on the train. . . ."

Anna was going to miss Mrs. Carey. In June she was moving to California to live with her son. Forced to find another place to live, Anna had searched the town over for an apartment. Uptown was one old house that had been divided into six apartments and, fortunately, one of them was going to be empty in June. It seemed like an answer to prayer.

The upstairs rooms were large with high ceilings, four closets, and a few furnishings. Windows let in light from three directions; windows on the bedroom faced Trade Street on one side and Cypress on the other which meant traffic noises. Beneath the windows on the Cypress side was the roof of the porch. Made of tin, the sound of rain on it was noisy. *But*, Anna thought, *I can get used to it.* Shades to the tall windows did not come all the way down to the sill and that bothered Anna— there was a two-inch space not covered. *I'll try not to think about it,* she told herself. *After all, nobody can see in the windows from down there.*

Anna scrubbed and waxed the rubber tile floors but there was little improvement. Clara thought she knew someone with discarded drapes that would fit the windows. In the end, Clara brought Miss Pendergraft with boxes of gray moire drapes trimmed in ball fringe; not what Anna would have chosen but better than nothing.

Miss Pendergraft steadied the ladder while Anna pinned the drapes to the rods. Miss Pendergraft was doling out gossipy tidbits in a miserly fashion designed to tantalize. "I hear Marge Penry's doing all right for herself."

Anna asked for another drapery hook.

"I say, Marge Penry's doing all right for herself."

Anna ignored the comment and asked, "Do you think this one's straight?"

Miss Pendergraft eyed the gray moire from top to bottom and nodded. "They say Harry is mopping up in shore property and between the two of them they own most of an island."

"Could you drink a Coke or something?" Anna asked.

She shook her head. "It's a shame about Marge. She seemed like such a fine girl when she first came. Just goes to show you how fast—"

"If you don't mind, Miss Pendergraft—"

"Oh, I'm not telling you anything that the entire town of Sumter doesn't already know. Even his wife knows. How a woman can put up with a man like that is beyond me. Just a meal ticket, that's all. He's her meal ticket and she'll put up with anything so long as she can drive a Cadillac and buy anything she wants."

Anna changed the subject. "It's going to be so nice to have a place where I can make my own meals. You'll have to come and have dinner with me sometime."

"What are you going to do with these floors? This tile will never hold a shine. Look at those squares popping up from the floor."

"Yes, I saw that. Maybe the landlord—"

Miss Pendergraft laughed her little cackling laugh. "Honey, you can forget about your landlord making any repairs on this place. He's tight as a tick. I heard this place is as cold as the North Pole in winter. All these windows need caulking and there's no weatherstripping. I just hope you don't freeze."

The drapes were all hung. Anna folded the ladder and took it downstairs. Coming upstairs again, Miss Pendergraft asked, "What're you going to use for furniture? This love seat is the poorest excuse for comfort I've ever seen. And that lamp, the shade's been wet. See the stain?"

"My aunt is sending me a bedroom suite and some tables. I'll make do."

"You'll need pots and pans, dishes."

"I know."

When Chicora Pendergraft left, Anna collapsed on the love seat and heaved a sigh of relief. Sitting there with only the old lamp and a brand new telephone was amusing. *Marge'll get a kick out of this,* she thought, and picked up the phone.

"Hi, Marge. It's me, Anna."

"Anna! I was just thinking about you. Every time I buy a pack of cigarettes I remember how we used to blow our cigarette money every Saturday."

"That was fun, wasn't it?"

"Tell me, what's the occasion? You don't call long distance without a reason."

"Well, I'm celebrating moving into an apartment."

"Great! I didn't know Scotsville had apartments."

"Well, it's not an apartment complex, it's in the old Siler home."

"Oh, not that old barn. How much are you paying?"

"Sixty-five a month. Two rooms, a bath, and a kitchen."

"That's no bargain."

"Maybe not, Marge, but I'm fortunate to find anything."

"Did you sign a lease?"

"No."

Marge laughed. "That's good. When the pipes burst you can move. Anna, you ought to get out of that town— go up north where the salaries are better. I bet you could get a job in New Jersey now."

"You have to have a master's."

"Well, get a master's."

"Where? The nearest school is the Indian College and they don't offer graduate work. I'm going to save as much money as I can and maybe someday I can spend a summer at Chapel Hill."

When Anna hung up, she felt unsettled but she shook off the feeling. Marge seemed natural, as if everything were going well. Yet, she felt sad when she thought of Marge.

She pulled down all the shades as far as they would go, put on a housecoat and slippers, and began arranging things. *This apartment may not be the Waldorf*, she told herself, *but it is definitely an improvement over living in one room and eating at the Greasy Spoon.*

Above the sealed fireplace was a mantel and Anna placed the conch there. Then she unzipped her cello case and placed the instrument beside the fireplace. *Now*, she said, *I feel at home.*

Anna did not fall asleep easily. The strangeness of the room, the traffic on the street below, and the curious insect noises outside made it hard to sleep. Even after she had been asleep for some time, a noise from the tin roof woke her up. She got up and looked out the window. The moon shone silver on the roof and she didn't see a thing. Of course, there was a low gable in the center of the roof where a person could hide. It was silly to think it was *someone*. More than likely it was a squirrel. She went back to bed and lay there, uneasy.

In a few minutes the tin snapped again and alarm pulsed in her throat. She jumped up quickly and went to the window. There was nothing to be seen. She searched the overhanging limbs for a squirrel but there was nothing to see or hear.

When she didn't hear anything more, she went back to bed but she lay there wide awake, unable to fall asleep.

If the apartment was downstairs she might suspect that Miss Letitia was prowling about, but the porch roof could only be reached by a fire ladder on the side of the house. Surely, Miss Letitia would not climb up that ladder to peep in her windows! Miss Letitia was not as shy as she once was with Anna—she knew she would be welcome inside.

In the morning sunshine, Anna forgot her fears. The furniture from Aunt Helga arrived and Anna spent the day unpacking and arranging it, rearranging it. Finally, she sat down to enjoy the satisfaction of having her own place, her very own furniture.

The phone startled her. It was Marge. Her voice was low and desperate. "I have to get away, Anna. Will you go with me?"

"Where, Marge, where?"

"The west coast. We'll drive my car."

"Well, I dunno—it's all so sudden."

It was the desperation in Marge's voice that persuaded her. Marge didn't ask many favors and if she was in trouble of some kind, Anna wanted to help. Still, she worried about spending the money.

In the night Anna talked to God about the decision. Somehow she felt at peace about it. "Lord, if you want me to talk with Marge about spiritual things, give me the opportunity and help me to say the right things."

The next afternoon, Marge arrived in a yellow Volkswagen. Nut brown, her hair streaked by the sun, she looked healthy and well. Then she took off her dark glasses and Anna saw in her eyes the tension and turmoil inside.

Marge chatted about the drive up, the apartment, and helped Anna finish packing. Anna mentioned the noises that had kept her awake. Marge looked outside, saw the tin roof, and laughed. "Anna, you have a tin roof—something a city girl like yourself has never had—so let a country girl like myself put your mind at ease. In the daytime the tin gets hot and expands but when the sun goes down, it cools. As it cools, it contracts and that makes it pop. Was it a snapping, popping sound?"

"Yes, but it gives you the creeps. You think someone is walking around on it."

"Nothing to worry about."

For the first two hundred miles of the trip, Marge lapsed into silence. Anna did all the talking. Marge was drinking cocktails at lunch and dinner with beers in between and nightcaps before she went to bed. It worried Anna.

When they came to nature country, Marge came to and took over with detailed explanations of the flora and fauna. Whatever troubled her, Marge was leaving it behind. She was drinking less and laughing more. Anna was glad. If stopping at every overlook on the scenic highway was what it took to loosen Marge from her worries, Anna was more than willing to patiently endure. In fear and trepidation, she followed Marge into the bowels of the earth to explore caverns only bats inhabited. Along the Gulf coast Marge wanted a guided tour of every antebellum home and traipsed the gardens identifying every bush and shrub.

Anna lived from one meal to the next. No sooner did they finish breakfast than Anna began planning where they would eat lunch and what they would eat.

Marge teased her. "I never knew anybody who lived from one meal to the next. When we get home you'll be able to tell exactly what we ate at every meal stop all across the country."

It was the truth. Anna was gaining weight and, for the first time in her life, not worrying about it.

Through Texas they drove early in the morning, not only to escape the heat but to enjoy eating breakfast steaks in the company of handsome ranch hands. Anna discovered hash browns. "I might as well rub them on my hips—that's where they're going."

In Mexico the poverty and dirt were appalling but Marge kept running from one tourist shop to another buying tooled leather and silver jewelry. Anna put her foot down. "We're not eating here! Marge, get me back to the U.S. of A. Pronto!"

Ecstasy returned to Marge in the Carlsbad Caverns, Los Alamos, Painted Desert, Petrified Forest. Anna took pictures of Marge inspecting lava flows and questioned her sanity as Marge loaded the car with rocks for souvenirs.

At the Grand Canyon, Marge was enthralled by the view. "Shall we go around the north rim?" she asked.

"Marge, if you've seen one Grand Canyon, you've seen 'em all."

Marge would not be put off and insisted on riding a burro to the bottom of the Canyon. Anna balked. "You go. I stay."

Anna sat on a bench all day reading and munching candy bars. It gave her time to think and pray. Marge Penry was every bit the mystery woman she had always been, but Anna wasn't so much interested in what

Marge was but what she might become.

Marge finally came up from the Canyon. "What're you reading?"

"A book."

"What about?"

"The Lordship of Christ."

"Oh, that. Well, Anna, I'm not ready for that."

"You're not?"

Marge shook her head. "I'd rather not discuss it."

As they were crossing the California desert, Anna felt depressed about Marge. She was getting nowhere with her spiritually and Marge's admission indicated a kind of rebellion, a revolt against God.

Marge was bragging about the VW and how it was performing. Other cars were overheating and stalling alongside the road, but the VW zoomed past them unaffected by the heat. "I would have brought the Lincoln but I knew you'd want the economy of the Volkswagen. Glad now we're in the VW."

After Disneyland they were trying to decide on which route to take—stay on the freeway up the coast or go to Yosemite. Suddenly they came within an inch of their being killed! The screech of brakes, the jolting, more than unnerved them! They got off the freeway as fast as they could and headed for Yosemite.

After that scare, Anna prayed all the more for Marge. What if they had been killed? Where would Marge be?

Sitting on a rock before the falls, Marge was entranced by the view, while Anna figured the car expense for the cross-country trip. "Eighty-two dollars, sixty-five cents, Marge. Divide that in two and it means we each pay forty-one dollars. You can't beat that, can you?"

Coming home, the Volkswagen was again tested, this time on the mountains of Colorado, and it took the Rockies in stride. As they approached Denver, Anna was thinking about Roger. She was wishing they would pass a hospital on the slim chance that it would be the one he practiced in. There might be one chance in a million that she would glimpse him.

They did pass a hospital and Anna drove slowly, taking a good look. Afterward, she felt foolish. It was silly even to think about it, but for the next few miles she was quiet. To be so close and to be so far—she couldn't get Roger off her mind.

For six thousand miles the two friends talked about everything and yet never about whatever it was that troubled Marge. Anna respected Marge's reserve; it was at least one thing they had in common and the bond forged by it was strong.

After six weeks of travel, Anna felt good about coming home to Scotsville, if not excited. She was anxious to get back in her own apartment. As they drove into town the familiar trees arching overhead and the lazy, sleepy look of the place gave Anna satisfaction even though she knew she would never feel as if she belonged in Scotsville.

As the car turned at Cypress and slowed for the apartment, they pulled up behind another car parked by the curb. Anna recognized it as Chicora Pendergraft's and a strange foreboding came over her.

As the girls got out of the Volkswagen, the older woman met them on the sidewalk. Her mouth twitched and without being told anything, Anna knew Miss Pendergraft had urgent news.

"It's about Clara. I'll tell you inside. It's terrible. Worse thing that's ever happened in Scotsville."

Only after they had brought in the bags and Miss Pendergraft was seated on the love seat did she speak. She looked from one to the other of them and in a voice hardly audible, spoke. "Clara Campbell's been murdered!"

"Murdered! What do you mean?" Anna exclaimed.

"Murdered in cold blood. Floyd Berry did it. Drowned her. Drowned her in a bucket of water."

"Oh, Miss Pendergraft, that's not possible," Marge said.

"Oh, yes, it is. Poor Clara—"

Anna couldn't believe her ears. "You say Floyd Berry did it? But why?"

"It happened on the night of July fourteenth. Floyd Berry sneaked up on her in her own house, held her head in a bucket of water till she drowned."

Anna felt weak and sat down. "Why? Why would he kill Clara?"

"Spite. You know what a temper he has. They say he got mad because she short-changed him on his pay. And, you know Clara was—what shall I say—close with her money; not stingy but close. She had to watch her pennies like the rest of us."

Marge was stunned. "Oh, how horrible!"

The realization that Clara was indeed dead hit Anna and she began shaking. "Oh, it can't be! It can't be!"

"There, there, Anna, I'm sorry to be the bearer of such sad tidings. Please don't cry."

Anna couldn't help it. "Clara was such a good friend. Oh, I can't believe this."

For a moment Anna had an irrational hatred of Chicora Pendergraft. Angry, she looked straight at the woman. "I can't believe Floyd Berry would kill Clara over something like that. I can't believe that boy would kill anyone!"

"Oh, Anna, how can you say such a thing. That boy's been nothing but trouble from the day he started school. I know him from 'way back."

"But he's no murderer!"

"Anna, these Indians are hotheads. That's exactly the kind of thing they will kill over. If they think someone's cheating them they get even. They don't take anything off anybody. You just don't know Indians, does she, Marge?"

"When's the trial?" Marge asked.

"Oh, there's not going to be any trial. The case is already wrapped up. Floyd pleaded guilty and they took him to Central Prison to begin a life sentence. Hmph. If I'd had anything to do with it, that's one Indian boy who'd have gone to the gas chamber. Killin' poor Clara who spent her life trying to help children. Good Christian woman, if there ever was one. Now she's dead and that Floyd Berry'll be free as a bird in a few years.

"He had a good lawyer or he'd wind up on death row. You know that Benjamin Lawton's smart. He advised Floyd to plea bargain, otherwise there'd have been a trial and Floyd would have gotten the death penalty." As if on cue, Chicora Pendergraft began sniffling, dabbing her eyes with tissue.

"I saved you all these newspaper clippings," she told Anna, handing them to her.

Anna could not look at them.

"I know you don't feel like reading them now but you may keep them. I'd like to have them back when you're finished. . . . I thought about you as soon as it happened but there was no way to get in touch with you. Guess you told your aunt where you'd be but I couldn't remember how to get in touch with her. Next time you go off, please, let me or somebody know where you are.

"It was a beautiful service. Reverend Mr. Jackson conducted the funeral. Oh, I know Clara would've wanted you there. Of course, there was such a crowd the church couldn't hold them, and there were newspaper reporters from Charlotte and Raleigh. I haven't seen a crowd like that at a funeral since Ted and Eddie were killed. I saw people I hadn't seen in years. Children Clara had taught over the years—many of them gray-headed, some with grandchildren, but they all remembered and loved Miss Clara, as they called her. She hated that, you know. Just like you probably hate 'Miss Pete,' but they only nickname the ones they like. . . ."

She was making Anna nervous.

"I don't know if you know this or not, but Clara went to the cemetery nearly every week with a flower for Ted's grave. She never forgot those boys." Miss Pendergraft blew her nose. "Well, I guess that's the last violet that grave will ever see."

When Miss Pendergraft was gone, Marge decided to stay overnight so Anna would not be alone. After they were dressed for bed, Marge was trying to make conversation. "Why don't you play the cello for me?"

Marge cared nothing for the cello. "Not now," Anna answered.

"I see you still have the conch. It really is quite beautiful. Reminds me of our room at the teacherage. I remember you told me where you got it but I forgot."

"My father and I found it on the beach at Ocean Grove."

Somehow that comment was where it began—before the night was through, Anna had told Marge everything about her childhood and youth. They talked past midnight on into the wee hours of the morning, and not until they stopped talking did it occur to Anna the change that had taken place. After being together for six weeks, and never confiding anything personal, they had sat up nearly all the night telling everything—all about Aunt Helga, the Parkinson's, about Roger Metcalf and how she came to Scotsville.

Long after Marge's steady breathing signaled that she was sound asleep, Anna pondered the strangeness of it. Marge had successfully taken her mind off the grief she felt for Clara, but somehow in the transference of emotion, everything spilled out. She was amazed at herself for sharing so intimately and confounded that not once had Marge reciprocated. Not once had she let down her guard to say anything about her own personal life.

For a long time Anna sat up in bed hugging her knees against her breast, thinking of Roger Metcalf.

# CHAPTER
# TWENTY-FIVE

David McBryde came running across campus calling, "Miss Pete! Miss Pete! Wait a minute!"

Anna waited, watching the handsome, long-legged boy racing toward her. So, David was calling her "Miss Pete." *Well, okay*, she thought.

"Boy, am I glad to see you!" He was breathing hard. "Oh, Miss Petersen, we gotta do something!"

So, she thought, the "Miss Pete" was a slip. "About what, David?" she asked.

"Not here."

David was terribly agitated—so nervous he was not aware of calling her "Miss Pete."

They climbed the old uneven steps into McAdden High and welcomed the cool interior of the place. She unlocked her classroom door and they went inside. David closed the door behind them and pulled up a chair close by the desk. "Miss Petersen, it's about Floyd Berry. I know Floyd Berry did not kill Miss Campbell."

"How do you know that?"

"Floyd couldn't kill anybody. He was even opposed to war. All that big talk about him being a troublemaker, Miss Petersen, was only Floyd's reputation. Think about it. Did you ever know him to start a fight? All he had to do was threaten somebody and they'd back off. Floyd couldn't kill anybody."

"But, David, aren't you forgetting something? Floyd confessed. He confessed that he killed her."

David shook his head vigorously. "Miss Petersen, I

went to see Floyd in jail. Had a hard time getting in to see him, but my daddy knows the chief and he let me stand outside and talk to Floyd. Floyd told me he and Andy Lawton were drinking that night—that he passed out and doesn't remember a thing that happened."

"Then why would he confess?"

"I don't know unless it was because he was afraid they'd give him the death penalty. Oh, Miss Petersen, I know Floyd's innocent. You've gotta help me!"

David was beside himself.

"Just calm down, David. Let's think about this for a while."

But David was too impatient. "Miss Petersen, you know Floyd couldn't kill anybody, now, don't you?"

Anna couldn't answer. No, she didn't think Floyd could murder but if the boy, out of his own mouth, said he did it, what could she say?

"I'm no lawyer, David. I'm not a detective—"

"Miss Petersen, you're the only person who knows Floyd the way I know him. If you and I don't try—"

"I'll write to him, David. I'll pray for him, send him magazines and things, but I don't see that I can do much more."

"Miss Petersen," his earnest young face was taut with emotion, "I believe God's on our side!"

"David, David. Let's make sure we're on God's side. The facts in this case all seem to be against whatever hunches you or I may share. Only God himself can prove the case to be other than what it has been decided at this point."

After he left, Anna dismissed the matter from her mind. Nevertheless, she did get Floyd's address and wrote to him. When that did not quell the nagging suspicion that she could do more, she visited Floyd's mother. Floyd's mother was a woman accustomed to hardship. "I nevah knowed my boy to do no harm," she said, "but you don't know what they'll git into oncet they start to drinkin'. He bees right smart like his Uncle Troy. Troy been in an' outa jail most of his life, fust one thing, then another."

The woman's acceptance bothered Anna. Driving home from the visit an increased sense of responsibility burdened her.

Nor could Anna shake David's confidence. Every day after school he waited until all the other students had cleared the room, then he talked about Floyd. Little by little he told her about the cockfight and about the night they spent in the graveyard. "Don't you see, Miss Petersen, as brutal as cockfighting seems to you and me, Floyd had a point—it's natural for those roosters to kill. But Floyd showed his true self to me when he said war was barbaric to him—that it's not the nature of men to kill each other. I know Floyd Berry could never kill another man, much less a woman."

"But if he were drinking—?"

"I still don't believe he could do it. You can't make a man go against his true self even when he is drunk."

"Or so you may think. If you want to prove Floyd's innocence, you must come up with solid evidence. Perhaps you can find a witness or . . . Well, I don't know what else, but—"

David was frustrated. "I know it, Miss Petersen. We have to have facts."

That night Anna lay awake trying to think of some way to relieve David's mind. The tin roof was popping. It had not been hot that day so why would the roof be popping? Anna smiled. *So, Miss Letitia has climbed the ladder and is clambering around on the roof. Too bad Letitia wasn't prowling around Clara's house the night she was killed. Come to think of it, it wouldn't be a bad idea to ask Miss Letitia if she saw anything that night.*

The roof popped again but Anna rolled over and went to sleep.

It was late October before Anna saw Miss Letitia. Anna had been to Charlotte to the Ice Capades and it was one o'clock in the morning. After letting the other women out at their homes, she drove Penny Slowpoke to the post office to mail a bill payment that was due. Miss Letitia startled her. Wild-eyed and stringy haired, she was going through the wastebasket.

"Hello, Miss Letitia," Anna said and dropped her letter in the box.

Letitia looked frightful, her witch-like features sharp, great dark circles framing her eyes. Furtively she glanced about, her movements erratic. The baggy clothes and flailing arms gave her the appearance of a scarecrow come alive.

Anna hoped to calm her. "I've been wanting to talk with you, Miss Letitia."

Miss Letitia stopped clawing the wastepaper and looked at Anna, her eyes wild and fierce.

"It's about Floyd Berry. I was wondering if—"

Miss Letitia dropped the paper on the floor and in her haste to get outside, knocked over the trash basket.

Hurrying after her, Anna was not fast enough. Miss Letitia was already too far away. In a minute she was out of sight, the wagon clattering after her.

*Well, I never!* thought Anna. *Why did she run like that? Could it be that she did know something about Floyd Berry? Hardly. Maybe she was just frightened.*

The experience haunted Anna. In class, seeing Floyd's empty desk every day kept bringing his case to mind and, with it, the odd behavior of Miss Letitia. She told herself over and over that the woman was only frightened.

The year before, Floyd and David had sat across the room from each other during study hall and they had talked across the empty rows about all sorts of things. Floyd began opening up, relating to her and to David.

Now the desks were filled with history students—David in his usual seat next to the windows and Floyd's empty. It was not by chance that it was empty. Billy Williams had wanted his seat but, on an impulse even Anna could not explain, she refused him.

The November sun streamed through the windows as if it were May. Someone called the season Indian Summer and she rather liked the name. Anna wiped dust from the wide shelf beneath the windows, waiting for the last students to return from lunch. David was behind her, poring over a book, or at least she thought he was until she turned around and caught him looking at her. Poor David, he needed a girlfriend.

The tardy bell rang. Anna called the roll, skipping the names of home ec girls who were at a district meeting and cheerleaders who were somewhere else. There were more students absent than present. Anna sighed.

Across the hall the math teacher was hawking her favorite slogan, "Students, you must have clear thinking and sound reasoning." A long line of students was waiting to sharpen pencils. It was test day in math, too.

Billy Williams craned his neck to see the girls across the hall. Billy was a cross to bear—Anna was well into the school year before she realized how impossible he was. He hated Negroes and the Kennedys. If he were more intelligent Anna would have held out hope for him, but he was lazy, ignorant, and stubborn. You couldn't tell him anything. David tried to help but Billy wouldn't listen even to a peer.

Before school started that fall, Oren Wallace was killed in Vietnam. Scotsville was not aroused but Billy was. "Where's Veetnam?" he asked but he could never keep it straight. "What's our boys doin' over there anyway?" he asked every time the subject was mentioned. Billy said Oren was his first cousin once removed and the fires of resentment Billy felt for the President were made to blaze by his cousin's death. Today, of all days, Anna hoped Billy would not argue. With so many of the girls coming in late, they'd have to wait to pass out the tests and if he started an argument—well, she'd cross that bridge when they came to it.

"All right, class, while we wait for the girls I'll hear your current events."

Billy lounged on his desk, his head on his arm. "They sent George to reform school for the bomb scare."

Anna ignored him. "Anything on the national scene?"

"My sister had a baby," Billy persisted.

David raised his hand. "President Kennedy will be in Texas today."

"Weather man said it's gonna rain tomorrow." Anna looked at Billy trying to determine if he were trying to be obnoxious or if he didn't know any better.

Someone from across the room asked, "Miss Petersen, who do you think'll go to the Rose Bowl this year?"

The cheerleaders were coming in the door. "Where's Mildred?" she asked them.

"She stopped by the water fountain."

The girls were warm from practicing.

"Big game tonight, girls?" Anna asked. Mildred was coming in the door. "Okay, turn in your news items and get out a sheet of paper for the test."

"We can't have a test today," Billy protested. "There's too many absent."

"Billy, how many times do I have to tell you we don't stop school because some people are missing?"

The intercom crackled and the principal came on to tell teachers to excuse the tardy cheerleaders.

"Can I go get some water?" Billy asked.

"No, Billy, we're starting the test."

"You let Mildred get water."

Anna was getting exasperated. In addition to Billy's

irritation, the speaker was crackling again. Mark Secrest could think of more reasons to interrupt class.

He hesitated, then began. "We have just heard over the radio that the President has been shot." Another pause. "I repeat, we have just heard that President Kennedy has been shot. . . . It is thought that the President may be dead."

They were stunned. David Robbins burst into tears. The impact was one of total shock. No one moved or spoke. Then Billy Williams blurted out, "Let's get on with the test!" His words ricocheted in Anna's head like a swirling dervish that would not stop.

Too numb to speak, Anna did not notice when the students resumed taking their tests. She sat at her desk praying. Before the end of the period, the speaker sputtered again and all heads looked up to listen. "The news has been confirmed. President Kennedy is dead. He was shot by an unidentified gunman while his motorcade was passing through Dallas." Secrest paused. "School is dismissed."

Billy Williams jumped up, grabbed his books, threw his test paper on Anna's desk, and left. The rest of the students sat still at their desks, thunderstruck. Anna walked to the front of the room, too shaken to speak. "You may go," she whispered. They moved quietly, picking up their books, handing her their test papers, and leaving the room without a word.

After they were gone, Anna glanced down at the papers. She would have to throw them away; the answers were all smeared from tears.

Anna pulled herself together, then hurried to the teachers' lounge to hear the details. Some people were crowded around a small radio in the principal's office hearing the information above the sounds of hysterical confusion. People dispersed quickly to get home to a television set.

Anna drove to her apartment, put on the tea kettle.

Since she didn't have a television, she would have to wait until her next-door neighbor came home. The neighbor arrived soon after Anna and Anna met her in the hall. "Oh, do come in," the neighbor insisted. "I don't want to be by myself."

The scant information was repeated over and over, and there were reporters who could not control their emotions. As the rapidly escalating situation developed, the newsmen relayed it, their voices excited and out of control. The pictures of the awful events, the terror-stricken faces of eyewitnesses, struck horror in her heart.

Anna smelled something burning. "Oh, my! I left the kettle on!" The apartment was filled with an acrid smoke and the bottom of the aluminum kettle had melted on the stove. Coughing, she raised the windows, opened the doors, and went back to the neighbor's.

The neighbor was sure the acrid smoke would poison Anna and insisted she spend the weekend with her.

All weekend there was continual coverage of the shooting on all the networks, and somber music. Late Sunday night, when Anna returned to her apartment, the phone was ringing. "Miss Petersen, I've been trying to get you all day," Mark Secrest began. "I feel we must bring the students together tomorrow morning for an assembly. Since you're the history teacher, it seems appropriate that you should speak to them about the assassination. I know this won't be easy for you but someone has to do it. Sorry I couldn't reach you earlier."

"Me? You want me—"

"Yes, Miss Petersen, I want you to talk to them. You're the logical person to do it."

Anna hung up the phone and fell limp in the chair. *What in the world can I say?*

She was up half the night writing her speech and praying she would get through the next day without falling apart. Sitting on the platform looking down on the upturned faces, Anna had never seen the young people so stricken, so subdued. While Mark Secrest read Psalm 46, Anna prayed that her voice would not crack, that what she said would help.

Anna stood quietly before the podium, taking time to look at the young people staring back at her, then she spoke. "Young people, we are gathered together to pay respect to our fallen Chief Executive, John Fitzgerald Kennedy.

"To the very young all of this sobriety has probably become tiresome. We are all accustomed to a thirty-minute program packed full of hatred, violence, running, hiding, and then a quick wrap-up by a vague justice.

"This weekend there has been no other channel to turn to. If you have become impatient with a grieving world, let it be known that one day you will understand the infamy.

"In one terrible moment we have seen the violence of our age take epic form with shock upon shock. For these hours in history all Americans have huddled together to weep and the world has wrapped its arms around us.

"God has looked down and we have looked up, stunned and helpless. Some have looked to God only briefly and turned away, seething with hatred and frustration. It was hatred that killed our President. 'Liberty and justice for all' are not pretty words but truths we must live by.

"Who is to say what we will have learned when this is past? Will vengeance be drained from us? Will we be united under God? Will we walk more slowly and take a second look at all these issues we have talked about so glibly? Will we retain our sense of helplessness and our sense of dependence on God?

"What can we do? We can pray. This is no last resort. Prayer is the means of our greatest help. If, in our hearts, we shared the revenge of the man who killed the assassin, then we need to pray for ourselves. Taking the law into our own hands is not the way of God.

"We cannot personally comfort the loved ones of the late President, the family of the police officer who was killed, nor can we offer solace to those who loved Lee Harvey Oswald—his widowed mother, his wife, and children. But God can comfort.

"Pray for our nation, shamed by these crimes, and pray for President Johnson."

Anna had not meant to invite them to pray aloud, but spontaneously, all over the audience, students and teachers rose taking their turns to pray.

Anna looked at Mark Secrest. "It's okay," he whispered. His eyes were brimming with tears.

# CHAPTER
# TWENTY-SIX

Horace Wigglesworth had outgrown the shadow of Miss
Amy at Montgomery School and on his own was making
strides in public relations. He, too, insisted on one
hundred percent membership in the local, state, and
national professional teachers' organization and attendance at all PTA functions.

Every summer he went to the University of North
Carolina and racked up credits toward a doctorate in
education. It was tough, and he passed some courses
and failed some. It was also expensive and that's why
he put off getting married, but now Gilchrist told him
he needed a wife. Said she'd see that he wore the right
tie, make a home for him. Well, he didn't need any
woman to tell him how to dress, but Gilchrist was undoubtedly grooming him for something better and it
would pay to go along with his advice.

Finding a girl was no problem, even though he was
forty-three and nearly bald. Yul Brynner made baldness
something to be desired and it never bothered Horace
that people made jokes—it only meant they were en-
vious of his male prowess. He never had trouble getting
dates. He considered himself to be a good dresser with
a flair other men didn't have, and he was fun to be with
and that's all that mattered with girls. The right kind
of girls, that is. The other kind wanted money to spend
and places to go. He could do without that kind. He
was thumbing through his little black book. It would
not be an easy choice but he didn't have to worry about

being pressured—most of the girls thought he was a confirmed bachelor and had given up hope of ever catching him. He licked his thumb and turned a page. With a pencil he drew a line through one name after another. If he had his druthers he'd ask Marge Penry—there was something about that girl that excited him. But Marge lived in Georgia and if he brought her back to Scotsville she'd take a while to live down all the talk that had gone on about her.

Anna Petersen's name was not in the book and he considered it a stroke of genius on his part when her name occurred to him. Right away he knew she was the number-one choice. He glanced in the mirror, adjusted his narrow tie, wet his fingers and slicked down some strands of hair across his head, slapped after-shave lotion on his face, and dashed out the house.

Anna lived in an apartment on the street across from the police station. As he pulled up to the curb, he glanced at the upstairs windows in case she might be looking down and he could wave, but he didn't see her. Banging the screen door behind him, he yelled up the stairs, "Anna, ya home?"

The door opened at the top of the stairs and Anna stuck her head out. "Horace, is that you? Come on up."

Horace sat on the short couch and crossed his legs.

"What's on your mind?" she asked and sat down by the dining table.

"You got supper cooked?"

"As a matter of fact, I have."

"Too bad. I was going to ask you to go out to eat."

"Well, stay and have dinner with me."

"Okay. Believe I will."

"I haven't seen you lately. You must be busy."

"Busy as a one-armed paper hanger. Being a principal is no little job, Anna. I stay at that school from mawnin' to night. No small thing tryin' to fill Miss Amy's shoes. I hung a two-hunnert dollah oil paintin' o' her on the wall just as you come in the door. You've seen it theah. Well, the way parents come in and gawk at it you'd think Miss Amy was some kinda saint.

"It's not been easy tryin' to satisfy Gilchrist either, that old mossback. You know, Anna, things are happening in education that's gonna curl his hair."

"What kind of things?"

"Integration is the big thing. It's coming, Anna. There's been this flood-tide of legislation. That Civil Rights Bill sets it in cement. You'll see. There's the devil to pay."

Anna was putting the meal on the table. "You probably never ate anything like this before, Horace."

"Lord, have mercy, it looks like wallpaper paste. What is it?"

"It's fish balls. My Aunt Helga sent me a can of it. Norwegians love fish balls. They make it out of haddock—scrape it and make it into round cakes. I love it fresh but you can buy the fresh only in Norwegian delicatessans."

Horace asked the blessing, then helped himself to the fish and carrots. "You eat carrots?"

"Yes, don't you?"

"I don't go for 'em much."

"Do you like rhubarb?"

"Never ate it."

Anna looked really good for her age. *Must be nearly forty*, he thought. *Nice smooth skin. A little plump, but a man likes an armful. Yes, she would fill the bill. In fact, she'd be a downright asset, what with her reputation as a teacher and all.* He was trying to remember why he hadn't been attracted to her before—when she first came to the teacherage. He must have been put off by the fact she was a Yankee. Maybe it was the cello.

He took a forkful of the fish and in his mouth it felt like a blob of foam rubber.

"How do you like it?" she asked, smiling.

It was tasteless. It was terrible! He swallowed it whole. "Tastes like wallpaper paste."

She laughed, then smiled again.

She did have a very nice smile. Come to think of it, Horace couldn't understand why somebody else hadn't led her to the altar. He was trying to remember if she had gone with anybody. Woodall Jackson had taken her to a program or two and he'd seen them driving around together but Woodall, being a preacher and all, he didn't think of him as a romantic kind. Besides, no woman would be interested in a man with a patch over his eye—a man with no personality, no ambition.

She passed the applesauce to him. "Good," he said. "At least applesauce's got taste. How 'bout some more potatoes?"

There was something very delicate about Anna—the way she wore bracelets and used her hands. *No, she would not be hard to love, really love*, he thought— *loved in the way you want to love the mother of your children.*

But that was another matter. He couldn't afford children even if there was time. Sometimes he wondered if the psychology prof had been right, telling him he had a subconscious aversion to children and that was the reason he didn't get married. "How can I not like chuldrun?" he asked the man. "I'm an elementary school principal—I'm with chuldrun all day long!"

Anna was clearing the table. "Will you have dessert? I have rhubarb pie—not fresh rhubarb but I'm trying a new recipe using a jar of rhubarb Aunt Helga sent me."

"Sure, I'll try it."

The reddish color looked strange to him. "Looks slimey like okra." He cut it with his fork, lifted it to his mouth cautiously. Sour to the taste, he washed it down with water and pushed aside the plate. "Not my cup o'tea," he said. "Guess it's okay if you're used to it."

After wiping his mouth with his napkin he crumpled it beside his plate. Pushing his chair back, he stroked the top of his head. Maybe he'd better think about this one. After all, a man has to think about his stomach. Three meals a day eating such things as fish balls, carrots, and rhubarb pie might do him in. No need to raise the woman's hopes if he wasn't going to follow through. Yes, he'd think it over a while—look over the field, consider all the options. He'd waited this long, a couple weeks more wouldn't hurt.

"Horace, what else is so new in education?"

"Individualized teaching, team teaching, open classrooms, that kinda' stuff."

"Don't you think Gilchrist knows about all that?"

"Yeah, but he's an old-fashioned school man. He thinks education is Latin, that kinda stuff. One time he told the English teachers all he expected them to do was get the chuldrun to love literature. Told 'em to sit on the desk and read poetry to 'em until they got an ear for it. You know how he's always quoting *Hiawatha* to 'em or 'Quoth the raven, nevermore.' There's not a graduate of McAdden High School can't quote Gunga Dinn fo'wa'ds and back'ards. Now what good's that gonna do 'em in the real world, I ask you?"

He stood up to stretch his legs and walked over to the mantel. "Where'd you get this?"

"It's a conch my father and I picked up on the beach at Ocean Grove."

"That in New Jersey?"

She nodded.

"How come you kept it so long?"

"Just a keepsake."

He returned it to the shelf. "It's a nice one. You ever hear from Marge Penry?"

"Not often."

"I hear she's mopping up in real estate. Did she ever get married?"

"No."

"Did you ever think about getting married?"

Anna laughed. "Well, I guess everyone thinks about that."

"Even Miss Pendergraft?"

"Even Miss Pendergraft."

"I hear Gilchrist is bringing her back to teach Latin next year. She must be a hunnert."

"What makes you say that?"

"Well, it's a known fact she taught Cecil McCurdy in first grade and he's older'n I am."

"She probably started teaching when she was very young."

"Even so, if McCurdy is forty-five and she started teaching when she was twenty, she'd have to be —let's see—well, I know she's older'n any other teacher.

"By the way, I got an idea Gilchrist is groomin' me for Secrest's job. Man like Secrest will move up. If Gilchrist retires they're sure to make Secrest superintendent." He sat down on the couch and leveled his eyes on Anna. "Anna, I don't intend to get stuck at Montgomery the rest of my life. I got plans. Soon's I get my doctorate I'm either gonna move up in this system or I'm gonna find another ladder to climb. Do you blame me?"

"No, Horace, if that's what you want."

"Anna, Mark Secrest told me he offered you the head of the department last year and you turned him down. What was back of all that?"

"Horace, I like the classroom, that's all there is to that."

"Oh, good night, don't you care about advancing? You'll never get up in the world if you don't grab every rung up."

"What's so bad about loving your job?"

"Nothin', I guess." He stood up again. "This apartment's so squeaky clean it smells fresh as longleaf pine after a rain. Now, my place looks like a tornado struck and it smells, well, it smells like fried ham grease—like it smells all over town when they're ginnin' cotton. I think you and I ought to merge—balance out the equation."

Anna laughed. "Tell me, Horace, do you think Scotsville will vote a bond issue to build a new high school?"

"I doubt it. Gilchrist thinks they will but he's an idealist. Voting the bond issue is not the big problem—it's consolidating all these schools. None o' these towns wants to give up their high school and come to Scotsville. 'Course, the power structure being what it is, they might pull it off. It depends on what Cecil McCurdy wants."

"He strikes me as a smart man."

"He's smart all right and I guess you'd call him progressive in some ways. But with the niggers rioting all over the country, he might think twice before he decides to build a school for the whole county. It might mean the niggers would pour into it and if the Croatans take a notion to give up their school, they might pile in on us, too.

"By the way, somebody told me you write to that Indian fellow that killed Clara. Is that true?"

"Yes, I write to Floyd. He seems to be a changed person."

"In what way?"

"Well, he told me he accepted Christ."

"So?"

"Well, he speaks so personally about God. In every letter he says something—he's had an answer to prayer or the Bible encouraged him in some way."

"Fox hole religion. I've seen a lot of that kind."

"That's what you said about Lester McKenzie and look at him—he's finished college and seminary—

serves in the Army as a chaplain. Who would ever have thought he could do all that? I have high hopes for Floyd. I think his conversion is real."

"Did you know David McBryde is waging a one-man campaign to get Floyd outta prison?" He grinned. "That boy won't see the outside o' them walls the rest of his life. If you ask me, he shoulda got the death penalty. Gives me nightmares thinkin' about him holding Clara's head in that bucket o' water till she drowned. He musta been roarin' drunk."

"Could he have been on drugs?"

"Indians'll drink anything; guess they'd take pills, too, if they took a notion to. There's dope to be had aroun' here."

"Horace, is it true that a person can't be held responsible for a crime they commit if they were not conscious when they did it?"

"Whadda you mean?"

"If a person is under the influence of drugs and blacks out, can he be tried for crimes he's accused of committing at such a time?"

"I heard there was some kinda law like that. Didn't that fellow that killed all those nurses in Los Angeles get off on some kinda grounds like that? Of course, when you say a man's not responsible you make him something less than a man." He sat down. "What're you sayin', that Floyd Berry didn't know what he was doin'?"

"No, I didn't say that."

"But you have reason to believe that was the case?"

"I'm not in a position to say what the case was. It's just that I thought I knew Floyd. . . ."

Horace laughed. "Anna, don't nobody know an Indian unless he's an Indian himself. Take it from me, I don't pretend to know what makes a Croatan tick."

A hot rod, tires squealing, roared down the street, radio blaring. Horace leaned out the window. "Looks like a Ford." He came back to the couch. "They're still at it—dragging every chance they get. They're wild all right. Wilder than those poor boys were who got killed on the Old Mill Road. Every time I think of that night, I get the awfulest feelin'. I don't know of anything that ever upset me like that did. Ted was such a nice boy, not smart, but nice. Let's see, he was about fifteen, wasn't he? Sixteen? He'd be twenty-six now—through college."

"How do you think Andrew is doing?"

"I hear he's some better. Marryin' Anita made a difference. I hear they have a baby on the way. The last I heard, Andrew was traveling for some company—meat packing plant—something like that."

Anna turned on another lamp.

"How's yer car doin', Anna?"

"Penny Slowpoke? Well, she's on her last legs, I'm afraid."

"You plannin' to go see your aunt this summer?"

"I was thinking about it."

"You ought not to get out on the road in that car. What you need is one o' these new Ramblers. What say I come by one afternoon and we go up to Weston and look at 'em?"

"Well, okay. I've been thinking about it."

Horace was enjoying himself and if for the present he had changed his mind about marriage, he'd keep Anna on the back burner in case nothing better showed up.

"Well, Horace, this has been nice but I need to wash the dishes and grade some papers."

"Oh, sure. Tell you what, I'll come sometime next week and we'll go look at cars."

"Okay," she said and opened the door.

# CHAPTER
# TWENTY-SEVEN

It was really too funny for words that Horace should come calling but typical that he would come unannounced. Thinking about his outfit, Anna giggled. *Wouldn't Marge get a good laugh out of this?* she thought. She decided to splurge on a call.

No sooner did she tell Marge that Horace had been to see her than Marge asked, "What was he wearing?"

"No, not white bucks—white patent leathers! And the irony is, he thinks he looks great! Can you imagine white patent leathers with white socks! He must still have athlete's feet!

"No, I don't know why he came—he just appeared downstairs. He didn't like my dinner. As luck would have it, I was having Norwegian fish balls and you know nobody likes them who isn't Scandinavian. And I had rhubarb pie, something he's never eaten before and that didn't go over either. He's coming next week to take me to Weston to look at cars. Yes, Penny Slowpoke is about to give up the ghost. I'd like to go up to see Aunt Helga this summer and Penny Slowpoke would never make that trip. Of course, if I buy the car there won't be money to make a trip.

"The other day I had trouble with Penny on the Old Bridge Road; you remember the one that runs by the cemetery? I had been to Ted McGill's grave to put a flower on it for Clara. Well, when the car wouldn't start, I walked a distance before I came to a house in McCrory Quarter. Marge, a little Negro boy let me in to use the phone and it was one of those dingy little houses, all dark and grimy inside, but there on a rickety table was a shocking pink telephone and above it, pictures of Jesus, J.F.K., and Martin Luther King. It was like a shrine and that shocking pink phone seemed all out of place."

"You ought to leave, Anna. Think what McAdden High will be like when they integrate. You need to get back in the world where you'll meet someone your own calibre and get mar—"

"I'm forty, Marge. It's too late to think I'll ever get married."

"With an attitude like that, you won't, but you're selling yourself short. Go up to Charlotte or Greensboro or back up north."

"Oh, Marge, the grass is always greener on the other side of the fence. I know there's no culture here in Scotsville, but it could be worse. Most of these people are the salt of the earth."

"You don't need salt, you need a little pepper!"

"Let's get off this subject, Marge."

"You wait until they start bringing Negroes into McAdden High School and then you'll be sorry you didn't get out when you could."

Talking with Marge invariably led to the same impasse, yet it disturbed Anna. Maybe she was letting the world pass her by, but as for going someplace to meet a husband, well, maybe she was the kind of person who could never love but one man and if she couldn't have him she wouldn't have anyone.

Anna was not proud of herself on that score. From time to time she thought about Roger Metcalf, even fantasized about him—daydreamed that he'd come walking in the door, free to marry her. It wasn't right of her, she knew, to think of Roger. She had no reason to hope, much less to feel anything. She tried not to think of Roger, but in her heart she knew she was somehow still waiting for him. What would it be like to open the door and find him standing there, arms outstretched?

Of course, after so many years, Roger couldn't possibly be anything like the man she had known. Then he had been a struggling student, now he was a successful surgeon, with a wife and two children—a man with a family.

*I wonder if he ever thinks of me?* she wondered. The fantasy kept surfacing—*his wife will die and he'll come back to me. I'll open the door and he'll be standing there. He'll open his arms and take me in.*

She broke off the dream. It was a silly, childish game.

Anna went over to the windows to pull down the shades. Down on the sidewalk beneath the trees she could see the light of a cigarette. She pulled down the shade as far as it would go and went in the bedroom to undress.

Anna took a leisurely bath and, wrapped in a towel, dried her hair and brushed it. The roof popped and she looked out to see if she could see anything. There was nothing and no one in sight.

When her hair was dry, she dressed for bed and crawled between the sheets. A breeze billowed the curtains and light from the service station cast shadows in the room. The roof popped again. She ignored it, rolled over, and went to sleep.

Sometime in the night, a noise wakened Anna and she lay in bed trying to determine what it was. If Miss Letitia was prowling about the roof, she didn't care to catch her. Anna was thinking again about that night when she saw Miss Letitia in the post office. The poor soul had acted so strangely at the mention of Clara's name. The poor dear looked like a witch and just the mention of Clara's name had sent her running. How different she was from the Letitia who sat in Mrs. Carey's parlor enraptured by music.

Unable to sleep, Anna got up and sat on the side of the bed. The tin popped again. Again she went to the window and stood there for some time looking down on the street below. The noise did unnerve her. If she had not been standing there she would never have seen him, but the tin snapped in a way that startled her and she leaned her head far out against the screen and there he was, a man in khaki pants! Only his legs showed as he flattened himself against the side of the house. Anna was petrified!

Her heart pounding, she reached for the phone and dialed the operator. "Get me the police!"

She could hear the man scrambling down the fire ladder.

"I'll send someone," the dispatcher was saying.

Anna stood at the door, her hand gripping the knob, shaking from head to toe.

*What's taking them so long?* she thought.

It seemed like an hour before a policeman arrived. He had in tow a black man, eyes wide with fright.

"Is this the man? He was over at the station in the phone booth."

Anna looked at the frightened man. "Were you up on my roof?" she asked.

"No, ma'am. No, ma'am," he said, as scared as she.

Anna remembered the khaki pants. "No, Officer, he isn't the man. The one on the roof was wearing khaki pants."

"You can go," the policeman said and the man leaped off the porch and ran down the street.

The policeman asked questions, wrote his report, then put the tablet back in his pocket. "You got nothing to worry about, Miss Petersen. We'll put a stake-out in your apartment. If he comes back, we'll catch him."

But the stake-out didn't catch him. It was Miss Pendergraft who solved the case. "It's your next-door neighbor," she said. "I taught Elmer in the fifth grade. He's been peeping in windows all his life—made a career of it. The cops know who it was. What we have to do is find you another place to live and in this town that won't be easy."

# CHAPTER
# TWENTY-EIGHT

The new Rambler was parked under the oaks near the porch. Anna hated the new apartment but had no choice; it was the only available place in town. The apartment was on the first floor in a barn of a house. The porch around the house made access easy—all anyone had to do was open a window and step inside. Anna wondered how long it would take Elmer to find her.

The police assured her that Peeping Toms were harmless. "They only want to look," the dispatcher said. Small comfort, at best.

As if that were not enough, for weeks Anna was terrified at night by sounds outside. The noises sounded like babies crying! Yet, when she opened the door, the noises hushed. As baffled as she was, she wouldn't tell anyone for fear they'd think she was crazy. But, finally, trying to sound as casual as possible, she told Horace about the noise and he said he'd come over and take a look around.

"I only hear it at night," she said for the tenth time.

He was walking around in the yard, poking a stick around in the leaves, looking up in the trees. Stooping down, he picked up a dead bird. "Here's your problem," he said. "You got screech owls." He held up the bird for her to examine. "This is a baby owl." He looked up at the trees again. "Uh-huh. Every one o' these hollow trees is infested with owls. You're right. They sound just like babies crying. If you'd look out at night you'd see the grown birds flappin' around. They're nocturnal."

"Will they hurt you?"

"No, not 'less they got rabies, somethin' like that."

Anna wrote Marge about the whole affair.

> *Dear Marge,*
>
> *The way I got the apartment in the big Wilkes house—the teacher who lived here before went away to summer school and died. (She taught in a county school and I didn't know her.)*
>
> *It's a big apartment with high ceilings, lots of space I haven't furniture for. There's no closet and the kitchen is made from a narrow hall. Chicora's drapes fit some of the windows and we used striped sheets for the rest. The bedroom is on the front, the living room in between the bedroom and the bathroom. Inconvenient but the other place was worse.*
>
> *There are lots of doors and that's scary. Especially after the Peeping Tom at the other place. I'm afraid to look behind one door for fear some weirdo will reach out from behind another door.*
>
> *Only one lady lives here—in number six. The other four apartments are not habitable because of broken pipes or fallen plaster.*
>
> *And you wouldn't believe how far from the street this house is and how far it is from the nearest neighbors. It's in the middle of a spooky grove and it's hard to sleep when the screech owls are screaming and flapping around the hollow trees at night.*
>
> *I'd like the bathroom all right if there weren't holes all the way through the floor. Marge, do you think any kind of animal could crawl up through those holes? If they might, please don't tell me. I never told you but at the other place I woke up one night with something splashing in*

the bathroom. When I turned on the light, would you believe a great big wharf rat was in the commode? I nearly died! I slammed down the lid, called my neighbor, and we left the apartment while the plumber came and killed it. Marge, I don't like to think about it but what if I had gone in there in the middle of the night and sat down?!

In this bathroom the tub perches high on ball and claw feet and its sides are painted yellow. At night I sit in it, waiting for the warm water trickling from the faucet to fill it. As soon as there's enough water, I wash my underwear and stockings and hang them on the towel rack above. Then I wait some more, the water rising slowly, and I think.

I think about the woman who sat as I am sitting—wanting to soak in the warm water—soak away the stress of one more day of school. Wanting the luxury of a quarter hour without questions, without noise, the smell of tennis shoes and bubble gum. A few minutes to ponder the car payment or professional dues or the wedding present a former student expects.

Sure, she washed her underwear and hose, hung them limp and wet on the towel rack—wished the water would come faster and be warmer—worried about getting all those papers graded.

Then she went away to summer school and died.

There's a lesson in this somewhere but I think it's the one I always hear from you!

Love,
Anna

Adjustment to the apartment was almost as difficult as the new situation at school. One Negro teacher was added to the faculty and two Negro students were in Anna's classes. Joe Ellsworth was a tall, satin-black boy, brash but brilliant. On the first day he brandished his own checkbook in an effort to impress and the white students looked at him and smirked. The next day he left the checkbook at home.

As for the girl, Yolanda Smith, she was frightened speechless. Anna asked her to remain after class and, alone in the room, the girl began shaking all over. "Oh, Miz Petersen, I ain't nevah been aroun' so many white peoples! I so scairt!"

"I understand, Yolanda."

"Don't nobody understan'. My momma, she don' understan'. She say, 'Yolanda, you go to dat white school an' you hol' up yo' haid cuz you is as good as anybody.' But it ain' dat easy, Miz Petersen."

Too afraid to eat lunch in the cafeteria, Yolanda came to Anna's room every day. Anna didn't have to ask her why; the teachers' room was rife with reports of harassment, name calling, fights. The poor girl stayed pale with fear throughout the first six weeks. After that she began to relax. In class she sometimes slept. Her grades were poor but the other teachers said the girl was slow. Only Mrs. Simmons, the Negro teacher, disagreed. "That girl has plenty of sense," she said but would say no more.

Anna sent Yolanda to talk with Mrs. Simmons but it did no good. Yolanda continued to sleep in class and when she was awake she seemed dull and uninterested.

Joe Ellsworth talked with her. "Girl, you gotta make a showing," he told her but he got nowhere with her.

Joe was doing well. By the end of the first six weeks he was on the honor roll; by the end of the semester, he was leading the class. The fact that he was smart did not endear him to white classmates. "He cheats," they said, and only David McBryde came to his defense. That sealed David's fate. Students turned their backs on him.

It was not until February that Anna found out Yolanda Smith's secret. Anna chaperoned a trip to the State Fair and when none of the white girls would room with Yolanda, Anna invited her to share her room. Almost by accident, Anna noticed a string dangling from the lid of the toilet tank. Curious, she opened the lid and there was Yolanda's bottle inside the tank. Anna couldn't believe her eyes!

Coming back in the room she confronted the girl. "Is this yours?" she asked.

The girl hung her head.

"So this is the problem?"

Yolanda's head hung low on her chest and she would not look up. Anna sat beside her on the bed. "Yolanda, I'll have to report this to Mr. Secrest."

Still no answer.

"I'm afraid he'll have to expel you. The rule says no alcoholic beverages on campus or any school activity."

Yolanda burst into tears. "Oh, Miz Petersen, my momma'll kill me!"

"Yolanda, why do you drink?"

"You ought to know. It's de onliest way I can get through all dem classes."

"Do you drink at night?"

"No'm. My momma'd kill me."

Anna emptied the bottle into the sink and thought about what she would say.

"Yolanda, did you know that drinking is forbidden by school rules?"

"Yes'm, I know dat."

"Yolanda, I'm sorry this happened. I want you to know, I'll do anything I can to help you."

The girl pled with her. "Miz Petersen, if Mr. Secrest expels me, my momma'll kill me."

Looking in the girl's stricken face, Anna did not doubt that the girl believed what she said. "I'll do whatever I can, Yolanda."

Mark Secrest did expel Yolanda. Nothing Anna said

to him would change his mind. "Miss Petersen, we have to enforce the rules. If I let one student get away with a thing like this there'll be others. Besides, she's a Negro student and the town won't stand for special treatment of Negroes."

After school, Anna drove to Yolanda's house. The tar paper shack perched on cement blocks with three feet of space beneath. A dog lay underneath the porch thumping his tail. Anna was afraid to get out of the car and waited to see if Yolanda would come outside.

The wooden porch leaned away from the house and the front door was a gaping black hole. The screen bulged and holes in it were plugged with cotton. The two windows looked like eyes in the ramshackle shack and two children peered out at her. She tooted the horn and the faces disappeared. Shyly, one of the children came to the door. Anna rolled down the window and asked him to hold the dog. He obeyed.

Even then, Anna was reluctant about getting out but, mustering all her courage, she opened the door. Walking across the bare ground she could hear the television inside. The boy opened the door and a woman's voice invited her in. Anna introduced herself and the fat woman sitting on a broken down chair called Yolanda.

The house smelled of cabbage and the walls were smoked and streaked. The woman asked Anna to sit down and she did, in a straight-backed chair by the door. Over the television set, the faces of Martin Luther King, Jesus, and John F. Kennedy stared back at her.

When the girl came in the room it was obvious that she had been beaten—her lip was swollen and she moved slowly as if she were sore.

"Mrs. Smith, I'm sorry this happened. I wish there was something I could do to help," Anna began.

"Miz Petersen, dere ain' nuthin' nobody kin do wid a no 'count chile what ain' got sense. I works hard bringing up dese chuldrun right. I go outta here at six o'clock in the mawnin' a'ter I done make dere breakfus' and I works two jobs evah day doin' day work. Come home heah an' dese chuldrun bees evah wheah 'cept wheah dey 'spose to be. Dat Yolanda spose' to clean de house, mind de knee baby and wash or iron de clothes, cook dey supper. But I come home after dark and wheah she be? No tellin' wheah. Den she gits de chance for a education and what she do? She bring down my haid wid drinkin' likker! Got no pride."

The woman's face was stormy with anger and hurt. "I whup her good but it don' do no good."

"I know life is hard for you, Mrs. Smith. I guess none of us knows how hard life is for another person. You have a daughter to be proud of despite this. She's like a pioneer, the first student from McCrory's Quarter to come to McAdden High. I guess you and I can't understand what it's like for her being surrounded by all white students."

Yolanda's mother stiffened. "My Yolanda's jest as good as any o' them white chuldrun. She got no reason not to hold her haid up high."

"That's right, but young people can be cruel. There's name calling and prejudice."

"Dat ain' nuthin' new. All my life I be called names. Here my chile gits to go to school an' me, I worked in de fields when I was her age—don' nevah see de inside o' no school. I works to sen' her to school and dis is what she do. She got no call to do dis to me. Yes'm, I whups her good!" She turned to Yolanda. "What cha got to say for yo'se'f?"

Yolanda hung her head. Her mother took a swipe at her with a flyswatter.

"Momma doin' what she think bes'. I ain' no good. You'll see."

Anna felt a lump in her throat as she looked at the pitiful girl. "No, Yolanda. You're wrong." But Yolanda only hung her head.

Mark Secrest would not relent—a rule was a rule and drinking alcohol on a school-sponsored trip was punishable by expulsion. Finally, Anna asked him, "Would you mind talking this over with Mr. Gilchrist?"

"It won't do any good, Miss Petersen, but, yes, I'll talk it over with him. Lord knows these people come from a culture that doesn't fit our middle-class standards. I guess every teenage black knows what it is to drink."

"I wouldn't know about that."

"Would you care to go with me to Gilchrist?"

"Yes. I would like to speak in Yolanda's behalf."

"What can you say?"

"I can say how difficult it is for a Negro student to come to an all white school—how it's enough to drive them to drink."

"Well, I don't think Gilchrist will change the rule for one student. As you know, the whole town is up in arms about this integration and if we show favoritism we'll get a lot of criticism."

But Gilchrist did understand and was willing to risk public disfavor. "That colored girl needs an education, Mark. If we don't take her back she'll never get another day of school."

Secrest was surprised. When they came out of the office, he shook his head. "Well, it's a whole new ball game, Miss Petersen. Brace yourself. There's no telling what kind of fireworks this'll cause."

Fortunately, no one learned what offense Yolanda had committed and since she was out of school only two days, no one except teachers knew she had been expelled. Of course, they talked and their curiosity led them to Anna and the trip to Raleigh. "What did Yolanda Smith get expelled for? Did she do something on that trip you took them on?" they asked.

Anna kept mum. "I really can't say," she answered.

Yolanda did not improve appreciably. Anna talked

with her, worked with her, but Yolanda was always tired. In the weeks that followed, she lost weight steadily. Anna sent her to the visiting nurse.

In the spring, David McBryde ran for student body president and lost to a girl. "It's humiliating," David admitted. "Proves I'm not cut out for politics."

Everybody knew that his friendship with Joe Ellsworth had cost him the election but if he knew it, he didn't let on.

"What are you going to do with your life, David?" Anna asked.

"I think I'll study medicine or criminal law or Chinese. I found this great book on China—"

Anna laughed. "David, David, how long are you going to go in all directions? You're a junior. It's high time you settled on one subject."

"Miss Petersen, it's hard for me to go on with my life knowing Floyd is still in prison. There ought to be some way we could help him. If I have to, I'll study law—at least long enough to find out what to do. I tell you, Miss Petersen, there's no earthly way Floyd Berry could have killed anybody. Even if he was drunk, I don't believe he'd do something that went against everything he believes."

"Why don't you give up on that, David? It's hopeless."

"Maybe, but I'm not giving up."

Anna admired the boy and, secretly, she was not willing to give up either.

In May, Mrs. Carey wrote that she was coming to Scotsville for a visit and wanted very much to see Anna and, if possible, Letitia Oakes. Well, getting Letitia to cooperate wouldn't be easy but Anna would try. There was no use going to her house; Letitia wouldn't come to the door.

First, Anna called Miss Letitia but she would not answer the phone. She drove past Letitia's house hoping to catch her coming or going. At last she resorted to parking down by the corner after dark and waiting until Letitia came out for her nocturnal rounds. It worked. Anna succeeded in getting Letitia to come to the window of the car. Nervously, she listened to Anna, shook her head vigorously at the invitation to come to Anna's house to see Mrs. Carey. Then Anna coaxed her with the promise of nothing but music and shamed her with recalling her lifelong friendship with Mrs. Carey. Finally, she was persuaded.

The day before Mrs. Carey's arrival, Anna was in the store shopping for groceries when she met Anita. The girl's lip was swollen and Anna might not have suspected anything had she not remembered Yolanda's beating. "I ran into a cabinet," Anita explained.

Anna turned her attention to the baby in the grocery buggy. "Isn't he precious!" She studied his features. "Looks like Andrew."

"That's what everyone says."

"How is Andrew?" Anna asked, concerned.

"About the same, Miss Petersen."

Anita looked worn, older. Anna touched her arm. "Anita, I just pray things will get better."

The girl's eyes filled. "I'm pregnant again."

"Oh?"

"I just found out today."

Anna didn't know what to say. From the sadness in Anita's face, congratulations were not in order.

"Andy isn't working now. He's going into service."

"Well, maybe that will be helpful."

"He'll have a commission." The dullness in her eyes betrayed her hopelessness. Anna hated to leave her.

"Anita, if there's ever anything I can do—"

"Thanks." The girl reached for Anna's arm, grasped it as if desperate to say more. But then she let go and nodded good-bye.

When Anna came home from the grocery store Miss

Pearl McCabe called to say Mrs. Carey wasn't coming. She had called the night before to say she'd have to postpone her trip because she wasn't feeling well.

Anna was disappointed. As she put up the groceries she debated what to do about Miss Letitia. She decided to let the invitation stand. It was a risk; Letitia might think it was some kind of trick but Anna wanted to see her, wanted to talk to the lonely woman.

When Letitia arrived, it was dark. Parking her express wagon by the steps, she glanced about warily. Before she asked, Anna explained Mrs. Carey's absence. Letitia frowned, stood up to leave but Anna insisted she stay. "Please, Miss Letitia, I have this new music and there's no one to hear me play. Would you do me the favor of listening?"

Letitia hesitated, then eased down into the chair. Letitia was transfixed by music, unaware of anything else and even as Anna tuned the cello Letitia wet her lips with anticipation.

After the first sonata, Anna offered Letitia refreshments. "Coffee? Tea? I have some cake."

Miss Letitia shook her head, impatient for the music to continue.

Anna found Stravinsky's *Orpheus* and as she played, Letitia's eyes misted. "I met him," she whispered. "I met Igor Stravinsky."

Still whispering, she continued. "Stravinsky studied under Rimsky-Korsakov, both Russian, you know. I met Igor Stravinsky in New York during the war, don't you know. He upset the musical world, you know, with his *Rite of Spring*." Merriment danced in her eyes. "He used different things like irregular, changing meters, don't you know, and numerous keys—caused a riot at its first performance.

"I never liked his later work." Letitia's face clouded. "I think he wrote for money, don't you know."

Anna continued to play one piece after another and

from time to time Miss Letitia interrupted her, pointing to the score and humming the nuances Anna had missed.

When it was past midnight, Anna expected Miss Letitia to get up and go and when she didn't, Anna did not know what to make of it. Miss Letitia sat quietly, perhaps still hearing the music in her head.

Anna put the cello in its case and zipped it shut. Still Miss Letitia sat, twisting a handkerchief in her lap and saying nothing.

Anna felt awkward. Then it dawned on her—Miss Letitia had something on her mind.

"Miss Petersen," she began, her voice husky, "I do not have long to live."

She waved away Anna's protest, pressed her palm against her breast.

"I have something to tell you. It must not go out of this room." She glanced about furtively. Then her eyes met Anna's and would not let them go. "Except you must carry it to Judge Hall," she whispered.

"Judge Hall?"

Letitia pulled Anna down on the couch beside her. Her breath was sour and she spoke jerkily, agitated by what she had to tell. "I saw Clara die." Her voice was dreadful, sounding hoarse and hollow. "It wasn't the first time I saw her on the floor. Once before I saw her get out of the tub, don't you know, and fall down unconscious. That time, I went inside and helped her up only I told her that if she ever did that again she needn't to count on me. She promised me she'd never do that again and she promised never to tell anyone, don't you know.

"She was a foolish woman, Clara was—water scalding hot—she'd lie in the tub, don't you know."

"Soaking her bones, I remember. She had arthritis."

Letitia was distracted by a noise outside.

"Owls. It's only owls screeching."

Letitia cupped her ear to listen. "Yes, owls in the hollow trees."

Anna could feel her heart beating. If only Letitia would get on with the story.

"The night Clara died, I was near her house and looking in the window. She stayed in the tub a long time. Everything was all steamed up, don't you know. Finally, she climbed out of the tub and no sooner did she get out than she leaned over this way and fell. I knew she had passed out but I thought she would come to, don't you know. I waited. All I could see were her legs, don't you know, sticking out from behind the cabinet. In a few minutes, I decided to go in.

"Clara always kept a key under the flower pot, don't you know. But it was dark and I had a hard time finding the key. By the time I got inside, don't you know, I found Clara lying face down, her head in that bucket of water—dead! Oh, it was a shock! Drowned in a bucket of water! A freak accident, don't you know. A freak accident."

Miss Letitia was overwrought and the distress in her face made Anna want to comfort her.

"Oh, Miss Letitia, how awful for you."

The woman drew back like a caged animal.

Anna waited for her to calm a bit but she felt she must ask. "Tell me, Miss Letitia, why didn't you report this to the police?"

Letitia stared at her incredulously. Anna repeated the question, "Why didn't you report it?"

Letitia flayed her arms about wildly, made as if she would jump up and leave.

"No, please. Please don't go."

"I've told you everything," she whispered. "I stayed in the house with her all night and in the morning I slipped home, don't you see." Saliva wet the corners of her mouth as she spoke. "When the neighbor noticed that Clara did not bring in her paper, he checked on her. That's when they found out, don't you know. I never dreamed they'd think it was murder and when they did, I was afraid they'd think—"

Letitia's face was twisted with anguish. "They think I'm a crazy old woman, but if you told them, they'd believe you."

"I'll tell them, Miss Letitia, but if the judge wants to see you will you go to him?" Letitia looked the other way, twisted the handkerchief and did not answer. Anna touched her arm. Letitia looked at her, still distraught. Anna pled with her. "You must save that boy," she said earnestly.

In the silence that stood between them, only the screeching owls could be heard.

"What if Floyd were your son, your very own son, Jim. What would you think if someone knew how to prove his innocence but kept quiet. Miss Letitia, are you listening?"

At last, Miss Letitia drew in her breath and held it ever so long. When she exhaled there was an ever so slight nod of the head. Anna had won!

Miss Letitia stood up to go. At the door, she paused, turned around, and stood for a moment. The layers of clothing made her look larger than she was and the disheveled hair gave her a harried, scarecrow look, but to Anna, she was beautiful.

Anna barely caught her words when she spoke. "Now I can die in peace."

Anna moved toward her and as she did, Letitia opened her arms and the two women hugged each other.

Suddenly embarrassed, Letitia flung open the door. The owls hushed and, in the light from the open door, she made her way down the steps and disappeared in the night.

Anna closed the door softly and leaned against it. The little wagon was clattering onto the street.

As soon as Judge Hall heard Anna's story, he sent for Miss Letitia. Once she signed a sworn statement, the judge reopened the case.

The news swept Scotsville like wildfire. The story in the *Herald* was picked up by the wire services and reporters came from all over to follow up on the case. They hounded Miss Letitia and spread her picture in all their papers; wrote stories about the "Scotsville Eccentric" and about kleptomania.

The town rose up in arms. Cecil McCurdy sent security guards to Miss Letitia's house. Local policemen arrested the reporters on trumped-up charges. In three days they were run out of town but not soon enough.

The notoriety was too much for Miss Letitia and she did not live to see Floyd Berry released. One rainy night Roosevelt Carey stumbled on Letitia's body down by the express office. Dr. Jennie examined her. "Apparently, her heart simply gave out."

The whole town turned out for the funeral but Letitia's son requested a private service. The Baptist pastor read the Bible, Anna played two selections on the cello, and Woodall Jackson prayed.

Months later when they were cleaning out Miss Letitia's house, rumor had it that in the attic they even found embalming fluid but no one had it in his heart to make fun of Miss Letitia.

# CHAPTER
# TWENTY-NINE

The same year David McBryde graduated valedictorian, Joe Ellsworth was salutatorian. David went to Brown to study Chinese and Joe joined the Army which was the only way he could go on with his education. Yolanda was in the sanitarium, one lung destroyed by tuberculosis. With their departure, an era ended.

In the fall, McAdden High as they knew it would be a thing of the past. All the schools in the county were merging into one and moving into the big new building constructed on McCurdy property.

As Anna walked up the steps with their irregular rise and pitch, she held onto the railings bequeathed the school by the class of '56.

Inside her classroom, she looked at the cracks in the plaster, observing how they had widened during the years. Overhead were the long fluorescent lights that periodically crashed to the floor. Miraculously, no one was ever hurt, but how well they might have been sitting in desks beneath the lights.

Anna had listened to all the administration had to say about the advantages of consolidation: the variety of curriculum offerings, the modern facilities possible with pooled resources. To express how she felt would brand her, as Horace would say, a "mossback," not forward-looking.

She opened the windows wide to let in the good fresh air, then sat down at her desk for the last time. The ancient desks facing her were marked with names, initials, and dates, some carved before her time, others since her coming. "Pluto" was plain to see on the back of his curved arm desk and whenever it was moved from the front of the room, Anna invariably put it back where it belonged. On one of the back seats were Sue Marie Ellsworth's initials " + A. L.," permanent witness to first love.

Anna's apprehension about consolidation was not due to sentimentality. A part of her security was found in the predictability of life and what lay ahead was anything but predictable. Everyone knew they were making a giant step and were intrigued by the prospects for the future, but did they realize that never again could they leap back across the chasm? They were leaving a way of life they could never go back to. Nor could they take it with them. Certainly not the sense of the personal, not in a student body of fifteen hundred.

The librarian was coming down the hall. "Anybody seen Roosevelt Carey?" she called out. She poked her head in Anna's room. "Hey. Have you seen Roosevelt? I just took down the pictures of the boys and I want Roosevelt to take them to their families." She saw Roosevelt come in and she went after him.

So, they had taken down the pictures of Eddie and Ted that had hung in the library since the accident. A heavy sadness bore down on Anna.


In 1967, the Vietnam War was heating up and "flower children" were everywhere, advocating love, not war. Hippie styles became the rage and the spread of drugs became alarming.

Anna understood the young people who were disillusioned by the "power structure" and the materialism of the older generation. The answers were not easy. The questions were even harder.

# CHAPTER
# THIRTY

Since the riots in Watts, the new slogan was "black power" and militant organizations were sprouting all over the country. As for the Indians, no one had doubted their power since they ran the Ku Klux Klan from Beaver County in the '50s.

Local tensions abounded, each community resentful at having to give up their school. Philip Gilchrist succeeded in getting the school board to merge the schools gradually, one at a time, and that lessened all-out revolt at the start.

"Freedom of choice" was a thing of the past and yellow buses patroled the county, criss-crossing neighborhoods, splitting up children within a family.

In such a climate, school began in the fall of '67. In the beautiful air-conditioned auditorium, dignitaries dedicated, in deathless prose, the new McAdden High School to Minerva and all the gods and goddesses of wisdom, learning, and light. Prognosticians of the highest degree gave voice to lofty dreams and expectations for the student body now that they had air-conditioning and carpeted labs.

Coming down from the stage, Anna heard Mark Secrest say to his new assistant, Horace Wigglesworth, "Let's see now if we can make it through the first week."

Horace laughed. He was confident. In fact, Horace had never been more confident. Anna didn't know if it was due to his having acquired his doctorate in education or his marriage to a woman from Weston. He was the only man on the platform wearing an academic robe on the opening day of school and whether it was the warmth of the robe or the weight he had put on since his marriage, she did not know, but Horace's face was florid. The high color did not seem to go away even after he took off the robe. Undoubtedly, Horace was being well fed and he was also middle-aged, a combination that could produce high blood pressure and all the related conditions. But Anna had more things to worry about than Horace's health.

Despite every effort to plan ahead, the opening of school was total confusion. Nothing worked: not the schedules, not the equipment. It was the confusion that held the students together and brought them to the playing field on Homecoming Night without incident. That the queen was white made no matter so long as there were different colors in the band and on the playing field. Seeing black and Indian band members in Scottish kilts came as a jolt to spectators, unaware as they were of how far the social experiment had come.

In her class was the most intelligent girl Anna had ever taught—an Indian girl named Delores. The girl bore the strong features of her hardy stock and carried herself well, but Anna sensed that the reserve was a mask for the fear the girl felt in the presence of town students.

Anna spent hours breaking through the girl's reserve. Every afternoon Delores had to wait for the last bus, the one that made two round trips, and she spent that time in Anna's room. It was then they became friends. Little by little Delores told Anna about herself and her family. Delores's father was a tenant farmer with a house full of children. In the isolation of that house, set in the middle of the field, there was only work, some books, and love. There was no time for social life except church and theirs was an Indian church with only people like themselves.

Delores finally opened up and talked about what she knew best, her Indian culture. "Our dialect is pure Old English, Miss Petersen," she said, "which makes it different from the speech of whites or blacks. In written language our way of talking is obsolete because in the swamps where our people lived, colloquial English has been preserved for centuries."

"I wish you'd explain all this to me."

"We Lumbees drawl the first syllable in every sentence."

Anna had not heard Delores drawl anything.

"Usually when we meet someone we say, 'Mon-n-n,' which means 'man' and we might say something like, 'Mon, my fayther told me that his fayther . . .'" She thought a moment. "Another thing we do is add a 'y' as they did in Anglo-Saxon. My father told me it's something about the palate; the way the palate sounds consonants causes us to say 'cow' as 'cy-ow' in a kind of glide, don't you see? 'Cart' is 'cy-art' and 'card' is 'cy-ard.'"

"Yes, I've noticed that. I've heard students say 'girl' as 'gy-irl.' Years ago, a boy I taught used to always say, 'ky-ind.' His name is Floyd Berry. I guess you've heard of him?"

"Oh, yes. He's my mother's cousin. Since he got out of prison he's doing real well selling used cars. On weekends he speaks in churches over in Beaver County.

"We have a lot of relatives in Beaver County. They use words you never heard of. Did you ever hear the word 'crone'? It's a word that means to push down."

A bee was buzzing in the room and Anna swatted it. "Delores, you talk like a college professor. Why is it that you speak so well?"

"Miss Petersen, I guess it's because our mother and father saw that our generation would have to break with the past. They taught themselves how to speak properly and they never allowed us to talk any other way.

"Because we live on the land, my family always has plenty to eat if not much more. My daddy buys books and when he comes in from the field, he reads and my mama always sees to it that we children read. My sister who's in the Air Force gave us a TV last Christmas and that cuts down on our reading time, but you almost have to have a television nowadays."

"How long has your sister been in the Air Force?"

"Quite a while. She's made the rank of major."

"Major?"

"She's very smart. Mama worries about her in Vietnam. Sissy doesn't write Mama anything that might make her worry but she tells me plenty.

"She said the pilots have it the hardest. They sit around bored between missions but then, when they fly they come back emotional wrecks. Sissy says they either go crazy or they become cynical."

"It must be awful."

"I couldn't do it. When they press the buttons to drop napalm, they know it means the lives of people like themselves."

"Delores, what do you think of the war—all the protesters?"

"I've thought a lot about the war, Miss Petersen, but it seems to me that if we believe in freedom for ourselves we ought to believe in it for everybody. Protesters call Vietnam an immoral war. Well, there can be immoral peace, Daddy says. He said we should have helped the Hungarians when they revolted. Daddy said we kept an immoral peace. I'm proud of my sister and what she's doing. I hope we win over there. I hope Vietnam can be free.

"Sissy said the media don't give the real picture of the war. Once she went up to a fire base with some Red Cross workers. They took a band to welcome troops coming back from a land mission and camera crews were there to film the event but the reporter who came along had already written the story back at the base. He wrote what he wanted to write.

"Sissy said they were terrified because the enemy could be anywhere around them and their group had no weapons. When the troops finally arrived, they were high on Cambodian grass, too stoned to care.

"A cameraman stood on top of a bunker taking pictures of the Chinook helicopters and tanks returning, but the girls had the good sense to hit the ground. Sissy felt something under her and when she got up again there was a man's severed hand lying where she had been.

"Sissy said there was a crewman in the crowd from Scotsville. I forget his name. This fellow seemed okay at the time but when they got back to the base he went to pieces."

"Was his name Ellsworth? Joe Ellsworth? He's a black soldier from here. I taught him several years ago."

"No, not Ellsworth."

"Was he a chaplain?"

"No."

"How about Andrew Lawton?" Before Delores answered, Anna sensed it was he.

"Yes, that's the name. Do you know him?"

"Yes. I know him well."

"Sorry I can't tell you much about him. Sissy said he was incoherent when she tried to talk to him. She couldn't get much sense out of him. Sissy said he stood on a table pointing to Red Cross workers shouting, 'She's a communist! She's a communist!' When a commander came in, he was a communist, too!"

"Well, what did they do with him?"

Delores shrugged her shoulders. "Sissy said there're so many men who have episodes, as they call them, they have to ignore them."

The news depressed Anna. She thought of Anita and wondered how she was faring. The last she heard, Anita and the two children were in Texas.

"Delores, do you think you might go into service when you graduate?"

"No, Miss Petersen, all I want out of this life is to have a child of my own."

"Well, Delores, there's nothing more precious than human life and if you bring a child into the world you have something of eternal value."

If Delores was the most intelligent girl Anna had taught, she thought Bobby Shelton must be the most unintelligent boy. He was in his sixth year of high school and his third course in U.S. history. Bobby's two-hundred pound body bulged on all sides of the new plastic desk. He sat slovenly, enjoyed being the center of attention.

Students were checking answers to homework questions and Bobby was reading his answer aloud. "Why was Saratoga the turning point of the war?" he repeated. "The turning point meant that the point of the war was directly there. When they had to meet, they changed their mind and started pointing for somewhere to have the war. You could only turn but so much to beat the turning point of the war. They fought at a point in order to fight better. They called it that because they were turning at the point when they was at war."

The class started laughing. "Would you run that by me one more time?" someone asked and he did. The students laughed so hard they cried.

Anna wondered if Bobby did not try to be ridiculous or if there was some irregularity in his thinking apparatus. She talked to Bobby's guidance counselor. "The other day," she said, "I had drilled the class in the 'A, B, C' islands, Aruba, Bonaire, and Curacao, and I asked Bobby to give me their names. He answered the first one right, then added 'Benezuela and Corea'!

I thought the class would have hysterics. And when I asked him the cause of President Roosevelt's death, he said, 'He had a cerebral hemorrhoid.'"

"A cerebral hemorrhoid? That's nothing," the counselor said. "He was telling me about somebody getting shot nine times in his intertestaments!" He was looking for Bobby's file. "Aw, yes, just as I thought. Here's his psychological." He scanned the form. "Bobby has a learning disability."

"Well, how can I help him?"

"That's hard to say, Miss Petersen. He probably has a chemical imbalance—maybe a birth defect—or it may have been caused by improper diet. We really need to send him downtown for further testing."

"If you just give me some pointers in how to help him now—"

"Well, you know, Miss Petersen, kids like Bobby need a lotta love. They need to have a good self-image. They've experienced nothing but failure, so give him a lotta praise. You can do a lot for that boy with a little TLC."

"But isn't there some technique, some way to get through or around his disability?"

"I'll check his reading scores. Maybe he should be in Special Ed."

Anna felt totally frustrated. Bobby Shelton was not stupid but she did not know how to teach him and there didn't seem to be help from any source. She sought out Bobby's homeroom teacher whose opinion was quite clear. "He plainly doesn't want to learn, Anna. I call it unadulterated ignorance. I wish I could help you but in all the education courses I took, not one of them ever addressed the problem of ignorance. Did yours? Ignorance is made up of a lot of things—prejudice, laziness, superstition, but most of all, stubbornness. I'm sure you'll agree that Bobby is stubborn."

Anna agreed that Bobby was stubborn and had other

undesirable traits, but he was accomplished in one area—the art of making trouble. Bobby draped a Confederate flag over the balcony of the commons and in five minutes fights were going on all over campus. Student mobs surged through the halls knocking down everything and everyone in their way. By noon, there was a walkout by black students. They crossed the highway and lined the road looking back at white students lining the other side. Mark Secrest persuaded the black students to assemble at the stadium where school officials could come and talk with them. As talks progressed, Horace acted as courier to report back to the teachers. "We're listening to grievances," he said, tight-lipped.

Horace, as assistant principal, felt the responsibility to assure the school's good image, and the only way to do that was by minimizing difficulties and by keeping information under tight security.

The walkout was not something easily concealed. After all, the whole town saw the students out on the highway in the face-off and they saw black students transported to the stadium in buses. And the most disconcerting part of the whole affair was that students were roaming the streets, upsetting the Scotsville routine.

Mark Secrest was a reasonable man but he and Philip Gilchrist thought it necessary to get to the bottom of the trouble, nip things in the bud by disciplining the ringleaders. Investigation and negotiations took time. It was important to weigh every concession carefully and make crystal clear any agreement under which students would be permitted to return to class. Gilchrist told the faculty, "It would be a fatal error to minimize the situation."

The town was not pleased. Mark Secrest came under fire and nothing Philip Gilchrist said made any difference. Parents of both races kept their children at home.

Horace kept up a good front and when he was asked, he repeated again and again, "Other schools are having riots. McAdden High has had a walkout. That tells you something right there, dudn't it? There's been misunderstanding but now that we've listened to both sides, we're ready to forget the whole affair, get the kids off the street."

That was what they wanted to hear. Of all the school personnel, Horace Wigglesworth was getting the highest marks. "Get the kids off the streets" ricocheted all over Scotsville. And, back in school they went.

Tensions mounted. White students were antagonistic, black students belligerent. Incidents happened daily.

"Liver lips!" Bobby Shelton called out in class and a black girl hit him over the head with a dictionary. Anna had to haul both of them to the office not knowing if they would go with her and fearing for her own safety. Before they reached the office, they saw a group of boys, jeering, threatening Horace who was pinned against a wall. "Pink cheeks! Pink cheeks!" they taunted and Horace could only stand there and endure the indignity.

Anna pushed her way through the crowd. "Let Miss Pete through!" somebody yelled.

"Go on to class, students. You've had your fun," she said, repeating it several times until they heard.

Still poking fun at Horace, the boys began to turn away. When they looked as if they were dispersing, Anna went on to the office. *It must be very humiliating for Horace*, she thought. Women were not challenged the way the men were. Students enjoyed pitting themselves against male authority.

Later in the day, Mark Secrest called a faculty meeting. He asked for reports of incidents and in his grave manner, made notes. "Mr. Wigglesworth, do you have anything you'd like to say?"

Horace stood and his new-found authority was intact. "I'd just like to say, 'Keep your shirt on.' By now you should know that Mr. Secrest and I can handle it."

Two weeks later there was a full-scale riot. Rocks were flying, shattering glass. Belts and chains were swinging. People were screaming! Anna was pushed by the mob to the railing around the balcony above the commons. The main confrontation was below—black students on one side, white on the other, edging closer together. Police were positioning themselves between the two attempting to hold them back but both sides overpowered them at once. The bedlam was savage: kicking, hitting, clawing, biting, hysterical screaming, running. In the melee, Anna saw Delores attacked by five black girls, vainly trying to defend herself. Anna pushed her way through the crowd trying to get downstairs to stop them.

By the time she got to them, a policeman was restraining Delores. What he did not see was a black girl swinging down on Delores's hair. The officer could not hear Anna for the deafening pandemonium, nor see the bloody bald spot on Delores's head as he forced his way through the crowd, taking her into custody.

Police herded people into patrol cars, carrying some of them bodily. Through bull horns they ordered students to go home. Those who were terrified ran to the buses; those who were enjoying the excitement did not leave until they were forced to go by the police.

That day, Anna went home a basket case. In the days that followed, there were hearings and trials, suspensions and expulsions and through it all Horace, whose responsibility was to report to the faculty, informed no one of anything.

Rumor and hearsay abounded. Anna was so shaken, she thought about quitting. Combat, not education, was the order of the day. To walk on campus and see guardsmen in riot gear created panic. If only the faculty had known the guard would be there, they could have prepared the students and themselves. As it was, the school appeared to be under siege and that struck fear in all their hearts. A guidance counselor saw the troops, turned around in the parking lot, and never came back.

Students huddled around Anna's desk, afraid to go into the hall. She was almost as afraid as they, yet she walked them to the restrooms and stood guard to protect them. When the final bell rang, she watched them until they were safely on the buses, then prayed for them as they rolled out of the parking lot.

The scuttlebutt had it that a student hit Mr. Secrest over the head with a drink bottle and that a policeman lost a tooth. Bobby Shelton said, "If this keeps up, somebody's gonna get killed!"

# CHAPTER
# THIRTY-ONE

No one was killed, but there were casualties. Philip
Gilchrist suffered a heart attack and was forced to retire. Mark Secrest, in line for the superintendent's position, was warned that he had one year to "clean up
the mess" at the high school or he would be replaced.
The town demanded an elected school board and the
only member of the old board to survive the election
was Dr. Jennie. The new board hired a Frenchman from
Canada as superintendent and sat back to congratulate
themselves.

The strife continued, taking form much as in a war
with battle lines drawn, issues that could not be ne-
gotiated, names that could not be tolerated. Negroes
and coloreds became blacks because black was beautiful. "Dixie" could not be sung or hummed or whistled;
a black male could not be called "boy."

In an effort to be conciliatory, Horace was at a loss
to know what to call students. He groped for the right
word. Up until then, he had called them kids, but then
he tried "young ladies and gentlemen," "young men
and women," and when that seemed too formal, he tried
"youngsters." It never occurred to him to call them
students.

Troublemakers established patterns to keep the strife
on-going. Assemblies, Homecoming, exams, and
Brotherhood Week were occasions for major outbreaks
of hostility. Even the U.S. Marine Band refused an
invitation to play after one concert was interrupted by

firecrackers, rowdy behavior, and yellow paint sprayed on the drum.

After several seasons of rampage, predictable factors in rioting were discerned that students seemed unaware of. Teachers observed that riots did not occur during cold or rainy weather. But, beginning with the January thaw, the alert was on and every defense mechanism was put in place. With warm weather, the slightest encroachment by either side ignited violence that would last for days.

To some students, the riots were exhilarating, an exciting way to get out of classes, to thwart the system. It was a chance for recognition, for bravado, for risking life and limb. To others, the violence was terrifying.

Polarized as they were, the black students congregated at their Silver Spoon night spot while the whites met in the sandhills in a deserted store called Dry Gulch. Neither place was dry. Beer flowed and pencil-thin cigarettes made of local grass were smoked. In the daytime, the two groups met on a homemade playing field to do battle on the diamond they had shared since childhood. Beyond that, the only show of friendship came when they tipped each other off about upcoming raids on their respective social centers.

In this milieu, attitudes were forged that would not change for a lifetime. Those not in an adversary position took the critical stance of observers, evaluators. Among them, Judyth McCurdy.

Judyth, at sixteen, knew all the answers. She was more than the proverbial sophomore; she was, by her own account, a committed Liberal. Her father, Cecil McCurdy, as a matter of course, subscribed to magazines representing the entire spectrum of political thought, and Judyth was well-informed. She was not unusual, only bright and strong-willed. Her affection for Anna bordered on adoration. "A mother fixation," Miss Pendergraft said, "and no wonder. The child has never had a mother except Aunt Charlotte, the colored woman."

Still, the relationship made Anna uncomfortable. Judyth left no stone unturned to have Anna's undivided attention. She brought copies of *The American Heritage* from her father's library for Anna to read and later discussed the articles with her in private. She joined the Debating Club because Anna was the sponsor. When the new Raefield Arms was built by McCurdy Enterprises, Judyth persuaded her father to put Anna's name at the top of the list, and Anna was given her choice of apartments.

As much as the girl annoyed her, Anna sensed that Judyth was as needy a student as any she had ever taught and she wanted to do all she could for her. It was gratifying that when Judyth learned Anna was a Bible-reader, she read the entire Old Testament in one semester. Judyth took issue with the Mosaic theocracy, and Anna struggled unsuccessfully to defend the Bible against her criticism.

The girl was forceful and there was little Anna could do to restrain her. She did refuse to give Judyth cello lessons although the girl kept asking. But Anna was vulnerable when it came to the girl's personal life and felt great sympathy for one so young bearing the sadness of an invalid mother.

"I hardly know my mother, Miss Pete," she said. "When she came out of the lung years ago, my father took my brother and me to see her. She lives in a very posh place on Long Island. But when I saw her, I cried, and that upset her. She told my father never to bring us again and, to tell the truth, I did not want to go. She's all in braces and her speech is slurred. She can't comb her own hair or bathe herself, can barely feed herself. She'd be better off dead."

"No, Judyth. Life is a sacred gift. No matter how limited we may be, there's a purpose for living."

"A purpose? What good does my mother do? My poor father has been married to a vegetable when he could have had a wife. He doesn't agree with me but I think he should have divorced my mother long ago. He could continue to care for her and see that all her needs are met but go on with his life. He's all hung up on what people will think."

"Are you sure that's the reason?"

"Well, he says the marriage vows forbid it—that he promised to 'love, honor and obey' until 'death do us part.'" She said it with contempt. "He visits her once or twice a month—gives her time he could give Cecil and me. It's all so cruel. Do you know what I think, Miss Pete? I think that when my mother was in that iron lung, it would have been best for her and for us if they had pulled the plug."

"Oh, no, Judyth. No one has the right to do that. Life and death are in God's hands."

"How can a loving God let people suffer like my mother—like my family has suffered? Tell me, Miss Pete!"

# CHAPTER
# THIRTY-TWO

Mark Secrest had not "cleaned up the mess," and when someone shot out the window in his office, he decided to resign. Horace Wigglesworth was the unanimous choice of the board to replace him, and when Horace was asked what it would take to bring things under control, he asked for a staff sufficient to run a school as large as McAdden. The request seemed reasonable and six men were made administrators. With such a staff, Horace spent most of his time getting the place organized. There were job descriptions to write, objectives and strategies to plan, and many committees to meet with.

The Frenchman had long since departed and the superintendent was a lazy, indifferent sort who gave Horace free reign.

Horace tried his best to ignore the unrest among the students and when there was a flare up, he sent one of the men to take care of it. After all, he was there to handle things from the top.

When violence broke out on a big scale, Horace was forced to give some explanation to the board. He wore his new leisure suit with a bow tie and he felt good about the way he looked when he addressed the board. "I inherited an unstable situation," he said. "Given time, everything will be under control."

That was good enough for the board. Horace was their man—they had picked him.

Back at the school, Horace let the faculty have it. "People," he said, "you've gotta stop all this talkin' over the bridge table! The next time my wife comes home tellin' me something that happened here at the high school, I'm gonna track down the source and if it's one o' you, I guarantee you, I'm gonna write you up. That reprimand will become a part of your permanent file and you get enough of them and it'll cost you your job! School business is school business, and I don't want you goin' outta here broadcastin' it all over town! We've got better things to do here." He wiped the sweat from his forehead. "Do you hear me?" he yelled. "Who's 'at talkin' in the back o' the room?"

Horace did not ask for loyalty from his people, as that was the mistake Secrest had made; he demanded submission. "If it's too hot in the kitchen," he told them, "you know what you can do!"

It didn't take Horace long to identify the problems at McAdden High. The number-one problem was not kids, it was teachers. The stupid teachers couldn't fill out a simple form. Talk about kids being irresponsible, teachers couldn't get stuff in on time or carry out instructions. If the teachers would only do their jobs—keep those kids in the classrooms, not let them run the halls—if teachers would stay on duty in the halls, there wouldn't be any trouble at McAdden High School. When he had the time he'd weed out the bad apples. Chicora Pendergraft was number one on the hit list. Next year he'd drop Latin from the curriculum and Lady Big Mouth would go.

In the uneasy quiet that followed his tirade, Horace proceeded to get the bureaucracy in place. He had made the mistake of trying to do everything himself, at least that's what his wife told him. A big man had to delegate authority. Well, not so much authority as responsibility.

Horace also worked hard on public relations. Cultivating the Rotary was not as easy as he thought it would be, but he found that so long as he talked about teacher accountability, behavior modification, and systems to improve reading scores the men gave him the benefit of the doubt.

He thought he had things pretty well under his command when the Briggs girl had the baby in the girls' washroom. He couldn't believe it at first. Who would ever expect a thing like that in a public high school! He was careful who he dispatched to the scene—two black women. When they reported back to him he knew he had to call the law. He asked for plainclothes men and the chief obliged. Horace let them handle it and he never left his office. They whisked that baby up to Chapel Hill so the medical officer could examine it, and Horace washed his hands of the whole affair.

In a closed session with the school board, he had his explanation memorized. "Gentlemen, you have to understand where these people are coming from. Most of these youngsters don't know what it is to have both a daddy and a mama at home. It's not like when you and I were growin' up. These kids come from broken homes and they live in a society that's got nothin' to offer but drugs, sex, and violence. You can't blame the school. Lord knows we're doin' everything possible to help these youngsters, but now and then you have a situation like this that gets outta hand."

No one blamed Horace for the scandalous happening, yet he knew he had enemies in town—parents of kids who didn't like the way he ran things. *Thing to do*, he told himself, *is bring those people in, have rap sessions, make them feel like we're listening*. And, he'd serve refreshments, show them around the building, ask their advice. If he had a long suit, he told himself, it was in public relations. He knew how to handle people.

He thought the whole business about the baby was

a thing of the past when out of the blue, Anna Petersen had to bring it up. She made an appointment with him on a Friday afternoon.

"What's on your mind, Anna?"

"It's about the baby."

*Uh-oh,* he thought. *She's gonna have some kinda moralist somethin' to say about this;* and she did.

"Horace, frankly, my conscience has been bothering me. Can you tell me if anything has been done about this case?"

"Oh, sure. The police took care of that a month ago."

"Well, there wasn't anything in the paper about it. Marge Penry said we ought to make sure."

"Marge Penry? She call you?"

"Well, no. I called her."

"You called her, eh? Too bad about Harry."

"What do you mean?"

" 'Bout him gettin' killed. Didn't you hear?"

"No. When did it happen?"

"Last week. I wonder if Miss Pendergraft knows—"

"I don't think so. I believe she would have told me. How did he die?"

"Car wreck."

"Well, I'm sorry to hear that, but what I came to see you about is—"

"Well, Anna, it's a bad thing all right but if you're thinking of getting mixed up in that baby thing, I'd advise against it."

"Can you tell me—"

"If the baby was drowned?" He leaned back in the chair and thought a minute. "Now, Anna, I wouldn't tell anybody else this but we've been friends a long time and I know it won't go out of this room." He lowered his voice. "The medical examiner did find water in the baby's lungs."

"Are they going to prosecute the girl?"

Horace shook his head. "Attorney General chose not to."

"For lack of evidence?"

Horace shook his head. "Didn't say."

"You mean it's a closed case?"

"It's a closed case."

Why that didn't satisfy Anna, he could not understand and it aggravated him that she was so obstinate. She wasn't like the others. Some teachers cooperated with him on everything, either because they felt it was their professional, ethical duty or because they wanted to stay in good with the principal. They knew they had to keep their jobs and keeping in good with the powers that be was good insurance. But Anna was a maverick. She'd be good to head up a committee except for her bull-headedness. He couldn't risk having her object, rock the boat.

Horace came back from the convention in New Orleans all fired up with the latest innovations in education. First, he had to get the faculty loosened up with sensitivity sessions, then educate them to the New Management System. Once he got the teachers on a first-name basis, willing to hug each other once in a while, their everlasting reserve would no longer be a barrier to good human relations.

He conducted the first sensitivity session himself because nobody else knew what it was all about. Things seemed to be going well until during the afternoon, he told them to blindfold a partner and lead them wherever they wished. That was to establish trust. What Anna Petersen did really made him blow his stack. She blindfolded Miss Pendergraft and the two of them walked right out of the building and went home! Talk about insubordination!

# CHAPTER
# THIRTY-THREE

Anna went by the supermarket and bought a violet for
Ted's grave. She went to the cemetery less frequently
than she once did but today she needed to be alone for
a while. As she drove toward the old tree where the
McGill plot was, she saw another car parked there. As
she got out, she saw Anita sitting on the coping. She
was holding a kitten in her lap and when she looked
up there were tears in her eyes. She put down the cat
and hugged Anna, too full to speak.

"It's good to see you, Anita," Anna said and sat
down beside her.

Anita stroked the kitten trying to get control of herself. In the late afternoon sun, strands of copper glistened in her chestnut hair. Finally, she spoke. "Want
to hold it?"

"No," Anna replied. "I'm afraid of cats."

"So is Andy."

Anna waited.

"I guess you heard?" Anita asked.

"Heard what?"

"Andy and I are divorced."

Anna shook her head. "No, I didn't know that. I'm
sorry it didn't work out, Anita."

She was fighting back the tears. "I tried. Oh, how I
tried, Miss Petersen!"

"Yes, I'm sure you did."

"Poor Andy, he tried too. He was pitiful. Some days
when he was not tormented by all his fears, we would

talk about the future and all the things he wanted for me and the children. He was a very loving and tender father. When he was well he couldn't remember what had happened when he was ill, but he knew he had behaved badly and he would cry and beg my forgiveness." She pulled a tissue from her purse and blew her nose. "When he was like that, I hoped my prayers were answered but then, poor Andy—he's a very sick man, Miss Petersen. When he came home from his tour of duty in Vietnam, he suffered terribly. Miss Petersen, sometimes, even when I was holding him in my arms, he'd get up, get his gun and roam the house, sure there were enemies outside. He was obsessed with guns and I was so afraid he would hurt someone or himself. He had this reflex action from the war—the slightest noise would startle him and he'd react without thinking. And there were times when night after night he didn't sleep.

"The Army sent him to psychiatrists but they only helped him temporarily. They finally gave him a medical discharge."

"Where is he now?"

"I have no earthly idea. I want him to see the children but when I divorced him he left and neither his parents nor I have heard from him."

"Are you living at home?"

"For the time being. You know my children are nine and seven now and it's important that they have the things they need. Mr. Lawton's going to pay my tuition at Beaver College so I can go back to school. As soon as I get a teaching certificate I'll go to work and make a home for us."

The kitten lay with its eyes half-closed, contented. "Isn't he darling? He was over there beside the railroad track half starved to death. I had stopped by the store on the way over here and had some milk in the car. I guess it's a kitten someone abandoned. They always did throw stray cats in the woods over there. I wish I could take him home with me but Mother would have a fit. She claims I collect strays. Maybe she's right but it looks like I've made a throw-away of Andy." Her eyes were misting again.

"No, Anita, you can't blame yourself. You did everything you could for Andrew."

"Nothing short of a miracle will help Andy now."

"Anita, do you believe in miracles?"

"Miracles? This may surprise you but I've seen a few. There were times when the children and I were in danger for our lives and I couldn't do anything but pray. Remarkable things happened. Once we had to spend the night in the car. A very bad storm raged around us and we were terribly afraid. I cried out to God to protect us and just then a huge tree came crashing down right in front of the car. I was so frightened I grabbed the children and jumped out of the car. All around us live wires were strewn about and in the dark I could not see them. We ran to the nearest house and a woman took us in. It was nothing less than a miracle that we were not electrocuted." Anita stroked the kitten thoughtfully. "Miss Petersen, there's something I want you to promise me."

"Why, of course, Anita. I'll do anything I can for you."

"Promise me that if ever you see Andy, you'll talk to him about the Lord."

"That's not a hard promise to make."

"It's his only hope, Miss Petersen." Her chin was trembling. "And, I do believe the Lord can change his life." Then she quickly changed the subject. "What a pretty violet. I'll bet it's for Ted's grave. Mother told me how Miss Clara started this and how you've kept it up. Poor Miss Clara. Wasn't that dreadful?"

"Oh, it was."

"Miss Clara was one of my favorite teachers. Of course, you were my favorite. And I liked Miss Penry.

I can't believe Mr. Wigglesworth is a principal. Does he still wear those white buck shoes?"

"No, not white buck." Anna smiled. "Do you often think of the old high school?"

"Hmmm. And the people. Whatever happened to Sue Marie?"

"Oh, Sue Marie was in a stock company last summer and she's doing an off Broadway musical soon. I hear from her at Christmas."

"I hear David McBryde is a surgeon."

"Yes, he's a surgeon but he wants to study psychiatry. His father calls him a professional student. He's married now. Lives in California."

"I wonder if he still plays cello? We used to tease him about that. We thought he took lessons because he had such a crush on you."

"Yes, he not only plays cello, he's done some composing. He plays with an ensemble but if he had the time he'd do concerts. He still calls me occasionally but he rarely gets home. You know David—always has a million things going at once."

"Is Lester McKenzie still in the chaplaincy?"

"Yes, and he has his doctorate now. When he retires he'll be a marriage counselor. And Pluto, do you remember Pluto?"

"Wasn't he the one with big ears?"

"Yes. Well, Pluto has a drinking problem and several years ago he called me from Wisconsin. I pled with him to go to a Christian alcoholic treatment center but so far as I know he hasn't."

"Well, I need to get home with these groceries. *And* this kitten. I know Mother'll have a fit but I can't leave the little thing out here to starve. Can I help you with the plant?"

"No, I can manage."

# CHAPTER
# THIRTY-FOUR

Judyth McCurdy was rebelling against everything her father stood for, and Anna Petersen was in the middle. Every afternoon she went to Miss Petersen's classroom on some ruse or another—either an article she wanted her to read or with a question about something. There was no disclaiming the vehement idealism with which she defended the rights of women, the economically disenfranchised, the causes of the handicapped, children, *ad infinitum*. The girl was driven by unyielding passion to right all wrongs.

Cecil McCurdy stood it as long as he could but when Judyth led the Debating Team to victory in the state finals on a platform advocating socialized medicine, he had his secretary set up an appointment with Miss Petersen. He was ready when she arrived.

"Miss Petersen," he began, fingering the letter opener on his desk, "ever since my daughter, Judyth, has been in your American History Class, she's been reading books that have inflamed her emotions and radicalized her thinking."

Anna Petersen looked back at him as if that was not the end of his sentence. In the silence that hung between them, he studied her, reflecting on the times he had encountered her before. For some reason he remembered those times with the utmost clarity. She had been a slip of a girl, a freshman teacher, when the board called her on the carpet about the retreat. Never would he have remembered such an incident except for the woman's extraordinary mastery of the game they were playing. Animated with feminine innocence, she had totally disarmed the board. He would wager that not one of those men had forgotten the way she pulled the rug out from under them. Even now, after twenty years, her naiveté seemed intact. He admired the fact that back of that pretty face was a clear-cut sense of right and wrong and the courage to say what she thought.

"Miss Petersen," he said, and smiled. "I'm calling you to account."

"Mr. McCurdy, your daughter has a mind of her own. She reads widely and, being immature, she's persuaded by arguments she's incapable of refuting."

"What do you suggest that I do?"

"Well, you can censor everything she reads—weed out all contrary views, or you can take the time to discuss with her the issues that concern you."

"Miss Petersen, my daughter looks upon me as a robber baron. Nothing I say convinces her that our capital has been used for the common good."

"Judyth and I disagree about many things, but—"

He put the letter opener aside. "But not about empire towns."

She returned his direct gaze. "You're right, Mr. McCurdy. We agree that an empire town is oppressive."

There, she had said it, and it did not surprise him. Unlike other people, she was not intimidated by him.

"Miss Petersen, would you explain to me how the town of Scotsville would survive without the mills and other enterprises my family and I operate here? Because of the capital those businesses generate we provide jobs, and we are also privileged to provide schools, churches, and other facilities that otherwise would not be available. We're Christian people and have always looked upon wealth as a stewardship. My sisters and I live unpretentious lives as members of this community."

"Mr. McCurdy, what you're describing is not capitalism but paternalism."

That angered him. "Miss Petersen, that is a serious accusation." He checked his anger, leaned back in the chair, and spoke more softly. "If you were in my position, what would you do differently?"

"Perhaps, Mr. McCurdy, your money would be spent more in keeping with biblical principles if you shared the profits of their labor with the people who earn those profits."

"You mean, give the money directly to people who work for us through salaries and bonuses, that sort of thing?"

"Yes."

"But you don't know these people. They'd spend that money foolishly—on big automobiles, nonsense, not education—"

"That would be their responsibility, not yours. Every person is responsible before God—no one needs a caretaker."

He looked at her for some time and she did not waver. He did not like the way she disturbed him.

When he said nothing more, she broke the silence. "Is there anything else?"

"No, Miss Petersen." He stood up. "Thank you for coming."

After she was gone, he moved to the window and waited. He watched her all the way to her car. Miss Petersen was, indeed, a remarkable woman.

# CHAPTER
# THIRTY-FIVE

Samantha Johnson came into homeroom, bubbling. Under her arm was a large sheet of poster paper. Securing her books, she came up to Anna's desk. "Miz Petersen, is there any part on your car you don't need?"

"Well, no, Samantha. I need all the parts to make it go."

"Don't you have a spare tire?"

"Yes, I have a spare tire."

Samantha looked at her as if she were lunatic. "Well, Miss Petersen, it is a *spare* tire isn't it?"

"Yes, it is, but I need it."

"Well, Miz Petersen, it's all right that you can't help me. I'll go by de gas station, they'll give me a spare tire."

"What do you need a tire for?"

"For my project in Drivers Ed. I'm making a poster and I'll put part of the tire on my poster."

"*A part of the tire on your poster?* Well, doesn't the part have to illustrate a point? What will part of a tire illustrate?"

"To show them what a flat tire looks like."

Ken Tompkins had come in and was listening. "Hey, Samantha, I saw you last night."

"Where?"

"In your brother's car. You musta been coming from the hospital."

"Well, if I had knowed it was you, I woulda flang out my arm an wove to you."

He laughed. "What cha got there?"

"My project for Drivers Ed."

"Tell you what, Samantha, I'll help you. I'll get Louvenia and Miss Pete here and we'll help you."

Every morning during homeroom, they worked on the poster. Instead of a spare tire, they drew highways and roads making an intersection. Ken brought toy cars and glued them to the board to illustrate a traffic violation. Samantha beamed. "Oh, Miss Petersen, isn't it nice to have a man around!" She held up the finished project. "It's fatatic!"

The next day, Samantha was absent. When she returned, her mouth was swollen. "What's the matter, Samantha?" Louvenia asked.

"I been to the dentist and he grilled my teeth."

"*Grilled* your teeth?" Alfred Stegall repeated. The students chuckled. "Well, Samantha, you look beautiful anyway. 'Black is beautiful,' they say."

"Honey, I ain't black, I am pecan tan!"

*Come to think of it, she is,* Anna thought. And in the bright pinks she wore, Samanatha seemed to have a faint blush to the cheeks. Despite the very thick lips, she was a neat, attractive girl, but more important than her appearance was the enthusiasm she brought with her.

"Miz Petersen, I can't give you no kiss today because my mouf is swoll shut but tomorra I'll give you two— one for today and one for tomorrow."

"Be thankful for small favors, eh, Miss Pete?" Ken said and laughed. "Hey, Judyth, Mr. Nesbit's hittin' the bottle again. I met him in the hall and he's weavin'. Bet your class goes to the library today."

"Ken, I'd be careful how I talked about Mr. Nesbit," Anna warned.

"It's the truth, ain't it, Judyth? He keeps likker in a Listerine bottle in his desk."

"Ken, if Mr. Nesbit has a Listerine bottle in his desk, it has mouthwash in it."

Samantha interrupted. "Miz Petersen, when did you ever see somebody drink moufwash? You spits out moufwash. The dentist dat grilled my teeth tol' me, 'Samantha, spit the moufwash here,' and I did.

"Miz Petersen, dat dentist gimme a diabolic. How come he gimme a diabolic?"

"That's an antibiotic to arrest disease," Judyth informed her.

Samantha looked at her as if she were an imbecile. "Judyth, you don't arrest a disease—you arrest criminals. If you want to arrest somebody you call de police."

After school Samantha came again to Anna's room. That was the only time they could be alone. Usually, it was the time when Samantha confided about her mother. "Oh, Miz Petersen, my mother—do you know what she called me? She called me a dummy." Samantha began to cry. "Oh, if she knew how that hurts me, she wouldn't do it."

Anna tried to console her. "Well, Samantha, when you are a mother you will know how to be a good mother and not say the wrong things to your children." Anna's heart ached for the girl because her mother constantly belittled her. "Your father is nice to you, isn't he?"

"Yes, but you know he don't live with us and he never comes to see me."

"Doesn't your brother take you to see him?"

"Sometimes. My brother he is very nice to me." She was sniffling. "When I get off my candy stripe job, he be right there to take me home and he talks to me 'bout me growin' up and gettin' a husband and having childrun. He don't want me to get a baby like some o' dese high school girls—he wants me to graduate then I can have a baby."

Anna smiled. "First you have a husband."

"Oh, Miz Petersen, I ain't nevah gonna do nothin' I be ashame' of when I have my baby." Samantha remembered something. "Miz Petersen, if I tell you somethin' you won't tell nobody will you? The other day Louvenia an' me wuz passin' dis gull in de hall an' Louvenia say to me, 'Hmph, Gloria's losin' her waistline.' Now, Miz Petersen, can't nobody lose dere waistline, can dey? Do you s'pose Louvenia don' know dat girl's gonna have a baby?" She thought of something else and distress filled her eyes. "You don' s'pose dat girl'll throw her baby in de john, do you?"

"No, Samantha, of course not."

Suddenly, her lips were quivering and her eyes were puddling. "Oh, Miz Petersen, when I think of dat gull droppin' dat baby in the john, I want her to know dat dat's just plain murder. She should not get away wid dat, Miz Petersen."

"Samantha, it is hard to understand how this can be, but you and I can't do anything about it."

"You could, Miz Petersen, you can go to the police and make dem do right by dat poor little baby."

"Samantha, the police know all about this and they've decided not to do anything more."

Big tears rolled down the girl's cheeks as she insisted, "You could write your congressman."

Samantha could be very disconcerting. At night Anna lay awake wondering if she had, indeed, done all she could. Even now she was haunted by the sight of the baby lying on the floor and many nights she buried her face in the pillow to black out the mercury light and the mauve shade it cast.

Judyth McCurdy's opinion in the case was as disturbing as Samantha's. Judyth advocated sterilizing the mother because she was "obviously unfit" to be a mother.

There were times when Judyth sounded like a Nazi, yet she was a kind and loving person. She took Samantha under her wing and helped her with her schoolwork and saw to it that she had nurses' shoes to go with her candy stripe uniform. "Learn all you can in that hospital, Samantha, because some day, you and I will have our own place and take care of people together."

Judyth's ambition was another source of trouble for Anna. Judyth's father wanted his daughter to become a doctor, but Judyth insisted on becoming a nurse in order to have "hands-on" experience in the care of patients. Nothing her father said would convince her otherwise and he sought Anna's help. He called her at home.

Anna protested, "But, Mr. McCurdy, that's Judyth's decision. What's wrong with her becoming a nurse?"

On the other end of the line there was a tightness in his voice. "There is nothing *wrong* with becoming a nurse, Miss Petersen, but Judyth is capable of much more. Right now she's an idealistic young girl, but you and I both know that a few months of performing the distasteful chores of nursing and she'll see her mistake."

The man made her nervous. "That may be true, Mr. McCurdy, but your daughter has to make a few mistakes in life and we can't be sure that Judyth will feel that this is a mistake."

McCurdy ended the conversation abruptly. Anna held the receiver a moment, then placed it back in its cradle. To Anna, it seemed odd that he would call her and out of character for him to become exasperated. Cecil McCurdy was an enigma.

The phone rang again and Anna picked it up. "McCurdy here," he said in a clipped, tight voice. "Miss Petersen, if I sounded short with you, I beg your pardon."

"No offense, Mr. McCurdy."

"Very well . . . Good night, Miss Petersen."

Anna hung up the receiver and whispered, "Well, whadda ya know?"

# CHAPTER
# THIRTY-SIX

It was midnight when the doorbell rang. Anna peeped
out to see who it was and at first did not recognize her.
The woman was leaning against the wall across the hall,
a suitcase at her feet. It was Marge!

Quickly, Anna unlocked the door and let her in.
"Oh, Marge," she said as they hugged each other.
Marge was reeking of liquor and she did not look like
herself—her face was puffed and she looked fat in the
stomach. Anna took her coat and Marge dropped into
a chair. Bleary eyed, she rested a few minutes, lit a
cigarette, her hands trembling. She drew a long
draught, inhaled so that hardly any smoke escaped,
then began to talk.

"I came to you, Anna, because I need help and you're
the only person I know who will help me." Despite the
liquor, Marge's speech was nearly normal. Anna could
tell she was fighting for control. "I've lost everything
except the property, Anna, and that's not worth living
for . . . Have you got some coffee?" Anna went to the
kitchen and plugged in the pot.

"If you have an ash tray . . ."

Anna found a clam shell and brought it to her. The
humor of it brought a faint smile to Marge. "That the
best you can do?" Drawing on the cigarette, her eyes
on Anna, she studied her thoughtfully. "Anna, I guess
if I had it all to do over again, I'd do it the same way,
but I've made a mess of things. You, here, you've got
it all together. Nice apartment, you have peace of mind,

something I've never had." She took a deep breath. "Maybe it's too late for me. I took down the gun to end it all and I might have done it but I have all these cats to look after. If I blew my brains out, the poor little things would starve. I thought about it a while then put up the gun. I was in a pretty bad state, as you can imagine. I remember crawling on the floor to get to the phone to call you. Then I decided to get in the car and come. I took the cats to the vet's and headed this way. . . .They took my license six months ago so all the way here, I prayed I wouldn't get stopped. I guess Somebody up there likes me. It's not the first time I prayed to get home when I was loaded, you know, and how I got home I'll never know, but I did."

Anna handed her the coffee.

"Anna, I gotta have a drink." She fumbled to open the suitcase, finally got it open, and took out a paper bag with the bottle in it.

"Do you want a glass?" Marge was already drinking from the bottle.

"I don't want to get mushy on you, Anna. I try to be a decent drunk."

"Oh, Marge." Anna didn't know what to say. "I'm really sorry."

"Don't feel sorry for me. Lord knows I feel sorry enough for myself." She took another drink from the bottle.

"Well, Marge, I think I know where you can get help."

"I've tried 'em all, Anna." She lit another cigarette. "I've taken all the cures, gone to shrinks." It was hard for her to get the cigarette to her mouth.

"This is a Christian place."

"Ha! They give me the creeps." Marge's speech was slurring. "You always were religious, as I remember."

"I don't like to be called *religious*, Marge."

"None of 'em do, but you are religious. Now admit

it, Anna, you *are* religious!" Her head was wobbly as if she were having a hard time keeping Anna in focus.

"What do you say we go to bed?"

"Oh, the night is young. You sleep your life away. Tell me 'bout Horace. What's old athletic socks up to now?"

"Well, he's principal of the high school and some day he'll probably be superintendent." Marge was looking around the room, not listening. "Marge, getting back to the place I was telling you about—it's called Carolina Colony. It's up near Boone in a beautiful place in the mountains. Dr. Hodges runs it and he's a real man of God. In fact, he's speaking tomorrow in Woodall Jackson's church. I want you to hear him."

"I'll tell you right now, Anna, that's not for me." Marge drained the last drop from the bottle.

"Well, why don't we go to bed? Maybe if you sleep on it you'll think differently about it."

Finally, Marge agreed to go to bed. As they were undressing, Anna asked Marge not to smoke in the bedroom. "If you have to smoke during the night, Marge, how about going in the living room?"

Marge agreed and in the night, when she couldn't sleep, she got up, went in the living room, and lit a cigarette. Then she decided to make some coffee. Without anything to drink she'd have to smoke it out until morning.

She roamed from the living room to the kitchen to the bathroom, back and forth, restless. Anna had a neat apartment. There was the conch she was so fond of and her cello. On the wall near the door was a plaque of some kind. Without her glasses she couldn't read what it said. A pretty little thing. Curious, Marge fumbled in her pocketbook for her glasses. The plaque was a verse from the Bible, "By grace are ye saved through faith and that not of yourselves, it is the gift of God." *Very nice.*

Marge went back to the couch. *She was a good girl, Anna Petersen. One in a million. All these years she's stuck it out in this mean little town and she's won.*

On the marble top table was a Bible. Marge picked it up and leafed through it. She tried to read the markings in the margins. They were few and far apart, neatly written and the underlining was straight. *That was like Anna, she'd use a ruler.* Marge smiled to herself. She decided to read a psalm and turned at random to Psalm 116.

> *I love the Lord, because he hath heard my voice and my supplications.*
> *Because he hath inclined his ear unto me, therefore will I call upon him as long as I live.*
> *The sorrows of death compassed me, and the pains of hell gat hold upon me: I found trouble and sorrow.*
> *Then called I upon the name of the Lord; O Lord, I beseech thee, deliver my soul. . . ."*

Marge felt drawn to the words personally and felt strangely touched by them. For a long time she sat smoking and thinking about them, turning them over in her mind. It was as if they said exactly what she felt and after a while she was just sitting there crying. Just before daylight, Marge made up her mind. Crushing the cigarette in the clam shell, she went in the bedroom.

"Anna," she called but Anna was sleeping soundly. Marge touched her shoulder. "Anna."

That woke her up. Marge sat down on the bed. "Anna, I've decided to do what you said. I'll go to that Colony."

"Oh, good, Marge. I was praying you'd decide to go."

Marge got up and went to the other side of the bed.

"Sorry to wake you up, but I had to. Maybe now I can go to sleep."

When Marge woke up the next morning, she heard Anna in the kitchen and smelled bacon frying. *My, it's been a long time since I smelled bacon frying*, she thought. Then she remembered the night before and her promise and she was sorry she'd said she'd go to that Colony. When she came out of the bedroom Anna had the radio on and was singing along with it. "It's right ready to put on the table," she said, and Marge helped her carry the food to the other room. She was ravenously hungry.

"This is the first time I've eaten breakfast in months," she confessed. "Boy, is this good."

"Can I fry you another egg?"

"Yes, I believe I could eat another one."

When breakfast was finished, Marge lit a cigarette and took her coffee to the couch. "I don't know when I've enjoyed anything so much. Do you cook like this every morning?"

"Well, more so on Sunday mornings. Sometimes I'm rushing to get to school and . . . say, we better get a wiggle on. I'll quick wash these dishes—maybe you could go in the bathroom while I'm doing this and then I'll get ready."

"Anna, I'll do those dishes. I decided I'm in no shape to go to church. I'd shake 'em off the pew."

"Oh, Marge, you'll love Dr. Hodges."

"Oh, I'm sure I would but I don't have anything decent to wear. I should've brought something."

"Marge, I know what you can wear," and she went to the closet. "Here's something I've never worn and it's sharp. We're about the same size. I know it'll fit you."

"Gee, Anna, that is pretty but I don't want to wear your new outfit. You just run on. I'll go with you some other time."

Anna hesitated, then spoke softly. "Marge, just do it for me, will you?"

"Well, all right!" she said crossly and went into the bathroom.

Dr. Hodges was a wonderful man. She liked the way he looked and the way he talked and after the service when Anna asked if she would like to make an appointment to see him in the afternoon, she agreed.

But after lunch, when it was time to go, Marge begged off. "Anna, it's no use. I've been to all kinds of places—religious and otherwise. Alcoholism is a sickness and you have to treat it like any other sickness. I can lick this thing, I know I can."

"Marge, all I ask is that you go and keep an open mind, that you just listen to Dr. Hodges. Then make up your mind. I'll drive you over there and I'll sit in the car."

Anna was persistent and Marge was getting a bit tired of it. "I went to church and it was a beautiful service, but that's enough for one day, Anna. Why don't you just sit there and read the Bible to me. I'd get more out of that than going to see that man."

Anna saw that she had lost. Sitting in the chair across from Marge, she took the Bible and opened it. When she began to read it was the same psalm Marge had read the night before.

> . . . *The pains of hell gat hold upon me: I found trouble and sorrow. Then called I upon the name of the Lord . . .*

Marge interrupted her. "Anna, I think I'll keep that appointment after all."

Anna's eyes were wide with surprise. Without a word she got up and they left.

After the interview with Dr. Hodges, Marge knew

she must go to the Colony. Never had she met such a winsome person, such a man of God. She felt good about her decision, but back in the car with Anna, she began to shake uncontrollably.

"Well, how'd it go?" Anna asked.

Marge couldn't say anything. Anna kept glancing at her, waiting for a response. "Anna," she asked, "will you drive me up there?"

As soon as they reached the apartment, Anna called Horace and made arrangements to be out of school the next day. Then they got in the car and drove far into the night to reach Carolina Colony.

# CHAPTER
# THIRTY-SEVEN

In the fall of '78, Aunt Helga died and Anna flew up for the funeral. When she returned, another funeral awaited her. Cecil McCurdy's wife had died and Judyth, in her senior year of nursing in Chicago, was home for the services.

As could be expected, the McCurdys went through the services with dignity—no eulogies were given, no tears shed. Judyth was tall and willowy, as beautiful as her elegantly dressed aunts. Cecil McCurdy stood in the November sun, the wind stirring his gray hair, and Anna wondered what was left for him. Both his children were in college and the one human responsibility he had was now gone. Perhaps he'd marry again.

After the graveside service, Judyth walked over to Anna and embraced her. Her father joined them. "Ah, Miss Petersen," he said in a courtly manner and reached to shake her hand.

Before Anna had time to express her condolences, Judyth was chatting enthusiastically about nursing school. "Miss Pete, Cook County is the best hospital in the country. I'm so fortunate to be there. And the city is so exciting. I think even my father realizes this is the place for me."

McCurdy smiled. "No, Judyth, I still think you should be in pre-med." His eyes fastened on Anna. "Miss Petersen, you will probably be happy to hear that my son has no interest in taking over the mills. With that development, I'm divesting myself of several companies and McCurdy Enterprises will no longer be the main-stay of Scotsville. I've encouraged the Chamber of Commerce to explore the possibilities for bringing new industry here."

His arms were folded across his chest as he looked down at the ground and moved a stick with the toe of his shoe. "It seems to be the right thing to do."

Anna felt strangely uncomfortable that he was telling her all this. Judyth took Anna's arm. "Miss Pete, we want you to come for dinner. When can you come?"

Anna felt a sense of apprehension and answered quickly. "I can't come this week. How long will you be here?"

"I leave Saturday. Sure you can't come? Any night would be fine for us, wouldn't it, Dad?"

"Of course," he answered.

"I'm sorry," she said simply and let it go at that.

Anna drove back to her apartment so absorbed in her thoughts she was unaware of anything else. If she didn't know better, she might think Cecil McCurdy had some sort of personal interest in her. She had thought that once before, she remembered. It made her feel uncomfortable.

There was a letter from Marge waiting for her. It was always a boost to hear from Marge. She had suffered ups and downs but had come a long way since she accepted Christ. "Anna, where can I get a motto like the one you have in your living room? You know the one—Ephesians 2:8, 9." On and on the letter continued. Three single-spaced typed sheets. When Anna finished, she went over and took down the plaque, wrapped it, and addressed it to Marge.

"I needed that bright spot," Anna said aloud, and went to answer the phone. It was Horace. "Anna, I just wanted to make sure you were back in town. I'm coming to the high school with a proposal that some teachers might not like. I know you'll be on my side but I might need a little extra support for this thing. I'm callin' around to different ones—people I can depend on—the regular stand-bys. You know there're some people who might make waves."

"Sure, Horace. I'll back you if I can."

Horace Wigglesworth had finally become superintendent, moved his wife into a bigger house, and joined the country club. He was still a "good old boy" and what he didn't know about curriculum he made up for in public relations. In the long parade of McAdden County superintendents there had been all kinds and some with sticky fingers. At least Horace was honest and the money he spent might be wasted but never stolen.

Horace presented the proposal in faculty meeting and Anna was not only appalled, she was incensed. Management Systems was the name of the program and he planned to implement it over the entire county.

Horace liked the program with its objectives, strategies, and projections because it made teachers accountable and the public was clamoring for that.

From the top down, from the central office to individual schools, departments, courses, and objectives—goals to attain and strategies to achieve the goals were being formulated. From these were to come projections, percentiles. For instance, if good citizenship was a goal set for students of American History, the teacher was to predict how many students would indeed become good citizens as a result of the course.

Anna dreaded taking issue with him but when she could stand it no longer, she spoke out. "Mr. Wigglesworth, this is not fit for human consumption." Teachers laughed but Horace was annoyed.

"Whadda ya mean?"

"This is based on experiments with animals. You can't teach students as if they were mice in a maze trying to reach the cheese."

"I don't know, Miss Petersen. Some o' these young-sters remind me of monkeys." More laughter.

"Humans are not animals—they're complex creatures made in the image of God. There are too many variables to program them, put them through the same grid, and predict the results. You mustn't do that, Mr. Wigglesworth."

"Well, I don't wanna get into all that moralizing. Lord knows I was glad to get outta that philosophy class at U.N.C."

Anna knew she couldn't go along with Management Systems, but to buck the superintendent went against every ethic she had ever been taught. Yet she couldn't sit there and say nothing. She raised her hand again.

Horace could not ignore her; she was on the front row. When he looked at her, his displeasure was obvious. "Miss Petersen," he said, lowering his voice, "you and I will discuss this in private. We gotta get through with the agenda."

They never discussed anything. Every time Anna went for an appointment Horace's secretary told her he was tied up. Finally, she gave up. All she could do was pray, but she knew she couldn't conscientiously go along with Management Systems.

At a PTA meeting, Horace saw that it was impossible to avoid Anna. When he approached her he said, "Anna, you of all people got nothing to worry about. In my book you're an A number-one teacher, but you know as well as I that I gotta hold some of their feet to the fire. If I can get them, out of their own mouths, to say what they're gonna do in that classroom, then I've got something to evaluate their competency by. Don't cha see? Lookit Nesbit—how we ever gonna get rid of that lush if we don't have somethin' concrete? We can say, 'Now look, fella'. . . you said you were gonna to do so an' so and you haven't done it.' Then we can terminate him. Otherwise—"

"Horace, I understand your reasons for all this, but, don't you see, you're dehumanizing people, expecting them to perform like machines."

"No, I don't see that at all, Anna, and I'd appreciate it if you'd just keep your mouth shut about this. My job's tough enough without you opposing my biggest number. People listen to you, Anna. They look up to you."

"I'm sorry, Horace. I can't cooperate."

"Kitchen gettin' too hot for you, Anna?"

The threat shocked her.

Anna went home with a certain panic inside. Horace had, indeed, eliminated Chicora Pendergraft and, if forced to, he would get rid of her. The prospect so disturbed her she could not eat. Despite tenure or anything regarding her record, Horace had an effective way of hassling. He could have the principal assign her an impossible work load—give her several preparations, six classes in six different classrooms, to force her to resign. Whether or not she could get a job somewhere else was a moot question. She was fifty-four years old and social studies teachers were a dime a dozen.

Yet the longer she thought about it the more she was convinced that she must take a stand. The next day, she did what seemed to be the best of all options. In an elaborate brief, she detailed her objections and the reasons for them. Then, after reviewing the brief many times, she mailed a copy to Horace and asked him either to respond or have the school board respond.

Horace called her. "Anna, I got cher stuff and I'm gonna go you one better. I'm gonna send it to the state department. Whatever they say we'll abide by it. That fair enough?"

Anna couldn't believe what she was hearing. Sending her stuff to the state department was a twist she hadn't anticipated. In a flash it came to her—*perhaps Horace thinks I'll chicken out if he says he's sending it to the top.* "Okay, Horace, that's fair enough," she said.

In a month's time, the answer came down the line and by the time it reached the teachers, all that was said was, "The state department has ruled that Management Systems is not a valid criteria for measurement of values." Horace announced, "We've decided to scrap it for now. Maybe they'll perfect it later on."

On the way out of the meeting, Anna hoped she wouldn't encounter Horace, but he called to her. As they walked out into the sunlight together he made no reference to her winning the battle.

"My wife was telling me some news I thought you might be interested in, Anna. Judyth McCurdy's home for the weekend. Seems she brought home a Jewish boyfriend and Mr. McCurdy won't even speak to him. My wife says McCurdy's warned Judyth about fortune seekers and I guess to him some smart Jewish boy might be just that."

"I wouldn't know about that. And, Horace, about Management—"

He waved it aside. "It's all right, Anna. In the game you win some, lose some. When I was a coach I taught the boys to be good sports. I gotta practice what I preach." He was climbing into his car.

# CHAPTER
# THIRTY-EIGHT

With the January thaw, young people all over the country were streaking, running about naked. Even so, Anna was not prepared for what happened at McAdden High.

Standing on duty at the half-way point of the first floor corridor, Anna's responsibility was to keep students out of the hall during lunch. The institutional bleakness of the empty hall with the long tile floor stretching the length of the building, the walls lined with rows of lockers, rectangles of ceiling board matched with rectangular light panels—was as stark as a Mondrian painting. Double doors at each end of the hallway led onto the playing field and outside, a motor was sounding.

Suddenly, one of the double doors bounced open and a motorcycle burst through, roaring down the hall! Anna jumped to one side and, flattened against the wall, felt the rush of air as the streaker roared past her. Head down, his bare back bent over, he headed for the doors at the other end of the hall. Students rushed from the commons, jamming the hall trying to see what was happening.

As he slammed outside again, the mob stampeded after him, trying to glimpse the male Godiva racing across campus. As quickly as he came, he was gone!

Pandemonium reigned and Anna escaped to her room. Shutting the door on the bedlam, she sat down at her desk and laughed until tears rolled down her face.

In a few minutes a reporter appeared at her door. He was one of Charles Simpson's boys, and she couldn't refuse to talk to him. Quickly repairing her face, she straightened her skirt and put on a very serious face.

"Miss Petersen, I'm Charles Simpson, Jr., and I work for the *Herald*," he began. Tall and slender, he bore no resemblance to his father. "Sorry I never had you for history. My Daddy said I'd have learned something if I'd had you."

"Thank you, Charles. Now what brings you here?"

His face reddened. "It's about the streaker, Miss Petersen. They say you saw him?"

"Hmmmmm."

He shifted awkwardly. "They say he didn't have on a stitch, is that right?"

She answered gravely. "No, that isn't correct."

"It ain't? What'd he have on?" Whipping out a pencil and pad, he held the pencil poised, ready to write down every word.

Anna paused. He eyed her expectantly.

"A helmet, Charles. A big blue helmet."

His mouth fell open. He looked astonished. "That's all? A helmet?"

She nodded.

Confused, he looked at her, then the pencil. Quickly stuffing the pad in his hip pocket, he backed out the door and left.

Anna closed the door behind him, sat down at the desk, and laughed some more.

The streaker was the only incident to interrupt the monotony of the long period between Christmas and Easter break. The weeks and months were interminable, and by April Anna was beside herself with boredom. Even so, when Cecil McCurdy called and asked her to go to the Country Club of North Carolina with him, she was shocked and was definitely going to say no, when he began explaining his reasons.

"Miss Petersen, I would like to discuss a serious problem involving my daughter. I feel that you know her well and care—that you can provide helpful insight."

Well, that made the date feasible, Anna thought; Judyth's on some wild tangent and he needs help. *All right*, she thought, *I'll go this once.*

No sooner had she accepted his invitation than she regretted it. Not knowing what to wear or what to expect, Anna was in such a stew she couldn't sleep. *If only I could ask someone what people wear in a place like that*, she thought. *But that's out of the question. The minute I ask they'll want to know why I'm asking and if anybody in Scotsville found out that I'm going to the Country Club of North Carolina with Cecil McCurdy, the whole town would start buzzing!*

But the more she thought about it, the more desperate she became. *I could call Thelma. She knows all about things like that. I don't have to tell her I'm going*, she reasoned. *I can just ask casually.*

Thelma did know; her sister was a waitress there. "The men wear jackets and ties but not formal dress unless there's a wedding or something like that. Women wear nice dresses, and I guess they're stylish, but they don't dress formally. You know, some of the people come in off the golf course and eat dinner. Why're you asking?"

"Oh, I was just asking."

Anna relaxed. *It can't be too stuffy if golfers can come in off the links and go in the dining room.* Thelma's sister being a waitress there worried her. *If one word of this gets out in Scotsville there'll be no end to the gossip. I'll just pray that if she's there she won't know who I am. Maybe she won't be working Friday.*

For two days before the date, Anna suffered bouts of anxiety. At school, she was absentminded, had to be reminded about several important things. If only she could talk with somebody, release the tension. Going through her wardrobe fifty times, choosing first one dress, then another, wishing a thousand times she had never accepted the invitation, Anna was a nervous wreck.

Finally, she sat down and talked to herself. *You got yourself into this and all this stewing about it is not going to change one thing. Just pull yourself together and try to be calm. Maybe Thelma's got a tranquilizer.*

Anna came home from the beauty parlor in plenty of time to get dressed, but she hated the way the girl had fixed her hair. There was nothing to do but wash it again and fix it herself. By the time she finished with her hair, she had to hurry to be ready on time.

Her nails were polished, her makeup carefully applied, and jewelry selected with utmost pains. She had pressed the dress twice—once before hanging it in the closet and once after taking it out again. After she had it on she wasn't sure it fit right. With her graying hair she wasn't sure orchid was her best color nor if the colored beads were right for the dress. *I could use Marge Penry right now*, she fumed as she slipped on pumps.

Anna looked out at the parking lot. On a strip of grass to the side were three women from neighboring apartments sitting in lawn chairs. *Oh, they're going to see him!* she fretted.

And they did. Cecil McCurdy arrived on the minute and as he got out of the car the women recognized him. He spoke to them and as he came into the building, their heads turned to follow his direction.

Anna groaned. *Uff-dah!*

But she couldn't worry about the women, McCurdy was at the door. Straightening her dress she glanced once more in the mirror, patted her hair, pulled in her stomach, and went to the door.

McCurdy came in and sat a few minutes making small

talk. Finally, he said, "Well, shall we go?"

Leaving the building with him, Anna did not look at the women, but she sensed they were well aware of who was going out with Cecil McCurdy. She could well imagine how curious they would be and how their tongues would wag.

On the drive to Pinehurst, Cecil McCurdy came directly to the point. "Miss Petersen, Judyth is going to marry a Jewish man. I know this sounds anti-Semitic but I can't have this. I'm not against Jews but the differences in religion are crucial. Judyth doesn't realize what it will mean to her and to her children to have a divided household, or what it will mean if she gives up her Protestant faith. You know the Bible. Christians are forbidden to marry anyone who denies that Jesus is the Christ."

"I agree with you, Mr. McCurdy."

"Then will you tell her that?"

"Isn't that something you should explain to her yourself?"

"She won't listen to me. In fact, the last time she was home I behaved badly. She brought Seymour with her and, quite frankly, I couldn't handle it. I was rude. Now she's going to marry him."

"Does she understand your reasons?"

"Miss Petersen, we've discussed it at length, but Judyth has always rebelled against me. I think she puts me in the category of Moses—closes her mind to anything I have to say."

"When is she getting married?"

"In June. If I can persuade her to come home for a weekend, would you be kind enough to try to get through to her? As you can understand, this matter is of utmost concern to me, and you are the only person I know who might help in the situation."

Anna hesitated. "Mr. McCurdy, it seems to me that if Judyth is twenty-two and you've done everything you

can to teach her, then Judyth is responsible for this
decision and there isn't anything you or I or anyone
else can do about it."

"But she loves you so, maybe she'll listen to you.
Miss Petersen, you're my only hope."

"Judyth has a mind of her own."

"Yes, I believe you've told me that before." An ironic
smile crossed his lips. "But I'm desperate. Judyth is
my daughter and if I lose her—"

Anna weakened. "All right. If Judyth comes home,
send her to see me."

Cecil McCurdy heaved a sigh of relief.

They were turning in the gate of the club and did
not slow down as the guard waved them through. The
drive to the clubhouse was breathtakingly beautiful with
red and white shrubs in full bloom. "I want us to take
a little walk before dinner. The dogwood is at its height
and the way the azaleas bloom along the little creeks,
well, it's just beautiful."

As the car came to a stop before the clubhouse, a
doorman opened the door for Anna, waited for her to
get out, then hurried around to the other side to slip
under the wheel and drive the car away. Mr. McCurdy
motioned toward the golf course. "Shall we walk down
toward the lake?"

The flowers were pretty and he talked about the
landscaping and how it was designed, who built the
club, and some of the people whose homes were there.
"Now, Miss Petersen, may I call you Anna?"

"Of course," she said.

"And do you mind calling me Cecil?"

"Well, that won't come easy."

He smiled.

"Anna, this is a beautiful place and I come here
occasionally with associates, but the people here are a
different lot. They must think of themselves as the
beautiful people and some of them are, but they're not

happy people. They dress well and live well, if creature comforts are what you call living well. Knowing the right people is important to them and excluding others is a necessary evil."

Anna wondered if he was trying to tell her something—perhaps in his own way to put her at ease. They came to a foot bridge and he helped her across. Standing beside the little creek, he did not let go of her hand.

"They always travel in groups. They're like adolescents who have their own language, their right labels, go to the right places. Out of their element, they can't function. Here we have the horsey set. The hunt gives them a reason to wear sporting habits and show their fine dogs. It gives them a reason for getting together to drink cocktails and make conversation. Golfing gives them a reason to follow the sun—go from one club to another."

She hardly heard what he was saying, she was so nervous standing there with him holding her hand.

"They can't stand to be alone, Anna. To spend an evening at home would be agony for them. If they aren't dressing up and going somewhere they're miserable."

"Shouldn't we go inside?"

He took the hint and dropped her hand. "Yes, it's time."

When they entered the clubhouse, Anna was awed by its splendor. On all sides there was glass letting in the beauty of the lake, the golf greens, trees, and shrubs. "Good evening, Mr. McCurdy," a waiter said, and he nodded in return.

"We'll have dinner in the ballroom," he said, and Anna preceded him.

Band music was coming from somewhere and when they entered the ballroom she saw the musicians, six of them, a jazz combo.

The bamboo furniture and bright chintzes, fresh flowers, and gorgeous buffet were elegant. From the buffet they were served scrumptious hors d'oeuvres—anchovies, caviar, crab meat. The table was laden with shrimp, roast beef, chicken, lamb, salads, vegetable dishes, fruits, cheeses, sauces, desserts.

Anna's dress was nothing like those the other women were wearing. There were diamonds galore and designer clothes, and people drifted by their table in a practiced casualness that belied their meticulous protocol. Young women on the arms of elderly men walked like birds on crane legs, their long necks craning to survey the crowd.

"Anna, what're you thinking?"

"I was thinking, what a different world this is."

"It isn't real, Anna. It's sheer fantasy."

"I was thinking how different it is from the world of classrooms and school corridors. It's all so elegant."

"But not real."

Anna smiled. "I think I could stand it."

He chuckled. "Not for a steady diet, could you?"

"Maybe."

A waiter interrupted them. "There's a call for you, Mr. McCurdy. Do you want to take it in here or there?"

"I'll take it in the office. Will you excuse me, Anna?"

After he left, Anna took a deep breath. *Well, so far, so good. It's a wonderful experience being in such a place but I'll be glad when this is over.* She tried to dry the palms of her hands on the napkin.

Pretty young waitresses, looking like maids in their black uniforms and white aprons, were serving drinks. *It's a wonder some former student is not working here,* she thought. *That's all I need! I wonder which girl is Thelma's sister. I imagine it's that one with the sandy hair, she looks a bit like Thelma from the back.* The girl kept smiling at Anna each time she passed the table. Anna smiled back self-consciously.

*It must be an important call, he's staying so long. So*

*far, so good,* she thought. *No spills, no* faux pas—*if I can manage not to trip and fall flat on my face, I'll make it okay.*

When Mr. McCurdy did not return, the waitress slipped a drink off the tray and served it to Anna. "I didn't order—"

The girl winked. "It's on the house."

The tiny glass held only a few swallows. *It can't be wine,* Anna thought, *it's creamy, looks syrupy. Is it amber color? . . . Must be one of those after-dinner things. Really looks good . . . Can't be much to it. Might calm me down a bit . . . I feel like a fool sitting here looking at it.*

The waitress swept by the table again, glanced at Anna.

*Oh, good grief! I guess I better drink it.* Turning up the glass she drank it straight down! *Whew!* The drink burned like fire! She grabbed the goblet and gulped water. Cecil McCurdy was making his way through the crowd back to the table.

"Sorry. That was Judyth. She got so excited when she heard we were here together she just kept talking." He looked dejected. "She won't be coming home, they're going to be married in Chicago."

"I'm sorry, Mr. McCurdy."

"I'm sorry, Cecil," he said.

Anna felt the room sway. It was getting warm.

"Judyth wants you to come with me to the wedding. I don't suppose—"

"No. Thank you, but, no." It was getting warmer by the minute. She slipped off her jacket.

He looked very downcast but for some reason Anna couldn't feel sad. "Now, don't take it so hard, Cecil. Judyth's going to be all right."

Looking at his woe-begone face struck her as very funny and she was having a hard time suppressing giggles. This was no time to be giggling when the man was down in the dumps, so she kept as straight a face as possible.

"It's awful hot in here!" Anna complained. "I'm going to speak to the manager. Miss! Oh, Miss, could you come here, please?"

"Anna, I'll speak to the manager," Cecil said in a low, firm voice.

Anna was in a talkative mood and when the manager came, she told him to turn down the heat. "I'm burning up!" she told him. Then it struck her funny that here with all these women walking around like models, she was the only one who had the nerve to complain. She had a fit of laughing that made tears roll down her cheeks.

Cecil did not see anything funny in it and after a while he said, "I think we better go."

On the way home, she was in such a silly mood she was out of control. *I've got to stop giggling! Oh, good grief! What's the matter with me?* Everything he said was funny and the harder she tried not to laugh, the more the giggles came.

The next morning, Anna remembered what happened and realized it was the drink. *Glory be, I was tipsy! Downright tipsy! Oh, good night, whatever does Cecil McCurdy think?* Her cheeks burned just thinking about it and she held her face in her palms. *How will I ever face that man again? . . . How could I be so stupid!*

No sooner did she step out of the house than a neighbor came running out. "Hey, Anna, didn't I see you going out with Cecil McCurdy last night?"

"You did," Anna acknowledged and kept right on walking as fast as she could to the car. Before the woman could catch up with her, she shut the door and drove out of the parking lot.

Of course, Thelma heard about the date and was

waiting at the apartment when she came home from school. "Anna Petersen! Aren't you the foxy one! Now I know why you wanted to know what they wear at the Country Club! Aren't you foxy! As soon as I heard about it, I called my sister and asked if she saw you there. She said McCurdy was there with a woman but then she said the woman created a bit of a scene. I told my sister that couldn't possibly be you because Anna Petersen does not make scenes!"

"I created a scene, Thelma. You can believe I did."

"Not *you*, Anna!"

"Yes, me, Thelma. I drank something too fast and it made me tipsy." She felt like adding, "Now go and tell that all over town."

"Well, I'm sure it wasn't as bad as you thought—" Then she was snickering. "Oh, Anna, this is too funny for words!"

*Big deal!* Anna thought.

# CHAPTER
# THIRTY-NINE

Anna was depressed. The wild stories circulating about her were too much. To hear them tell it, she got drunk and kicked up her heels. One rumor had it that she passed out. When a student asked her if it was true that she was going to marry Mr. McCurdy, it was the straw that broke the camel's back. She felt like closing the door and never coming out again.

Flopping on the couch, she looked at the drooping red roses Cecil McCurdy had sent. She wasn't crazy about flowers but somehow she couldn't throw them away. He was such a nice man and none of this was his fault. Three times he had called and three times she had said, no, she wouldn't go out with him.

The mail lay on her stomach unopened. *Probably only bills*, she thought. Finally, she lifted one of the envelopes to see what it was. The return address was some place in Connecticut, probably a playbill from Sue Marie—she always sent one if she were in the cast. Anna opened it and that's what it was—an off Broadway production and there was Sue Marie's picture and a write-up about her. She didn't feel like reading it— maybe later.

There was a card from David McBryde telling her he'd been to Salzburg, the city of Mozart. Another birth announcement from Delores—a girl this time. *Must be her third*, Anna thought, trying to remember.

*Wish I'd hear from Anita.*

There was a wedding invitation from Judyth. She

almost decided not to open it but when she did, the groom's name aroused her interest. Dr. Seymour Metcalf. *The only Metcalf I ever knew was Roger, but there couldn't be any connection. Cecil said this fellow's Jewish.* Then it dawned on her! *Roger married a* Jewish *girl!*

Anna sat straight up and adjusted her glasses to see better. *It can't be!* she thought. This man lives in Chicago. Roger lives in Denver. Her heart was pulsating in her neck. But he is a *doctor* practicing in Cook County. She stood up. "Lord," she asked, "is it possible he's one of the twins?"

Anna couldn't wait to find out. She called Thelma. When she answered, Anna asked, "Thelma, did you and George get an invitation to Judyth's wedding?"

"Sure did but she's crazy if she thinks we're going to Chicago to see her tie the knot. Are you going?"

"Don't be silly. I'm sorry the wedding isn't going to be here. Do you know where the groom's from?"

"He's from Colorado some place. He's a doctor, you know."

"Yes, I know," Anna replied weakly.

"I understand his father's a doctor, too. A surgeon."

"Oh?"

"And he has a twin brother. I think his brother's a geologist or something."

Anna felt weak. "That's interesting," she managed to say and ended the conversation.

She lay back on the bed. *It's incredible! Absolutely incredible!*

# CHAPTER
# FORTY

A year passed before Judyth and Seymour Metcalf moved to Scotsville, he to go into private practice and she to open a resident facility for patients recuperating. They bought a modest home and Cecil McCurdy financed the purchase of the McAllister place near town, a beautiful old colonial home set in a grove of live oaks. Judyth busied herself in the remodeling of the house and within six months it was ready for occupancy.

It was at the dedication of Metcalf Residence that Anna first met Seymour. Except for unavoidable encounters, Anna had succeeded in keeping her distance from the McCurdy family. Judyth called repeatedly, inviting her to dinner but Anna declined. Anna anticipated meeting Seymour with mixed emotions. As soon as their eyes met she recognized him as Roger's son, and the sight of him brought a lump to her throat. Seymour was not as blond as Roger but he was the same height and build. When he came across the room to greet her, he carried himself just as Roger did and, unconsciously, she glanced at his feet remembering the built-up shoe. He was smiling and looked down on her with the same blue eyes, the same shy charm she remembered.

Anna had to turn away. "Excuse me, please," she said and hurried to the ladies' room.

Judyth saw her and followed. Anna wet a towel and was holding it to her eyes hoping to stop the redness. "Miss Pete?" Judyth was looking at her in the mirror.

She put her arm around Anna. "Whatever is the matter?"

Anna shook her head.

"Don't you feel well?"

"I'm fine."

"You've been avoiding us. Poor Daddy, he doesn't know what else to do. Why won't you see him?"

"Judyth, you need to get back to your guests."

"Say you'll come for dinner. Wednesday—come Wednesday."

"No, Judyth. Thank you, but I cannot." She was emphatic.

"How do you like my husband?"

"I've only met him."

"Isn't he handsome!"

"Yes, he's very handsome."

"Samantha Johnson is helping us here at the Residence. She's in her glory, Miss Pete, and she's dying to see you. When you're finished here come along and let me show you the rest of the house." She turned to go. "Sure you're okay?"

Anna nodded and smiled.

Shortly after Judyth left, the door was flung open and Samantha burst upon her. "Oh, Miz Petersen!" she cried as she fell in Anna's arms. "Oh, let me kiss your face!"

After several wet kisses, Anna was able to disengage herself and look at the dear girl. "Samantha, have you been a good girl?"

Samantha drew in her breath and stood straight. "Miz Petersen, I lives a good mortal life!"

"How many children do you have?"

"Two, a boy and a girl. They lives a good mortal life, too, because I am their mother and I teach them to do right." She was wagging her finger in motherly fashion.

"The Residence is beautiful. I'm sure you will enjoy working here."

"Oh, Miz Petersen, it's fatatic! We got patients already and I make them laugh. I make them laugh every day. Now we got one man that is old and he forgets. Judyth say he's crazy as a bedbug. Now you know she know better than that. Bedbugs ain't crazy, Miz Petersen, they know exactly what they're doin'."

Anna smiled. Samantha had not changed.

The facility was lovely. Vibrant colors and white wicker with fresh flowers everywhere reminded her more of the Country Club than a place for the infirm.

When Anna came out to mingle with the guests, Seymour sought her out. "Miss Petersen, I can't understand why we haven't met before. I've been looking forward to knowing you because my wife talks about you as if you are a legend in your own time. If I may say so, you seem to be younger than most legendary figures."

The sound of his voice was so like Roger's it was uncanny.

"May I get you a drink?"

"Perhaps a ginger ale."

*I must get hold of myself,* Anna thought. *Oh, I just wish he'd go talk to someone else.* She tried to turn her attention to Samantha, serving hors d'oeuvres with ecstatic joy. Every person Samantha served was left with a face wreathed in smiles.

Seymour returned bearing the glasses. They stood away from the milling visitors behind palm fronds and sipped the drinks. "Isn't Samantha something? She's so sociable. The patients love her. I tell Judyth she's a national treasure."

"I quite agree."

"We're sorry our folks can't be here today. Mr. McCurdy's in Japan and, unfortunately, my parents are in the process of getting a divorce."

"I'm sorry," she said and set down the glass. Her hand was trembling.

"Well, it's all very amicable. Mother has her interests and of course Dad keeps busy. My brother and I are established so it's not quite like the breakup of a growing family."

"No."

"As soon as things are straightened out, I expect they'll visit us. I want you to meet them." Judyth was beckoning to him. "Will you excuse me? My wife wants me."

As soon as Anna could leave gracefully, she did and on the way home she let the tears roll. It was hard to believe that after all these years news of Roger could affect her this way. Looking at Seymour simply brought it all back to her and to think that one day she might see Roger—well, it was overwhelming.

Safe at home in her cozy apartment, Anna sat in the dark for awhile trying to sort out her feelings. It was futile. "Lord," she said, "only you are sufficient for this. You know how much I would like to see him but you know how vulnerable I am. Please, don't let me do something foolish or wrong."

The prayer gave her peace. In a little while she turned on the lamp and reached for the cello. Tuning the strings, she was hearing in her head Franck's *Panis Angelicus,* and as she played, she hummed the words, "O Lord, most holy . . . "

In the months that followed, she did have lunch with Judyth several times on Saturdays, but Anna refused to discuss Cecil McCurdy with his daughter. "But, Miss Pete, why not be friends? My father is a very lonely man and he's fond of you. Since my mother died he hasn't shown an interest in any other woman."

"But he should, Judyth. Someone who can entertain his friends, move in his circles."

"I'm looking at the lady who fits that bill perfectly."

"Let's get off this subject, Judyth."

The next fall, Anna determined to bury herself in school. All the apathy, all the nonsense going on in education, all the stress of the work she was going to take in stride. A positive outlook, a little more sense of humor, and she could live above it all and at least survive.

The opening day activities did not promise any improvement over the past years but Anna wasn't going to let it get her down. Sitting in the auditorium with a clipboard on her lap to take notes, she soon realized there would be nothing noteworthy that day.

There were seven hundred and fifty teachers from all over the system in the high school auditorium. Air-conditioning vents blasted cold air from every direction, turning August into February. Horace Wigglesworth was proud of McAdden High facilities and he was fond of standing before an audience in the auditorium as superintendent of schools. Seeing Horace in his plaid polyester sports jacket and green school-color pants made Anna think of Marge Penry who would enjoy the humor of it all.

> Dear Marge,
>
> School opened today. Among the speakers was the spokesman for the school board. He wanted to tell us their dreams. No, school boards do not have nightmares—teachers have nightmares. School boards have dreams.
>
> There were forty-three new teachers today. Each one was given a carnation. In thirty years, when they retire, they may be given another carnation. What happens between carnations changes history, but only students and teachers know that.
>
> The second speaker, a professor of education,

found it "delightful" to be with us. Of course, he is not staying long—45 minutes, tops. He spoke of our talents and called us heroes and saints. He tells us we are now "high" but by January we will be "low." True, Horace will probably see to that! The professor advises that when the January "low" comes, when we're on our way home from school we should roll up the windows, turn on the radio, and scream.

If I am "high" now, by "scream time" I will do well to whimper.

An alcoholic sits across from me picking his nose. That's what he does when he's sober. I like him better looped.

The assistant superintendent, whose job is to think up things to do, tells us to greet those on the right, left, front, and back. We do. Then he tells us to touch them or hug them. It has been observed that some faculty members have been doing this all along but only behind closed doors. Does this mean they can come out of the closet?

Administrators are to cook lunch for us but "Miss Nan," the library supervisor, is holding forth. She won't quit. First, Horace left the platform. Then, one by one, the other administrators went to their assigned duties, leaving no one in charge. We are held captive, not by eloquence but by Horace's lieutenants guarding the doors.

The way the lieutenants spot-check attendance is by giving door prizes—valuable stuff such as a yardstick from McCurdy's Furniture Store and key chains with Central Bank printed on them. Quite a few numbers were called and the owners were absent. Horace has as much fun catching recalcitrants as he used to have bebopping in the teacherage. Remember?

Miss Nan is pigeon-toed. She reads to us a lot.

*I guess she wants to prove that she can. She's ambidextrous—she can hold up a laminated, hand-lettered poster in one hand and point at us with the other, all the time talking in the Barbara Jordan manner, end syllables emphasized with warbling resonance. Miss Nan tells us the alert teacher "SPOTS THAT CHILD" and in my view that works both ways. What we're "spotting" each other for is never made clear but the slogan is drummed into our heads never to be forgotten!*

*Miss Nan's voice booms over the mike and even the mike can't take it—it spits back! Finally, Miss Nan moves away from the mike to our great relief.*

*On an amateur show, she would definitely get the hook.*

*The supervisor for staff development reappears but she doesn't have a hook. She tells Miss Nan she has wandered from the mike. Nothing dampens the woman's enthusiasm. She has no terminal facilities.*

*In the end, the supervisor sidles up to Miss Nan and tells her to "Shut up!" This startles Miss Nan and the two of them discuss the matter. The supervisor wins but Miss Nan is not convinced and refuses to give up even as she is departing. Leaving the stage she keeps holding up one laminated poster after another with frantic running comments.*

*We cheer!*

*Horace comes back to the podium, hush puppy dough on his cheek, and tells us we have a new wrinkle this year. The administration has added German and Latin to the curriculum; the theory being, "If they can't learn our language, maybe they can learn somebody else's." Good thinking, huh, Marge?*

*We have yet another speaker. This one from Raleigh. He says that if he reads the crystal ball* correctly (when you can't read writing, you read glass balls, etc.) the '90s will be the best years yet for education.

That's good to know. It means, "Cheer up," "Pull up your socks," or "Get with it!" Marge, the golden years are just around the corner. Sound familiar?

I am real excited about school. Can you tell?

Love,
Anna

# CHAPTER
# FORTY-ONE

In the spring of '81, the inevitable occurred—Roger Metcalf was coming to Scotsville and he had asked to see her. Anna wanted to see him and if it left her scarred more than she already was, she was willing to risk it.

Seymour's Volvo turned into the parking lot just as Anna drew the drapes. Peeping between them, she watched Roger climbing out from under the wheel. He was thick-bodied now, square shouldered but favoring the bad leg. Pausing to flatten the flaps on the pockets of his sports coat, the spring breeze played with his thin hair, and as he moved toward the door he smoothed his hair with the palms of his hands.

Anna had rehearsed a hundred times how she would greet Roger, what she would say, how she would behave, but when the buzzer sounded, she froze. In a minute, it rang again. Still she stood, unable to move. Finally, he knocked. Anna glanced down at herself one more time to make sure she looked all right, then opened the door. "Roger Metcalf! Do come in. It's good to see you."

"Anna." He came inside and she closed the door.

"Please sit down. Here." As soon as she was seated, he settled himself in the big upholstered chair. For the moment he seemed as shy as when she first met him. Stroking his hair nervously, finding it hard to look at her straight on, he said, "It's good to see you, Anna. You're looking really good." There was an awkward pause. "Seymour tells me you're the most beloved teacher in town. I'm not surprised."

The sound of his voice was as she remembered it. In all her imaginations she had not expected the sight nor the sound of him to move her this way.

Roger tilted back his head to look through the bifocals and nodded toward the end table. "Your Aunt Helga's marble top?"

"You remember that?" she asked, surprised. "It's been how many years?"

"Thirty." He looked at the table thoughtfully, touching it with his fingertips. "I remember everything, Anna." His head swung round for full-fledged eye contact.

"Can I get you something to drink?"

He shook his head. "No thanks. Seymour made reservations for us in Pinehurst. We'd better be going, that is, if you're ready."

In the comfortable darkness of the car, he began talking more easily. "Anna, I want to tell you everything and there isn't much time. I didn't come here to see the kids nearly so much as I came to see you.

"As you know, Lenta divorced me and, I'm sorry to say, with good reason. I'm not the man you knew at Rutgers. I want to be that man, though.

"Our marriage went sour six months after the wedding. We both agreed that we'd made a mistake but we hoped to work it out. Then she became pregnant with the boys. When the babies came we wanted to do what was right for them. Lenta still held hope that the marriage would work, but I could never be what she wanted me to be and, quite frankly, I knew our differences were irreconcilable.

"I put everything into my practice, my time, energy—everything—trying to forget. Lenta and I lived under the same roof but I was not a dutiful husband. The only woman I ever wanted was you, Anna."

Anna did not want to hear more. There was something irresistible about him, something that made her weaken in his presence. Over and over she had told herself that all she wanted from him was one visit to satisfy her curiosity, to let the closed book lie still and flat where it had been for thirty years, but in his presence that was not possible. The book was open and he was thumbing through the pages.

"Do you remember, at Rutgers, how I wanted to help in the war or go to Europe afterward—do something to help? Well, I should have followed through on that. Marrying outside my faith was the next mistake. Then I became ambitious. Lenta wanted things and it was the least I could do for her. I could give her what money could buy. . . .

"But now I'm free, Anna. I'm going to pick up where I left off, put the pieces back together."

She weighed her words before she spoke. "That's not possible, Roger. You can never go back and start all over again."

"You can if you find all the pieces," he insisted, striving to convince her.

"No, you can't. Not even if you find all the pieces."

"Well, I'm going to try." They were rounding a curve and he slowed the car. "Anna, I'm going overseas to one of those mission outposts and give what time I have left to the destitute."

"Do you think a mission board will accept you?"

"You mean because I'm divorced?" She nodded. "Well, I don't know. I am a surgeon and they have a hard time finding missionary doctors, much less surgeons. Also, I can go at my own expense. That's a plus factor.

"It's a new generation, Anna. People don't frown on divorce as they once did." Then he tried harder to persuade her. "I don't need a mission board, Anna. There's a hospital ship that travels the Amazon, sponsored by an outfit in Seattle. I can sign on with them.

"I don't need a mission board," he repeated, his voice softer. "But I do need you, Anna. All through the years, I've yearned for you as no man ever yearned for a woman. Isn't it time that I had a little happiness in my life?" Then he grew angry. Pounding the steering wheel with his fist, he said, "Why should one mistake sentence a man for life? Why, Anna? Why?"

She could not answer for fear her voice would quiver.

"You gave the ring back, Anna, but I let you. Will you forgive me for that?"

She nodded and managed to say, "I forgave you a long time ago."

"When I gave you the ring that night in the cafeteria, do you remember I told you we'd have to wait a long time? Do you remember you told me you'd wait for me forever? Did you mean that?"

Anna took a deep breath and felt the sob that was in her voice. "I meant it, Roger, but that's all changed now." Her voice did quiver.

He drove the car off the side of the road, cut off the motor, and dimmed the lights. Reaching for her, he took her in his arms. "Why, can't it be? You're free, I'm free. Tell me you don't love me, tell me anything, but don't say you won't marry me."

The coarse tweed of his jacket, the feel of his face against hers flooded her with a sense of belonging. Life would be so much easier if there was someone to share it with, someone to love, someone to lean on.

Gently, she drew back from him. "Roger, you're not making sense."

Letting her go, he agreed. "You're right. I'm talking like a fool. I hadn't meant to rush you. It's just that there's so little time." He started the car and pulled back onto the road. "I don't want you to answer me tonight. For that matter, you can take all the time you want. But, Anna, I will do anything I have to, to have you."

"Roger—"

"Not now. Don't answer now. Take your time. Pray about it." They were slowing down on a narrow, winding street. "We won't talk about it anymore tonight. We'll just enjoy ourselves."

Enjoy they did. There was good food, music, candlelight, and Roger regaled her with one story after another. If anything, the years had sharpened his wit, matured his charm.

By the time they were turning into the Raefield Arms, Anna was happier than she had been in a very long time.

At the door, Roger took her in his arms and kissed her. Not waiting for another, she said, "Good night, Roger."

Inside the apartment, Anna sat down on the couch in the darkened room. Never, in her wildest imagination, had she dreamed he would affect her like this. How could he rekindle the old feelings so easily, so quickly? Wrapping her arms around her knees, she hugged them to her chest, leaned her head back, and closed her eyes. To imagine what it would be like to be married to Roger had always been a dream—now the dream could be realized. *Why would the Lord let him come back like this if it wasn't meant to be? Why do I still care for him if we aren't to get married?*

The phone ringing startled her. It was nearly one o'clock in the morning. *Who can this be? Marge. Probably Marge*, she decided.

It was. Nothing urgent, just another of Marge's spontaneous indulgences. "Where've you been? I've been trying all night to get you."

Anna hedged. "I was out."

"Of course, but where?"

"Pinehurst."

"Out with the girls?"

"Not exactly."

"Anna Petersen, don't tell me you've been out with Cecil McCurdy again!"

"No."

"Come on, you're being evasive. Who were you out with?"

"It isn't nice to put a person on the spot," Anna teased.

"Are you going to tell me or do I have to find out some other way?"

"Well, if you must know . . . Roger Metcalf was in town and we had dinner together."

Marge was flabbergasted. *"Roger Metcalf?* Seymour's father? Your old boyfriend?"

"The same."

"Well, whadda ya know! Do you want to tell me about it? Is he still married?"

"No, he isn't married. He's divorced and—" Anna's voice broke.

"Anna, you're crying. Now tell me, tell me exactly what's bothering you."

"It's nothing."

"Then why are you sniffling? I bet I can tell you what it is. He wants you back and—"

"He's divorced, Marge, and not for the right reasons."

"Since when is there a right reason? On second thought, there is a right reason, isn't there? Matthew 6, somewhere along there. Are you sure? Oh, Anna, I know how much you cared for him and I know what a temptation this is, but Anna, don't weaken. No one would be happier to see you married than I, but, honey, you can't do this—God wouldn't bless a marriage like that. . . . Anna, are you still there?"

"I'm here, Marge. I know you're right and I know

my conscience won't let me marry him, but Marge, it hurts so bad. Marge, I can't talk . . . I'll call you over the weekend."

Anna lay back on the bed exhausted. Overhead the ceiling was mauve, and the unsettling effect that had upon her made her pull up the covers and bury her head in the pillow.

Hours later when she was still wide awake, Anna got up, found her father's concordance, looked up all the scriptures on divorce. When she was through, her mind was made up but her heart kept arguing.

Roger came by the high school on his way out of town. Seymour was driving him to the plane in Charlotte. Anna felt uncomfortable seeing him there in the office. Every secretary was trying to get a glimpse of him and students stared unashamedly. Anna walked him out to the car and on the way she told him, "Roger, there's no need for us to string this out over a long period of time. I've made up my mind. I can't marry you."

"Oh, but you don't have to answer now. Give me more time, Anna. I rushed you. You'll see this differently in time. Give me a chance to show you. Let's just be friends for a while—"

If he only knew how hard it was for her to give him up he would not torment her. She shook her head, too full to speak.

They stopped under the pecan tree, a discreet distance from the Volvo. Roger took both her hands and held her eyes with his. His voice was husky. "I think I knew all along." His eyes were misty. "But I had to find out. Anna, I'll never give up trying. If you change your mind—"

Her chin was quivering. She couldn't talk. He dropped his eyes to the pavement. "Anna, would you tell me one thing?" He pressed her hands in his. "Do you love me?"

Anna waited for him to look at her. "Roger," her voice was shaking, "I mustn't answer that."

He stared at her longingly. Brushing her cheek with his hand, he turned and walked toward the car. As she watched him go she hoped she had freed him to go ahead without her and she prayed his leaving would free her once and for all.

When he reached the car, he turned and looked back. Seymour opened the door for him and he got into the car. As she stood gazing after him, the Volvo rolled slowly over the speed breakers and when it reached the highway, it turned west and, picking up speed, moved out of sight.

# CHAPTER
# FORTY-TWO

At three o'clock in the morning, the phone rang. It was Cecil McCurdy calling from Tokyo.

"Anna, I know it's an unearthly hour to be calling but I had to speak to you. Judyth called me when she found out Roger Metcalf was a friend of yours and that he was going to see you.

"Anna, please don't commit yourself to someone else until you've given me a fair chance. I want to see you in the worst way. Is there any way—"

At first she thought to refuse, then thought better about it. "Cecil, I'm right here."

"But you've refused so many times to see me."

Anna thought about it.

"Anna, are you there?"

"Yes." Finally, she answered, "I guess I've been rude, Cecil. When are you coming back?"

"I'll be home as soon as I can—probably Wednesday."

"Call me when you get home."

"Thank you, Anna. I've waited a long time."

Anna lay back on the pillow exhausted. There were a lot of things to be done before Wednesday—she'd try to get them all done and have everything sorted out so that when she faced Cecil she could think clearly. "Lord, help me do the right thing," she prayed and rolled over, trying to go back to sleep.

# CHAPTER
# FORTY-THREE

The trucker let him off on the by-pass and Andrew Lawton stood there until the eighteen-wheeler pulled away, dust flying in his face. It was somewhere near, he remembered. Following the ditch beside the highway, he came to Bridge Road. There, he knew the way.

Andrew felt his heart beating, something he had not felt for a long time. Pressing his hand against his chest he could feel it thumping. Even the darkness in his head seemed to open and let in light again. In the spring air he felt exhilarated, higher than he had ever been before. At last he would be free! Free!

Ahead of him was the railroad crossing. Heading toward it, the ground rising and falling beneath his feet, Andrew clenched the penny deep inside his pocket and held on to consciousness. The wine bottle, still unopened, bulged beneath his coat and with his free hand, he clasped it, making sure it did not fall. Stumbling onto the tracks, he flushed a covey of quail feeding in the broomstraw. The fluttering upsurge of their flight did not startle him; rather, he felt a certain glee that it was he who frightened them.

Soon nothing would frighten him. Leaving the tracks he pushed through plum bushes on the bank and, confused, stood swaying, unbalanced in the wind. Where was the big tree? Where? Where? An iron fence enclosed a plot just ahead of him; it came in and out of view as the land heaved upward in front of him and lay back down again. Gravestones swayed from side to side,

rocking, tilting, leaning forward, leaning backward —
gray, white, black, red in the late light.

Was that the big tree? It was! Fat oak solid against
the sky. He was giggling now, wiping his mouth on his
sleeve. The wine would wash away the smell of blood
but that could wait now. He was plunging forward,
breathing hard. The tree moved, taking the bushes
around its roots with it. Saliva oozed at the corners of
his mouth and he wiped at it as he kicked aside a
basket of plastic flowers. Nearing the place, he tripped
over a coping—fell sprawling. Stunned, he lay on the
ground feeling for the bottle. It lay intact beside him,
his dear and faithful friend. Hugging it to his chest he
sat up and, laughing, unscrewed the cap. Swallowing
enough to wash his mouth, he fumbled as he screwed
the cap back on. Holding the bottle by its thin neck,
he crawled on hands and knees toward the gravestone.
With a trembling finger tracing the letters, he spelled
out THEODORE MCGILL.

Giggling again, he clawed the ground with his fingers
until he spied an iron pipe lying beside the coping.
With it he began to bore into the ground. Sweat beaded
his forehead and wet his upper lip as the pipe cut deeper
and deeper in the dirt. Panting, Andrew leaned back
on his heels, wiped his oily face on his sleeve, and
reached in his pocket for the penny. Rubbing the surface of the penny, Andrew, for the last time, stared at
the Indianhead. It lay warm in his palm, the Indian in
headdress as alive as ever. He pressed his lips against
the coin, then carefully placed it heads-down in the
hole. Filling the hole with dirt, he packed it with his
thumbs, then hammered it with his fist, packing it solid.

His task finished, Andrew fell face forward on the
grave. It was over! The hell was over. He had done it!
He had done it! Laughing and crying, Andrew's body
jerked convulsively. Rolling over on his back, the
spasms subsided and he could feel again his heart

pounding in his chest. As he lay glancing from side to side, he saw the broad expanse of sky drenched in wine, red wine, old and dark. He closed his eyes, his heartbeat growing fainter, numbness creeping over him.

When Andrew stirred again, the sky was darker, the wine drained out of it, leaving only dregs. Rolling over on his belly, he inched himself forward on his elbows. The smell was coming back, rising like vapor from a stagnant swamp, the strong, dark smell of blood. Clutching the gravestone in his arms, Andrew pulled himself to his knees. Leaning heavily against the cold stone, he pressed his cheek against it and, sobbing, cried out for Anita.

A car was turning off the Bridge Road and heading into the cemetery. When he finally saw it, Andrew reached for the bottle and on hands and knees, crawled behind the shrubs at the base of the tree.

The car stopped by the iron fence and he could see a woman getting out, the breeze whipping her coat. He knew the woman. In his mind he knew the woman! Peering through the leaves he could see her clearly. His heart was pounding like a hammer, sounding in his head. *She's come to dig up the penny!* He had to stop her! When she reached the grave, she knelt down to dig and he made his move, coming up on her from behind just as she turned.

"Why, Andrew Lawton! I didn't expect to see you here." She was smiling, or was she laughing? The ground pitched forward beneath his feet but he leaned backward against the force.

"I'm Anna Petersen. You remember me, don't you?"

He remembered and contempt rose in him like the smell of the blood. There was that smile on her face that sickened him.

"I do this every now and then for Miss Clara. Did you have her? Perhaps you don't remember, it's been so long ago. How long, Andrew? Let's see, you graduated in 1959, or was it '60?" She stooped down again to dig.

The land was swaying. Andrew eased himself down on the coping. The woman got up, stood above him, quiet, her feet near his. Was that her hand on his shoulder? "Andrew, is there anything I can do for you?"

Fury rose in him. She was sitting down beside him, her voice soft and tender. "Andrew, I promised Anita I would talk to you about the Lord. May I?"

Andrew opened his eyes wide to glare at her. That frightened her; he could see the fear in her face. It delighted him! Everything about the woman rushed through his head, the fear and pain she had caused him. "Yankee witch! Get me yet, will you?" The smell made him see the fresh red blood oozing from the mouth and nose, pooling beneath the head. He was breathing hard, licking his lips. Pointing his finger in her face, his voice rasping, he swore. "I can tell on you, know that? I can tell on you, too! You scared all those kids with that bomb, remember?"

Close up in her face he spoke and the spit made her flinch. "Tried to scare us. Wanted us to run like rats in a hole. Well, we didn't!" He laughed. "We had our war and we're still here. We've been to hell and back and no Yankee woman dropped a bomb on us."

Her voice shook. "Was Vietnam hell?"

"There's no hell, woman! There never was and never will be." He licked his greasy lips and whispered, "I buried the bomb."

He was giggling now, rolling against her, his arm around her shoulders. Her body was shaking.

"Where did you bury the bomb, Andrew?"

"You know where," he snarled, locking her neck in his arm. "That's why you came here. You know. You know everything. 'Ask Miss Petersen,'" he mimicked in a high pitched voice. "'Ask Miss Petersen. She'll know!'" he taunted her.

"Andrew," she began, her voice quivering, "the Lord Jesus Christ can wash it all away—all the guilt—make you clean."

He stopped laughing and glared at her. "Don't talk to me about him! I'm the Lord Jesus Christ! I buried the bomb!"

The smell made him want the wine. Opening the bottle he turned it up and drank in great gulps. Then he took hold of her wrist, squeezing hard, watching her face whiten. It pleased him that she was afraid and he felt good now that the wine had washed him clean. He fondled her neck. "Tell me, Miss Petersen—what's it all about?"

"What's it all about, Andrew?"

The fool woman made him wait.

"There was once a song with a title like that—do you remember, Andrew?" Her voice was quavering. "Andrew, it's about you and me, heaven and hell." She made a sweeping gesture with her arm as she spoke. "None of this had to be—"

"Then tell me, tell me!"

"Sin caused all this. It didn't have to be—not death nor pain nor sorrow. But even now, the blood of Christ can save you—change your torment into peace."

Andrew threw back his head laughing. "I told you! I'm the Lord Jesus Christ! I buried the bomb. There's no hell left!"

"Oh, Andrew, Andrew . . . " She was weeping now. "Pin all your hopes on him—he alone can help you."

He was hearing her and the darkness in his head was opening, a sunbeam was streaming in, and he was quiet. Andrew lost the sound of his heart beating and he leaned toward the woman, wanting her to cradle him in her arms. She held him against her breast, and he lay there moaning.

How long he lay, he did not know, but when he roused he could hear the woman whispering to God.

Suddenly, she jumped and when she did Andrew saw the cat. He leaped to his feet, grabbed the pipe, and swung hard. The cat bounded in the brush unscathed, and when he turned to see what he had hit, the woman lay crumpled on the ground. He stared at the dark blood staining her hair and he wanted to help her. But for the blood he would have.

# CHAPTER
# FORTY-FOUR

Anna Petersen was found by Eddie McLaughlin's father when he went to visit his son's grave. How long she had lain there, no one could tell, certainly all night. There was little hope for her survival and Seymour Metcalf did only a cursory examination before rushing her to the hospital in Chapel Hill. For three weeks she lay in a coma, unaware of the furor her accident caused.

Police found the pipe, identified it as the weapon but the prints were poor and there were no other clues. "A transient," they theorized but were at a loss to understand why her purse was not stolen nor the car. "No sign of struggle," the paper said.

Messages and flowers poured in from all over the country. A prayer vigil was begun and lasted throughout the three weeks.

Judyth, the logical person to take charge of the case, assessed the situation. On the day Anna showed signs of consciousness, Judyth had a long conference with the doctors. The language was technical but Judyth understood, and when she told her poor father, devastated as he was, the prognosis, she made it as optimistic as she dared.

"Her speech is gone, Dad, and the paralysis of the face will not improve. If ever she walks again, she will drag one leg. Other than that, they cannot say." She laid her hand on his arm. "Seymour and I will give her the best of care."

"When can I see her?"

She hesitated. "Wouldn't you rather remember her as she was? If you see her now, the shock would make it harder for you."

"I want to see her."

"No, Dad. She wouldn't want you to see her like this. Don't you understand? A woman's beauty is very important, and Miss Pete was so beautiful it would be criminal for anyone to see her as she is now. Dad, she wouldn't even be able to speak to you. Why don't you give her time? Maybe in a few months we'll be able to communicate with her and let her decide if she wants to see you."

Cecil McCurdy put his head in his hands and wept.

McCurdy was not the only person Judyth kept away. When Anna was transferred to the Residence, Judyth gave her a lovely room on the second floor and made it clear to everyone that no visitors were allowed. In the mornings, Anna could sit on the sun porch with the other patients or enjoy the game room where the television was, but during visiting hours she was not to be available.

Samantha Johnson could not understand although Judyth patiently explained. "Samantha, do you love Miss Pete? I know you do. Don't you want to do what is best for her? Think about it—what if your pretty face was ruined and looked ugly, would you want people staring at you?"

Samantha thought a long time. "I wouldn't care if they looked at me. If they loved me they would come to see me and make me happy inside."

"Samantha, do you remember how brilliant Miss Pete was? How she stood up there and told us all about history and government and other things as well? Do you remember how funny she was—made us laugh? And remember how caring she was? Well, look at her now. She doesn't know anything. At times she acts crazy—locking herself in her room—

"Now look at her, Samantha—that fine brain is gone. It can't be repaired. Poor Miss Pete can't even talk. What good is she to anybody? I think if she could speak for herself she'd say she'd rather not live than be this way."

"No, Judyth, life alway mean somethin'. Miss Petersen ain' what she once was but she still be livin', an' dere's no tellin' what's goin' on 'tween her and God right now."

"Samantha, that's just wishful thinking. When the brain is damaged the way hers is, she doesn't know she's in this world. You ask Dr. Metcalf."

"Hmph. Don't Dr. Metcalf nor nobody else know all dere is to know."

"Well, Miss Petersen wouldn't want people to see her this way." She could tell she was getting nowhere with the girl.

Judyth tried again: "Samantha, dear, if you love Miss Pete you will help me protect her. This will be our secret and when folks come to see her we'll just say she's resting or she doesn't feel well."

Samantha shook her head stubbornly.

Judyth grew firm. "Samantha, Dr. Metcalf and I order you to do this. If you want to work here, you must abide by the rules. Do you understand?"

Big tears rolled down her face. "Judyth, if I don't work here, how will I feed my childrun?"

"I don't know, Samantha, but if you work here you must obey the doctor's orders."

When Marge Penry heard that Anna was in a convalescent home she drove all the way from Georgia to see her. Judyth met her at the desk. "I'm sorry, Miss Penry, Miss Petersen is not feeling well. It's been a very bad day for her."

Marge stayed in town six days but Judyth held firm and Marge did not suspect the truth.

Judyth turned Floyd Berry away every day for a month until he became disgusted and stopped coming. And when he called David McBryde and David called Judyth, she had a hard time explaining the protective custody in light of the medical records. Fortunately for Judyth, he could not come east for awhile.

Woodall Jackson, being a minister, felt he had *carte blanche*. Judyth purposely scheduled Anna's medication to coincide with his regular visit so that when he came, Anna was asleep.

"Men do not understand these things," she told Samantha. "They mean well, but we know Miss Pete, and if she could speak for herself she would say we are doing the right thing."

Samantha thought on the subject and after making her rounds, she announced to Judyth, "If Miss Petersen can't be pretty it don't mean she can't be happy on the inside. What makes you happy on the inside got nuthin' to do with what's on the ouside."

"I know you mean well, Samantha, but I think I'm in a better position to judge this than you are. Now run along—take Miss Pete out in the fresh air."

Judyth left no stone unturned to provide everything possible for Anna. There was a radio and a stereo in her room, fresh flowers every day, and she would have left her cello in the room but the sight of it distressed Anna. When Anna scribbled music notes on a paper, Judyth went to the trouble of getting ruled paper for composing music. Anna showed her delight by locking herself in her room and scribbling half the night. When she finally got her to open the door, Judyth took the sheets and started to throw them away but on second thought, she didn't. Of course, it was sentimental, but Miss Pete seemed so passionately absorbed in the scribbling there was a slim possibility that she was, indeed, composing music. Judyth stuck the sheets in an envelope and mailed them to David McBryde. He, of all people, would know if they had any value.

A week later, David called. Samantha answered the phone and heard all he said. "Tell Mrs. Metcalf, I am keeping these scores to send to my publisher. Miss Pete has written some extraordinary music. I've played it and it is outstanding. Tell her to hurry up and finish! Miss Johnson, I'm delighted that Miss Pete is doing so well. I'll be coming east soon and I'm coming to see you folks."

Samantha put down the phone and glanced about to make sure Judyth had not heard. *If dat man come,* Samantha said to herself, *I'll let him in. David McBryde he be a nice man.*

Judyth was hurrying down the hall to the sun porch. "Who was that, Samantha?"

"Some man," she answered.

Judyth was in too big a hurry to find out more.

Samantha had other worries to think about. Toby, the cat, was about to have kittens, and Judyth was simply not going to have that! she said. *Of course,* Samantha reasoned, *there's nothin' she can do about it. Them babies is goin' to be bawn whether she likes it or not.*

That night they were born, and the next morning she told Judyth. "There's five little kittens down dere in a box in the pantry. Toby try to hide dem but dey bees lyin' one on toppa de othah, pullin' at dere mama. Toby, she be so tired she jes' lie dere lettin' 'em tug at her."

Judyth made no comment and when she was finished with the chart she was reading, she shut it and filed it with the rest. Leaving the desk she told Samantha, "I'll be back in a few minutes if anyone calls."

Samantha was humming as she placed roses in a vase. The smell of them gave her special delight and arranging them made her feel important. Taking them to Miss Petersen's room, she announced, "Miz Petersen, look how God loves you—look at all dese flowers he done sent you! Dem folks what paid big money for 'em, dey thinks dey sent 'em but dat ain't true. Only God makes flowers. He sent you dese flowers, Miz Petersen. Here, lemme give you one big kiss to go wid dem."

Miss Petersen never said anything, but Samantha could feel what she wanted to say and understood how it was with her. "You lives on de inside, like me. I think to myself 'cause don't nobody on de outside know what it bees like inside."

As she went back to the desk she wondered what was keeping Judyth. Suddenly, it dawned on her, and she rushed down the hall. Taking the elevator to the basement she fretted. "Can't you go no faster? Get down! Get down!"

Bursting into the pantry, she discovered Judyth and hollered, "Leave dem kittens be!"

Judyth was sitting in a chair, holding a wet wash cloth over the mouth and nose of the last kitten. At her feet lay the lifeless bodies of the other four.

Samantha snatched her arm away and took the kitten but the poor little thing was already dead. She burst into tears. "You killed dem kittens!"

"Samantha, listen to me! I know what's best. Do you understand? We can't have cats running all over the place."

"You got no right!"

"Indeed I have. There's no need to stand there blubbering. We have work to do. Now, if you don't mind—" She was dropping the kittens in a plastic bag. "Take these creatures out to the dumpster. If you behave yourself, you can keep Toby. She gets rid of mice but you must keep her down here. And for heaven's sake, don't let her get pregnant again!"

# CHAPTER
# FORTY-FIVE

Samantha Johnson wheeled Miss Petersen to the front door but then she let down the foot rests, helped her out of the chair, and let her walk with her cane. True, she could not talk but that did not mean she did not hear and understand, Samantha reasoned. "It be all right, Miss Petersen, that you can't say my name. What do a name mean anyway? 'Samantha' don't mean nuttin'. Why my mama don't call me 'Pecan Tan' or 'Brown Sugar,' somethin' like dat, I don't know. I call my babies Sweet Angel and Bit of Heaven 'cause dat bees what dey is. Now, if I was to call Judyth what she bees, I might say she bees Book Smart or Miss Do Good. What would you call her, Miss Petersen?"

Anna was thinking in her head what she would name Judyth. Perhaps, she would just call her the Other One. Yes, that would do very well.

"I don't like all dese people callin' you Miz Pete like you was a man. Yo' name be Miz Petersen."

They were on the sidewalk that led to the garden. In the grass were wild violets and Anna thought of . . . The woman's name would not come to her. She would like to go and put a flower on the grave but no one could hear her when she asked to go. Everyone in the Residence was deaf. Brown Sugar could talk like all the others but she could not hear.

Anna could hear everything they said and the music besides. Walking along the path she could feel the music deep inside her not yet ready to be heard. How it swirled inside, bits and pieces of melody, linking up into patterns but it took solitude . . . Yes, soli . . . The word would not come. Oh, well, she knew what it took. In the room with the door locked, the music would come to the surface and write itself, only she must be alone. Thinking about it made a fluttering in her chest, as if a bird were caught in a cage.

"Dese yalla flowers bees marigolds, Miz Petersen. Dey smells so good. Don't you want me break one o' dem and pin it on your dress? Heah . . ."

Anna did not like the odor of the flower but who could refuse Brown Sugar? Patiently, she let the girl put a flower on her dress and one in her hair, and when Brown Sugar kissed her Anna could not feel the wetness but she knew it was there.

There were many things jumbled in her head and Anna could not sort them out properly. It wearied her to try so she finally gave up. What if she did get confused? What was important was never confused. If only David would come . . . , Dav . . . ? She couldn't remember his name but he was a boy—yes, a boy. The boy would help her make the music. He would play and she would play and the whole world would hear what she heard.

And there were others. Where were they? Where was Sue Marie and the Wheatley girl? They sat side by side. What a lovely voice the girl had. Perhaps there would be words for her to sing.

"Miz Petersen, now when we turn aroun' I don' want you take off like you usually do, rushin' to git back to dat room. It ain't good for you stayin' inside listenin' to music all de time. And I tell you one thing, you bettah not shet yo'se'f in like you done dat las' time or Judyth make me guard you like you was a crim'nal. Now, wait, Miz Petersen. Don' go so fas'."

Anna could not wait to get back within the walls because that was where the music was. But the Other

One met them at the door and scolded Brown Sugar. "Samantha, how many times have I told you not to take Miss Pete out front this time of the day? It's almost visiting hours. What if someone drove up now and saw her? If you must take her outside see to it that you go out back in the grove. It's shady there and Miss Pete will enjoy the birds. Take her out to Seymour's dog pens—show her the bird dogs."

Brown Sugar led her through the house and out the back door but Anna refused to go farther. "Miz Petersen, you be de most stubborn lady roun' heah. Why don't you let me take you down yonder? Well, dere ain' no way I kin stan' heah an' make you go. If you be wantin' to go to yo' room den dat's wheah I'll take you."

Brown Sugar was frowning but she would not stay that way. Soon she would be laughing or singing. Anna could have her own way.

Going up in the elevator, Brown Sugar's face clouded and by the time they were in the room, the storm was ready to burst. Carefully, the girl closed the door behind them. Then she poured out her heart.

"Miz Petersen, I don' mean to cause you no grief but I got to tell somebody. I done cried till my eyes puff up and dat don't do no good. Judyth she done kilt evah one o' dose wee little kittens. Snuffed out deah life like dey got no right to live. She so smaht she t'inks she be God hisse'f, goin' roun' doin' only what God hisse'f got a right to do. God gib 'em dere life, she take it. Miz Petersen, she ain't got no right to do dat!" Brown Sugar's cheeks were wet with tears and her troubled face distressed Anna.

Fumbling with the flower in her hair, Anna succeeded in getting it free. Handing it to Brown Sugar, she told her how to pin it to her dress but Brown Sugar couldn't hear and put it in her hair. Then smiling through her tears, Samantha hugged Anna and kissed her several times.

# CHAPTER
# FORTY-SIX

Brown Sugar was early—the stripe of sunlight had scarcely peeped inside the room. Before Anna could talk to the Lord Jesus, Brown Sugar had her in the boat soaping her so fast, rinsing and wiping her dry, Anna had no time to feel the heat of the water loosening the wires that held the tree limbs stiff.

"Baby, Baby, dis is de day! Dis is de day! Samantha gonna gib you a pahty such as you ain' nevah had no time, no place!"

Her hands were velvety soft patting Anna's back, dusting her with flour. Putting on her clothes, Anna knew she was a guitar whose cat gut strings were stretched too far. Brown Sugar must know that because she knew everything and she took care that the strings did not snap. Once Anna was in the chair, Brown Sugar was again a flock of sparrows in a hedgerow chattering, swooping up and flying away in loud laughing Anna could not follow, yet she laughed because Brown Sugar was a magic flute, full of gladness. Her wet kisses took Anna home to bells, metal doors slamming, a sweetish-sour smell of the place that was her own. "Home," she told Brown Sugar. "Home! Home! Home!" she insisted but the girl was deaf like all the others—chattering, patting Anna's head as she raked her hair straight out from her head. Sitting in the chair before a mirror, Anna could see another woman with Brown Sugar raking her hair, tying strands of it with colored ribbons.

"It's gonna be some pahty, Miz Petersen, but we

dasn't tell nobody. Baby, if we tells you-know-who, we bof be in trou-ble! It be your burfday an' it be de bigges' burfday pahty you evah seen."

The Other One bounced open the door. "Oh, no! Not that way again! Samantha, how many times have I told you that's not the way to brush Miss Pete's hair!" She snatched the rake from Brown Sugar's foot and untied all the strings, dropping them in Anna's lap. Brown Sugar made her cheeks fat, punched out her lips, but Brown Sugar could not stay that way. Soon she would be going down the tunnel singing.

And she did, leaving the Other One raking the hair. She was sweeping it up, piling it on the woman's head, cupping her hand beneath the hair, lifting it, eyeing the woman—liking what she saw. "Now, that's nice," she said, handing Anna the glass. "Look at the back." Anna did not try to understand. The Other One lifted the glass before her face and she saw the same woman in the mirror. The woman didn't know that her hair would not stay that way—that it would fly free and hang loose like feathers.

The Other One smelled as fresh as Cushman's Bakery. There it was, plain as day, *Cushman's Bakery*.

The Other One was telling Anna to eat and she would wait to see that she did. This one took no chances. If only she would leave, but, no, she had to raise the shade and let the flat sky show against the line of the land and say, "What a lovely day."

It would be a lovely day if she could see them all— the one with ears—or the red-haired one she dreamed about. Was she all right? And the Boy—the Boy, oh, if she could see the Boy! He would make music for her and they would see if Letitia was at the window!

If only the Other One would leave and let them come, but no, she had to scold—"Oh, dear, you've spilled down the front of your dress," and wiped Anna's mouth.

All the food was gone now. Anna smiled at the Other

One but she only shook her head . . . distressed. *Distressed*—there! It was as plain as day with all its parts front and back. The Other One was *distressed*, she repeated, rolling the word over and over, savoring it. Tiny lines marking the girl's forehead showed that she was . . . The word was hiding. The Other One patted her shoulder. "If only we could help you," she said sadly. "If only something could be done. Miss Pete, promise me, dear, that you won't barricade yourself in here. You could hurt yourself. You could fall. Please? Promise me?"

Anna smiled again but the Other One was . . . was still . . . The word was slipping away out of sight. Would it come back again? Anna felt the bird inside her chest fluttering its wings against its cage. The girl was stacking the dishes on the tray getting ready to take it away. She would leave now. Only she would not go far. Stepping outside in the tunnel, she would stop and listen to make sure—then go swishing down the tunnel. It was a trick.

"Can you reach the radio, Miss Pete? Here's your *Smithsonian*. No, not that way, that's upside down."

What did it matter? *Go now*, she thought. *Go, go, go!*

The sadness of the Other One—Anna knew she was the cause and sometimes she knew why but not today. Even as the girl stood there now, white in the morning sun, there was only dis . . . The word bobbed under again. It was drowning and would soon be dead like the others. It would never come back. All the more reason she needed to get on with the music. What if it came no more? What if, in the fretting worrisomeness of the Other One, it, too, died?

The girl leaned close to fuss with Anna's hair and with both hands Anna pushed her away. "Go away!" she screamed. But the girl was deaf like all the others and stood there struck with grief. Where was her cello?

She needed a cello. That would help her. Did she know? The Other One walked to the door, looked back at Anna and her eyes were filled with tears.

The footsteps halted a step from the door. Anna reached for the radio, turned it on because that would make her leave. Fingers in her ears, Anna waited until she could bear it no longer, reached for her cane beside the chair, and pulled herself up. At the window she pulled down the shade shutting out the flatness. Facing the door, she waited to see if anyone noticed, if any of them were coming back. Then quickly she snapped each of the locks on the wheels of the bed. Still undiscovered, she made the move! Rolling the bed against the door, wedging the foot of it beneath the knob, she locked the wheels and shouted for joy! Safe! Safe! Safe!

Tremblingly, making her way to the chair, she took care to ease herself down without falling.

Already they were trying the door, shouting at her. She shut them out—must not hear them or the music would not come. Turning off the radio, Anna pulled the sheaf of papers from beneath the mattress. The "Unaccompanied Sonata," she had named it.

First the courante sounding the undulating roar of the conch, shifting from treble to lower parts like the tides, alternating from soft to loud, crashing on the beach *pianoforte!*

Then the sweet rhythms of the curling conch, symmetrical and spreading fan-shaped, a tracery of violet edging. The pearled pink lip of the conch like the inside membrane of a baby's mouth, smooth harmony swelling and falling sweetly into place. She leaned back, hearing the music in her head, wave after wave washing over her.

When the first movement had spent itself she moved feverishly to the second. The saraband made her weep—the slow stately dance in triple meter mourning for the dead child. Andante? Largo? She must choose. Oh, the mauve shade of light that mourned, the morbid dirge weaving back and forth.

Then came the joy! And, oh, what joy it was! She laughed and cried as she watched—that little black baby was dancing a minuet with a flock of angels singing "Alleluia!"

Today the third movement must come. The bird fluttering in her chest said it must come today or it would be too late. Outside the door, the banging stopped, then the voices moved away. They would try something else.

The morning din pushed in—breakfast trays clattering, cart wheels screeching, a voice calling names— or was that Michael, the archangel calling for her? No, no! The Lord Jesus Christ himself will come for me. Oh, how he loves me! How much longer must I wait?

Mop pails clanging, elevator doors opening, shutting—she must set her will against the noises, turn them into cymbals and brass to help the music struggling inside to be heard.

Obsessed with energy, she pressed the pencil to the paper and the vigor was well controlled. Waiting, poised, she trembled, watching noiseless explosions of color in her head like fireworks in a night sky too far away to be heard. Terrified, the bird flew into a frenzy. Was this the death? Was the music dying? Was it dead?

As if in answer, a faint stirring began, sounds mumbling, moving; steadily growing stronger, dark rumblings of clouds down river moving up river, mounting. No vision, this—clear, crystal memory! The storm growing, churning, building to the first great thunderclap! Forked lightning racing top to bottom! God of the Seven Thunders! she shouted. Surging wind, roar of rain! For her pleasure they were and are created! Over and over again they came—sounds of force and power.

How easily she recorded it on paper, no erasing, no

adding—not even a flag on one stem! The Lord was helping! Whole notes, round and open; fortissimo; staccato in all the right places. Perfection! Perfection! The Boy will know. . . .

The pencil broke and more was coming, it was not finished.

They were knocking, banging, begging again. Fumbling for another pencil, Anna found a pen. Putting it on the paper, it would not write. "Lord Jesus Christ!" she prayed.

Falling back in the chair, panting for breath, she thought to let them in. Brown Sugar would get her a pencil. But, no, Brown Sugar would also take her to the sun porch or to that other place where sick people went to watch a box. No. Anna began working with the pen. The phone was ringing. They thought she would lift it and listen as Brown Sugar loved her into giving up. Let it ring, she said.

"Get a ladder, Tom," Judyth said. "You can go in her window."

"Only ladder'll reach that winder is at the fire station."

"Well, we can't let them know this. Don't you know a painter, a carpenter who has a ladder?"

"I know a Indian feller but he's working in Weston."

"Well, can't you think of something?" Her patience was wearing thin. "We've got to get her out of there."

"Might as well buy yo'se'f a extension ladder. This ain' de las' time Miz Petersen gonna hole up in dat room."

"Nonsense. There's a way to fix those wheels so she can't move that bed. We'll think of something. Tom, I know there's someone besides—"

"Go 'head, Miz Judyth, ask anybody in town."

"You know we can't ask just anybody." The man provoked her. "Now, it's up to you, Tom, to get Miss

Petersen out of there unharmed and unhurt."

He leaned on the mop handle. "That Indian won't be back 'fore sundown. Sundown's best I can do."

Samantha had to make one more phone call. Mr. Wigglesworth had made the list and invited them all but Samantha had to call Floyd Berry one more time or she would burst. Sneaking into the utility room, she made sure the door was fast shut and no one was in the closet. Punching the number made no noise but the ringing in her ear sounded loud enough to be heard down the hall. Her heart pounded in her chest. Would he never answer? "Hello? Dat you, Floyd Berry?"

"Samantha?"

"I axed you, is you Floyd Berry?"

He laughed. "The same. Floyd Berry. Is everything ready for the party, Samantha?"

"Evahthin'. Cake's done hid in de laundry room. I got de room beautiful. Did you practice yo' speech?"

"It's down pat, Samantha."

"I don't axe you nuttin' 'bout Pat, I axe you did you practice yo' speech?"

"Yeah, Samantha, I practiced."

"An' don' you let none o' dem mens bring no likker 'bout dis place. Miz Petersen, she don' nevah like likker, you know dat."

"And the battle axe?"

"What choo talkin' 'bout?"

"Judyth."

"Judyth don' know nuttin' 'bout dis. Do as I say an' she won' know."

"I can handle Judyth," Floyd boasted. "This time there's no way she can stop us. We're all coming— Marge Somebody from Georgia, David McBryde, my old buddy all the way from San Diego, some gal who's an actress—all the locals, even Old Lady Pendergraft."

Samantha heard someone in the hall. "I gotta go."

Anna roused from sleep. "Miss Petersen, it's lunch time," Brown Sugar was calling from the other side of the door. "Won' you please lemme come in? I got you some nice turnip greens, po'k chops, and red jiggly Jell-O."

Anna did not move. More voices in the hall. A sharp rapping. "Miss Pete, this is a lovely meal." The Other One. "Samantha's brought you daffodils. Come now, please. Open the door while the food is hot. You don't like cold food."

"No," she said as nicely as she knew how, but, of course they did not hear her. More talk, more knocking. Finally they went away.

Anna pressed the pen to the paper and the ink came in tiny spurts, enough to make the marks if only the storm would come again. The bird was quiet, nestling inside her breast. Then it roused, began to stir. The storm had passed, gone rumbling up river beyond where they stood, leaving a trail of sobbing, sighing trees. Was that all? Only sobbing and sighing? She waited and waited. Closing her eyes, leaning back in the chair, Anna could not keep awake. Somewhere in the deep recesses of dream were floating soft thin strains of harmony more beautiful than ever she had heard. They rose imperceptibly over Manhattan and arched across the river, broad bands of color in a bow—sapphire fused with lavender bending to touch the other side. The span, forming a pristine sound no mortal ear had ever heard, drove Anna frenziedly as she strained to match and blend the notes, meter the measure—bring it all together as God had.

The pen slipped from her hand. She was feeling for it in the cushion when—

The window was flung up and The Man was crawling inside, ripping the shade as he came. Switching on the light, he grinned. "Well, little lady, you done yourself up proud, that's all I got to say."

Samantha, for the fortieth time, rearranged the green and red streamers strung from the light fixture in the servants' kitchen. There was no one to talk to but the cat and she did not seem the least bit excited. "Toby, you go right in the yard soon's I bring Miz Petersen down here. Bless Gawd, Judyth be so busy gittin' Miss Petersen outta dat room she ain' got no mind 'bout dis here pahty." Samantha laughed. "Toby, you know Miz Petersen don' like no kin' o' animal and dat's what you is. You is a animal. I," she said, pointing to herself, "I be a person, made in de image o' Awmighty Gawd. Miz Petersen, she done taught me dat when I was a young gu'l. I knowed I was somebody but don't nobody tol' me dat till Miz Petersen come along. Dat is one fine lady, and if I'd listened to her and not got in no trouble wid mens, I'd be more better today. I don' know how de debbil made dem mens look so good to me. I knowed all along dem mens be jes like those tom cats goin' 'bout cross de creek an' all ovah leavin' chuldrun an' wimmins all by theyse'f."

A car sounded on the gravel in back. Samantha grabbed Toby, rushed through the pantry, unlatched the door, and dropped the cat outside. They were coming as she had told them to, up the back road to the service entrance. There were no headlights shining, only red flickers of brake lights. Bumper to bumper they came in a steady stream.

Judyth, in the utility room, heard a car in back. Disregarding the sound, she went about scouring the bedpan. Then she heard another and another—many tires crunching on the service road. Pulling the curtain aside, she looked down on them, a long file of cars, lights off, creeping up the road. So, she had done it! Samantha had gone against orders and done it— planned a party despite what Judyth had said.

There was Louvenia and Ken Tompkins . . . looks like that Berry fellow. Blood surged at her temples as she watched shadowy figures emerging from the cars. All along the road cars were backed up as far as she could see. There would be no stopping them! Judyth felt sick. Why couldn't that simpleton get it through her head how inhumane this was!

She turned quickly from the window. She knew what she must do and she must hurry! No matter what it cost, she must do it for Miss Petersen. At the door she did not pause but slipped quietly into the room. The poor dear was sleeping in the chair, her breathing erratic and shallow. Judyth took one long, last look at her, smoothed hair. . . . But there was no more time. She went to the sink, wet the towel with warm water, wrung out the excess.

Standing beside the chair, Judyth paused, then leaned down and kissed her brow. "Good-bye, Miss Pete," she whispered, then placed the towel over her mouth and nose and held it firmly.

Miss Pete did not struggle. Surely she wanted to go.

Judyth waited longer than was necessary and, still holding the towel firmly, felt Anna's wrist. There was not a flutter. For five minutes she waited, then removed the towel and dried the white face.

The elevator was whining up the shaft. It stopped and the door opened. Samantha must be bringing a wheelchair. The door rolled shut again. Judyth wrung out the towel and hung it up to dry. Samantha was racing down the hall. In a minute the door bumped open and she burst in the room. "Miss Petersen, git in dis chair! You is in for a big surprise!"

She was busy positioning the chair, locking the wheels, lifting the foot rests.

"It's her burfday, Judyth, and I don't care what you do to me, Miss Petersen goin' to have a pahty! They's all come—Louvenia, Mr. Wigglesworth, Rev'rend

Jackson, dat chaplain—all dem chuldrun!"

"Samantha," Judyth began, her voice calm. "Samantha, I'm afraid it's too late."

At first Samantha did not hear but when she did, she froze.

"I'm sorry, " Judyth said softly.

Samantha stared at Anna, gray as stone. Judyth turned her back to avoid the shocked girl's wide-eyed grief. She felt the room sway then right itself. A sheaf of papers slid to the floor—Miss Pete's scribblings. Gathering them up carefully, Judyth stacked them, a flood of tears threatening.

As she reached for tissues, she could feel Samantha looking at her accusingly. "What is it, Samantha?"

Samantha's pale lips parted. "God won't like this."

Floyd Berry had quietly come in the room and was standing behind Samantha. "What happened?" he asked.

"She killed her!" Samantha screamed and going to the towel bar she yanked down the wet towel and thrust it toward him. Then her knees buckled under her and she crumpled to the floor in a faint.

"Help me lift her, Floyd. We'll put her on the bed." Together they settled Samantha, and Judyth glanced about for a pillow. "Hand me that pillow. We have to prop up her feet." Tucking the pillow under Samantha's feet, Judyth shook her head. "Poor girl. She's distraught."

Judyth spread a sheet over Miss Petersen, the Indian helping her. "Perhaps you'd better go downstairs and break the news to the others," she told him. "I'll call Dr. Metcalf and the funeral home. When the business is taken care of, I'll join you."

Floyd Berry could not be brushed aside. He looked back at her threateningly, his voice brittle. "Judyth

McCurdy, if there's foul play here, I'll not rest till justice is done."

She didn't answer.

After he was gone, Judyth filled a syringe and thrust the needle in Samantha's arm. The sedative would keep her quiet for a while.

Seymour came right away and certified the death. "Her heart just quit on her," he said and, looking at Samantha, he asked, "What's the story on Samantha?"

"Poor girl. She was so distraught I had to give her something."

Seymour looked at his wife sympathetically. "Why don't you go along downstairs. I'll wait for McSwain."

"All right, I will," she said and picking up the sheets with the scribbled notes, she took the elevator down to the basement. In the elevator, she checked the fear rising in her. It was an act of love, she told herself. The only decent thing to do.

She arrived in the servants' kitchen soon after Floyd had made the announcement. Everyone looked her way and she knew she must say something. Speaking in a strong voice, she said, "Miss Petersen will always live in our hearts—" Her voice quavered. Their hard, cold looks frightened her.

"She was a beautiful, intelligent woman who loved us."

Marge Penry, livid with anger, rose half-way from her chair. David McBryde, weeping unashamedly, stepped between them, and taking the sheaf of compositions from Judyth, said, "Miss Petersen will live in this music." He held the sheets above his head for all to see. "What she has written here will live forever."

# Other Living Books Best-sellers

**THE ANGEL OF HIS PRESENCE** by Grace Livingston Hill. This book captures the romance of John Wentworth Stanley and a beautiful young woman whose influence causes John to reevaluate his well-laid plans for the future. 07-0047 $2.95.

**ANSWERS** by Josh McDowell and Don Stewart. In a question-and-answer format, the authors tackle sixty-five of the most-asked questions about the Bible, God, Jesus Christ, miracles, other religions, and creation. 07-0021 $3.95.

**THE BEST CHRISTMAS PAGEANT EVER** by Barbara Robinson. A delightfully wild and funny story about what happens to a Christmas program when the "Horrible Herdman" brothers and sisters are miscast in the roles of the biblical Christmas story characters. 07-0137 $2.50.

**BUILDING YOUR SELF-IMAGE** by Josh McDowell. Here are practical answers to help you overcome your fears, anxieties, and lack of self-confidence. Learn how God's higher image of who you are can take root in your heart and mind. 07-1395 $3.95.

**THE CHILD WITHIN** by Mari Hanes. The author shares insights she gained from God's Word during her own pregnancy. She identifies areas of stress, offers concrete data about the birth process, and points to God's sure promises that he will "gently lead those that are with young." 07-0219 $2.95.

**400 WAYS TO SAY I LOVE YOU** by Alice Chapin. Perhaps the flame of love has almost died in your marriage. Maybe you have a good marriage that just needs a little "spark." Here is a book especially for the woman who wants to rekindle the flame of romance in her marriage; who wants creative, practical, useful ideas to show the man in her life that she cares. 07-0919 $2.95.

**GIVERS, TAKERS, AND OTHER KINDS OF LOVERS** by Josh McDowell and Paul Lewis. This book bypasses vague generalities about love and sex and gets right to the basic questions: Whatever happened to sexual freedom? What's true love like? Do men respond differently than women? If you're looking for straight answers about God's plan for love and sexuality, this book was written for you. 07-1031 $2.95.

**HINDS' FEET ON HIGH PLACES** by Hannah Hurnard. A classic allegory of a journey toward faith that has sold more than a million copies! 07-1429 $3.95.

**HOW TO BE HAPPY THOUGH MARRIED** by Tim LaHaye. One of America's most successful marriage counselors gives practical, proven advice for marital happiness. 07-1499 $3.50.

**JOHN, SON OF THUNDER** by Ellen Gunderson Traylor. In this saga of adventure, romance, and discovery, travel with John—the disciple whom Jesus loved—down desert paths, through the courts of the Holy City, to the foot of the cross. Journey with him from his luxury as a privileged son of Israel to the bitter hardship of his exile on Patmos. 07-1903 $4.95.

# Other Living Books Best-sellers

**KAREN'S CHOICE** by Janice Hermansen. College students Karen and Jon fall in love and are heading toward marriage when Karen discovers she is pregnant. Struggle with Karen and Jon through the choices they make and observe how they cope with the consequences and eventually find the forgiveness of Christ. 07-2027 $3.50.

**LIFE IS TREMENDOUS!** by Charlie "Tremendous" Jones. Believing that enthusiasm makes the difference, Jones shows how anyone can be happy, involved, relevant, productive, healthy, and secure in the midst of a high-pressure, commercialized society. 07-2184 $2.95.

**LOOKING FOR LOVE IN ALL THE WRONG PLACES** by Joe White. Using wisdom gained from many talks with young people, White steers teens in the right direction to find love and fulfillment in a personal relationship with God. 07-3825 $3.50.

**LORD, COULD YOU HURRY A LITTLE?** by Ruth Harms Calkin. These prayer-poems from the heart of a godly woman trace the inner workings of the heart, following the rhythms of the day and the seasons of the year with expectation and love. 07-3816 $2.95.

**LORD, I KEEP RUNNING BACK TO YOU** by Ruth Harms Calkin. In prayer-poems tinged with wonder, joy, humanness, and questioning, the author speaks for all of us who are groping and learning together what it means to be God's child. 07-3819 $3.50.

**LORD, YOU LOVE TO SAY YES** by Ruth Harms Calkin. In this collection of prayer-poems the author speaks openly and honestly with her Lord about hopes and dreams, longings and frustrations, and her observations of life. 07-3824 $3.50.

**MORE THAN A CARPENTER** by Josh McDowell. A hard-hitting book for people who are skeptical about Jesus' deity, his resurrection, and his claims on their lives. 07-4552 $2.95.

**MOUNTAINS OF SPICES** by Hannah Hurnard. Here is an allegory comparing the nine spices mentioned in the Song of Solomon to the nine fruits of the Spirit. A story of the glory of surrender by the author of *HINDS' FEET ON HIGH PLACES.* 07-4611 $3.95.

**THE NEW MOTHER'S BOOK OF BABY CARE** by Marjorie Palmer and Ethel Bowman. From when to call the doctor to what you will need to clothe the baby, this book will give you all the basic knowledge necessary to be the parent your child needs. 07-4695 $2.95.

**NOW IS YOUR TIME TO WIN** by Dave Dean. In this true-life story, Dean shares how he locked into seven principles that enabled him to bounce back from failure to success. Read about successful men and women—from sports and entertainment celebrities to the ordinary people next door—and discover how you too can bounce back from failure to success! 07-4727 $2.95.

**THE POSITIVE POWER OF JESUS CHRIST** by Norman Vincent Peale. All his life the author has been leading men and women to Jesus Christ. In this book he tells of his boyhood encounters with Jesus and of his spiritual growth as he attended seminary and began his world-renowned ministry. 07-4914 $3.95.

# Other Living Books Best-sellers

**REASONS** by Josh McDowell and Don Stewart. In a convenient question-and-answer format, the authors address many of the commonly asked questions about the Bible and evolution. 07-5287 $3.95.

**ROCK** by Bob Larson. A well-researched and penetrating look at today's rock music and rock performers, their lyrics, and their life-styles. 07-5686 $3.50.

**SHAPE UP FROM THE INSIDE OUT** by John R. Throop. Learn how to conquer the problem of being overweight! In this honest, often humorous book, Throop shares his own personal struggle with this area and how he gained fresh insight about the biblical relationship between physical and spiritual fitness. 07-5899 $2.95.

**SUCCESS: THE GLENN BLAND METHOD** by Glenn Bland. The author shows how to set goals and make plans that really work. His ingredients of success include spiritual, financial, educational, and recreational balances. 07-6689 $3.50.

**TAKE ME HOME** by Bonnie Jamison. This touching, candid story of the author's relationship with her dying mother will offer hope and assurance to those dealing with an aging parent, relative, or friend. 07-6901 $3.50.

**TELL ME AGAIN, LORD, I FORGET** by Ruth Harms Calkin. You will easily identify with Calkin in this collection of prayer-poems about the challenges, peaks, and quiet moments of each day. 07-6990 $3.50.

**THROUGH GATES OF SPLENDOR** by Elisabeth Elliot. This unforgettable story of five men who braved the Auca Indians has become one of the most famous missionary books of all times. 07-7151 $3.95.

**WAY BACK IN THE HILLS** by James C. Hefley. The story of Hefley's colorful childhood in the Ozarks makes reflective reading for those who like a nostalgic journey into the past. 07-7821 $3.95.

**WHAT WIVES WISH THEIR HUSBANDS KNEW ABOUT WOMEN** by James Dobson. The best-selling author of *DARE TO DISCIPLINE* and *THE STRONG-WILLED CHILD* brings us this vital book that speaks to the unique emotional needs and aspirations of today's woman. An immensely practical, interesting guide. 07-7896 $3.50.

**YES** by Ann Kiemel. In this window into Ann's heart, she tells—in her usual honest, charming way—how she has answered a resounding YES to Jesus in the various circumstances of her life. 07-8563 $2.95.

The books listed are available at your bookstore. If unavailable, send check with order to cover retail price plus $1.00 per book for postage and handling to:

Tyndale DMS
Box 80
Wheaton, Illinois 60189

Prices and availability subject to change without notice. Allow 4–6 weeks for delivery.